CODE BILLY

BEN HUBER

MMXVIII

Code Billy/ Ben Huber -- 1st ed.

ISBN 978-0-9993204-0-2

For my brothers

CODE BILLY

BILLY

Poppycock.

As in, "That, ladies and gentlemen of the jury, is absolute poppycock."

Billy imagined himself saying it in a Southern drawl, which would lend an extra patina of authority to the statement. Not that there weren't other words to describe his mom: Preposterous. Ludicrous. Unfair, unjust. Partisan, hypocritical, absurd. Prejudiced, farcical, discriminatory, shambolic, selfish. Inane. Insane. The point was, she was being irrational.

Or maybe the situation called for something stronger; maybe the ladies and gentlemen of the jury needed to be shocked. And there was nothing that shocked people more than swear words. Billy knew all the swear words, or most of them anyway; just because he was young didn't mean he was ignorant. Bullshit, for example, would be appropriate. Though he probably shouldn't say that to his mom. Not unless he wanted her to have a conniption and punish him again. He was just finishing his last punishment! A month without his Xbox for one small piece of lasagna, well thrown, had been draconian enough. And now, just when it was supposed to be over, the punishment was extended. Sure, she would say that this trip to the store wasn't part of the punishment. But what was being forced to do something you didn't want to do, something against your will, if not punishment? It was going to ruin his whole Saturday, probably his whole weekend. It was bullsh—crap!

"We've had this discussion, Billy; please don't use language like that."

"But I don't want to go. And besides, I said crap. That's not that bad. It's not like I said the s-h word."

"Watch your mouth, young man. This isn't up for debate. Now get your coat."

The problem was that there was no jury, just stupid Mom. She was jury, judge, *and* executioner—the whole freaking body politic. This was supposed to be America. What about his rights? But there was no separation of powers from where he was standing. The lasagna incident should not have been that big of a deal. There were some families where that sort of native athletic talent would be nurtured. Billy's was not one of them.

"But, Mom, you're supposed to give my Xbox back; it's not fair, taking me to the store and not letting me use it."

"Oh, that's right. Well, I'd think you would not be so argumentative in hopes of keeping it a little while this time."

Was that a threat? He was pretty sure it was a threat. He needed to try a different tack.

"But, Mom, Mary doesn't have to go. So it seems to me that—"

That was as far as he got.

"Your sister is fourteen and has to study and then go to her play rehearsal. You are too young to be left home alone. And since your father can't give up his precious golf, you're coming with me."

Billy didn't know where to begin in picking apart his mother's argument. Her rhetoric was so flawed it was like trying to build a TinkerToys tower with half TinkerToys and half marshmallows. Billy knew from personal experience that *that* was a recipe for disaster. The tower was completely structurally unsound, and cleaning off the marshmallow took weeks.

But where to begin taking apart his mom's tower? First of all, his sister was just barely fourteen. Her birthday was only last week. So she was really more like thirteen. And Billy would be eight in less than a month. So they were basically the same age. Second of all, Billy was pretty skeptical about "play rehearsal." Allegedly, Mary was in some kind of play where a pair of teenagers fell in love, but their families were enemies, and their parents wouldn't let them get married. And so they ended up killing themselves. It seemed pretty farfetched that they would want to get married so young and overly dramatic that they'd then kill themselves, like that solved the problem. Double suicide was not romantic. Billy could relate to the controlling parents part, but the rest just didn't seem realistic. He suspected she might be sneaking off to do pot. Or worse: cigarettes.

But he couldn't worry about Mary right now. He had to persuade his mom that going to the store was a bad idea. If she wasn't going to bow to the overwhelming genius of his logic, then he would have to resort to an emotional appeal. It was cheap, and not nearly as satisfying, but time was of the essence. She had her purse out and was looking for the car keys.

"But, Mom! I really don't wanna! You're treating me like a little kid! Please don't make me. Don't you—"

"Billy. You're seven years old. You can't stay home alone. Your father isn't here, and your sister is busy. You're coming with me. Enough arguments."

"I'm almost eight!"

"Enough!"

"Joan of Arc! Alexander the Great! Both great by the age of eight!" Billy knew he was grasping at straws. Well, more like he had a straw, but it lacked the requisite cutting edge to pierce the overly robust juice box he was up against, and so it crumpled.

"Billy, they lived more than a thousand years ago. Things were different then. And the last time I checked, you were still seven."

A Kevlar-reinforced juice box. He needed a knife.

"What about the next Dalai Lama then?"

Zing. Had her there.

"You are not the next Dalai Lama."

Ouch. Maybe if she would let him be a little more in control of his own life he would be! Moms. His friend Chris's mom wouldn't let him do *anything*. He went from piano to soccer to a special tutor for math to swimming. And that was just Saturdays! Chris only had like half an hour per week when he got to do what he wanted. Billy shook his head. Poor Chris.

"Don't shake your head at me, young man," his mom said. "Seven is too young to be left alone. So it'd be great if just this once you didn't try to fight me. Please?"

Billy balled his fists and ground his teeth. She talked to him as if his opinion didn't count for anything. He was beginning to suspect it didn't. And now she was trying to manipulate him! That's what "please" was for. He had just said it himself, a minute ago. He ground his teeth harder, working his jaw slowly left and right, hearing a gratifying click when his upper molars slipped off the ledge of the lower ones. Dr. Mulligan, his dentist, would probably have a vaguely condescending comment about it at his next appointment, which he would make to his mom, instead of to Billy, like he was too stupid to understand. Something like, "Now, Mrs. Anderson, little Billy here, we may have to put a ceiling on his molars, and he's going to need braces." Dentists. Such a racket.

"And, Billy? Please don't grind your teeth. It's unpleasant."

Billy clenched and unclenched his fists.

"BUT I DON'T WANNA GO!"

His protests came to nothing. His mom found the keys, and before he could argue any more, he was strapped into the back seat. What a stupid way to spend a Saturday.

RUSTY

Today was the day! Rusty felt great. Did he feel great? His toes felt a little stiff. Was that bad? No. Couldn't be. Probably just normal sleepy stiffness. Today was the day. It was probably just that he had slept so well. Yeah, he was fine. Better than fine. He was great. He sat up and sprang out of bed. He did a cartwheel and a backflip. Yep. He was great. The power of positive thinking! His wife, still asleep, groaned softly. She wasn't into mornings.

Rusty went into the bathroom. He looked in the mirror. He looked great. Did he look great? What was that on his cheek? Was it rabies? He pawed at it. Nope. Just dirt. His teeth needed brushing. He brushed. He turned to check out his back. All okay. More than okay. Strong. Lithe. Powerful. The power of positive thinking! And today was a big day.

Rusty reached toward the ceiling and stretched his body, head to toes. He gave a shake and flexed his tail. Was it less bushy? Did rabies make your tail debush? He'd have to ask Raccoon sometime. That guy knew everything. Oooh, he should wash his paws. Raccoon was always washing his paws. And he had given Rusty the inside info on the job. And what a job it was! Rusty would have to ask him about rabies some other time. He had to get going. His tail was fine. It was just the light. His tail was bushy. Silky. Sexy. Rusty swooshed it and grinned. Today was the day. It was all happening. He would be the prince of squirrel thieves. He went back into the bedroom.

"Today's the day!" he said and kissed his wife softly on her cheek.

"Hmmmm?" His wife groaned again. She was warm. Too warm? Was it rabies? Rusty almost recoiled, then remembered that she had just been tested last week as part of her checkup. She was pregnant, not rabid.

"Be careful," she mumbled. "I love you."

"Don't worry. I will be. You're the chestnut of my heart. Love you too!"

He kissed her again and left the nest.

It was a beautiful morning. The sun was shining. Birds were singing. It augured well. He checked for hawks. A hawk could really ruin his day. No hawks. All clear. Another omen. Today was the day! The day he would put himself on easy street. Not just himself. His new family. And he'd probably kick something back to Raccoon for setting it up. Why not? When you were rich, you could afford to be generous. A dog was barking, but Rusty could get to where he was going by hardly touching the ground. He would have to cross the road, but he was fast. Too fast, too pretty. They couldn't stop him.

"Light as a feather and quick as a squirrel!" he cried.

He leapt straight up, landed on the same branch, and took off at a dead sprint. With a whoop, he launched himself from the end of the branch, tail streaming behind him. He landed softly on the end of the next branch. He paused and checked for hawks. Still clear! He took in the brilliance of the world around him. Was that a twinge in his neck? Didn't he hear last week that a neck twinge was a symptom? He slowly twisted his neck, side to side, front to back. All smooth. Pain free. Still no predators. He needed to stop worrying. Worrying wasn't a symptom too, was it? No, yes, everything was good. Today was the day. Rusty let forth a chatter of pure joy to show the world how good he felt.

"Oh be quiet, you gall-derned squirrel!" a woman yelled from the house next door.

Rusty could see she was about to slam the window shut. She couldn't! He needed that window open: It was part of the plan. He had to get into that house. He accelerated into a dead sprint and leapt from the end of the branch, his tail billowing bushily behind him.

He wasn't gonna make it! Oh, nuts. Wait! Rusty's front paws touched the sill. He scrabbled. He thrashed his tail as a counterweight. Success! He hoisted his back paws up and shot into the house, tucking his tail to stop the woman from slamming it in the window.

"Eeek! Aaah! Get out of here, you little varmint!" she screamed. Rusty was trying to obey. It wasn't like he wanted to be in there. He just had to go through the house to get where he was going. All part of the plan. Raccoon had thought it might work. Good old Raccoon. Though now that he was inside, Rusty wasn't so sure quite how good either the plan or Raccoon's endorsement of it were.

The house smelled like overripe fruit. The kind that might poison you. Poison! That would be awful. Not today. He could not get poisoned today. Rusty had to get out of there. And fast. It was part of the plan. But the woman was blocking his way. There was nothing for it but to go straight at her.

Rusty ran. He hopped: once, twice. The woman had enormous mammary fat pads on her upper torso. Why humans kept them there was beyond him, but he had no time to contemplate the engineering flaws of humans. The fat pads were like a pair of trampolines. He launched off the second trampoline and onto a table. He skittered on some papers, scattering them everywhere. The woman was shouting, but Rusty paid no attention. Through the house and out the window on the far side: that was the plan. She had a broom! That was not the plan. Rusty had to improvise. Duck! *Wham!* Bob and weave. *Wham!* Light as a feather, quick as a squirrel. *Wham!* Missed again.

Rusty perched on the arm of a chair and chattered. She swung again. He dodged again. She was clumsy with the broom. Or he was just that good. Better than that good. Great! He faked left. Predictably, the woman swung directly at him, left; Rusty juked right. There was a huge crash as the broom hit a lamp. It fell to the floor and smashed open—would that work for acorns? Rusty shook his head; he could worry about that later. He darted across the back of the couch. Then he was on the counter, out the far window, and onto the rope that humans used to dry their clothes. Clothes, only fools needed them. He sprinted along the rope, swishing his tail to keep his balance. Tails were awesome. His tail was awesome. He reached the fake tree at the far end of the rope, the fake tree that carried the wires with sweet, sweet electricity.

No. Rusty couldn't. Not now. Not today. Not anymore. He was done with electricity.

He shot up the fake tree, ignored the pulsating wires, and jumped into a natural pine tree on the other side. Once there, he paused, catching his breath. He checked his tail. Still silky. Sexy. He checked for hawks. All clear. The woman continued to yell.

Rusty ignored her. She couldn't bring him down. She couldn't stop him. She couldn't hope to contain him. He was going to pull off the greatest nut heist in squirrel history. Heck, in any species' history. Today was the day!

SANDY

"Lord Jesus, hear me now. I've been faithful to you since you showed me the light. And I will be faithful forever more. Thank you, Lord Jesus. Please smile on and help me, your humble servant. Help make today a blessed day. Amen."

"I sure do need it," Sandy added under her breath. Light filtered through the fraying curtains, and she got up from beside her uncomfortable bed. The carpet she walked from her bedroom to her kitchen was threadbare. She wished she could replace it all, frayed curtains and threadbare carpet and uncomfortable bed. And while she was at it, why not also her rinky-dink house and piece-of-junk car and everything else? But the pile of bills waiting for her on the kitchen table reminded her that it wasn't an option. Prayer didn't seem to be helping, but if she was going to talk the talk, she knew she had to walk the walk.

And there was hope. Her latest sermon had gone if not quite viral, then at least mildly contagious on the YouTube. At least by her standards. Four hundred thirty-seven views in the first twelve hours alone! And three likes. Against only one dislike. She hadn't checked yet this morning, but she could be approaching the magic five hundred number. Sure, it still wasn't quite enough to monetize with advertisements and whatnot, but it was improvement in the right direction. Baby steps.

Preaching to the masses and being well paid for it besides— that was her destiny, her fate. But in the meantime, she also needed to eat and stuff. That was the hard part. Today was Saturday, and she was hoping she could kill two birds with one stone, so to speak. Because what better place to bring the message of the Lord Jesus to the masses than in front of the SuperMart on a Saturday? And having heard that message straight from her lips, how could they not buy a DVD or two? Maybe she'd be really blessed and a TV executive or someone would come by and she would end up with her own cable show. Maybe.

Sandy couldn't resist anymore. She fired up the YouTube. Nervous with anticipation, she drummed her fingers on the table while she waited for her latest sermon to load—748 views! And six likes. Against only two dislikes, who were probably just good-for-nothing heathen trolls. She wasn't going to let those bother her. The likes were still winning three to one. That was what was important. All in all, it was even better than she had hoped. Truly a blessing. Truly a sign. What was the minimum threshold for advertisements anyway? She should really check on that. Later.

"Oh, thank you, Jesus," Sandy whispered. Adrenaline coursed through her. It was like being touched by an angel. She clicked play. Self-idolatry was bad, but Sandy was pretty sure the Lord Jesus would understand in this case. She watched herself speak from the same kitchen. The lighting was maybe a little bit harsh, but her hair looked nice. It was straight and lustrous, hanging down to frame her full cheeks with their dimples, curling up just so at the exact same level as her chin. The effect was a pleasant one, welcoming, professional. Classy.

"Hey, y'all. Sandy Newman here, bringing the word of our Lord Jesus to you! Now, when you think about Jesus—which I encourage y'all to do as often as you can—what do you picture? A man. Jesus was a man. A man with a beard. But he was so much more than that. He was a man with a beard who died. For our sins. Think about that for a moment. He had a life, performing miracles, loved by thousands..."

Yes, the lighting in the video was a bit harsh, Sandy decided. She'd have to adjust that before her next video. Was her kitchen really that color? She supposed it must be. When she got money, she'd have to repaint. Maybe even remodel. Heck, maybe even move.

"Loved by thousands," Video Sandy repeated. "Can you imagine what that'd be like? To have the love of thousands and to choose death? Not because he was suicidal like those emo teens I keep hearing about. Stay positive, kids, and let Jesus into your life. No, Jesus chose death because he knew, he knew, that for us to be saved, he had to sacrifice. Sacrifice himself. For us. Think about that."

Video Sandy was in full flow; her cheeks were flushed, but only slightly.

"We must be thankful every day." Video Sandy punctuated her point by bumping her fist on the kitchen table. Real Sandy mimicked her. It was a good piece of theater. It was a good sermon.

"Every day, we must be thankful for that sacrifice. Seems so easy. But it isn't. To be a good Christian is hard. Squirrels can't do it. That's right. Squirrels can't be saved. No, sir, and no, ma'am. They might be God's creatures, and you can be sure that he loves them as he loves all things, but they can't go to heaven. Not like we can. They might sit and chatter and shriek outside our windows, but that's not believing. That's not accepting Jesus into their hearts. We are blessed. We have the gift to be *able* to accept the word of the Bible and Jesus into our hearts."

Sandy thought about the squirrel that had inspired this part of the sermon and shuddered. He chattered outside her window pretty much every day. Worse than those internet trolls, that vile little creature. No, she had to be more forgiving than that. Squirrels might be annoying and disgusting, but she needed to practice tolerance. It was like Video Sandy said: they couldn't know Jesus. So that must be hard for them, even if they were still creepy.

Video Sandy kept talking. Real Sandy watched: a good performer knew how to critique herself. Her voice was good, animated and friendly. Her posture was exemplary. But she really would have to figure out a better way to do the lights.

Even still, it was a good video. No wonder it was so popular. Video Sandy had reached the closing.

"I ask y'all to pray with me now.

"Dear Lord Jesus, who has sacrificed so much for us. Forgive us our daily trespasses, as we work to live better by your example. And help us forgive the obnoxious little squirrels who chatter on and disturb our rest. For we must know and practice forgiveness to all of God's creatures. Even the annoying ones.

"Praise you, Jesus. Thank you. Amen.

"And thanks to all y'all for prayin' with me. Be sure to check out my other clips here on the YouTube, and like me on Facebook. Just search for me, Sandy Newman, or my ministry, Blessed Prayers. I'll be praying for you. Y'all have a most blessed day."

The video ended. Sandy knew it was a little tacky to end with such blatant salesmanship, but the money wasn't going to make itself. And she had wished her viewers a *most* blessed day. Besides, if the Lord Jesus disapproved, would he have blessed her with so many views? She was up to 750! That was, why, that was three quarters of the way to a thousand! And it meant that someone had been watching at the same time she was watching herself. And well, what do you know, another like. That blessed soul.

She really ought to beef up her social media presence. She had a Facebook page, but for now, it was just bare bones and directed people to her YouTube channel. She didn't cultivate it at all. Besides, who had heard of anyone getting rich off of Facebook? There were new YouTube millionaires every day. She was going to be one of them. The rest of the social media, the tweeting and the chappy snappy and the instant grammar, all that was for later, when she really needed to crank up the PR machine. Right now she was building her brand.

The YouTube was suggesting clips of other sermons, by her and others, but also, strange as it seemed, clips of "cute baby squirrel" and "water-skiing squirrel." Sandy didn't understand it, but there it was. A staccato burst of squirrel chatter interrupted her train of thought. She looked out the window. Sure enough, there he was. Twisting his little bug-eyed head back and forth. Little devil wouldn't leave her in peace.

"Oh be quiet, you gall-derned squirrel!" she yelled at him. She knew she should try to be more forgiving, but squirrels did try her patience.

Forgiveness and sacrifice were hard. But if Sandy wasn't going to practice what she preached, who would? Plus, maybe it was the plight of the squirrel that had resonated with viewers. Or maybe others found squirrels just as annoying and creepy as she did. Hopefully someone would let her know in the comments section of the YouTube. Either way, she should probably try a few more rodent sermons, just to test out their marketability.

Then again, maybe this particular video had been such a success because of her hair. It did look amazing. She was blessed to be a natural blonde, but it still took work to make it look like that. She hoped she could replicate her look from the video again today. It might help sell some DVDs at the SuperMart.

She looked out the window again. The squirrel was running at her. He was really—oh, Lord! What if it was rabid? She had to get the window closed. She pulled at the bottom of the frame. It was stuck, warped by the humid weather they'd been having. She dug her fingers into the wood; splinters dug back into her fingers. It budged an inch. She leaned, adding her body weight to the strength of her muscles. The squirrel was five feet away! She gave a little jump. The window yielded another couple of inches, then caught. The squirrel was three feet away. She jiggled the window and leapt, putting all the force she could into it. *Wham!* The window was shut. The squirrel...the squirrel had beaten her. It was in her house. In. Her. House! She couldn't breathe. No, she was hyperventilating. She had to calm down. She had to breathe.

She screamed! That wasn't calm, but it helped regulate her airflow.

Sandy and the squirrel stared at each other. It was a showdown. Eye to eye. Then a most disgusting thing happened: the squirrel leapt at her. On her! She screamed! She could feel its dirty little claws on...on her...on her bosom! That was most un-Christian of him. Groped by a squirrel. Defiled! She screamed again and swatted at her breasts, but the squirrel was already gone and onto her table. He was scattering her papers all over.

"Somebody help!" Sandy screamed. No one came.

"Jesus, help me!" Sandy screamed louder. He didn't answer. He was probably busy. She had to handle this herself.

She hefted a broom. She swung and missed. He was a quick little devil. She swung again. Miss. The little brat was now on the arm of her chair. Was he puffing out his chest at her? She would wipe that little squirrel smile right off his little squirrel face. He chattered. Sandy wound up and swung.

Crash! She missed the squirrel but not her lamp. It crashed to the floor and shattered. The squirrel was away, out her window and across the clothesline, heading up a telephone pole. Sandy looked around at the mess. She screamed again, this time in frustration. She hated squirrels.

Sandy bent to pick up the papers that the little vermin had scattered. Gas bill. Late. Water bill. Due. Internet. Due. Phone. Late. And the big one. The mortgage payment for her ramshackle house. And now she needed a new lamp. Great, just great. At least she had an electricity credit: after all the power outages last month, the utility company had given everyone a rebate. But that wasn't really much consolation. Sandy sat down. Where was the money going to come from? She felt her eyes starting to well up.

No, she had to pull it together. God worked in mysterious ways. He would provide. He had certainly provided a glorious day, gross little vermin notwithstanding. Sandy looked in the mirror. She was disheveled. No one was going to want to hear the word and buy DVDs from a disheveled woman. The devil was in disheveled, if you rearranged the letters a little bit. Her hair no longer had any of the smooth, controlled elegance of her YouTube hair; it had regained its natural, frustrating frizz and was sticking all whichway, in defiance of gravity, in defiance of her! No, calm and composed: that was what would move merchandise. And Sandy needed money.

She looked at the neckline of her sweater. It wasn't sinful, but that squirrel...she should take a shower. And then she needed to hurry. To make her hair look that good did take time, after all. If she was going to get to the SuperMart and be all set up by the time shoppers arrived, she'd have to get a move on.

TIM

In the immaculate one-bedroom apartment with an eat-in kitchen, not much of a view but convenient to transportation and many other amenities, the mortgage for which cost less than five hundred a month, Tim was running late. This was normal, though he hated it; things just always seemed to take a little longer than he thought. He tried to live a well-ordered life. He had routines and rules to follow, which made things a little easier. Like washing the dishes: six times clockwise for plates, seven times counterclockwise for bowls, and straight into the dishwasher. Sometimes the rules and routines were what made things take a little longer, but he couldn't help that. More important to get the job done right. Besides, Tim knew how to compensate. He just had to plan to get places an hour before he needed to be there, and then he'd usually be on time. Most of the time anyway. Today was gonna be tight though. He couldn't stop watching the most recent YouTube video from the beautiful, blond preacher lady, Sandy Newman. In fact, he'd left it on loop for most of the night.

Tim was Christian, but that wasn't the only reason he liked to watch the Blessed Prayers channel. He knew it was wrong to like a lady preacher like that, but he couldn't help it. In this latest video, especially, her hair was amazing. And so were her... her boobs! Tim blushed, then shook his head, trying to focus on her words. It was a little weird the way she went on and on about squirrels, but Tim didn't really mind. Love could do that to a guy. Tim's breath caught at the thought: is this what love felt like, for real? He flicked his wrist and the cursor hovered over the little thumbs-up icon on the screen. He had never actually

rest of the management team was relegated to cubicles behind the customer-service desk. Tim and Mr. Spooner had the privacy of the balcony *above* the customer-service desk. From there, they had views of the entire store. Well, there were views of the whole store from Mr. Spooner's offices. Tim's office didn't have a window, so to speak. But when he went up the stairs to the executive suite, he could see a bunch of the store.

Tim punched in the electronic code for the front door and entered the mega super store. The first thing to do was turn on the lights. It was his favorite part of the day. They had recently installed extrapowerful new lights: Sun Series SuperBrights. The description on the box said the lights were a "technological marvel." And boy, were they ever. They saved energy *and* money. Plus, the improved visibility meant the store was safer for everyone. It was a win-win-win. The round globes lit up one after another, illuminating row upon row of goods. It was magical. What a great place to work! He took the stairs up to the executive suite two at a time.

There was a box on the desk in the central space where the coffee maker lived. The lid was slightly askew, and it looked like someone had been pawing through the manila envelopes inside. The box was labeled. Accounts. Tim furrowed his brow. That shouldn't have been there.

"Golly, it must have been Mr. Spooner, working late on a Friday night, making sure everything was shipshape!" Tim said out loud to himself, shaking his head. He wished Mr. Spooner would give him some more responsibility to help ease the burden. But his boss liked to do things himself. Oh well, he'd just have to help in the ways he could. Tim straightened up the box and put it in his own office, closing the door behind him. No need for Mr. Spooner to work himself to death.

Smiling, Tim made the coffee. Then he turned to the peripherals: a cinnamon-vanilla-potpourri air freshener and a machine that jammed people's cell phone signals in the store. He plugged them both in and turned them on. He took a deep breath and drew in the heady cinnamon-vanilla scent. It was like his grandma's house. Literally: she had the same potpourri air freshener. Tim had spent part of his bonus on a box of them to give to all his family. Tim loved cinnamon-vanilla potpourri.

He was more ambivalent about the cell phone jammer. It meant he had to deal with a lot of complaints from people about why their cell phones didn't work in the store, and Tim hated seeing customers unhappy. But Mr. Spooner said they needed the machine so people wouldn't be able to comparison shop on their phones. It was a way of leveling the playing field, he said. Tim didn't really understand, but then, that was why he wasn't the boss. And it was true that if they just told people the store was in a dead spot and they were working with the cell phone companies to try to get it resolved, then people tended to understand. Tim didn't like lying, but it did placate people. Plus, the fact that Mr. Spooner trusted him with the reasoning behind the machine was better than a year's worth of free cinnamon-vanilla potpourri! Tim realized he was just standing there like a silly person with a smile on his face. He had to get moving. People would be arriving soon!

He grabbed a broom and went to sweep Mr. Spooner's parking spot. Fifty strokes up the left side, fifty back down the right, twenty-two down the middle, and maybe one or two extra and the spot would look newly paved. Mr. Spooner never thanked him, but that was okay. Cool guys didn't have to say thanks. Tim knew it was appreciated.

Tim savored the view over the store as he headed back down the stairs, broom in hand. The new lights really were a technological marvel. Everything was so bright, so welcoming, and at this hour, so still. In just a little while, the store would be packed with customers, waiting to be satisfied. But for now, it was calm, peaceful.

Something was wrong. A prominent sign, advertising a sale on summer beach towels, was lopsided. The raincoat display beside it featured a rather realistic mannequin. Disturbingly realistic really. It had a moustache. Admittedly, it was at the other end of the registers from where he was standing, so he couldn't really tell, but, gosh, it almost looked like it was *breathing.* Mannequin realism, while maybe tipping toward the creepy, wasn't the problem though. Even the crooked sign, though a problem of course, wasn't the *real* problem. It was the positioning of the displays. No one would want to be reminded of rain if they were going to the beach. The whole thing didn't work. It was incongruous. He might have to have a word with whoever was in charge of that section. Hopefully it wouldn't come to that but...jiminy! He was standing on the stairs with his mouth open like a big dumb-dumb head! First things first: Mr. Spooner's parking spot.

Up and down and down and up, across and back across, soon the parking spot was spic-and-span, and yipes, time was running short. Reentering the store, Tim upped his pace to walk-skip. The towel sign was still off kilter, Tim wasn't surprised to see. But the raincoat display was gone, which was a surprise. It must have fallen over. He really would have to have a word with someone. Or maybe he could just take care of it himself. That would be easier, and there would be no argument. But he didn't have time for that now.

Tim returned the broom to its place and checked to make sure the coffee was ready. Then he tried to make sure his office was neat and tidy and ready for the workday. The door was locked.

"Oopsy daisy," Tim said and reached for his keys, which he kept clipped to a belt loop for easy access. "Oh fiddlesticks!"

In his haste leaving his apartment, he had grabbed the wrong set of keys. He had all the keys for the various locks and drawers and doors and whatnot in his apartment, not the SuperMart keys. He was locked out.

"Oh, for Pete's sake! Golly gee whiz, heck!" Tim felt his face grow warm. This blessed day had taken a turn.

"Get it together, Timothy," he scolded himself. It would be okay. It was a Saturday, so only Mr. Spooner would be there. Maybe he wouldn't need to go into his office. He could just spend the day on the store floor, talking with employees and customers. Mr. Spooner would like that. Or he could just hang out in the cubicles behind the customer-service desk. No one else would be in today.

Tim remembered the box that Mr. Spooner had been working on.

"No! Bad! Idiot!" Tim berated himself aloud and was on the point of banging his head against the door but managed to stop himself. He couldn't let himself get down. He took a deep breath. It would be all right. He'd just have to skip lunch and run home and get the right keys. There. Problem solved. It wasn't the normal routine, but it'd be okay. Tim was whistling again as he went back to the front door to welcome employees and wait for Mr. Spooner's triumphant arrival.

MITCH

Mitch was hungover. The alarm sent bolts of pain ricocheting around his foggy skull. Was it 8:30 already? Whatever. It was bullshit he had to go to work on a Saturday anyway. Wasn't he supposed to be in charge? But no, *Corporate* had ordered him to be there, to receive a phone call or some other BS. Financial irregularity? C'mon. What did they know? Nothing, 'cause they were punks. God dammit, his head hurt. But it had been worth it. Applebee's had been off the chain last night! What's-her-name hadn't come home with him, but Mitch was pretty sure that the conquest would only be sweeter for the chase. Though now that he thought about it, he might not even have gotten her name either. Oh well. It'd be that much more sweeter for not knowing.

Mitch sat up and the room spun. He hunched over, sitting on the side of the bed, head in hands, elbows on knees. Play through it like a champion. He reached over to the bedside table for some ibuprofen. SuperMart brand. Didn't work as well as the name-brand stuff, but whatever. He was a team player. Plus, he got it for free. The childproof cap gave him some difficulty.

"Sonofabitch! Bastard. C'mon!"

Mitch put everything he had into it, and finally the cap gave way. He slammed back a couple of pills and swallowed them dry. They burned his throat as they went down. No candy coating. It was a good burn though; how else could you tell if the medicine was working? He burped, then stretched his arms up and over his head and back down to his sides. He felt better already.

He still didn't want to go to work. It was Saturday, after all. But whatever, he could nap there. Mitch's second-in-command was a total chump, but he could handle the store for a couple of hours while Mitch slept.

Mitch stumbled into the bathroom and found the shower. He turned on the water, superhot. That was a great thing about the condo: an endless supply of scalding water. That scalding water might have been burning him a little bit, but Mitch gritted his teeth and embraced the pain. It was just weakness leaving the body. He felt his head clearing. He grabbed the soap—another freebie from work—and lathered up. The bubbles swirled and disappeared down the drain. It was like a kaleidoscope. Mitch liked it. Real Italian marble in his shower—bubbles didn't swirl like that over bullshit fake marble. Mitch shut the water off and got out.

He wrapped himself in a deluxe Egyptian cotton towel (freebie) and admired himself in the mirror. "Spoon" they had called him back when he was playing tailback for Central High. Those had been the days. "Spooooooon!" the crowd would shout after a big play, which was pretty often. Old two-four really brought it, back in the day. He still looked pretty good. Maybe his definition wasn't quite what it could be. But he didn't look bad. He could definitely still bring it if he wanted to. He was still more jacked than probably like 95 percent of guys out there. Ninety percent anyway. Mitch turned and looked at himself from another angle. Fine, not what he could be, but he was definitely in better shape than at least half the guys out there. He thrust his jaw forward. Good-looking dude. Still, probably should hit the gym a little harder before going back to Applebee's. That chick wouldn't be able to resist him. Work hard. Play hard. Mitch made a couple of seductive faces in the mirror—pouty lips; squinty eyes; one eye winking, opposite eyebrow raised, corners of his mouth slightly raised—so many options, he should really name them. He flexed one more time and left the bathroom. Stud.

"Morning, Charlie!" Mitch hollered to his pet piranha. Charlie was swimming slowly back and forth in his tank, the murderous little bastard. Mitch tossed a handful of cubed steak into the tank. Charlie destroyed it in about five seconds.

"Hell yeah!" Mitch shouted. He kinda wished he and Charlie could high-five. But after the last time, he was not sticking his hand in that tank again. "Daddy's gotta go to work. I know; it's dumb. But I'll be back later. Stay cool."

Mitch grabbed a bar and a banana. He descended to the garage in the elevator, chomping on the powdery powerbar. SuperBrand PowEnergy bars weren't tasty, but they were free. And free, after all, was tasty. He swallowed the last of it as the doors opened, and he stepped out into the garage, leaving the wrapper on the floor of the elevator. His Hummer was waiting for him, parked sideways across two spaces. Like a boss.

It was an H3. Mitch had considered getting the H2 or maybe even an actual decommissioned military model but, in the end, decided that might be too showy. He did like to keep it classy, after all. And it wasn't like his truck wasn't cool as hell all the same. Mitch had tricked it out: matte-black paint, supertinted windows, license plate that read SPOON24. And the rims. Twenty-inch spinners, also matte black. Boss: for a boss. Sometimes Mitch wished someone else would drive just so he could see it go by. Not that he would ever let someone else drive his truck.

"Sup, buddy," Mitch said to the parking attendant, Johnny or Matty or something like that. He hopped into the driver's seat and turned the key. The deep-throated rumbling of the double-barreled chrome-plated exhaust filled the garage. That was not a freebie from work. SuperMart exhaust systems sucked. This was custom. Only the very best for Mitch's wheels. He turned up the bass; Z107, Today's Best Hit Music, blared the Top 40 countdown out of his speakers, also custom—truly only the best for his wheels. He checked his hair and sunglasses in the rearview mirror, which was the thing's only purpose, really. Looking back was for losers. Mitch Spooner looked ahead. He flexed his calf then tromped on the accelerator. A small screech reverberated after him as he sped out of the garage.

A similar screech echoed around the parking lot of the Cup-a-Joe just around the corner. One could only get so far on a PowEnergy bar. Mitch looked in the rearview again. One beautiful man looked back.

Coffee in one hand, bagel in the other, steering with his knee, Mitch headed for work. Haters gonna hate, but playas gonna play. And Mitch Spooner was definitely a player. He tossed the half-eaten bagel out the window—they were never as good after the first couple bites—and floored it.

CLEM

Clem was getting too old for this shit. The alarm went off, but he was already awake. He just couldn't seem to sleep like he used to. It wasn't what he'd expected. He thought he'd be more into sleeping as he entered his so-called golden years. But it wasn't the case.

"Turn that cursed thing off!"

"Sorry," Clem said and did as he was told. His back was sore. It was probably that newfangled bed they were sleeping on, with its firmness control and auto tilt; it was a surprise it couldn't fly. His hips and knees were achy. That probably wasn't the bed's fault. He hauled himself up and sat on the side of the bed. His rear end sank into the foam. Stupid bed.

"I don't see why you have to get up so early," his wife, Else, said, propping herself up on pillows. She didn't need the auto-tilt feature to do it.

"I've got to go to work."

He looked down at his legs and feet. When had he gotten so droopy? Even his feet had wrinkles. He wiggled his toes. Getting up was no fun. Neither was getting old.

"I don't see why," his wife said. "I thought you were retired."

"Oh, come on, you wouldn't want me hanging around here all day, would you?"

Else knew better than to answer that question. She was right; he had retired. And, truth be told, he didn't even want to go to work. The store was a wreck, and there was little to nothing he could do about it. He should probably have just taken his money and walked away, found a hobby or something like that. That was why they called it selling out, after all. And the money had

27

been very, very good. It let them start the Foundation. That had been all Else's idea, and she was doing tremendous things with it. But he would have just been in the way there. It was just... how was he supposed to just give up his life's work and watch it get perverted into its current state? The money, the Foundation, and the store. Clem wished he could have it all three ways. He wished his back wasn't so sore too, but if wishes were fishes, he'd have fried up a mess ages ago.

Well, now he was up. Things would get better as he moved around and loosened up.

"Should I bring you some coffee?" he asked.

"Yes, please."

He shuffled off to make the coffee. Even after fifty-plus years of marriage, there were few things coffee couldn't fix. They used to have a live-in housekeeper, but that all seemed a bit much now. It was still a big house, but walking was probably good for him.

When he returned with the coffee, his shirt and tie were laid out for him, as always. Else was a sweetheart.

"Have a good day, darling," he said and put the coffee on the nightstand.

"Thanks, Clem. You too. Don't work too hard."

"I'll try not to. You too."

Clem left his wife and headed off to his job, such as it was.

DIRK BLADE

It was better to have work. Dirk Blade had to remind himself of that sometimes. Standing in the semidarkness of the Mega SuperMart at 7:30 a.m. was one of those times. He could already tell it was going to be a long day; heck, it had already *been* a long day. He'd been awake for five hours, driven 150 miles, and so far was none the wiser for it. His stomach rumbled.

Everyone knew the key to a calm mind and comfortable spirit, not to mention finely tuned body, depended upon just the right morning alkaloid regime. Get it right and your mind was clear, your spirit charged, and your body ready for action. Get it wrong and, well, morphine and strychnine were alkaloids too. They had their uses, sure, but not in the morning. Dirk Blade's preferred morning alkaloid cocktail was a mix of $C_8H_{10}N_4O_2$ and $C_{10}H_{14}N_2$, in the form of a double espresso and a Chesterfield. This morning had not allowed for it. Not that his wife really ever much allowed the $C_{10}H_{14}N_2$ anymore.

Usually the jobs were something pretty small potatoes, barely enough to get by, but work wasn't there unless you took it. It was good to have work, and this job was no small potatoes. Sometimes he missed the surety and security of working for the department, but the independence he got from being his own boss more than made up for that. Most of the time.

Not that he was really his own boss. His wife ran the office and took care of the books. She was a constant nag and rarely gave him a moment's peace. So he needed to appreciate the moment of peace here in the empty store. Yes, it was good to have work, even if it had meant waking up way too early and a three-hour drive, broken up only by a 4:00 a.m. Denny's breakfast. The

29

coffee had been indifferent, and the mess they called eggs and hash browns was doing weird things to his GI tract, but it was all part of the job. He hadn't had a cigarette in...way too long. That was his wife's fault too. The e-cigarette she had given him for his birthday just didn't do the trick. That was probably why they worked so well. No satisfaction, so everybody just quit.

The drive had been tense, and not just because he missed his usual alkaloid regimen, but also because he never knew when the hunk of junk he called a car might finally give up. It shuttered and sputtered, but it got him there, though who knew if it would get him back. He might have missed a company car, but he had never had one.

Dirk Blade was not his real name. But no one came to Bob and Marnie Johnson's Detective Agency with their tough-to-solve cases. They had found that out the hard way. The new identity had to sound professional, yet dangerous. Germans were professional, yet dangerous. Dirk was a German name. When they had looked it up in the dictionary, they were pleased to discover its English meaning was also fitting. And so Dirk Blade, PI, was born. Lots of people, it turned out, were willing to turn to Dirk Blade, PI, with their tough-to-solve cases, and business picked up. It had been a little tricky at first: Bob Johnson was not the sort of man who could simply take on a name and impersonate a great sleuth. To do the job right, he couldn't just pretend. So when he was working, Bob Johnson didn't exist; there was only Dirk Blade.

No case too big, no case too small. That was the motto of Dirk Blade, PI. The motto had been his wife's idea. It meant he spent far too much time climbing trees after widows' cats and spying on suspected philanderers, very few of whom were actually philandering. He hadn't thought that the *too big* modifying clause would ever be a problem. Standing by a display of cut-rate towels in the semidark of the Mega SuperMart, he was starting to wonder if maybe this was the case that called that assumption into question.

He had been working it for nearly two weeks, poring through mountains of paper work and getting nowhere. Everything was redacted, redacted, redacted. Even still, Dirk Blade could tell: something was missing. His wife kept yapping at him to look at it again. He told her to look at the paper work herself, which was the sort of thing Bob Johnson never would have dared to do. She hadn't appreciated that suggestion so much, judging by the force of the rolled-up magazine across the back of his head after he had made it. He rubbed the spot—maybe Bob Johnson had the right of it, sometimes—and could almost still feel the sting. Not content with physical violence, she then began hectoring him to go to the scene of the crime. Relentlessly. Dirk Blade hadn't liked it, but nor could he say she was wrong. Visiting the scene of the crime was basic gumshoe stuff, and his client hadn't given him the access code to the store for nothing. Likely, there was something there.

So far though...Dirk Blade had spent his first couple hours in the store looking through boxes of files in the executive office. He hadn't found anything. It had to be there somewhere though. Unless his big corporate client was setting him up, most likely at the behest of the feds. Dirk Blade didn't think it was likely, but neither could he discount the possibility; professional jealousies ran deep.

There was nothing in the boxes. Well, not *nothing*, the boxes weren't empty, but the personnel files within didn't tell him anything he didn't already know. Something—call it intuition, call it a sixth sense developed after twenty years of sleuthing, call it his wife's nagging—told him the information he needed was in the store. But it wasn't in that office, wasn't in that box. He had left the box out, as a warning. Maybe he could get the perp to panic and make a mistake. That would be the best. But for the moment, he had to wait.

The store lights lit up. Dirk Blade held still. He had long since trained his inward-looking eye. The idea was that you focused so intently on yourself that no one else would notice you were there, rendering you virtually invisible. It worked best with some sort of camouflage; you could blend in with the drapes for example, if there were drapes. Or a coat rack, if there was a coat rack. Dressed as he was in his usual costume, a tan trench coat and a fedora, Dirk Blade always blended in nicely with a coat rack. But as the lights came on, he was standing next to the towel display. All he could do was be still and hope no one saw him.

Dirk Blade watched as a slight man in a white shirt and black tie walked through the empty store, whistling. The whistler disappeared up the stairs to the office. *Ho ho!* The first suspect. But it wasn't time to bust him yet. He needed more proof, more evidence. He needed to find the smoking gun. Smoking. Dirk Blade's fingers twitched toward his pocket, but he stilled his hand, focused his inward-looking eye. The nicotine fix could wait. After what felt like an interminably long time, the man came back down, carrying a broom. Why had he taken so long? What was with the broom? What was he trying to hide? Dirk Blade held still, and the man went back outside with the broom.

Maybe the day would turn up something after all. And it felt good to have work. Dirk Blade retreated deeper into the store. He had to remain unnoticed until it filled up with customers. Then he would carry on his investigation.

RUSTY

Rusty was freaked out. Some crazy human—adult, female—had just tried to run him over. Then she got out of her car, determined to finish the job! Rusty took his pulse from the safety of a leafy branch while he watched the psycho woman look for him on the ground—272. That was high, even for a squirrel. Was that a symptom of early onset rabies? He had to calm down. Take deep breaths. Or could it be that bird flu thing he had been hearing so much about? Please not bird flu! He'd have to check with Raccoon at some point about prevention. It probably wasn't bird flu. Rusty wasn't sure, but he thought that you could only get bird flu by making out with birds. So he was safe.

Maybe his heart rate was just spiking from nearly being assassinated. That made sense. The human woman got back in her car and began to drive off, painfully slowly. Probably on the lookout for him! Rusty checked for hawks. Still clear. He'd have to be careful. Obviously his plan wasn't as top secret as he thought. He might have to talk to Raccoon about that. The guy was clever, but his problem was he couldn't help but show it off all the time. Rusty didn't think Raccoon would have tipped anyone off on purpose, but he might have blabbed inadvertently, especially if he'd been into the corn liquor he liked to distill. Focus! It was not the time to worry about Raccoon. Rusty would just have to be vigilant.

Besides, the woman had missed. She couldn't kill him. She couldn't stop him. Rabies...Rusty compulsively checked his tail. Still bushy. Silky, sexy. Rabies couldn't stop him. Bird flu either! Rusty was agile. Virile. Unstoppable. Light as a feather, quick as a squirrel. The power of positive thinking! Who da squirrel? You da squirrel. Rusty took off through the trees. Branch to branch and tree to tree. The sun shone bright.

Rusty burst through one last clump of foliage and stared out at the view. There was an empty expanse of blacktop and then the mark. The SuperMart. There was some human over by the door, sweeping. Sweeping the parking lot? Humans didn't make sense. But they were clearly going to be guarding their nuts. That made sense. Human nuts were roasted *and* salted. You didn't have to smash them or anything either. If Rusty had nuts like that, he'd guard them too. *When.* When Rusty had nuts like that, he would guard them too. Rusty chuckled to himself. Not all of his plans were revealed. The human was guarding the door. Rusty wasn't going in that way. Their pitiful human security could never stop all of the avenues open to a squirrel. He was going in through a hole in the wall. Literally.

They couldn't stop him. They couldn't even hope to contain him.

Rusty checked his pulse again—199. Back to normal. He checked his tail. Still silky, still sexy. But now was the hard part. He had to cross the pavement without getting run over or eaten by some predator. There were no cars yet. But there hadn't been any when he was crossing the street either...until there was. Cars were quick. He'd just have to be quicker. Rusty took a deep breath. No guts, no nuts. He tensed. Was he ready? He could use a pick-me-up. He shouldn't. He had promised to quit once the kits arrived. And he would. But they hadn't arrived yet. And it wasn't dangerous. Not really anyway. Just a quick, little hit. The job was more stressful than anticipated, and electricity would really help. There were some power lines running to the big red-white-and-blue sign. Maybe just a little pick-me-up. Rusty scampered up and started nibbling on the wire. Pulses of electricity coursed through him. His fur tingled; the day grew brighter; the white lines demarcating where humans should park their assassination machines were crisper. His tail bushed out a little more fully. He nibbled a little more. The metallic tang of current flooded his mouth, his tongue growing sensitive to the edge of numbness. Oh yeah! Felt good.

Now Rusty was jacked up. Ready to go. Rusty checked for predators. Skies clear. On the ground...a few cars were arriving. Store workers, Rusty reasoned. More guards. Well, you didn't become the prince of squirrel thieves because it was easy. A huge black SUV screeched into the parking lot, nearly sideswiping a lamppost and then roaring down to where the man had been sweeping. Rusty took one last nibble off the wire. Time to go. There was a grassy median strip that would be free of cars if he wanted to run down that. Not much cover, but there was a solitary oak about two-thirds of the way toward the store. He didn't really have a choice. Fortune favored the bold. Time to bust a move. The wire was almost completely chewed through anyway. Plus, he was trying to quit.

Rusty, amped up, shot down the telephone pole and across the parking lot toward the grass median. A car came into the parking lot as he hit the pavement and almost got him. Again! Rusty didn't stop this time. He was going for glory. He was going for nuts.

Pavement. Pavement. Car! Grass. Pavement! Grass. Female human foot! Scream! Grass! Tree!

Rusty raced up the trunk and perched on a low branch. Safe. He took his pulse. It was creeping above three hundred. But that was probably just the electricity. Or rabies! He checked his tail. Still bushy, silky, sexy. Not rabies then. He couldn't believe some idiot had almost run him over a second time. They really were trying to stop him. Flippin' Raccoon and his big mouth. But they hadn't gotten him. Rusty was on it. The prince of squirrel thieves. And he was almost inside, only one last sprint to the nut house. He circled around and up to get a better look at his route. The pit of his stomach dropped. He was staring straight at a hawk. And the hawk was staring straight at him.

MITCH

"Wooo! Yeah, boy! That's what I'm talkin' about!"

Mitch was amped up. It'd been one hell of a drive to work: fast, aggressive, on the edge. Just like Mitch liked to live. And Z107 provided one hell of a soundtrack. The Top 40 countdown had just reached number 24, his lucky number, when the SuperMart came into sight. Coincidence? No way. It was fate. Today was gonna be a good day. The song was catchy and fly. Just like Mitch. Hammering the gas, he nearly flipped the Hummer right there in the parking lot but, instead, he just came out looking like a badass. Right on. Mitch waited for the song to end before he got out.

"Yo, Timmy! My man. Give me some skin, dog!"

Timmy gave Mitch a high five. It was weaker than watered-down wine cooler.

"Timmy, you pussy. I said give me some skin! Slap like you mean it, bro!"

Mitch had to make Timmy slap his hand twice more before he was satisfied.

"Good morning, Mr. Spooner," Timmy said. "Coffee's made, and I hope your parking spot is clean to your satisfaction, sir."

Mitch looked at Timmy. The guy was pathetic. Nothing masculine about him. He probably pissed sitting down. Mitch laughed. Still, Timmy did the crappy jobs that Mitch didn't want to do, and his parking spot *was* clean. So whatever. Timmy might be an idiot, but he was Mitch's idiot.

"Cool, Timmy," Mitch said. Timmy's smile made Mitch uncomfortable. He was like an overattentive golden retriever or something.

"You see me come in? Tell it like it is, Timmy. Balls to the wall or what? Was I on two wheels, or was I on two wheels?"

Timmy shrugged. He apparently had been rendered speechless by Mitch's awesomeness. Whatever. Mitch ran a hand over his hair. The gel—freebie—had held. Mitch suspected it might be because it was actually glue, but whatever; the point was that he was still stylin', still baller. But now the thrill from the reckless commute was wearing off. His headache was creeping back.

"All right, Timmy. I'm gonna be in my office for a while. Don't come get me under any circumstances until lunchtime."

"But, Mr. Spooner, sir—"

"God dammit, Timmy. I can't make it any clearer. Do I have to write it down for you too?"

"No, sir. I'll handle everything, sir. Don't worry, sir. But, Mr. Spooner, sir, did you want to lead the cheer this morning? I think the staff likes it better when you lead it."

Yeah. That was probably true. They probably did like their cheer led by a certifiable badass. More meaningful that way.

"Okay, but then I'm gonna need the office until lunch. You'll have to find some other place to be."

"Yessir. No problem, Mr. Spooner. What about the Golden Snacks delivery?"

"Jesus Christ, Timmy. You can handle a little shipment of goddamn peanuts, can't you? Just make sure the door is open. There's no handle on the outside."

"Yipes! You just took his name in vain!"

"What? Oh for Christ's sake, Timmy. Just make sure I'm not bothered."

Timmy had clasped one hand to his mouth. What the hell was wrong with him?

"Timmy?"

"O...okay, Mr. Spooner."

"Good."

Mitch went inside. The employees were all assembled. Waiting for him. Mitch smiled. He raised his hands for silence. It was already quiet.

"All right, people. Today's a big day. Saturday. Remember to push the...the...what was it Timmy?"

"Bananas, sir?"

Oh yeah. Goddamn nanners were about to go rotten. Shouldn't they have figured out how to stop that at this point? Whatever.

"Right. Bananas, people. Push the bananas. They're about to spoil, and we need to clear that inventory. Word. Now it's time to sell some shit and make some money!" Mitch knew his employees liked it better when he swore. It made everything seem cooler. Kept it more real. Mitch Spooner was nothing if not real. And cool. Really cool. He looked out at them. They looked as tired as he felt. That surprised him a bit. He hadn't seen any of them at Applebee's. Not that he necessarily remembered much after a certain point, heh. Still, tired or not, shouldn't they be looking at him with a little more respect and awe, like Timmy did? Whatever.

"Time for our cheer. Let's make some noiiise! Su, su, su!"

"Su, su, su," the crowd said.

"I can't hear you! Su! Su! *Su!*"

"Su, su, su."

It was as weak as one of Timmy's high fives, but Mitch's head was telling him he really needed to go sit in the dark for a while.

"Su, su, *super!*"

"Su, su, super," the crowd echoed. That was a little better. Must have been his charismatic leadership.

"Su, su, *super!* SuperMart! We're super!" Mitch yelled. The crowd parroted it back. Not everyone though. There was one young lady, hot too, who was not cheering. She looked familiar. But then all pretty girls looked the same. Still, he'd have to speak to her about not cheering. Maybe about more than that, heh, heh. He'd have Timmy bring her up later.

"Su, su, *super!* SuperMart! We're super!"

All his employees, except for the one hottie, held the last *r*, as was the custom for the cheer. In a fit of inspiration, Mitch punched his fist in the air and held it up as he turned and headed off to his office. He was exhausted. His head hurt. He needed a nap.

TIM

"Good morning, Brian."

"Morning, Amanda."

"Hi there, Jeff."

"Scarlett."

"Hey, Aidan, great day to come to work!"

Tim enthusiastically greeted the SuperMart employees as they arrived. His enthusiasm was not returned, on the whole, but Tim didn't mind. They'd round into form as the day went along. The guttural roar of an aftermarket exhaust system warned Tim that his boss was on the way. Everything was shipshape. Well, he was locked out of his office, and that wasn't too good, but maybe that wouldn't come up until he found a way to get his keys. Yep. There was Mr. Spooner. Just a little late. Whoa, he almost went up on two wheels!

"Good morning, Clem. Great to see you today."

"Good morning, Timothy. I hope you are in fine fettle today." One of the greeters, a genial old guy named Clem, returned Tim's greeting. Tim thought Clem was probably pretty good at his job; he was so warm and welcoming. And he appreciated that Clem took the time to call him Timothy. He liked Timothy. Or Tim. Either one. He hated Timmy. It made him feel seven years old. That was what Mr. Spooner called him, though Tim didn't complain. He didn't really have a choice; that was just how cool guys like Mr. Spooner talked.

"Yes, sir," Tim told Clem, not sure what a fettle was but imagined a fat kettle, like a cauldron or something like that. He didn't see how he was in a fine one; he was just standing on the sidewalk. Maybe Clem was getting a little dotty? He was old. But

40

the answer seemed to please him, so Tim decided not to worry about it too much right then.

The black Hummer was screaming down the parking lot toward him. What a cool car! Tim knew he would never be able to pull off a car like that, but he was glad Mr. Spooner could. Tim checked the parking spot. Spotless. Yipes, was Mr. Spooner going to crash?!

Tim jumped back only to see the Hummer lock its wheels, spin, and slide into the parking spot and the one next to it, which was reserved for Tim's use. He didn't mind if Mr. Spooner parked there too: he didn't have a car. The vibrations from Mr. Spooner's sound system shook the glass entrance doors, and Tim could feel them through his feet. If history were any precedent, it would still be a couple of minutes before Mr. Spooner got out. Tim ducked inside to get everyone ready for the cheer.

"All right, everyone, let's assemble here," Tim said, indicating the open area between the cash registers and the shopping carts. "Mr. Spooner will be coming in in just a minute and will lead the cheer."

The SuperMart employees shuffled together. Not quite shipshape, but it would have to do. Tim heard a car door slam and hurried back out to greet Mr. Spooner. Mr. Spooner had sprayed gravel all over the previously immaculate parking spot with his scary parking maneuver. Fiddlesticks! He braced for the critique he knew was coming.

"Wooo! Yeah, boy! That's what I'm talkin' about!"

That didn't seem too negative.

"Yo, Timmy! My man. Give me some skin, dog!"

Tim held up his hand, and Mitch slapped it, hard. It stung. Tim shook his hand to dissipate the pain.

"Timmy, you pussy. I said give me some skin! Slap like you mean it, bro!"

Tim tried again. And again. Owie! It stung. But finally Mr. Spooner seemed to be satisfied. Tim smiled. Mr. Spooner was still calling him Timmy, but he was also calling him dog and cat nicknames, which Tim knew were cool-guy code for acceptance, even affection. He smiled wider.

"Good morning, Mr. Spooner," Tim said. "Coffee's made, and I hope your parking spot is clean to your satisfaction, sir."

Tim looked at Mr. Spooner. He was so cool. Tim sure was lucky to get to work for such a great boss. He trusted Tim with lots of important jobs. But he looked tired. Tim worried that he was overworking himself. His mind drifted to the box locked in his office. Maybe Mr. Spooner could trust him with even more responsibility. He stretched his smile to the breaking point, to show that he was trustworthy.

"Cool, Timmy," Mr. Spooner said. He liked the parking spot! He didn't mind the gravel.

"You see me come in? Tell it like it is, Tim-may! Balls to the wall or what? Was I on two wheels, or was I on two wheels?"

The questions confused Tim. Of course he saw him come in. He didn't know what the second question meant, and the answer to the last two questions was the same. In fact, it was the same question! Tim didn't see the obvious right answer. So he just shrugged.

Mr. Spooner didn't seem to mind the lack of a verbal answer. He kept talking.

"All right, Timmy. I'm gonna be in my office for a while. Don't come get me under any circumstances until lunchtime."

"But, Mr. Spooner, sir—"

There was a big snack-truck delivery today, and Tim had never managed one of those all by himself. Plus, he needed Mr. Spooner to lead the cheer. It pumped everyone up so much more when he did it.

"God dammit, Timmy. I can't make it any clearer. Do I have to write it out for you too?"

"No, sir. I'll handle everything, sir." Tim swallowed. He'd figure it out, somehow. He hoped. "But, Mr. Spooner, sir, did you want to lead the cheer this morning? I think the staff likes it better when you lead it."

Mr. Spooner looked off into the middle distance for a moment. Tim waited.

Finally, Mr. Spooner said, "Okay, but then I'm gonna need the office until lunch. You'll have to find some other place to be."

"Yessir. No problem, Mr. Spooner."

That was fine with Tim. He had been planning on that anyway, what with being locked out of his own office and all. But he thought he really should double-check that Mr. Spooner didn't want to be there for the snack-truck delivery.

"What about the Golden Snacks delivery?"

"Jesus Christ, Timmy!"

Tim felt his face flush. Yipes! He had just taken his name in vain. Even cool guys shouldn't do that. But Mr. Spooner didn't seem very concerned when Tim pointed it out.

"For Christ's sake, Timmy. Just make sure I'm not bothered."

Mr. Spooner had done it again! It was like he was trying to sin. Even being cool couldn't save you in the final judgment. Tim thought maybe it might help a little bit, but golly, he wouldn't want to push his luck, even if he were as cool as Mr. Spooner. Mr. Spooner was probably just tired though; he sure looked it. Tim would try to help him with his soul later. Mr. Spooner's sinful language certainly didn't affect his ability to pump up the troops for a big day. Sometimes Tim wished he could inspire people that way.

After Mr. Spooner had gone up to his office, Tim adjusted his tie. Adjusting his tie always helped him calm down. It was something he could control. Mr. Spooner had left him in charge of the entire store for the whole morning! Tim needed to stay calm. He was also in charge of receiving the Golden Snacks shipment. That was enough to fluster anyone. He had wished for more responsibility, but now that he had it, he wasn't so sure it was a good idea. On the plus side, Mr. Spooner had told him explicitly to stay out of the office, so he wouldn't have to explain that he was locked out. He'd be able to sneak home and get the keys before Mr. Spooner even found out. Tim's tie was straight. He squared his shoulders. Customers would start to arrive any minute. He breathed deep and remembered his favorite internet preacher's words. Today was a most blessed day!

SANDY

Sandy wasn't so sure the day was really all that blessed after all. It had started at home when she had picked up her Blessed Prayer pamphlets. Well, no, really if she was being honest, it had started when she had been so...so *trespassed* upon by that filthy little creature. It had just gotten worse when she had picked up her Blessed Prayer pamphlets. Something had been chewing on them. Probably that same mangy squirrel. She couldn't bless him; she just couldn't. The Lord Jesus would understand. She had had to leave half of the pamphlets behind. They were garbage.

Recycling. Sandy wasn't so sure about recycling; it seemed like something the godless liberal elites were pushing to feel better about themselves. They weren't cleaning up the garbage that kept getting tossed in the ditch across the street from her house, or the toxic mess behind the garage down the road, the years of oil and gas and who-knew-what else. No money in that. Of course, if there was money in recycling, then maybe she should consider adding it to her portfolio. Just until she had her own radio show or a cash-generating podcast. Plus, recycling did seem like a good thing. So it was tough to know. To her knowledge, Jesus had yet to make a definitive statement on the subject, so perhaps it was best to withhold her own judgment. For now anyway. Try to remember to do it when she could. Yes, that was a decent compromise.

Not that it made losing half of her promotional materials any easier. They were expensive. Just like everything else in this unjust world. No. She couldn't be negative. Just like everything else in this *blessed* world: that was the right attitude.

Thank God her DVDs had been okay. Little squirrel teeth couldn't get through the hard plastic. The same could not be said for her big cardboard display, the one that said, "Sandy Newman. A preacher for YOU! Have YOU found Jesus?" with a pretty good and slightly larger-than-life-size photo of herself smiling blessings out from it. She had left it too close to that leaky window, and it was now stained and warped past the point of repair. She really should get that window fixed.

It had been a frustrating morning. But now, in the SuperMart parking lot, unloading her materials—the undamaged pamphlets, her DVDs, the folding card table that doubled as her kitchen table—into a shopping cart, things were getting better. Maybe the morning's trials had just been a test. Yes, that was probably it. A divine test. She would be equal to it.

Her car had been another test, though Sandy was pretty sure there was nothing divine about it. It had started fine for a change, which was truly a blessing. But there were clearly transmission issues. She hadn't been able to go much more than twenty-five miles an hour. And there was a pretty awful burning smell coming from somewhere too. The car was a piece of junk, and she didn't have money to fix it. Not yet anyway. It would probably cost less just to get a new used one. But she didn't have the money for that either. If only Jesus had been a mechanic! Sandy wondered if even he could fix her car. Even miracles had limits, after all. Oh well. It had gotten her there. Despite the big jerk-face in the Hummer who almost ran her off the road and the uppity woman in a minivan who tailgated her all the way into the SuperMart parking lot.

At least it was a beautiful day. The humidity of last week finally seemed to be gone. That boded well, not least for her hair. Sandy took the last box of DVDs from her car and put them into the shopping cart she was using to ferry her materials to the front door, from where she would minister to the masses as they came and went from the SuperMart.

"Eeek!" Sandy shrieked as something small and brownish red ran over her foot. She dropped the box of DVDs on the pavement. The squirrel darted up a tree and disappeared among the foliage.

"Oh gross, yuck!" What was it with squirrels today? She unconsciously brushed her chest off. She gave a convulsive little shiver, then straightened up. She had to keep it together. Confidence sold. She bent to pick up the DVDs.

"Oh, h-e-double hockey sticks."

The DVD cases all had cracks running through them.

"Little brat!" She looked up at the tree where the squirrel had disappeared. Squirrels. There just wasn't anything redeeming about them.

She popped one of the cases open and examined the DVD. It seemed okay. But it looked a little shabby. She'd probably have to put a discount on them. Was ten bucks too much for a possibly broken DVD? Hopefully not. She took out an antiseptic wipe from her purse and cleaned her foot. The little critters were full of germs.

"Oh, he...ck." Sandy had been about to name the infernal place again but managed to pull it back. Some DVD cases were really messed up. Ten bucks was probably too much. But then again, ten bucks for the path to eternal salvation was actually quite the bargain. Better than any of the so-called bargains people would be finding inside the SuperMart. Sandy decided it would be okay.

Just then, a big bird soared from the tree. It was majestic. A hawk or eagle or something. Auspicious, that was what it was. It truly was a blessed day. And it looked like it had something in one of its claws. She hoped it was the squirrel.

Sandy set up her folding card/kitchen table just outside the SuperMart's entrance, between the front door and that jerk-face's jet-black Hummer. What a son of a gun. He had parked in two spots reserved for the hardworking employees of the store. Sandy shook her head and spread a red-and-white-checked tablecloth over the table. She arranged her materials in an agreeable pattern, a smooth fan of pamphlets in the middle of the table, flanked by a couple DVDs stood vertically, to add a 3-D element to the presentation. It looked good. She checked her hair in the door's reflection. It looked good. She smiled. It was time to go to work.

The first folks who walked by were none other than the driver of the minivan, Ms. Uppity, and a small boy, her son, no doubt. The boy was complaining as they walked toward her. He did not, it seemed, want to go to the SuperMart. Sandy smiled. Just a little more divine retribution for Ms. Uppity.

"And besides, Mom, you almost ran over two squirrels! Isn't that enough stress for one day? Wouldn't it be easier if we just went home?" Uppity Jr. was arguing with his mother and walking with an exaggerated gate, as if his feet weighed as much as a whole stack of Bibles, the King James Version.

Ooh, but it sounded like they were having squirrel problems too. That made them prime candidates for her sermons!

"Hi," she said as they got close. "Could I talk to you both for a minute?"

They slowed down. That was as big of an invitation as she could hope to receive, though the boy was looking at her with green eyes set under eyebrows so furrowed that they almost met in the middle. The corners of his mouth were turned down, and she could see his little jaw muscles clenching and unclenching. It was kind of the opposite of friendly. Sandy didn't really appreciate it. But she had to wade ahead, dive right in. There was probably some other water metaphor, something to do with baptism, maybe, but she couldn't think of it. Instead she started talking.

"Now, I'm sure y'all know Jesus. But do you *know* him? Not biblically of course. Ha-ha." Sandy looked at Ms. Uppity; that joke had been for her benefit. Ms. Uppity didn't laugh. Tough crowd. Sandy pressed on. "Do you know what he has done for you? He loves you! Pure and true love. All you have to do is accept him as your personal savior. Pretty great, huh, little guy?"

"Jesus is a hippie!" the little boy yelled at her. Sandy straightened up. Ms. Uppity grimaced and seemed decently embarrassed.

"Billy, that's not how we talk to people. Say sorry to the nice lady. I'm really sorry about that, Ms...."

"Newman. Sandy Newman." Sandy extended her hand and shook Ms. Uppity's. "And that's all right. Don't worry about it. Now, Billy, how old are you?"

"I'm seven, but I'm almost eight! I'm not 'little guy'!"

Sandy struggled to keep what she hoped was a serene smile on her face. Did he always yell like that? No wonder Ms. Uppity was so, well, uppity.

"Of course you're not," Sandy said, crouching to be on his level. It was a little tricky in her pencil skirt. But she managed.

"Now why would you call Jesus a hippie? Do you even know what a hippie is?"

The kid rolled his eyes.

"C'mon, lady—"

"She is Ms. Newman," Ms. Uppity said, cutting him off more effectively and smoothly than a mohel at a bris. Whatever one might think about the tenets of Judaism—and Sandy was mostly a New Testament gal herself—one couldn't deny that it provided some useful metaphors. Sandy shook her head; that didn't matter right now. The kid glared at his mother. Sandy almost pitied her. Her erratic driving was becoming more and more understandable.

The kid said, "C'mon, Ms. Newman. Everybody knows what a hippie is. Just because I'm only almost eight doesn't mean I'm dumb."

"No, of course not," Sandy said. "But why would you say Jesus is a hippie?"

"Right," Billy said. "So here's why. Just look at Jesus. Long hair, beard, sandals. Classic hippie costume. I wouldn't be surprised if he had a hacky sack hidden somewhere in those robes. Hippies love hacky sack. Add in the message of peace and love, I mean, duh, lady—I mean, Ms. Newman. Looks like a hippie. Acts like a hippie. Probably smells like a hippie. Is a hippie!"

"I'm really sorry about this. He's in such a mood this morning. Please don't take any offense," Ms. Uppity said. "Come on, Billy, apologize to Ms. Newman, and let's go before you get into more trouble."

The kid just scowled. Sandy had to admit his logic was pretty ironclad. She was sure he was wrong, but she'd have to think about why. Better just to end this conversation and move on to the sales pitch.

"No, it's fine, ma'am. He's got a point. Maybe hippies aren't that bad. Maybe you'd like to buy a DVD that explains a little more about Jesus?" Sandy doubted it, but it was worth a shot.

"What?!" the kid yelled again. Maybe he needed therapy or something. "Hippies are lazy bums! Everybody knows that!"

"Billy!" Ms. Uppity said.

Darn it! The kid had caught her in a paradox. Ms. Uppity needed to be stricter. Bad parenting was probably the problem. Sandy knew she had to bring it back to Jesus if she was going to make a sale.

"But hippies can't offer you eternal salvation, can they? No, they can't. Not like the Lord Jesus, who died for our sins."

Ha! Hoisted by his own petard! Now to close the sale.

"Maybe you should get him one of these DVDs. Be something you and he could do together." Sandy stood up, offering her best smile and a DVD to Ms. Uppity.

"Oh, thanks, but we're really fine. Come on, Billy," Ms. Uppity said and pulled her little brat off into the store.

"Y'all have a blessed day!" Sandy called after them and kicked a small piece of gravel out of her way. She had been so close. Oh well. The Lord worked in mysterious ways. And a steady stream of cars was arriving. Some of them would want to buy a DVD or two or three.

BILLY

"Ow, Mom!"

He hadn't done anything wrong! All he had done was put the smarmy blond preacher in her place and point out that Jesus was a hippie and the inherent contradiction therein. He had just pointed it out; it wasn't his fault that the contradiction existed. Billy didn't have a problem with Jesus, per se; it was just that having to go and spend one of two precious weekend mornings listening to boring speeches and dumb songs was cruelty that borderline violated the Geneva Convention. But that wasn't Jesus's fault—that was his parents' fault. And he certainly didn't need to hear about it from a stupid, condescending blond preacher who smelled like one of his sister's teenage-girl magazines. So he fought back with the weapons he had: wit and the irrefutable force of his logic. And now Mom was overcoming his arm with the irrefutable force of her grip. It hurt.

"Ow! Mom!"

"Oh, please, Billy. I'm not hurting you, and you know it."

She wasn't really hurting him physically, it was true. She was just ruining his life!

He wrenched his arm free. His mom spun in front of him and kneeled down so their faces were level. She could be quick when she wanted.

"Listen to me, mister. You better to stop acting out, or there will be consequences."

That was definitely a threat. Billy was sure of it. He thought of several choice names he could call her. Like the b word. But that would definitely lead to trouble. Lots of trouble. Billy was working on a theorem of swear-word hierarchy, reciprocity, and escalation, but there were a lot of variables.

The b word, for example, was a first-tier word, right up there with the s-h word or the f word. What was confusing were the modifiers: *bullshit* seemed to be more of an everyday kind of word, one that didn't require such strict censorship, possibly because of the bovine connection. And while the b word was really bad, *sonofabitch* seemed okay—at least Dad had no problem shouting it, *shouting* it, whenever he was working on carpentry. Moreover, *sonofabitch*—and *asshole*—appeared to be appropriate for driving. Mom certainly hadn't held back when the big SUV almost ran them off the road on the way to the store and she almost ran over the squirrel. She hadn't hit it; that was good. Billy made her stop to get out and check to be sure. Squirrels were great. Mom thought they were little sonofabitches. An opinion she had repeated when she had almost hit another one in the parking lot. It was like she was gunning for them. And *she* had the temerity to swear at them! How did that make sense?

And then, of course, there were the Sunday-only swears. Those he knew from his parents.

"*God dammit*, Helena! Can't it wait? The game's on!"

"I worked all afternoon on this casserole, and you're just gonna sit and watch a game on TV? You can be a real *bastard* sometimes, you know that?"

That had led to a lot of yelling and cold cereal for dinner. And then the next night his dad brought home flowers, and his mom made a particularly tasty meatloaf. Swear words were powerful; the aftereffects lasted for days. And who knew how long the fallout from calling his mom the b word would last?

Dictionaries were of surprisingly little help, and it wasn't the sort of thing he could ask about. Least of all right now: The situation was still salvageable. They hadn't gone into the store yet.

"Mom, I'm sorry."

She raised an eyebrow. How did she know he wasn't actually sorry? It was like she was magic, like an ogre or something. Billy forged ahead.

"It's just, I really didn't want to go, and you made me, and I just wanted to stay home and play Xbox and work on my fort and..."

Billy trailed off. He didn't really have anything new to say. And it wasn't like his mom was going to change her mind for an apology she knew he didn't really mean.

"Your fort? You mean that pile of sticks in the backyard? Oh, Billy, I had your dad clean that up. It was so unsightly."

"What do you mean, 'clean it up'?"

"I had him get rid of it. Come on, we need to go in now."

"You. Did. What?"

"Billy, it was a mess so I had your father clean it up. Why are you being so obtuse? That's not like you. Now come on."

"THAT WAS MY FORT!" Like hornets from a nest that, having been struck by a well-thrown, if ill-considered, stone, plummeted to earth and smashed, Billy's rage burst forth, looking for things to sting.

"Billy, stop shouting."

Billy did not stop shouting. His rage, born of frustration, born of a thousand slights, massed and swarmed. It was his fort! It had taken him a month to build.

"HOW COULD YOU DO THAT?! YOU'RE THE WORST! I HATE YOU! I HATE YOU! I'M GONNA RUN AWAY!"

"Billy, that's enough." His mother's voice had changed: it was hard and sharp, like one of those pieces of shale rock on the hill behind his house; it had the strained tone that Billy associated with danger. He was in a delicate zone now—like when he didn't pick up his Legos before going to bed and then had to tiptoe blindly in the night to go to the bathroom, hoping not to step on one—but he also was close to the point of not caring. It was his fort. His eyes felt hot, and he had something in his throat. He swallowed. He didn't want to cry. Not here. Not now.

"But, Mom, that was my...I worked on it so long...why would you do that?" Billy's voice started to crack. He bit his lip. He really didn't want to cry. He didn't want to give her the satisfaction.

"I'm sorry, Billy. I didn't know it was important to you. I thought it was just a bunch of sticks. You can make another one."

That was a fake apology. She wasn't sorry at all. Just a bunch of sticks?! Billy wiped the corner of his eye.

"There you go; that's my big boy," his mom said and smoothed back his hair. Billy hated it when she did that. He hated her patronizing tone. It was as bad as that stupid preacher woman's, and Billy hated her. He hated his mom too. He hated everything. Except his fort. He loved his fort.

He wanted to scream. He wanted to kick and punch. He almost understood why that kid Jessica in his class would bite people. Maybe she just felt like this all the time. Maybe her mom constantly ignored her opinion, and the only way she could get people to listen was by biting. Of course, she usually got hauled to the principal or worse, to Dr. Bradley's office. Dr. Bradley was the school counselor and seriously annoying. If he were Jessica, Billy would definitely have bit him. Not that that would have helped. Biting may have been satisfying in the moment, but it ultimately didn't help accomplish goals. Jessica was a good example of how not to get what you wanted. So Billy didn't react outwardly. He didn't bite or kick or punch or cry. He might have only been seven—almost eight—but he could demonstrate self-control.

SCARLETT

Scarlett had remained tight lipped during the corporate cheer. It was asinine and degrading under normal circumstances. Today had been even worse. How that creep from the restaurant had managed to become the store manager was beyond her. As he led the cheer, his gaze had returned to her a few times. That had only made Scarlett angrier. Did he recognize her? She doubted it. He was so far gone last night that she would be surprised if he even knew which restaurant he had been at. But still...best not to make eye contact.

Scarlett was still angry as she set up her register. She couldn't believe she technically worked for him. *Baby, I never been with a black chick before. Wanna go somewhere?* It was probably the type of crap she should report, but it wasn't worth it. Nothing would change.

She didn't get along so great with Tim, the assistant store manager, either. She was over his always-on positivity, which was so over the top it had to be fake. So she stopped pretending to enjoy their interactions. That backfired, since it seemed to have made Tim redouble his efforts to be positive and cheery around her, when all she really wanted was for him to leave her alone. The extra attention was especially unwelcome now. Stealing from the store was wrong; she knew that. And yes, technically, taking the crib the way she had *was* stealing. But all she had really done was sort of slide the damaged box over from the stack of things to be returned to the warehouse to the pile of things to be put in the dumpster. No one ever noticed the difference, because it had ended up in the dumpster, and she just sort of took it from there. Plus, she really needed it. But if it were all that easily justifiable, why did she feel so guilty? And why had Tim started to count out her cash drawer so ostentatiously at the end of every shift? Did he suspect her already? Why hadn't he said anything? Did he not have any solid evidence? Was he just letting it go? Was she completely paranoid? Questions in your own head could drive you crazy, and three minutes into a ten-hour shift was *not* the time to start with them.

Scarlett fantasized daily about quitting but couldn't afford to get fired. Not with rent and loans for tuition, which had just gone up *again*, and with Rose and Julius staying with her "for now." No. She needed all the jobs she had and then some.

Tim brought her a tray of cash to make change.

"Make sure it's all there when you give it back. Have a super day!" he said, way too excited for the hour and the place.

"Yeah, okay," Scarlett said in monotone.

Scarlett's quitting fantasy changed in its details, but the main points went something like this: The store would be crowded, and one customer would be just a little too rude, pecking away ineffectually on a smartphone, which never seemed to work at the SuperMart, not even acknowledging that Scarlett was there, ignoring her question of paper or plastic, then looking up right as Scarlett scanned the last item—cheap makeup or a tablet computer that was only cheap because she and everyone else at the store weren't getting paid jack, or cheese puffs that were, like, 85 percent sawdust, or some other pointless crap—and then right as Scarlett put it in a bag, the customer would decide, "No, no, no, hon, I want paper." Instead of rebagging everything for the ingrate, Scarlett would dump everything on the floor, maybe give the bag of cheese puffs a satisfying kick. They'd fly up into the stupid customer's gut, eliciting a satisfying *oof*. Tim's spidey sense for an upset customer would alert him, and he'd come over to try to smooth things out and to reprimand her. But before he could, she would eject the cash register drawer and slam it at his feet. He'd drop to his knees and scrabble around, trying to pick up every last penny. Everyone else would just be standing there, shocked. Taking advantage of the silence, Scarlett would give a short speech, punctuating it with just the right amount of profanity. A few of the more enlightened customers would clap. A couple store employees would join in. Then she'd leave. Calm, composed, she'd walk out, shoulders back, head up. Maybe an employee or two would follow her. The story would get picked up by the national news. And then she'd get interviewed. Someone would see how criminal it had been that she had been working such a crappy job for such a shady corporation, and she'd end up with a real job. A better job. Like a clerk in a law office that was going to sponsor her law-school tuition.

That was her fantasy anyway.

Tim bustled off to continue his store-opening chores. He was so cheerful. Scarlett wondered if maybe there was something wrong with him, like maybe whatever part of his brain regulated dopamine was misfiring or something. No one was that happy all the time. But whatever was up with Tim didn't matter. Not her business.

Clem caught her eye. She gave a little wave and a smile. Sometimes—often—it seemed like Clem was the only nonidiot in her life. Well, him and Julius. But her nephew was only one and a half, so it wasn't like she could talk to him. At least, not if she wanted it to be a two-way conversation. Julius mostly smiled, giggled, and drooled.

Clem was definitely the only nonidiot in the SuperMart. He was the best part of this job. She felt like he was a grandfather she'd never known. He nodded at her and did a little shuffling moonwalk thing toward the door. Clem was the best. Scarlett felt her mood lift some. In her quitting fantasy, Clem was one of the ones who'd come with her, maybe smashing a window or something as he left.

The first half hour was the best part of the working day for a SuperMart cashier. No one ever arrived until twenty minutes after the store opened, and even the most expeditious of shoppers took a little while to find whatever crap they wanted to buy. Scarlett suspected the store layout was confusing on purpose, so customers would spend more time wandering around and end up buying extra stuff. And so for the first thirty minutes or so, Scarlett was free to zone out, wake up, and pretty much do whatever until the first customers started checking out. After that, it sucked, for nine and a half straight hours, but for now, she could just relax. Every morning was the same.

But today, she spotted something—someone—new. Who was that? Scarlett was sure he didn't work there. No one who worked at the SuperMart would wear a fedora and a trench coat. And he didn't seem like a customer either. He was too skinny, for one. And wasn't moving. SuperMart customers were always wandering around slowly, like zombies. Occasionally, they'd stop to hold some product or another, weighing it in their hands while they weighed in their minds whether to buy it. Almost always, they ended up tipping whatever it was into their cart. This guy wasn't holding anything. He didn't have a cart. And he was so still he almost blended into the row of basketballs behind him. If it hadn't been for his unusual dress, he might have been invisible. In any case, the doors had just opened, and Scarlett hadn't seen anyone come in yet. Should she say something? You kept hearing about stuff on the news. Like the crazy guy on the bus in Indianapolis who had attacked the driver with an umbrella and caused him to crash. One person had been killed and a bunch more hurt. See something; say something. That's what you were supposed to do. But maybe he was just an early shopper; she shouldn't profile; that wasn't what you were supposed to do either. The man looked harmless enough. Would it be worth the hassle if he were just another shopper, albeit an oddly dressed one? She decided that she should at least see what Clem thought.

"Good morning, young lady."

"Hey, Clem."

"You look like you've got the weight of the world on those shoulders of yours. You're too young for that. Everything all right? Is it your sister?"

"Yeah. No. I mean, it's just I'm tired is all. Don't worry."

The tired part was certainly true. It was her sister too though. And the stress from the other crappy jobs she had to work just to survive and how she'd probably have to keep working them forever because she was trapped, and poor, and it just sucked sometimes. But she didn't want to put that on Clem this early in the day. She looked down to keep him from asking more questions that she didn't feel like answering. His shoes looked expensive. So did his watch, come to think of it. How did he afford those? Not her business.

She looked over toward where the man with the trench coat had been. He was gone.

"Clem, did you see that guy over by sporting goods just now?"

Clem raised an eyebrow. "You mean Aidan?"

"No, not Aidan." Scarlett grinned. An accident-prone teenager who worked in sporting goods on weekends, Aidan was the source of a lot of amusement for her and Clem. "This guy doesn't work here. He was wearing, like, a fedora and a trench coat or something. About yea tall. Skinny, mustache. Midforties maybe. He looked kinda sketchy. Should I say something? Tell Tim or someone?"

Clem didn't answer right away. He looked tired too. How old was he? Scarlett realized she knew very little about him. He was always listening to her problems, but she never asked about his. Just because he was old, it didn't mean he didn't have problems. Hell, he probably had more. Scarlett resolved to ask him more questions, to be a good friend to him as well.

"Yes, I saw him," Clem finally said. "And no, I don't think it's worth mentioning."

"You don't think he's dangerous or anything? It's just, you know, with all the news lately..."

"Yes. But I don't think that's who that guy is. I'm pretty sure he's a government inspector. In my former life, I had to deal a lot with them. I think I overheard Tim mentioning something about that last week. An audit or something like that. I'm sure that's what it is. Nothing to worry yourself with."

"Okay," Scarlett said, not totally convinced but relieved. She didn't really want to do anything this morning. Clem was probably right. Then, remembering her new resolution, she said, "So what was that former life anyway, Clem?"

"Oh, nothing that interesting. I wouldn't want to bore you this early in the morning."

"I'm sure it wouldn't be boring," Scarlett said, and she meant it. "But have it your way. I gotta get back to the register. Looks like the hordes are arriving early today."

A woman was dragging a small boy into the store by his arm, whispering loudly and furiously at him.

"You do not talk to people that way, Billy. Do you understand? It is not okay. I know you don't want to be here, but you better start behaving, or so help me I will—"

"Hello and welcome to the SuperMart. Would you like a sticker?" Clem said, interrupting the woman's tirade with his deep baritone. Clem was the best.

"Billy, what do you say?"

"Hi. Yes, please, I'd like a sticker." The boy was sullen. Scarlett admired him. He wasn't sugarcoating anything. He wasn't pretending everything was fine when it wasn't.

Scarlett went back to the cash register. She looked over toward sporting goods. Nothing. The inspector, or whoever he was, was gone.

A steady trickle of people poured in. Only ten more hours.

CLEM

Clem watched the young boy and his mother push their cart off into the warren of shelves and racks that cluttered the store. The kid had spirit. Hopefully he wouldn't have to stay too long in this store; it seemed to beat people down these days.

Clem shook his head. These days. There was lots to worry about. Else and how she was getting on at home. She would be fine, of course—she had plenty to do between her friends and the Foundation. But he should really spend more time with her—he *wanted* to spend more time with her—maybe take her on that trip to Europe they always talked about but never seemed to have the time to do. Young Scarlett, wearing the world so heavy on her shoulders. That poor girl was tough as nails, but it sure did seem like she got dealt a bad hand more often than not. Didn't seem right. Wasn't right, in point of fact, and it wasn't fair, but if there was one thing Clem had learned over the years, it was that life wasn't fair. Scarlett was the closest thing he had to a daughter, or granddaughter more like, which was kinda sad. But he and Else had never wanted kids, and they certainly weren't going to start now. And besides, when life gave you lemons...Clem had always liked lemonade—the real stuff, not that powdered crap they sold at the store and that Tim mixed up as a "treat" for employees on the last Friday of every month. Scarlett was like real lemonade, sweet with an edge. She was a nice girl. And bright. She should not have been working the checkout at this soulless store. He wished he could help her, but not only was she tough as nails, she was as proud as a pack of lions. He doubted she would let him help, so he hadn't brought it up.

Clem also worried about what was happening to his beloved store. Not that it was his beloved store anymore, exactly. The SuperMart bore little similarity to the Patterson's that he had started so long ago. Clem had never imagined this when he sold his little chain to SuperCorp. Sure, he hadn't had much of a choice, and sure, it had made him richer than Croesus, but the homeyness and the friendliness, the warmth—what made Patterson's what it was—were gone. The store now was antiseptic, bland, and cold. A corporate cheer led by that meathead Mitch Spooner did not add to the atmosphere. Clem tried to make up for that as a greeter, but today people seemed pissed off that he was even saying hello to them. Plus, there was that government agent or whoever he was. Clem knew the type. Probably meant Corporate was doing some kind of audit. The world—or at least this store—was going to hell, it seemed. Maybe it was time for him to get out. What was there to save, really? And how could he do it as a lowly greeter? Especially today. People just didn't want to be welcomed anymore.

"I was already welcomed, thank you," a woman said. Clem suspected her thanks were insincere.

"Bro, step off. Once is enough. And I preferred my welcome from the lady with the big bazookas, if you know what I mean," a big lug in a State University sweatshirt said.

Clem didn't know what he meant. He was just trying to be friendly.

"No, thank you. Come on, Willow." A woman in a flowing Technicolor dress with a floral pattern stopped him from giving a sticker to her daughter. At least that thanks seemed sincere. Willow, a small girl of about seven or so, smiled at Clem and then skipped off. Clem smiled after her, shoulders slumped. It would be so nice to skip.

"Hello and welcome to the SuperMart," he said to the next shopper.

"I don't want another goddamn greeting. And I don't want a goddamn sticker," a larger-bellied man in blue sweat pants said. Clem hadn't even offered him a sticker. Those were for the children.

That was quite a few people who had complained about a redundant greeting. What was going on? Had that dope Tim put on two greeters? Clem wandered over to the front door to see what the deal was.

There was some sort of salesman who had set up shop in front of the store. Saleswoman. Clem stood behind the shopping carts and craned his neck to see what she was selling. Oh, sweet Jesus. Or severe Jesus, Clem couldn't tell from where he was standing. Either way, it was an odd thing to be selling, like one of those kids in the city with the stolen sunglasses. At least those guys were honest about what they were selling.

Clem started to march out to shoo her away but remembered it was no longer his jurisdiction. He was just a greeter. Greeter. The very existence of the position proved its impossibility. Used to be, you felt welcome in a store because it was a welcoming place. Not a job to be checked off. Greeter. In any case, a greeter wasn't supposed to chase away zealots. He was supposed to get a manager. That meant Tim. Meek and meager little Tim.

"Aw, really, Clem? You don't think we should just live and let live?"

"Ordinarily, I'd say yes, Tim. But customers have been complaining."

"Oh, well in that case, consider it done!" Tim said and hurried off, whistling. He was too happy for his own good.

Ten minutes later, Tim came back inside. He had one of the preacher's DVDs!

Clem swallowed his outrage and said, "Well?"

Tim looked from the DVD to Clem, then said, "Why don't you take your break?"

Always so damned peppy. Clem scowled back at him. He'd give Tim a break all right.

"She'll, uh, she'll be gone by the time you're back."

Clem scowled some more, put his batch of stickers on his stool, and stalked off. He did kind of need to use the restroom anyway. He hung his apron with the WELCOME TO SUPERMART and HOW CAN I HELP YOU TODAY? pins on a peg and made his way to the toilets. Just before he pushed open the door, he saw a small reddish-brown flash near the ceiling. It paused, then leapt onto a sprinkler pipe, and disappeared.

Clem shook his head. First a government agent. Now a squirrel? He was getting too old for this shit.

RUSTY

Rusty held stock-still. So did the hawk. Rusty's mind was racing. So was his heart. It kept doing that this morning. Rusty wondered if that was normal. He really needed to check and see what Raccoon knew about it. But first he had to get out of this tree alive. Options. Rusty needed options. The hawk blinked. Among the branches, Rusty was relatively safe. Hawks were morons. But they were dangerous. They could tear you apart. Or give you bird flu. Nuts! How many mortal dangers was he going to face today? The electricity rush was wearing off. Options. He was safe for now, but for how long? He couldn't stay here all day.

The hawk's stare seemed to be saying, "Duh. I'm a dumb hawk, and I'm gonna make you my snack. Durrr."

"That's what you think," Rusty said. "I'm the quickest there is. The prettiest there is. The humans and their cars couldn't stop me! Like some stupid bird is gonna do it."

The power of positive thinking. Rusty was psyching himself up and psyching the bird out. He was chattering. The hawk squawked. Dumb brute. Evolve already! Hawks didn't even have language. But Rusty wasn't about to teach it now. He darted down the trunk and clung on the far side, out of its sight.

Now what? He couldn't beat a hawk to the building by running. He checked his tail. Still bushy. Silky. Sexy. At least he didn't have to worry about rabies right now. He was still in a tough spot. Options. He needed options. A flat-out sprint to the store was out. That was suicide. Fortune favored the bold, not the recklessly stupid. And Rusty had so much to live for. He had to work the problem. Embrace the power of positive thinking. Expect the unexpected. What was it his judo teacher was always saying? "Be the squirrel your newt thinks you are?" No, that wasn't it. "Protect the tail?" Good advice for sure, but that wasn't it either. "Use your opponent to your advantage?" That was it! Turn the tables; turn the tide. Assets: brains, quickness, heart. Well hopefully heart. He couldn't worry about that now. Liabilities: fifty feet of pavement, crazy humans in cars, crazy humans out of cars, a bloodthirsty raptor.

Work the problem. See the solution. *Be* the solution. The power of positive thinking! Rusty needed to get to the store. Running was out. Blood was starting to rush to his head. It was a common misconception that squirrels didn't get head rushes. False. Rusty always got head rushes if he stayed upside down too long. That was normal. Wasn't it? Light-headedness wasn't a sign of rabies, was it? No: his tail told. And a meager squirrel got no nuts. It was time to bust moves.

He couldn't run. That was how one became roadkill. Or squirrel fricassee for a hawk. He couldn't fly. He wasn't that kind of squirrel. Or could he? Was it too crazy? Fortune favored the bold. Was this suicide too? Rusty didn't think so. To dare was to do. Don't think; just do it!

Rusty flipped himself upright. He held himself still a moment, letting the wooziness pass. The hawk was still there. Dumb mug.

"Killa, killa, killeee!" Rusty chattered a war cry and sprinted at the hawk.

The hawk, taken unaware, opened its beak and spread its wings. Sucker! Rusty faked left, went right, and wrapped himself around the raptor's leg. Protect the tail! Protected. Prince of squirrel thieves? Psshaw! After he pulled this off, Rusty was going to be the squirrel king!

But first he needed to pull it off. And the hawk wasn't cooperating.

"Fly!" Rusty said. He knew the hawk was too dumb to understand him, but he also knew it was dumb for a squirrel to attack a hawk. And his plan was not going to work if the hawk just sat there.

The hawk clacked its beak and tried to reach Rusty. But he couldn't. Rusty was too compact; his tail was too tucked. Nor could the bird get him with the other talon. Rusty was too clever. Too inaccessible.

"Fly!" Rusty said again and gave the hawk a motivating nip on the leg. He hoped that wasn't a way to contract bird flu. The hawk squawked again and took flight. Yes! Prince of squirrels! King!

"No! No, you stupid son of a opossum! Toward the store!"

The plan was going to hell. How did you steer a hawk anyway? Rusty clung on for dear life. The hawk banked and headed back toward the SuperMart. Hooray! Farther. Rusty needed him to go just a little farther. And lower. Lower would be better. Holy nuts, he was high! But there was nothing for it. He could see the woman whose shoe he had run over. She was down there, just in front of the store. If Rusty missed the building, he'd aim for her. Her blond hair would cushion the blow.

Rusty thought of his wife and his unborn kits. Light as a feather, quick as a squirrel! But mostly light as a feather. And he let go. Free! Falling! He was free and falling, fast! Focus. He had to focus on landing. The woman or the building? Did he have a choice? It became quickly apparent that he had misjudged his trajectory. He wasn't going to make the building. He had to hit the blond lady's head. The wind blew, and now he was over the building. If he spread his arms and legs and tail, he could control his descent a little. But only a little. Stupid cross breezes! Rancid nuts! The roof of the SuperMart was coming up fast.

Wham! Rusty landed hard. His right paw hurt. Broken? He flexed it. Painful...but not broken. Tail? Still bushy. Silky. Sexy. Head? Okay. He was okay. Was he okay? Better than okay. Great. Squirrel royalty! Oh nuts!

A shadow covered Rusty. The hawk was diving. Hell-bent on revenge, the sore loser. Rusty dove for cover, a silver hole in the side of the retaining wall. He was inside. The bird screeched in frustration. He was safe. But Rusty could get no purchase with his claws on the shiny metal. He began to slip, slowly at first, then faster and faster. He scrabbled, to no avail. Rusty slid backward, down the ventilation duct and into the SuperMart. He was spit out onto a ledge that was covered with dust. Rusty sneezed. He was inside. It was the strangest place he had ever seen.

There were no smells. No texture. Maybe a slight hint of cinnamon? Vanilla? Perhaps there was a bakery. Rusty did a quick head to toe. His right paw was sore, but everything was still operational. He did not like flying. Or hawks. Oh god, could he have bird flu now? No, he had just nipped the bird. He hadn't even broken the skin. They hadn't kissed. There was no exchange of fluids. He was okay. And he was in!

Rusty perched on the ledge. It overlooked the whole store. He closed his eyes and took a deep breath. No predators here. But still, it was a time for stealth. If Rusty knew one thing, it was that somehow the humans knew his plan and were going to try to stop him. Stupid Raccoon. He mentally ran through the schematic of the store that he had memorized. He opened his eyes. He was on the exact opposite side of the store from where he needed to be. Light as a feather, quick as a squirrel.

A latticework of pipes crisscrossed the store; they were for dispensing water in case of a fire. Sprinklers, they were called. They had been on the schematic. Practical, Rusty supposed, but a better idea would be to not start fires willy-nilly. Humans. No time for that now. It was go time. Rusty took off across the sprinkler system.

SANDY

As it turned out, the patrons of the SuperMart seemed much less interested in the bargain price for eternal salvation that Sandy was offering than the bargain prices on a wide variety of foreign-manufactured cheap goods inside the store. How shortsighted people could be. Sandy had managed to give away a couple of pamphlets but had sold no DVDs so far. She didn't even bother trying with the latest pair: a hippie woman in an ankle-length skirt printed with millions of tiny flowers and her little flower child. Whatever Ms. Uppity's little brat had said about Jesus and hippies, she knew these two weren't the type to spend money looking for salvation. Sandy wondered what they were even doing there. Shouldn't they be shopping at some kind of buy-local small business? As for the others...didn't anyone watch the YouTube? How was she going to get her exhaust fixed, much less pay the gas bill...and the water bill...and her mortgage...and fix that leaky window...and buy a new lamp?

At least, with the exception of Ms. Uppity and her brat, and an older SuperMart employee who kept coming over to the window to glower at her, people were generally being kind and sympathetic. And the prices inside the SuperMart were certainly enticing, Sandy had to admit, as she leafed through a weekend-specials flier during a lull in traffic. A beach towel for $4.99? Three for one on peanuts, almonds, and cashews. You didn't even have to buy mixed nuts; you could do it yourself! Sandy wondered if it would be worth buying a bunch and starting a mixed-nuts business on the side, just until she got a radio show or something. But it was fleeting. She just didn't feel any passion for snack food, not like she felt for preaching. There was a lamp on sale for $7.98. Well, there was one problem solved. If she could just sell a DVD.

Sandy was distracted from the flier by the throaty warble she associated with her piece-of-junk car. Sounded like she wasn't the only one who needed a new muffler. Sandy looked up and saw an enormous, loud red pickup truck. The body was popped up above wheels, making the whole thing absurdly tall. Dual-exhaust pipes stuck up next to the cab. It was possible that the guy intended for his truck to make that noise. Maybe he'd be interested in her car! No, no he wouldn't. And besides, she needed her car, even if it was a hunk of junk. Ugh. Why did men—and it was always men—feel the need to drive such big, loud things? Like that jerk-butt in the Hummer from this morning, who was really getting his money's worth by the look of it, since his big jerk-butt SUV was still parked askew next to Sandy's table. Sandy watched the truck in morbid fascination as it rolled down a row of parked cars until it found a spot.

The driver got out and hopped four feet to the ground. Seeing him, Sandy straightened up and unconsciously patted her hair. This guy could be the one. The critical first sale. No, she corrected herself, the critical first one to be saved. He was wearing jeans and a cutoff T-shirt. As he came closer, Sandy could see the T-shirt had a graphic of a bald eagle with an American flag streaming from its talons. The man was tanned and wiry and only a little taller than her. He was balding from the front, and what hair he did have was the same length as the few-days-old beard that covered his face. He was muscled, not like a gym freak or an athlete or anything, but muscled in the way that someone who worked with his body for a living was muscled...though on slightly closer inspection, it did appear to be a body that smoked and drank more than might be healthy. This was the sort of guy whose attentions Sandy usually tried to avoid. But this was also the sort of guy who believed in Jesus.

"And how are you this fine morning?" Sandy said to him as he walked up.

"Good morning! Oh, I'm pretty good. How are you doin'?"

A good start!

"I'm great," Sandy said. "Do you have a moment to talk about Jesus?"

"Yeah, I could take a minute to talk to you about almost anything." The guy smiled. One of his bottom front teeth had been replaced with a gold one, and he was slightly gap-toothed on top. The guy stopped close enough that Sandy could smell him. He smelled like tobacco and cheap aftershave—nope, he hadn't shaved recently. Must have been cheap cologne. The kind that usually would make her sneeze, but she seemed to be doing okay. A blessing. Sandy was only slightly uncomfortable with the way his gaze traveled up and down her body. Men. Best just to ignore that type of behavior.

"Well, that's great, because I have a question for you," Sandy said, smiling. Warm but professional. "Have you accepted the Lord Jesus Christ as your personal savior?"

"You mean, do I believe in God and shit?" the guy said.

Sandy tried not to grimace. She couldn't expect to be always helping the articulate.

"Hell yeah I do," the guy went on. "I'm American, ain't I? And God and Jesus are who made America great. Home of the brave and land of the free and shit! Hell yeah, I'm with them."

He turned his head and spit on the asphalt, just behind the jerk-butt's SUV. No, she could not always expect to be commercing with the articulate. At least she didn't need to change his opinions.

"Yes. He is. They are. And the Lord Jesus sacrificed himself for our sins! Isn't that amazing? And that's a part of our daily lives, isn't it?"

"Well, I guess so. I mean, the friggin' government keeps tryin' to mess with our freedom and shit, but we can't let 'em. Freedom ain't free, and we gotta fight for ours."

Sandy paused. It had been a rhetorical question. But she could meet him on his level.

"Exactly," she said. "Freedom. I mean, who likes freedom more than Jesus, right? Just think of Romans 8:1–2! 'Therefore, there is now no condemnation for those who are in Christ Jesus, because through Christ Jesus the law of the Spirit who gives life has set you *free* from the law of sin and death.'"

"Hell yeah! I mean, I didn't know that. But like I was saying before, freedom ain't free. And we gotta fight for ours. Friggin' democrat pricks in Washington tryin' to tell us what's good for us with communist health care and shit. Tryin' to take away our guns *and* our freedom. They won't listen to reason. But now we got another argument: it ain't what Jesus woulda wanted. I sure am glad I stopped to talk to you, lady."

That wasn't exactly Sandy's interpretation of that passage, but she wasn't going to argue with his politics; she hoped he wouldn't argue with her sales pitch. "Well, I sure am glad you stopped by too. Would you like to learn more about the life of Jesus?"

"Uh..."

"Because you can. I think he has a lot to say about things that might interest you."

"Like guns and America and freedom and the right to not have the government spyin' on my friggin' internet usage and shit?"

"Uh," Sandy said. "Well, yes, in a sense. I'm sure it could help your political arguments. But also on a more tangible basis than that."

"Tangerines?" the guy said.

Sandy ignored his confusion and kept going, "For instance, what brings you to the SuperMart today?"

"Well, it's what we've been talking about, isn't it? Freedom and America. And guns. It's all the same crap, right? I'm here to buy a gun. I got problems with crows hangin' around my trailer. Only bird that should be there is a bald eagle. Symbol of freedom, you know. But the friggin' crows keep squawking and wakin' me up when I'm tryin' to catch a few winks. It's wicked annoying. I've tried to shoot 'em with my friggin' pistol, but it don't work. I need something with a bigger bore."

"Praise Jesus, amen. I know what you're saying," Sandy said. "And I think Jesus would understand too. I mean, he has a lot to say on the subject of birds. How do you feel about squirrels?"

"Love 'em...in my grandad's squirrel stew! Huh-hah!" He chortled and slapped his thigh. "You ever have squirrel stew? Take two or three of the critters, throw 'em in a pot with some carrots and celery. Salt and pepper. Onion. Three, four hours later you come back and hoo-boy. Delish."

Sandy somewhat doubted his culinary acumen, but didn't want to say so.

"Well, Mr...."

"My friends call me Lee, but you can call me whatever you like."

He took a half step closer, and Sandy took a full step back.

"Lee. I think you have heard the word of Jesus already. You are on the path to salvation. This"—Sandy held up one of her uncracked DVDs—"can help you get there."

"Uh, that's nice and all, but really I'm on the path to buy a gun. I don't really have the funds to spend money on other stuff at the moment."

It was like she had just missed the last step of a staircase; her stomach swooped up to her neck, and she touched her table for balance. The sale was getting away. It couldn't. She had to meet Lee at his level. He was interested in guns? She could connect Jesus to guns.

She continued to speak, a little too quickly, "But, Lee, Jesus can help you *choose* the right gun. And with him on your side, your aim will be true. This DVD will only set you back fifteen dollars. It will help you answer all those questions I know you have."

"'Bout guns? Is it an NRA publication? What's on it anyway?"

"Oh, it's just a series of little sermons—talks—I've given. How to build your personal connection with Jesus and stuff like that. I..." Sandy paused, unsure of how best to convince him.

"You're on it? Hell yeah, I'll take one." Lee licked his lips and stuffed a crumpled bill into Sandy's hand. The lip licking creeped her out, but a sale was a sale.

"Oh, this is a twenty; let me get you some change."

"Naw, keep it, or maybe you could throw in one of those cracked ones to sweeten the deal?" Lee gave her a wink.

"Oh, okay. Well"—she gave him a particularly damaged-looking one. No sense in undercutting her bottom line any more than need be—"thank you, Lee. And you have a blessed day."

"You bet." Lee stuffed the DVDs into his back pocket and started to walk away, then stopped.

"Hey," he said. "You around later?"

"I, uh..." Sandy definitely did not like that question. "Why?"

"Oh, I just thought, you know, maybe we could go for a ride in my truck. Drive around and have a nice long...talk. About Jesus and shit? Maybe get to know him a little better...and each other?"

Unfortunately, Sandy was pretty used to getting offers like that. They usually had very little to do with Jesus. Consequently, she had become pretty good at dealing with them.

"Oh, that's real sweet," she said with a warm—but professional—smile. "But I don't know that today will work. Why don't you watch the DVDs and drop me a line if you have questions. My email's on the back cover."

"Oh, all right. Well, see ya."

Bullet dodged.

"And you have a blessed day."

"Excuse me, sir?" A SuperMart employee, a meek-looking little guy in a short-sleeved shirt and precisely straight tie, interrupted Lee as he was leaving. Maybe the little guy was coming to try to protect her. That was sweet.

"Huh?" Lee grunted.

"Is this woman bothering you?"

Sandy snorted to herself. So much for chivalry.

TIM

"Because if she is bothering you," Tim said, "I'd be happy to help."

"No, she's cool. We were just talking about freedom and Jesus and shit. Real cool chick," the guy said with a wolfish glance over at the woman. Then he brushed past Tim and into the store. The guy smelled like flowery cigarettes; it tickled Tim's nose. He sneezed.

"Oh, bless you!" the woman said.

Tim sneezed again.

"Thank you," he said, eyes a little watery.

"What did you mean, was I bothering that guy?" she asked him.

Tim gulped. He hated conflict.

"Yipes!"

The woman had moved closer while he was sneezing, and now she was right next to him. It startled him.

He looked at the woman.

"Yipes!" he said again. "It's you!"

She was even lovelier in real life. And unlike that flowery-cigarette guy, she smelled wonderful.

"What do you mean, it's me? Do we know each other?" The woman looked angry. This was not the way Tim had imagined meeting Sandy Newman would go.

He tried to speak. He failed. He just stood there, mouth slightly agape. He probably seemed a little foolish to her, but he was paralyzed. How was he supposed to shoo this woman off? Not Sandy Newman!

Clem had alerted him to the fact that the customers were upset with what they thought was a double greeting, which Tim would have thought was great. But what was it that one lady had said? "It seems like you're trying too hard, and it's annoying." Something like that. Which was certainly a stinging rebuke. And if the customers were upset and complaining to Clem, well then, Tim had to do something about it! But this was Sandy Newman! *The* Sandy Newman from the *internet!* Customers were customers, and they were always right; plus, the SuperMart had a policy of no unapproved solicitations, and she had certainly not been on the list; he would have noticed. But he couldn't just get rid of her. Golly, he was in a tough spot.

"Are you all right?" she asked him. She seemed less angry. That was good. She seemed...concerned. She touched his arm, and goose bumps ran up to his shoulder and then somehow seemed to jump to his belly. But as her touch lingered, the goose bumps changed to a warmth, which surged from his cheeks down to his...Tim shifted his weight from foot to foot. She removed her hand; Tim's body remained in a tumult.

"I'm...I'm good," Tim managed to say, absentmindedly putting his hand where her touch had landed.

"Oh good. Now, have we met somewhere?"

"No, ma'am. I mean, I feel like we have, but we haven't met, not for real. I just...you're...I'm...you're Sandy Newman! The Blessed Prayers lady! I've seen all your videos. I mean, your fruit sermon? The one where you talked about the parable of the pineapple and love? And your squirrel sermon from yesterday? You...you've changed my life," Tim said, speaking a little too fast, his voice a little too high-pitched. It wasn't how a cool guy like Mr. Spooner would act, meeting the woman of his dreams, but a tiger couldn't change his stripes in midstream. Tim hoped she wouldn't laugh at him.

Sandy beamed. It was like seeing an angel smile. Tim smiled back; his heart was thumping.

"You don't say?" Sandy said. "Well, I'm so glad. It's a pleasure to meet you too, uh..."

"Tim. Or Timothy. Timothy Phillips. You can call me whatever you like though, Ms. Newman. Though I guess I'd rather not be called Timmy."

"Well, Timothy, it's a pleasure to meet you. And please call me Sandy."

She was shaking his hand with both of hers. Tim dug the fingernails of his free hand into the back of his leg, because it felt like a dream. Ouch! The pain meant it wasn't a dream. He felt a little dizzy.

"Now what can I do for you?" Sandy said. "Was I causing a problem out here? I surely didn't mean it. Would you like a DVD? For you, I could do half price. Only five dollars for one of the damaged ones. Oh, it's purely cosmetic; don't worry."

"Yes, please," Tim said, flustered. He couldn't shoo her away. Not now. "Oh, Ms. Newman, I mean, Sandy...Ms. Sandy...I just... you never think you'll actually meet someone like you, you know?" Gosh, he sounded like an idiot. Too many *yous*. He handed over five dollars.

But Sandy Newman was gracious.

"Oh, I think we were probably meant to meet today, Timothy. Part of the Lord Jesus's plan. Thank you. Here's your DVD."

"Yeah! His plan," Tim said. His voice sounded distant, his own, but not his own; it was weird, but not unpleasant. He took the DVD and held it to his chest, like something precious. Like a...like a...like a Sandy Newman DVD! Which it was. Tim clutched it more tightly.

"Well, thank you so much, Timothy. Keep watching and keep praying. I'll be praying for you. Have a blessed day."

"You too, Ms.—I mean, Sandy."

Tim turned to go. But seeing Clem inside, expectant and frowning, made him stop. He couldn't put off all confrontation it seemed. Clem walked over.

"Well?" Clem said.

Oh, fiddlesticks! He'd have to do something. But what? Being in charge sure was tough. He needed a break. A break!

"Why don't you take your break, Clem? She'll, uh, she'll be gone by the time you're back."

Clem lowered his eyebrows but didn't say anything more. He just ambled off. Tim sighed. Problem solved. For the next fifteen minutes or so anyway. Surely by then he'd come up with some solution.

As it happened, it took only five minutes for Tim to solve the problem. He was adjusting a display of sun block cream, making sure they were all standing up straight, labels facing out, when it came to him.

"Yes?" Sandy Newman smiled at him as he came back outside to her.

"Oh, it's just, I was thinking. You shouldn't be out here in the hot sun all day," Tim said.

"Oh, you are so sweet," Sandy said.

Tim glowed.

"But I'm fine. Don't you worry."

Tim sunk. He turned to go. No. He couldn't. He had to stay in charge. He turned back.

"No, I have to worry. It's my job. I can't let you stay out here in the heat. It wouldn't be right. Please, come inside, and set up your table there. I have a spot at the junction of row seventeen and the main central corridor. There will be a lot of traffic there, and I can promise you'll be more comfortable."

"Are you sure?"

"I'm afraid I must insist," Tim said.

"Well, if you insist, I accept. Thank you kindly, Timothy."

Tim floated back into the store. If the rapture had come right then, Tim wouldn't have noticed, because he was pretty sure he couldn't feel any better.

LEE

Lee Rigg was having a pretty good day. Except for the friggin' crows, but he was working on that. He had woken up from a dream where he had totally been nailing Miss America. Hard. Those sorts of dreams always put a bounce in his boots. His back didn't hurt as bad as usual. He had only taken two aspirin and skipped the oxy entirely. He had found a half-full pack of cigarettes in a jacket pocket. And he didn't even need to wear the jacket; it was that nice out. His truck had been the envy of all who saw it as he drove to the Mega SuperMart. Course, that wasn't new. That was just normal. The chick with the huge knockers at the store's front door had been totally into him. She had given him—well, sold him—two DVDs, so he'd be able to check her out anytime he wanted. So what if she had done the same for that pipsqueak of a store manager who came and broke up his game? He could totally beat the snot out of that little twerp if it came to it. But he didn't have to worry. She was definitely into him. Yep, Lee Rigg was having a pretty damn-good day.

Except for the friggin' crows. Those damn birds, squawking and quacking and ruining awesome Miss America dreams. And then in the evenings, the friggin' woodpecker kept slamming his goddamn woodpecker head into the stop sign at the end of the road. Lee had tried to remove the sign, wasn't like he ever stopped there anyway. But the friggin' post was set in friggin' concrete, and the friggin' bolts were friggin' metric. In America! In the end, Lee had managed to get rid of the sign with his Sawzall, only to get cited for destruction of government property. In America, greatest country on Earth! Government of the people, by the people, for the people. All he had been doing was exercising his God-given rights as an American. But apparently *that* was a violation of his probation. To get rid of the crows, Lee would have to toe the line.

But, make no mistake: justice was coming for those birds. He was in America, greatest country on Earth, and he was going to buy a gun.

Lee scored a couple of stickers as he went into the store. Only in America did they give stickers out for free. They were just sitting there on a stool. Usually that stuff was jealously guarded as "just for kids," but Lee Rigg liked them. He stuck a dinosaur and a cartoon baseball player to the left and right of the bald eagle on his cutoff T-shirt. And now he was gonna go buy a gun. Those piece-of-crap birds weren't gonna know what hit them. Freedom!

But bringing justice to the squawking menace was proving easier said than done. Where did they keep the guns in this place anyway? The rows skewed left and right at all sorts of weird angles. It was like they were trying to make it confusing. Lee grabbed a pack of beef jerky to munch on as he wandered through the store. Everything was better with beef jerky. Kids' clothes, moms' clothes, tools, toys. He was trapped in a friggin' labyrinth. And he was starting to get a little annoyed. This was America; why the hell were there so many obstacles between him and shooting some friggin' birds? He chomped a little more fiercely into his jerky. IDEAS FOR THE KITCHEN! It was the third time he had seen that display. A sink in the kitchen? Didn't seem like much of an idea. Didn't anyone *work* here?

"Hey, buddy," Lee said to a man wearing a doofy hat and a long tan raincoat who was seemingly intent on picking out some bed linens across the aisle from the kitchenwares. The man jumped.

"Aaah!"

"Whoa, sorry, bud, didn't mean to scare you. You work here?"

The man stared at him. He had a thin mustache and shifty eyes, like he was looking for an escape. What was he trying to hide? When the man finally spoke, his voice seemed to come out of his cheek rather than his lips. The words were short, but they came rapid-fire. "No. I don't. How did you see me anyway?"

"You're just standing there. If you don't work here, you could just say so: no need to be so douchey about it. Good luck finding some sheets."

Lee rolled his eyes and walked off. People.

Fishing poles! They'd have to keep the guns somewhere nearby. It was logic, plain and simple. Lee made his way to the end of the aisle. A fishing pole might be cool to have. He didn't fish, but that was part of what he loved about America. If he wanted to, he could just grab a pole and go do it.

Sure enough, at the end of the fishing pole aisle was a long counter with handguns and ammunition behind glass panels. On the wall behind the counter was a big rack of rifles, shotguns, and assault weapons. It was like a friggin' armory. Lee was stoked. He adjusted his crotch and walked over to the counter. A bored teenager was standing a little way down, playing with his phone.

"Hey!" Lee said. The teen looked up. "You work here?"

The kid put down his phone and sulked over.

"Yeah," he said.

"Well, hallelujah!" Lee said. "I wanna buy a gun."

"Cool. What do you want?"

"How'm I supposed to know? Sell me something, kid. I wanna shoot birds and shit."

"I just work here, sir."

"Well, frig. Let's try that one then." Lee pointed to an all-black semiautomatic assault rifle in the middle of the shelf. It looked cool.

"Good choice, sir," the kid said flatly.

"Hell yeah it is! Looks friggin' badass, right?"

"Yes, it does." There was a clear lack of excitement in his voice. The hell? What was with the attitude? Did the little dink have a problem? Lee could totally beat the snot out of him if he wanted. But then he'd have to find another goddamn salesperson to get him the gun. This was supposed to be a country of the people, by the people, for the people! And he had the right to bear arms. He took another bite of jerky.

The kid started to walk away.

"Where are you going?!"

"I have to get another associate in order to unlock the gun rack, sir. I'll be back shortly."

Lee watched the kid head off through the fishing gear. What the hell? Where was he anyway? Friggin' Russia? Lee chuckled to himself. That was a good one. He'd have to remember it.

Lee admired the rows of weapons. What ever happened to bayonets? He didn't see any on offer. That was a shame, but maybe he could MacGyver something after the fact; that'd make any gun look even more badass. What was taking that pimply kid so long? Was he lost in the store? The layout was damn confusing. Or was this one of those garbage "waiting periods" the government kept trying oppress him with? Friggin' government, tryin' to take away his basic freedoms. But let them try once he had his hands on a gun! Where was that stupid kid? It wasn't like he could go looking for him. If he left the guns, he might never find them again. Lee peered down the fishing pole row. Nothing. His jerky was finished. Lee rubbed his bare arms. This was starting to get seriously annoying.

Finally. The pimply-faced kid materialized out of the row beyond the fishing poles, full of coolers and grills. With him was another blue-aproned SuperMart employee, Brian, by his nametag.

"Hi there," Brian said.

"'Sup," Lee said.

"Whattaya lookin' for?"

This Brian guy seemed halfway competent.

"Well," Lee said, "I got me a bird problem. They're always flapping and screeching and waking me up. Plus, they crap everywhere. So I wanna, you know, send 'em a message and stuff."

"Sweet, man. Did you have something picked out, or did you want to try a few?"

Yeah. Brian was all right.

"Well, I thought that one looked cool." Lee pointed to the black semi again.

"Oh, yeah," Brian said. "That's a badass gun all right. Semiautomatic. But they just say that to get around some of the regulations on fully automatic weapons. It'll shoot faster than you can pull the trigger."

Lee snorted a laugh. "That's what chicks sometimes say about me."

Brian looked away, then kept talking, "Yeah, well this baby can do 120 rounds a minute. Aim's pretty true. You could spray those birds full of lead, for sure. Why don't we grab that one and maybe another and you can hold 'em both and see what feels best? C'mon, Aidan, let's open it up."

The sullen teenager took out his keys and undid one of the locks at the same time that Brian undid the other. Then he went back to his phone. Kids today. Lee was glad he didn't have any. That he knew of anyway. He gave Brian a wink and a nod. Brian looked confused. Lee realized he had made that joke in his head.

"It's just, never mind," Lee said. Then, in a fit of inspiration, he added, "Two locks, you know? It's like we're in friggin' communist Russia!"

"Ha-ha! Ha-ha, ho." Brian slapped the counter, his eyes twinkling. Comedy gold!

"Here ya go. See how it feels."

Brian handed him the semiautomatic. Lee held it to his shoulder. It felt good. Powerful. Those birds might have won all the battles so far, but Lee Rigg would win the war. They wouldn't know what hit them. They'd have no friggin' idea.

"How's it feel?"

"Awesome."

Lee put it down and picked up another. This one was a shotgun and had a wooden stock.

"Genuine oak," Brian told him. As Lee put down the genuine-oak-stocked shotgun, there was a scream from across the store. A woman's scream. Lee tensed and looked at Brian. That scream had sounded real. Lee wondered if he would have to use his gun sooner than later. Freedom wasn't free, after all.

"I'm sure it's nothing," Brian said.

Lee picked up a third gun. Another scream, longer and louder this time.

"Aidan, why don't you go see what's going on. I'm going to help the gentleman get his gun," Brian said.

Aidan ignored Brian and kept playing with his phone.

"Which'll it be?"

Lee adjusted his crotch again; tighty-whities were ridin' a little snug. Shoulda free-balled it.

"This one," he said, selecting the first gun he had held.

"Excellent choice," Brian said. "I just have to enter your information into the system, and once your background check has cleared, you can come and pick up your gun."

"What?! I was joking about the communist Russia thing! At least I friggin' thought I was. Background check?! I thought this was the home of the brave and the land of the *free*!"

Lee's face was red, and he could feel a vein pulsing in his forehead. And he had thought Brian was a cool guy. Friggin' dink, sitting there with a smirk on his face. Lee knew he could beat the snot out of him if he wanted, and maybe he should. Punch him in the teeth and make him bleed blood.

"Naw, I'm just messing with you, man. There's no background check here. Maybe in California or somewhere, but we're good."

Land of the free, baby! Lee used his fist to pound Brian's, instead of to rearrange his dental work. It was a kinda funny joke. Not as funny as what Lee had been thinking to himself all morning, but kinda funny. Woulda been funnier said to someone else, but whatever.

Lee went and tousled Aidan's hair. "C'mon, you little tampon! Get in the spirit."

Aidan ducked away and shot him a sulky glare. Teenagers.

"I'll throw in a box of ammo, on the house," Brian said.

"Awesome."

There was another scream. It was different now—more of a holler or a yell. Longer, less frightened, more frustrated, less shriek, more bass. Someone needed help. And this was America. Land of the free, home of the brave. Of the people, by the people, for the people! Well, Lee was a person. He was the people. And someone was being oppressed. Without waiting for the receipt, he grabbed his new gun and sprinted off to find the trouble. And stop it.

BILLY

He wasn't going to cry: he was angrier than that. The only good thing that had happened to him all day was that the guy at the front door of the store had given him a dinosaur sticker, but it was scant consolation. He had thought he was the master of his own destiny, captain of his own ship. Not, apparently, if he wanted his ship to sail in a direction other than the one his mom wanted. She was the admiral of the fleet, and she was steering them toward the MEN'S AND WOMEN'S BARGAINS! section of the store.

"I wanna be admiral," Billy muttered to himself.

"What's that?" his mom asked. Her hearing was supernatural sometimes.

"Nothing."

"Good. Why don't you push the cart then?"

What was he, her slave? There were laws against child labor! He squeezed the bar with all his might; it didn't squeak or squeal or pop. It wasn't very satisfying, and his hands started to hurt, so he relaxed his grip. Maybe he should ram the display of SuperMart-brand cola. The cases were stacked like a pyramid, and it would be a pretty cool cascade if he hit it hard enough. It would be satisfying to release some of his bile into the world. His mom still had a firm grasp on the front of the cart though. Didn't she trust him at all?

Then Billy saw another better target. That smarmy blond preacher woman had set up her table at the end of the aisle. Billy disliked everything about her: The way she smelled like gross, dying flowers; her unnatural and unmoving hair; her condescending, fake-friendly tone. The way she had called him

87

little guy. The way she hadn't bowed to the apodictic truth of his logic. She was the worst. Ramming her table of DVDs and pamphlets and scattering them everywhere was a great idea. If only he could get Admiral Iron Grip to loosen her hold on the cart a little bit.

"Why hello again, little guy," the preacher woman said as they approached. "Bobby, isn't it?"

She smiled her fake smile. She raised the corners of her mouth and showed her teeth, but her eyes didn't change. Lots of grown-ups did that. The eyes. That was where you found the truth of a smile. He might have been only seven—almost eight— but Billy understood when people were lying with their faces. He scowled and tried not to breath in too deeply.

His mom started talking to her. Betrayal! Not that Billy was surprised. He was pretty sure his mom wasn't on his side at all; maybe she never had been. But...she took her hand off the cart. Slowly, carefully, Billy backed it up. He would need a running start. The stupid preacher was standing between him and her table. Well, he'd just ram her too. But what then? Billy knew the answer. His mom would shout at him, then lecture him, then ground him. They'd go home, and his dad would yell, then ground him. His sister would shake her head and say, "I don't know what is wrong with you." He had never actually rammed anyone with a shopping cart before, so there was no precedent, but judging by the great ketchup fiasco at Arby's—technically that had barely even been his fault—or the lasagna incident, which were the worst-on-record punishments, the punishment for ramming a preacher would probably be pretty severe. There was no food involved this time though, so there would be less of a mess, and maybe that would help mitigate the punishment? That was probably wishful thinking. He took his hands off the cart. It might not be worth it. He might not get to do anything fun for like...a year.

He looked around. Ten feet to the right was Men's Clothing. On the left were aisles of faucets and stuff. Maybe he should just run away. It seemed the only way he was going to get to do what he wanted would be to get out from under his mom's thumb.

It's not like anyone ever listened to him anyway. So why would they care if he was gone? He could build shelter for himself. His fort had taken a long time, but he'd only been working weekends. Food? He could find food. Food was everywhere. He might have to steal a little bit, but...those were details he could work out later.

Run away. It was perfect. Hadn't he already threatened to? Empty threats weren't worth the air expended on them. If he was ever going to get any respect, people had to know that he meant what he said. No time like the present to make a start on that. The only question was, why hadn't he thought of this years ago? Well, his mom was a good cook. And he would miss his Xbox and stuffed animals and stuff. So it wasn't a decision to take lightly. There would be no going back. But it had been building for a while—all morning in fact. Longer, really, if you counted the lasagna incident and the Arby's ketchup fiasco and about a million other things. Plus, they had destroyed his fort. And if he ran away, then there'd be no punishment for ramming the stupid blond preacher and her stupid helmet of perfumed hair. They'd never find him in Men's Clothing. Escape. And freedom. Ram the preacher woman and then disappear in the confused aftermath. It was the obvious choice, easy, and one he probably should have taken a long time ago.

He'd have to be quick. His mom would be quick. Billy took a deep breath.

"Billy, honey. Come back over here," his mom said.

"Okay, Mom," Billy said in what he hoped was a nonchalant tone. Ready. Aim...

As Billy set his feet and prepared to speed toward her, the preacher woman shrieked and pointed off to her right, Billy's left. Up over the faucets. His mom looked up to see what was the big deal. So did Billy. A squirrel was perched on the shelf at the end of the faucet aisle. It stared at them, then twitched, and looked a different direction, perfectly still. It moved so quickly Billy's eyes couldn't really follow it; suddenly, it was just in a new position, its bushy tail curled in an elegant *S*, a counterweight that helped it balance—it was like it was under a strobe light. Then it sprang and flashed away across the sprinkler system. Squirrels were so cool!

The preacher woman shrieked again. Jesus, she was loud. His mom went over and put her arm around her. Or tried to: the blond woman was waving her arms and almost knocked his mom in the face. Cosmic comeuppance! Billy didn't even bother with the cart. A clean escape was more important than venting his spleen. He might have been only almost eight, but he knew how to pick his spots. He just used the distraction to disappear into the middle of a circular rack of men's oversized T-shirts. It was so easy. They'd never find him.

DIRK BLADE

His hideout had been compromised. Dirk Blade held perfectly still, daring not even to breathe.

"Who are you?" the new arrival, a snotty-nosed little kid, said.

The kid was bluffing—Dirk Blade didn't move.

"Don't pretend like I can't see you," the kid said. "You can't fool me."

Little snippet was cleverer than he looked. Dirk Blade let out his breath. His inward-looking eye had failed him, but now was not the time to worry over spilt milk. If this kid was perceptive enough to see him in spite of the inward-looking eye, then he could be an asset.

"You got me, kid."

"Who are you?"

"I could ask you the same question, but that's not important right now."

"Okay," the kid said.

Good. The kid wouldn't blow his cover: that was critical.

"What are you doing here?"

It wasn't any of the kid's business. Maybe he should just kick him out of his hideout and be done with him, but no, this kid was perspicacious, and that could be of use. He had to try.

"I'm..." But what to tell him? And how much? "...searching."

That was good, honest enough to be defensible in court, yet sufficiently vague not to undermine his purpose. The kid rolled his perspicacious little eyes.

"Good for you, I guess, but you know Jesus is a hippie."

Dirk Blade did not need a sarcastic little whippersnapper fouling things up. Nor was a theological debate within his purview on this case.

"No, not like that. Listen, kid. I'm...there have been certain discrepancies. Here, I mean, in this store. Look, I don't know how much I can tell you. No one is supposed to know I'm here. But now that you do, I guess you could help me out."

There, that would be good. Make the kid think he was doing him the favor, not the other way around.

"Uh..." the kid said, looking around. "I don't know if that would be a good idea. No one is really supposed to know I'm here either. Maybe we should just pretend we never saw each other?"

So he was gonna try and play hardball, eh? Well, two could dance the foxtrot.

"Sorry, kid, that's not gonna work; my mind's a steel trap; I don't forget. So I'm sorry it's come to this, but the way I see it, you can help, or you can get out of my T-shirt rack. I was here first."

The kid blinked. Good, get the little punk on his back foot. Maybe he'd be more helpful. It worked: the kid nodded, once.

"Great, kid. It's like this, see—"

"My name is Will."

"Fine, Will. It's like this: someone in this store has been stealing, from the store and from the government." Dirk Blade emphasized the word *government*. The kid was still of an age where he probably had respect for that sort of authority. There was no need to specify that he wasn't, strictly speaking, working for the government. The kid stared blankly; hopefully first impressions were, in fact, deceiving, and he was indeed cleverer than he looked.

"There's gotta be evidence somewhere, but so far, I haven't been able to find it. You're perceptive, kid...Will. Between the two of us, I bet we'll be able to find it."

"What is it, exactly?" Will asked.

"Paper work. I've gone through everything in the office, but it's not there. So there's got to be some secret hiding place. That's what you're looking for. Find the place; find the papers."

"Wouldn't it just be on a computer somewhere? Paper seems kinda old fashioned."

"It'll be on paper. Just keep your eyes peeled, kid. If you find something, set off this."

Dirk Blade reached into one of his many pockets and pulled out an Orion self-propelled flare. It was supposed to be the brightest, most powerful on the market, though he'd never had cause to use one on a job yet. If the kid set it off, he'd be sure to see it. The kid took the flare, doubt writ large on his simple face.

"Just pull the ring. Make sure you've got the business end"— Dirk Blade indicated the nonring end—"away from you. Toward the ceiling is your best bet. Got it? Good. Thanks, Will."

"Wait, mister. What's..."

But he had already wasted enough times bandying words with this kid. Either he was going to help or he wasn't, and Dirk Blade had a case to solve. No one got paid for cases they didn't solve. Without waiting for the kid to finish, Dirk Blade whirled and pushed out through the T-shirts. He'd have to find a new hiding place while he thought up his next maneuver.

BILLY

The man in the goofy hat and the long tan raincoat was gone. Billy turned the stick of dynamite the man had given him over in his hands; instead of a wick, it had a ring on one end. He'd keep it; it might come in handy. But he wasn't so sure he'd use it to help that guy. At least he had the T-shirt rack to himself now. He could think.

"Hi. What are you doing?" a small voice said behind him.

Billy whirled. He couldn't get a moment's peace! The voice belonged to a small girl. She was probably six or something. She was dressed in a long-sleeved dress with sunflowers all over it. There was a big pocket emblazoned with a ladybug. But cool clothes didn't mean she could just barge into his space. What was she doing in here?

"I'm...never mind. Who are you? How did you get in here?"

"I'm Willow. I'm playing fairy princesses. I came in when the guy with the goofy hat came out. Do you wanna play? That's a nice dinosaur sticker. My mom wouldn't let me get one. What's your name? And what's that you've got behind your back?"

Willow? What kind of name was Willow? A willow was a sad tree. Billy had always felt bad for kids with weird names. In the second grade, there had been a girl named Buoyancy. Boy, did she get teased. She tried to pretend that it was like Beyoncé, but it didn't work. Billy didn't understand why parents did that to their children. There was also that kid Shiva, whose family was from India. That wasn't his parents' fault. Shiva was a normal name where they came from. But the whole year, Mrs. Archer, the gym teacher, had called him Shiver. "Shiver, pick up the ball!" "Shiver, stop picking your nose!" Poor Shiva didn't even

94

realize she was talking to him half the time. And then there was his cousin, Silvith, which wasn't even a word, much less a name, though it could have been a lot worse: Billy had heard his mom and his aunt talking, and apparently his aunt and uncle were gonna call him Artificial Insemination, so in that respect, Silvith wasn't so bad.

He felt a little sorry for Willow, but he did not want to play fairy princesses. He was trying to run away, and the last thing he needed was a six-year-old messing things up for him.

"I'm Will. I don't want to play fairy princesses. This is a stick of dynamite, I think. Be careful."

He held up the stick of dynamite for her inspection. The name change was natural. For his new life, he'd have to have a new identity. And William was his real name after all. The only great Billy in history was Billy the Kid, and he had to become an outlaw to get respect. Well, him and the Billy Goats Gruff. There were a lot more great Wills and Williams: William Tell, William Shakespeare, Will Smith.

"Cool. Why don't you want to play fairy princesses? It's fun. What are you, too old?"

She asked a lot of questions.

"I'm almost eight," Billy said.

"Oooh! I'm seven too. I just turned seven."

It wasn't the same. They were from different generations.

"So are you gonna play?" Willow asked.

"I don't want to be a fairy princess. Look, Willow, I've got things—"

"You don't have to be a fairy princess. That's just what the game's called. You run around through castles and have magical powers. You can be whoever you want."

Billy looked at her. She was talking about "superheroes." It was a good game. Plus, he needed to get a move on. His mom was going to realize he was gone any second now.

"Okay," he said. "I'll play. I'm going to be...The Squirrel. I have squirrel superpowers."

"I like squirrels! Did you see there's a squirrel in the store? It looked scared."

"Yeah! I hope it's all right. I hope the grown-ups don't hurt it."

"Yeah."

Willow seemed all right.

"Who are you gonna be?" Billy asked her.

"I'm the Fairy Princess Willow of course. I can freeze time and turn stuff into flowers."

Turning things into flowers seemed kinda pointless, but that was probably just some girl thing—to each their own. The important thing was to get going. Outside the T-shirt display, it sounded like his mom had calmed the blond preacher down some. Billy needed to put some distance between himself and her fast.

"Okay, Fairy Princess Willow. Let's go then."

"Wait, Squirrel. Will."

She giggled. Billy raised an eyebrow at her.

"I think it's funny how we kinda have the same name."

Will and Willow were sort of the same. But mostly different. One was a name, and one was a tree. It didn't strike Billy as funny. He hoped he wasn't making a mistake throwing in his lot with someone who had only just turned seven. He needed to make good on his escape.

"Where are we going though? What are we doing?" Willow asked.

Billy thought for a second.

"Maybe we can be looking for treasure?"

"Ooh, I like treasure. What kind?"

She asked so many questions. How was he supposed to know? But maybe...

"Papers? In a secret hiding place," he said.

"Not papers," Willow said.

Billy shrugged. Or not.

"Documents. It sounds more important if we call them documents. Can there be jewels too? Diamonds and rubies?"

Jewels—diamonds and rubies and whatever else—held no interest for Billy.

"There needs to be gold too," he said. Gold was proper treasure.

"Of course there's gold, Will. Some kind of treasure it'd be without gold."

"Okay. Documents, rubies, diamonds."

"And gold!" Willow finished. "In a secret hiding place!"

She clapped her hands.

"Let's go."

Finally.

"Okay. Let's move to the next castle."

"Fortress," Billy corrected her.

"No. Shirts are castles. Maybe pants can be fortresses?"

"Yeah, okay." Billy didn't have time to argue. They had to get moving. "To the next castle then. We'll make a quick stop there. And then to the blue-jean fortress!"

"Okay." Willow smiled. She was missing one of her front bottom teeth. The new one was half in. It was a good look. He spread the T-shirts apart slightly.

"Wait," Willow said.

"What?"

"We can't be seen by the grown-ups. They're bad ogres who want to steal our treasure."

Yep, Willow was all right. Billy grinned at her.

"Well, of course," he said. "I didn't think we even needed to mention that."

"Yeah, you're right. I'm gonna freeze time. That way we can go in secret," Willow said. She sat up straight; her face was solemn. She clapped her hands in front of her face, then extended her arms to the sides.

"Okay," she said. "We can go now."

Billy raced to the next T-shirt display. Willow came right after him. They paused. Willow froze time again, and then they raced to the blue-jean fortress. Inside, Billy sat down. Willow sat down next to him. Billy heard his mom shout from somewhere outside.

"Billy! Billy, where are you? Billy? Billly!"

TIM

Tim was killing it. Ordinarily Tim never meant to kill anything. But he knew "killing it" was cool-guy speak for doing a tip-top job. It was how Mr. Spooner would have described the current management of the store—if he hadn't been working so hard up in his office. In fact it was what Mr. Spooner had said that one time when Tim had managed to get the bathrooms clean after a bad shipment of rotisserie chickens had wreaked no small amount of havoc on the store's customers. "Timmy, I didn't think you would manage, but you killed it, dog." It had been glorious. And right now, Tim didn't want to get too cocky, but he had to admit everything was running super smoothly. He was killing it.

He had managed the double-greeter situation brilliantly by moving Ms. Newman—Sandy—into the store. She had shaken his hand and thanked him! He was considering never washing his hand again. Of course he would have to, because cleanliness was next to godliness, and Tim did the best he could. But maybe he would skip his usual midmorning handwashing and only do it when he had to, right before lunch. Lunch! His keys. No, not time to worry about that. He didn't want to step away from the store floor right now anyway. The store was busy, a freshly oiled machine. Mr. Spooner would be so pleased. Tim wondered if it was time to go check on him. The Golden Snacks truck would be arriving soon. No, he could handle it. Then he'd go see how Mr. Spooner was doing. Tim hoped he wasn't working too hard.

He wandered the floor: subtly adjusting displays that weren't at ninety-degree angles, making them right; talking to customers, wishing them tip-top days; checking in with associates, wishing them tip-top days. He was in the zone all right. The he heard the scream. He knew instinctively that it was bad. Screams were bad. And it was coming from the area where he had installed Ms. Newman—Sandy! Tim accelerated to walk-skip and headed in that direction. The screams kept coming. It was Ms. Newman! Gosh darn it, he'd have to get used to calling her Sandy.

"Oh turnips!" Tim said in a slightly higher-pitched voice than normal. Recognizing the creeping panic, he took a deep breath and spoke to himself aloud, "Keep it together, Timothy. This is your moment."

Ms. Newman—Sandy—was hyperventilating. Her face was wet with tears. She was bent over her table, huffing and puffing. A woman was patting her on the back. Tim grabbed a box of tissues from an abandoned cart and ripped it open. He'd have to remember to expense that to his charge account. He brought the box over to the stricken preacher.

"What seems to be the trouble, Ms.—Sandy?"

She was too overcome to answer, though she did snatch the tissues from Tim.

Tim turned to the other woman. "What seems to be the trouble, ma'am?"

The woman looked harried and somewhat angry. Tim braced himself.

"There was a squirrel up there." She pointed to Aisle 19: Kitchen Fixtures.

"A squirrel, you say?"

"Yes! A squirrel! And what, may I ask, is a squirrel doing in the store?"

"You're sure it was a squirrel?"

Tim couldn't believe what he was hearing. A squirrel in the store was highly irregular. And everything had been going so well.

"Are you suggesting I'm making it up?"

"No, ma'am. I mean, a trick of the light or something...it's just, what would a squirrel want with a new faucet?"

"Don't try to be funny with me, mister. She saw it too. And it really upset her, as you can see. I've half a mind to speak to the manager about this. I mean, I've got a child with me. What if it's rabid?"

Tim swallowed. The day was getting decidedly less blessed.

"I...I don't know. I'm terribly sorry, ma'am. And I, uh, I guess you sort of are talking to the manager already. So that's something, right?"

The woman's nostrils flared.

"Assistant manager," she read off his nametag. The skeptical, condescending tone was almost physically jarring. He had nothing to say to that. He felt helpless. And there was a wild squirrel, possibly rabid, running loose in the store. He should get Mr. Spooner. No. He had to handle this.

Sandy was saying something.

"Please don't fight," she said. "Mr. Timothy is a nice man. Oh, the little feet. So gross."

Both the woman and Tim turned back to Sandy.

"The claws. The teeth. Vile little rodents." Sandy was rubbing her hands on her shoulders, her arms, her chest, as if trying to brush off some unseen dirt. She rubbed the top of her shoe vigorously on the back of her other leg. Tim wondered if she was having a breakdown. That couldn't happen! Not now. Not today.

"There, there," Tim said. The woman patted Sandy on the back and offered her a bottle of water that she had grabbed off the shelf. Tim would have to bite the bullet and add that to his charge account too.

Sandy gulped down the water. Tim and the other woman exchanged a look. The look said, "Isn't she wonderful?" Though it could have meant, "Does this woman need professional help?" Tim had never been very good with nonverbal communication; it reminded him of sorcery. And he stayed well clear of the occult. Wizards and witches, magicians, all silently sharing wicked plans with winks and nods. What was speaking without words if not magic, dark and inaccessible to the honest man? Sandy's cheeks were red and wet with tears. Yet still, she looked lovely. Angelic. If there were a distraught angel, sobbing over a squirrel, this is what it would look like, for sure.

"I'm sorry, y'all. I just was overcome. It's the third time I've been in close contact with a squirrel today, and well, we don't have a great history. But I've got to be stronger. Help me, Lord Jesus, help me to be strong!" Sandy looked up at the ceiling.

Tim smiled. Of course. Jesus would help!

The other woman seemed to think so too, because she said, "You're right; squirrels do seem to be turning up all over the place today. Must be the time of year or phase of the moon or something. In any case, it's gone now. And you're looking better, Ms. Newman, so I guess you don't need my help anymore. Billy, we're going."

The woman turned and walked over to the abandoned cart where Tim had gotten the tissues.

Tim turned to Sandy. "Are you all right?"

"Yes, thanks, you're a dear. I'm sorry to have caused a scene."

"No, that's fine. Please don't worry about that. I'm just glad you're okay."

Her hand was hanging in midair, limp. Should he grab it? She was a lady preacher. But wasn't this compassion? Tim took a deep breath and made to grab her hand. But just as he did, she moved it and started fussing with her hair. Tim's hand lurched into space. Like a big dumb-dumb head. But Sandy didn't seem to have noticed. She was patting her hair. If an angel patted her hair in the wake of a squirrel-induced breakdown, that's what it would look like. Her hair was perfect.

"Hey, excuse me." The abandoned-cart woman broke Tim out of his reverie.

"Yes, ma'am?"

"My son, Billy, seems to have wandered off. Could you help me find him?"

"Yes, ma'am!"

Before Tim could start helping though, the woman began to shout.

"Billy! Billy, where are you? Billy! Billlly!"

She could yell really loud. Tim looked around. He didn't see any children. Sandy was still patting her hair. It was beautiful. She was beautiful.

"Billy, this isn't funny. You have to the count of ten. One."

"Timmy Phillips. Timmy Phillips to the office. Timmy to the office. Bring water." Mr. Spooner! He was calling for Tim over the loudspeaker.

"Two," the woman said, keeping on with her slow count. "Three."

So much was happening! Mr. Spooner needed him. Ms. Newman—Sandy needed him. This woman with the missing child. What to do?

"Timmy to the office."

Mr. Spooner!

"I'll be right back, ma'am," Tim told the woman. "I gotta run to the office for a second. I'll be right back, Ms.—Sandy."

Tim grabbed another bottle of water—his charge-account bill was going to be ugly this month—and walk-skipped as fast as he could toward the office.

MITCH

Mitch Spooner was standing at the top of a burning building. Ms. MacFarlane, his superhot tenth-grade English teacher, was with him. She was scared. He was not. They'd have to jump. But she'd be so glad afterward that...Mitch got his arm around her waist and pulled her close. She smelled like vanilla and cinnamon. The burning building was a bakery.

"Hold on tight, Ms. M.," Mitch said. She threw her arms around his neck. They jumped. Falling...falling...

They landed on a bed.

"Oh, Mitch. You saved me!"

Mitch smiled. It was time for the thank-you. He ran his hands down to the buttons of her blouse. She slapped them away.

"Mitch, answer the phone."

That wasn't the thank-you he was expecting. He leaned in.

She pushed him away and sat up. "The phone, Mitch."

Mitch blinked, confused. The phone was ringing, but it seemed like he and Ms. MacFarlane had a lot more important things to do right now.

"Answer the phone, Mitch."

Ms. MacFarlane flickered. No! She couldn't leave.

"The phone, Mitch."

"But I don't wanna; c'mon, Ms. M. I just saved you. Don't you want to, you know? Get a little freaky?"

Mitch gave what he hoped was a rakish grin. He didn't understand what women saw in rakes; he was more of a shovel guy, which was closer to a spoon, but that didn't matter. What mattered was Ms. MacFarlane not leaving. The phone was ringing louder. It sounded like the fire alarm that had triggered the whole thing in the first place. Make it stop!

"I don't wanna! No!"

Mitch awoke with a start. Where was the bed? Ms. MacFarlane? He was in his darkened office. There was a small puddle of drool on his desk. Mitch wiped the corners of his mouth and swallowed. His throat was dry. The phone was still echoing from his dream. It made his head hurt. Ms. MacFarlane was nowhere to be seen. Bitch. Mitch wondered if she was still hot. She had to be pushing forty by now. Yeah, she probably was. Was she married yet? Mitch had always had his suspicions about her and that lame-ass history teacher Mr. Brown. Why the hell wouldn't that phone echo stop?

"Oh," Mitch said. His office phone was actually ringing.

Mitch groaned, though he had to admit it made sense. He fumbled a desk drawer for some Tylenol—or whatever the generic form of Tylenol was, it was a freebie from work—and popped a couple in his mouth. The lack of candy coating was more unpleasant now than it had been that morning in his condo. They tasted not unlike mothballs, which he had tried on a dare back in the day. Mitch gagged. He had to play through it. He grabbed a handful of Skittles—or whatever the generic form of Skittles was, they were a freebie from work—and tossed them into his mouth afterward to cover up the mothball taste. Generic Skittles were delicious. He mashed everything into a paste with his molars and rolled it all around his mouth a couple times. It tasted like cherries and chalk. Much better. He could really use some goddamn water. The phone continued to ring. Mitch swallowed, then picked up the phone.

"Hel...hello?" Mitch's voice was froggy and thick with sleep and dehydration and hangover.

"Please hold for Mr. Wallace," a friendly feminine voice, not unlike Ms. MacFarlane's, said.

"Hello? Mitchell Spooner?" A gruff male voice replaced the friendly Ms. MacFarlane one.

"Huh? Yeah, I'm Mitch. Who's this?"

"This is C. Franklin Wallace. Where have you been? I've been calling for the last half hour. Do you think it's funny to make me wait, Mr. Spooner?"

Mitch's brain was still slow from the sleep and the dehydration and the hangover. Who was C. Franklin Wallace? A reporter?

"Sorry, C. Franklin, it's just...who are you again?"

"Do not jest with me, Mr. Spooner. You know exactly who I am. I have—that is my secretary, Mindy, has—been holding the line for the last thirty minutes. When I schedule a call, Mr. Spooner, by Christ, I expect my employees to be on time for it. My time is valuable. This will not happen again."

Oh, shit. Mitch's brain unfogged in record time. C. Franklin Wallace was the president and CEO of SuperGroup, the consortium behind SuperMart, SuperCinema, and SuperNews. When Corporate had said someone would be calling today, Mitch hadn't expected it would be him. Mr. Franklin Wallace didn't sound angry, exactly, but his calm, matter-of-fact tone was twice as unsettling as yelling would have been.

"Oh, Mr. Franklin Wallace. I'm so sorry. It's been a crazy morning, selling sh—stuff and making money, you know? And, uh, the connection, you know. I can hear you now."

"I'm sure, Mr. Spooner. I'm sure. And it's Mr. Wallace to you. Now let's get straight to business; I'm a busy man, and my time is valuable."

"Yes, sir."

"Mr. Spooner, as I'm sure you're aware, there have been some irregularities in the accounting of your store for more than six months now."

Well, no shit. He certainly couldn't afford his lifestyle on the paltry salary they were paying him, even with all the freebies. He was pretty sure he had covered all his tracks though. He should probably double-check, just in case. But to do that, first he would need to appease Mr. Franklin Wallace and buy himself some time.

"Irregularities, sir? You mean like we should be eating more fiber? Ha-ha, that's a joke, Mr. Franklin Wallace."

"Amusing, I'm sure. And please stop using my middle name."

He didn't sound amused.

"Yeah, well. I've noticed them obviously. It's certainly troubling, but I'm not sure it's necessarily sinister. Seems more like math tricks to me."

"Mr. Spooner, let's not beat around the bush. There has been a discrepancy between forecast and actual earnings for three consecutive quarters. The tax bill submitted by your location is nearly treble what our corporate action plan says it should have been. What's more, it's nearly eight times what the city and state say they've received. Someone is stealing from us, Mr. Spooner. I do not like to be made a fool of. And I also have a fiduciary duty to our shareholders, as do you. You were tasked several months ago with figuring out who the thief is. You have said nothing beyond that you're working on it. Which means you're either incompetent or complicit. We've opened our own investigation, Mr. Spooner. We will soon have answers. What I would like to know is, do you have any? Answers, that is. And be succinct. My time is valuable."

Mitch swallowed. His head hurt.

"Mr. Franklin Wallace."

"For Chrissakes, Spooner, call me Mr. Wallace. Franklin is my middle name, and only my friends use it. You are not my friend."

Jeez, he was touchy.

"Sorry, Mr. Wallace. But don't worry. I've almost got it figured out. I'll be sure soon. Just give me a little more time. I have a couple of promising leads. If I just had a few more—"

"You have until 1:00 p.m. to come up with something other than bland conjecture. That's when I will be arriving to talk with you. In person. So get it together, Mr. Spooner. I may arrive early. Someone will be calling every hour, on the hour, for updates. Make sure someone answers that phone. Good day to you."

"But, Mr. Wallace, wait a sec—"

"I said good day!"

The phone clicked off. C. Franklin Wallace had gone. Off to bang Mindy probably. Mitch needed a secretary. No. What he needed was to figure a way out of this mess. He *wanted* a secretary. Subtle difference. Mitch wasn't worried, per se. He had taken precautions; he wasn't an idiot after all. Still, he'd better check. And he hadn't been expecting the big kahuna himself to actually show up. Shit. He couldn't check the paper work without leaving the phone. Well, that part was easy anyway. It looked like Mitch's nap was over. He walked over to the intercom. It was a struggle. He really should drink some water. He cleared his throat as best he could and put his mouth next to the microphone.

"Timmy Phillips. Timmy Phillips to the office. Timmy to the office. Bring water."

***

"Here's the water, Mr. Spooner. Mr. Spooner, are you all right?"

Mitch grunted, chugged the water, burped, crushed the bottle, and stood up a little straighter.

"I'm great, Timmy. But look, I gotta check on some stuff. I'm forwarding all my calls to your phone. I need you to hang by it and answer when it rings. Can you do that?"

"I, uh, well..."

"Rhetorical question, Timmy. Just do it. Don't say anything specific about me when you answer. Just let whoever it is know that I'm working on the problem and will be back soon."

"What problem?!"

"Shut up. Don't ask questions. Got it? Good. I'm out."

"But—"

"Just do it, Timmy."

Mitch left the office. Why was he saddled with such a little bitch for an assistant? He bet Mr. Franklin Wallace's secretary,

Mindy, was hot *and* helpful. Timmy was neither. Answer the goddamn phone, dorkus. How hard could it be?

Once on the store floor, Mitch strode purposefully toward Aisle 15: Home Appliances.

Before he could get there, however, he was waylaid by a pushy woman. A soccer-mom type. Her hair was a little longer than it ought to be for her age. Her sweater left everything to the imagination. Her ass filled out her jeans—but in a soft, squishy way. Certainly wasn't what the designer of those pants had in mind. Mitch saw hundreds just like her every day. She probably drove a minivan. Ordinarily, her type held no interest for him. But before he could get past her and get on with his business, she stepped in front of him.

"Excuse me, sir. Do you work here?"

Mitch grunted. She might've been hot ten or fifteen years ago. Now...was this what had happened to Ms. MacFarlane too?

"I can't find my son, Billy."

"I'm sure he's around somewhere, ma'am. And I'd be happy to help. I just have one thing I have to do first."

"More important than finding my son?!"

Jesus. Soccer moms. It was like they thought they were the only ones whose biology was miraculous. But Mitch knew he had to be diplomatic.

"No, it's just—"

"Then help me find him! Your colleague already gave me the runaround once. He's missing!" Her voice rose in pitch to almost a shriek. Mitch grimaced; he should have taken more painkillers.

"Mr. Spooner? Maybe we should help?"

"Timmy? What the hell are you doing here? I told you to be in your office!"

"About that, sir, I was trying to explain, and you left the office, so I followed. It's like this. I—"

"Never mind, Timmy. Why don't you get this nice lady a water or a soda or something. On the house," Mitch said, smiling at Soccer Mom. She didn't smile back.

"And, Timmy, help her find her kid, Toby."

"Oh no you don't. You're going to help too, you bastard. This guy"—she was pointing at Timmy—"couldn't even do anything about the squirrel. You are going to bring me to the manager. And then we're going to find. My. Son. Billy."

Billy. Toby. Whatever. And squirrels? This chick seemed unstable. Mitch fought to keep his composure. He was getting sick of dealing with morons.

"Look, ma'am, I'm sure your little Billy is superprecious and all, but you're raving about squirrels. I can't help right now. Timmy here will—"

"There was a squirrel," a blond woman with a pretty face and huge boobs told him. While Mitch was on the fence about Soccer Mom, this lady was an easy decision. He would. He definitely would.

"Hey there," he said and pushed back his hair. It was still covered in gel, so it didn't really move.

"Mr. Spooner, sir, maybe we should do something about her son?"

Timmy was being a little prick and cutting in on him, messing up his game.

"Yes. You should," Soccer Mom said. "And take me to the manager."

"I'm the manager, lady," Mitch said. His patience was pretty much used up.

"Well, surely you'll help then, right?" the blond chick said.

Mitch thought of his office phone and the company investigation and the subterranean vault where he had covered all his tracks. He hoped he had covered them anyway. He thought about motorboating that blond chick. Everything was on him. Well, he did have strong shoulders. He did his shrugs at the gym.

"All right. Timmy, let's institute Code Bobby."

"Code Bobby?" Soccer Mom snarled. "Don't you mean Code Adam?"

"We subscribe to Code Bobby here, ma'am," Timmy, useful for once, said. "Slightly different protocols but it's largely the same thing. No one will come into or out of this store until your son is found. We'll all look for him. It's all set up. The protocols are all in place. Don't you worry."

"Oh, well. Thank you."

"Now, if you don't mind," Mitch said.

"Oh, I do," blond chick said.

"What?"

"Yes. We should all kneel and pray. The store manager especially. Certainly his prayers are important here. Let us pray for the deliverance of this poor little boy from whatever monster snatched him."

Mitch groaned. A Jesus freak. So much for the motorboating. She grabbed his hand. Timmy grabbed her other hand way too eagerly—which explained why he had tried to ruin Mitch's game. Soccer Mom was between Mitch and Timmy. She sank to her knees mutely. She had turned pale at the mention of the child-snatching monster.

"But, what about Code Bobby? Shouldn't we do that first?" Soccer Mom said. But she was already on her knees, holding Mitch's and Timmy's hands.

"The Lord will provide. Our duty is to him first," the blond chick said. Mitch rolled his eyes.

"Oh, Lord Jesus, please hear us now in our time of need. Protect and deliver us from evil. Protect us from the godless. And the squirrels. And the godless squirrels."

What was she talking about? Mitch started to get up. She pulled him back down and kept talking.

"Show us the path to righteousness and help us in our daily struggles. Help us find this boy and deliver him to us unharmed. Please, Lord Jesus, we pray. Amen."

"Amen!" Timmy practically shouted.

"Amen," Mitch said and gave the blond chick's hand a squeeze. She might be crazy, but she was still hot. A tumble or two with her would definitely be fun. Suppressed Christian chick? She'd be off the chain in the sack. She pulled her hand away. Well, just 'cause it would be awesome in the end didn't mean it'd be easy in the short term. And Mitch had other stuff to worry about.

"Okay. Can we *please* start looking for Billy now?" Soccer Mom asked.

Mitch nodded at Timmy, who walked over to a courtesy phone and made the announcement.

SCARLETT

"Attention SuperMart employees. Your attention please. We are initiating Code Bobby. All SuperMart employees. Code Bobby. Thank you.

"Also, could Billy Anderson please return to Aisle 17 and your mother please. Billy Anderson, if you can hear this, please come to Aisle 17."

The announcement sounded a little rushed, and Tim's voice was slightly higher pitched than normal, but overall, he sounded like he was keeping it together. Scarlett was mildly impressed. Her own heart was already beating a little faster and a little harder. A missing kid was terrifying. She thought of her nephew; he was probably tearing around her apartment on all fours and making a racket, the little gremlin. He was awesome. Kind of the complete opposite of his father. She wished Rose could make better decisions. But now was not the time to go down that rabbit hole. At least this Code Bobby broke up the monotony of the day. Scarlett wondered if that made her a horrible person. What if the kid had actually been abducted? No. That sort of thing didn't really happen. Please, let that not be what happened.

"Scarlett, you all right?" Clem asked, snapping her out of her own head.

"What? Yeah. Oh, I just...we better find that kid."

"Calm down, young miss. We'll find him. The doors are sealed. He probably just wandered off."

Clem was so calm, so serene. Scarlett had no idea how he managed. And he was probably right. Scarlett took a deep breath; it would be all right. And it was better than working checkout. Oh god, she really was a horrible person.

"C'mon then. Let's go find this little guy," Clem said. His old eyes twinkled.

Scarlett gave a small smile. Maybe she wasn't horrible. Maybe her regular job was horrible, and that's why she and, it seemed, Clem were excited about the change.

The two set off down Aisle 11: Legos and Other Toys. According to Code Bobby protocols, the store's employees were to partner up and then sweep the store, aisle by aisle, stopping all adults with children to make sure they belonged to them. Meanwhile, the doors remained closed, and the store went into lockdown. No one going in or out. And because it was a *Mega SuperMart*, sweeping the whole store could take as long as an hour. Scarlett was pretty sure that if they couldn't find the kid in the first ten minutes, they were supposed to call the cops. No, that was Code Adam. Code Bobby was more relaxed, which not coincidentally made Scarlett feel less relaxed. They were supposed to call the police "at the discretion of the manager" or something like that. There had been a training video about it, but Scarlett couldn't remember the exact wording. Besides, Clem was right, the child had probably just wandered off. He *was* right.

There was nothing in the Lego aisle, so they moved on to Aisle 33: Electrical Supplies. Nothing there either. At the end of the aisle, by Girls' Fashion, Scarlett stopped.

"Clem?"

"Yes?"

"You don't think this could have anything to do with that sketchy dude I saw earlier, do you? You know, the one in the store before we opened?"

Clem sighed. "No, Scarlett. I don't. But I don't know for sure. Seems I don't know as much as I think I do these days."

"What do you mean?"

"How old do you think I am, young lady?"

Scarlett had no idea. She'd have believed anything between sixty and eighty. Better to guess on the low end.

"Sixty-two?"

"Ha! Flattery'll get you everywhere. But no. I'm older than that. I won't keep you guessing though. I'm eighty-one."

Whoa. He looked great!

"Wow, I hope I look like you when I'm eighty-one. Heck, I hope I get to be eighty-one."

"Oh, I'm sure you will. And you'll be much prettier too; I have no doubt. But, Scarlett, my point is, why do you think I, at eighty-one, am standing at the front of a big-box store, greeting people who don't want to be greeted with an empty smile and fake enthusiasm?"

That was an uncomfortable question. There was only one reason anyone would work at this soul-sucking store.

"I, uh, probably you need the money." She figured Clem must have a point, but heck if she knew what it was.

"Heh, heh. No. I'm afraid not. I have problems, of course. But money is not one of them."

Well, that explained his fancy shoes and his fancy watch.

"Yeah," she said. "I thought your watch looked kinda expensive."

"My watch is expensive."

Scarlett didn't understand where he was going with this.

"This store used to be called Patterson's. That was probably back before you were born. And I, well, I'm Clem Patterson."

Scarlett opened her mouth and shut it again. Patterson's? Clem was a Patterson? At eighty-one, he was probably *the* Patterson. Her mom had shopped at Patterson's when she was a girl. It had been an institution. People her mother's age *still* talked about it with a weird sort of pride. Like they had owned it or something. And not only that, it had history. There had been a civil rights march that had started at Patterson's, an important one. Led by employees? They had learned about it in middle school. "A real turning point in the timbre of the movement," their civics book had said, something like that. Michael Gardiner had kept saying, "Timberrrr," and pretending to be a lumberjack to try to make the class laugh. He never was very funny.

Scarlett knew in the back of her mind that SuperMart had taken Patterson's over, and that people—like her mother—had been sad and upset about it. But if that was the case, it meant Clem...he wasn't just rich. He had to be...he had enough money to buy her whole building, much less just her apartment. He had enough money to buy all the cars in the parking lot. He could— why on *earth* was he working here?

"Please don't think less of me," Clem said.

"What? Why would I ever do that? If anything, this makes me think even more of you," Scarlett said. "You're, like, a gazillionaire. What are you doing still working here?"

"I, well, it's kind of a long story."

"Try me," Scarlett said.

Before either of them could say any more, Tim came hurrying by. His tie was crooked, his breathing heavy. His eyes kept darting left, right, up, down, like he was expecting the missing kid to suddenly materialize from nowhere.

"Any luck, you two?" he asked.

Scarlett shook her head.

"Fiddlesticks! Okay. Well, keep looking. I'll be by the front door if you need me."

Tim waved his hand hurriedly in front of his face—was he crossing himself?—and rushed off.

Clem shook his head.

"Well, we should probably keep looking. I came back here because I'm a damned fool. This store was the first one I opened, you know? My baby, so to speak. I could tell it was in trouble—nothing like the store I started, and I don't want to see it perverted into something terrible. Or shut down completely. Thought maybe I could help. Ha. Fat lot of good I can do greeting people at the front door. That guy you saw this morning? That's just confirmation—probably Corporate is running an audit, and given the meathead who's in charge here, I have no doubt they'll find all kinds of reasons to shut it down and move on. That's how it goes. Look, Scarlett, I don't think anyone kidnapped that child. But in my day, no one would ever do that kind of thing. This morning I saw a squirrel running along the sprinklers. That sort of thing never used to happen either, so I just don't know anymore."

Scarlett didn't pry. She just shook her head. Clem was really amazing. And life was always complicated, it seemed. She really hoped this Billy kid had just wandered off.

SANDY

Sandy's hair was still immaculate, like the baby Jesus's conception, but her heart was pounding like Pontius Pilate's at judgment day. She felt hot. If she was not careful, she might start to perspire. That would be unseemly. She needed to keep it together, for that poor woman if not for herself.

Ms. Uppity was all right. She was raising a little brat, to be sure, but to have her child abducted—Sandy was sure that was what had happened; children didn't just wander off in this day in age; she had seen enough prime-time news programs to know that—well, it was horrible. The store manager and that nice Timothy had just initiated a search, but Sandy knew it would take a miracle to find him safe and sound. They had prayed, but that was more for appearances—to walk the walk, so to speak. If it provided some comfort, well then, it was all to the good, but it wouldn't really help. Not that she could tell that to Ms. Uppity; outwardly, she had to be cheerful, hopeful.

"Don't worry," she told Ms. Uppity. "I'm sure we'll find him before...before something awful happens."

Ms. Uppity gave her a horrified look. Oh, how awful, that poor woman. It was awful. The world was a dangerous place, what with all the kidnappers...and the perverts...and the rapists...and the atheists out there. And the squirrels. Sandy couldn't help but put a little of the blame on Ms. Uppity though, for not having equipped her son with a tracking device or a cell phone or both. But she reserved blame for her private thoughts and was outwardly supportive. Oh Lord, how did you let it come to this? On top of it all, Sandy was still late on her mortgage and now unlikely to sell many DVDs with this unfortunate disruption. Why, Lord, why?

"I'm pretty sure he just ran away. He's been testing his boundaries a lot lately," Ms. Uppity was saying.

Sandy hadn't been listening, but she perked up at "testing." Of course! Testing. The Lord was still testing her. This was all part of his plan. She was meant to have been in the Mega SuperMart on this day. There were a lot of frightened people in there with her. Trapped. Probably searching for answers. Answers that only she could provide. She could help Ms. Uppity. She could help all the people stuck inside. Her flock. This wouldn't help pay the mortgage, but...if the story got big enough and her ministering proved influential enough, well, they might just make a TV movie out of it! And with that kind of exposure, her YouTube channel would explode. The YouTube would start paying her for advertising! She'd *have* to beef up her social media presence then. Her flock would want to hear from her unfiltered and direct, briefly and often, in addition to the videos. And with the groundswell of support that would come from hundreds and thousands of followers on social media, she could parlay that success into her own radio show. Or even better: cable! With the right time slot, her ratings would soar! She'd make the rounds on the late-night shows, and then the late-night shows would make the rounds to be on her program. She might even end up meeting Oprah!

"Oh, bless you," Sandy told Ms. Uppity.

"No, I didn't sneeze. I was just clearing my throat."

"But bless you all the same. Bless your heart."

Ms. Uppity frowned at her. Sandy understood. She was worried. Scared. It was her job to reassure and calm.

"Don't you fret," Sandy said. "This is gonna be all okay. Don't you worry. I'll pray for you. We'll all pray, won't we?"

"I really think it would be better if we left off with the praying for a little bit and just kept looking for my son," Ms. Uppity said.

That gall-derned know-it-all! Sandy had been trying to help her, and now she was trying to steal Sandy's moment? No siree, Bob! Sandy turned to the small crowd of shoppers who had gathered around after that nice Mr. Timothy's announcement. They were stranded. Lost. In need of help.

"No, I think prayer is exactly what we need right now, isn't it?"

In response to her question, a couple of people gave noncommittal shrugs and nods. They were not a very enthusiastic bunch. But then, they were scared. Heck, she was scared too. But she had to be strong. That's what the Lord Jesus would have been in this situation.

"I know this is scary," Sandy said, lifting her voice. She looked around. She needed something to stand on. Her flock needed to be able to see her, and even with her heels, she was barely five foot four. Sandy saw a display of a bunch of cases of pop. That could work.

"Hey, will y'all give me a hand?" she said to a red-haired teenage boy. He was standing next to a teenage girl, who also had red hair and was dressed in green and was cute as a button. They were holding hands. Well, time to nip that in the bud.

"C'mon now. Look alive. There's a good boy. Let's just stack up these pop cases. Yep, there you go. Thank you. Why don't you just stand over here, on this side of me now? Not you, missy, you can stay where you are."

The girl stuck out her lip, and the boy looked confused. But they did as they were told. Good. A minimountain of pop. The Sermon on the Mount of Pop: that's what the viral video would be called on the news. She could picture the graphic they would use for coverage already. Now she had to deliver. She climbed up. That was better; she could see the people now. And, more importantly, they could see her.

"Be perfect, as your heavenly Father is perfect," she began. If Jesus could end his Sermon on the Mount that way, she could begin her Sermon on the Mount of Pop that way too. It wasn't plagiarizing. It was homage.

"That means being free from sin." She paused and gave a significant look to the teenage lovebirds. Blank stares. Teenagers today. She might have to talk to them privately later.

"For while we are already forgiven, we must do our best to still please him. It makes customs and immigration at the kingdom of heaven go much more smoothly. Now, I know a lot of y'all will be more in favor of stricter border control. And here, on this mortal coil, that makes sense. I'm with you. We all gotta protect our livelihoods. It's hard. It is hard. The Lord Jesus knows. Believe me, he knows. He might not have struggled to pay his mortgage. Or have a broken-down, piece-of-junk car. The Lord Jesus might never have been plagued by obnoxious, rabid little squirrels. Godless, heathen squirrels. Yes, the Lord Jesus might never have felt their little paws and claws all over his body. And the Lord Jesus might never have been in a Mega SuperMart when a child was abducted! Our sufferings are different from the Lord Jesus's. And yet, they are the same. How mind blowing is that? I know. He feels what we feel. And more. He died. For *our* sins. So we're guaranteed entry into the blessed kingdom."

Sandy paused. This was good. She hoped someone was recording it: this was the sort of thing where a guerrilla video of it could launch her ministry into the stratosphere once it got put up on the YouTube. She really did need to beef up her social media presence. A couple of store employees, an old geezer and a young woman, had joined the crowd. So had a pimply-faced teenager, who wasn't going to be sinning like the redheads anytime soon. No sir, not with a face like that. Good thing he had a job. Sandy took a deep breath and launched back into her sermon.

"As long as we believe, we're in. How great is that? But that doesn't mean we don't try. Jesus might never have experienced being trapped inside a Mega SuperMart during his lifetime, but he is here with us now. He wants to be here. As long as we carry him in our hearts, we are not alone.

"That's the good news. The bad news is that there is evil in the world. A boy has been stolen. Snatched away. We don't know what will happen to him. There are sickos out there—"

"Hi, sorry!" Ms. Uppity interrupted. She was trying to hog the spotlight! And Sandy had thought she was all right. "I think Billy has just run away. I'm his mom. He has really been testing his limits lately. And thank you all for—"

"This is a test!" Sandy interrupted back. She was not about to let Ms. Uppity steal this crowd—steal this moment—away from her. "Not a test like back in school. Or a test like one of those that *you* might need if you and this boy don't embrace the Lord and his teachings."

Sandy nodded at the redheaded girl. She stared back. Was she slow or something?

"It's not even a test like one of those litmus papers that can tell you how salty your food is."

"That's not what litmus paper does," said the pimply teen. His nametag said Aidan. Impertinent little whippersnapper. Sandy chose not to correct him and went on.

"Jesus talked about salt too. The salt of the earth. Earthly salt. Pepper. Smoked paprika. Gotta have that smoked paprika. If we have it, we'll be saved." Sandy smiled broadly. She loved it when her free associations just worked. It was what made her such an effective preacher.

"And we will have our smoked paprika. For where there is light, there is hope. Let us count our blessings. And let us pray for young, little Billy. May he be delivered from the evil he's fallen into. And may God and the Lord Jesus bless you all. I'll be right here for y'all through this crisis. Right here at the junction of Aisle 17 and the righteous path. Feel free to stop by."

Sandy smiled again.

"And have a blessed day."

A couple of people clapped a couple of times. The rest just sort of stood there, then started to wander off. Ingrates. Well, you could lead a horse to water, but even if that horse happened to be trapped in a store with no chance but to receive the spiritual wisdom of a lifetime, you still couldn't make it drink necessarily. And showing that horse the light of blessed salvation...it was a lot to handle. Of course, horses were godless. Like squirrels. They couldn't know the Lord Jesus. Not that anyone could know the Lord Jesus in the biblical sense. That might make for a funny joke now and again, but if you really thought about it, that'd be messed up.

Sandy shook her head; she'd gotten so turned around in her own metaphor she didn't know what was going on. She'd almost had impure thoughts about the Lord Jesus. It was probably a good thing that she had ended her sermon when she did. As for her nascent flock, well, they'd come around. Sandy would get a chance to address them again. She knew it would be a while before they found that poor boy. That's just how these things went.

Sandy descended from the cases of pop. She should pray. Set a good example. Then she'd have to get back to figuring out how to help these people. And maybe sell a DVD or two.

RUSTY

The Mega SuperMart was not a red squirrel's natural habitat. The surfaces were all slippery smooth: half the time, Rusty could barely gain a purchase with his paws. The pervasive cinnamon-vanilla scent made him a little woozy. And that banshee howl from the blond woman had almost made him jump out of his skin. He knew, intellectually, that it wasn't the cry of a hawk, but that hadn't prevented instinct from taking over. He had fled blindly. Any progress he had made was lost.

Rusty took cover inside a pair of boots. Humans needed them to protect their feet. It was amazing how much *stuff* they needed to survive. There was a popular myth that humans were this ultimate apex predator, but the more time he spent among them—above them in this store—the more Rusty began to think it was a story invented, probably *by* humans, to disguise just how weak they actually naturally were.

Scrunched up in the toe of the boot, Rusty took deep breaths. It wasn't a hawk. There were no hawks inside. That was something. But then a second thought took hold of his overaccelerated heart and almost stopped it cold. What if the banshee howl—it had been picked up by another human female as he fled—had been a form of alarm? What if they were on to him?! This was a once-in-a-lifetime opportunity. The plan relied on the element of surprise. Raccoon? Didn't matter—even if he had spilled the acorns, there was nothing Rusty could do about it now. Rusty had to rely on himself. If he ever got out of this mess, he could deal with Raccoon then. When. When he got out of this mess. To get out of the mess, he had to get out of the boot. Squirrels didn't need boots. Be the squirrel!

Popping his head up, Rusty almost wished he hadn't. This place was perverse. It had fluorescent suns hanging every fifteen feet or so that made navigation impossible. Rusty suspected they were powered by electricity. His paws twitched. No! He was trying to quit. He was *going* to quit. The artificial suns had *not* been on the schematic. Stupid Raccoon. Rusty knew he had to get to Shipping/Receiving. But even before the banshee howl, he kept getting turned around. Apart from the omnipresent artificial suns, there were no real landmarks. And meanwhile, ticktock, ticktock, Rusty knew he had a finite amount of time to get to the nuts before they would be gone. This was a once-in-a-lifetime chance. And yet he had no way of telling the time; the artificial suns seemed to indicate noon.

Options. The sun and stars and trees usually told you where you were. Or the breezes and the water and the smells. Those were not options. He had only his wits, his eyes, his lightning-quick reflexes. His instincts. His tail. He had to get up high, gain a view, see if he could see something. That's what you did in a new place. You climbed. Surveyed. Watched for hawks.

Rusty went up and up. He regained the sprinkler system and followed a pipe east. Or west. Or north. It was impossible to know. But if he didn't make any turns, eventually he'd reach a wall. And by a wall would be a door. And the nuts were supposed to arrive at a door. The Shipping/Receiving door. It was sound reasoning.

Humans sure did need a lot of stuff. Rusty paused above a display of various boxes and platforms. Rusty knew the boxes were keepers of fire—hence all the sprinklers—and that humans used them to cook food. But not nuts. Rusty had never taken much interest in them. The platforms were because humans didn't have the ability to sit or lie on the ground or a tree branch or a tree trunk, like a normal animal. Rusty suspected they were allergic. Did contact with trees cause rabies in humans? They were obviously vectors for disease; the size of the Pharmacy Department in this store was enough to prove that.

On one of the platforms below, a human was reclined. It did look comfy. And this human seemed relaxed, in comparison to the rest of the humans. They sure had been frenzied since the banshee howl, probably looking for him. But he was too fast. Too pretty. Too clever. The human below seemed not to be interested. Perhaps he was asleep. Asleep in the open. He wouldn't last long in the real world.

But...oh! The man was wearing a coat with more pockets than Rusty had ever seen. Clothes were silly, but pockets...Rusty could appreciate pockets. That way you could carry stuff and still talk. Pockets weren't everything, of course; Opossum had pockets, and she was a moron. But still, the amount of nuts Rusty could have transported in one trip with pockets...he'd wipe the smug smile right off of Chipmunk's fat, skunk-striped face. Of course, the score today would do that anyway. He was gonna render pockets superfluous! He chattered in triumph. The man looked up.

Stupid! He needed to contain himself. Keep a low profile. He put a paw to his lips. The man nodded and lowered his head back down. Still, it would be best not to linger. Keep the straight path. Find a wall; find a door; get the nuts.

DIRK BLADE

Second thoughts could kill you in the private investigator game, but Dirk Blade couldn't help it. Had he told the kid too much? The kid seemed smart, but would he be smart enough to keep his mouth shut? He shouldn't have given him his flare. Now Dirk Blade was weaponless. Why hadn't he brought his nine millimeter? But how else was the kid going to signal him? No, he had to trust that it would work out. Precious little else was.

Dirk Blade was lying on a reclining deck chair in a display of patio furniture. It soothed whatever was going on in his intestines. Next to him was a large array of barbecue grills. His stomach rumbled, and he forced his mind away from food.

There was something he wasn't seeing. But what? And where? Dirk Blade furrowed his brow and thought hard. He just couldn't see the solution yet.

Remaining inconspicuous had gotten significantly harder since the store had gone into lockdown. That was the kid's fault. All the customers had been herded to the front of the store, to the café there. They were giving away free coffee. Dirk Blade would have loved some coffee, even the watered-down sludge they were probably offering. Coffee and a cigarette. That really would have made this day a lot better. And probably soothed his stomach as well. But it wasn't to be; he wasn't a customer after all. His hand had strayed into his pocket, fiddling with his e-cigarette. No. Not yet.

Probably he should have been looking for the kid. But that would blow his cover, and he was pretty sure the Good Samaritan payouts paled in comparison to what he would get paid for this SuperMart job. It wasn't right, necessarily, but it was the way of the world. Anyway, the kid had a good head on his shoulders; he'd be fine. Dirk Blade had bigger fish to fry.

A couple of store employees hurried by—he held perfectly still, and they didn't notice him. He saw a squirrel running along the sprinkler system that hung above the store. It stopped and looked at him. Dirk Blade stared back. The squirrel chattered. What was it trying to tell him? Unkown. Like so many other things. The squirrel took off, flitting along the sprinklers effortlessly.

Dirk Blade continued to stare after it. Besides the sprinklers, there was a pretty impressive industrial heating-and-cooling apparatus up there. It might be robust enough to support his weight...if he could get up there. And from up there, he would have a better view. He could see what he was missing. Moving only his eyes, he checked to see if there were any more store employees coming. There weren't. Dirk Blade got up and tried to climb up the nearest set of shelves, which was full of pool and beach accoutrements. No dice. He just wasn't any great shakes at climbing, not like that squirrel. A pity. All he succeeded in doing was pulling down six or eight Styrofoam noodles.

He kicked the noodles aside and smoothed his moustache. He couldn't get frustrated. But what to do? He should retrace his steps, see if he had missed anything. That was Private Investigating 101: when in doubt, go back to the beginning. He'd have to go back to the executive office and have another look at that paper work.

It took him longer than it should have to reach the office. The setup of the store kept turning him around; it was worse than a corn maze on Halloween. And on several occasions he had to duck into various displays—including, awkwardly, women's underwear—to avoid being seen by the store's employees. That kid had chutzpah—and talent—they were putting on the all-out press, but they couldn't seem to find him. A kid after his own heart.

The box he had left in the office as a warning was gone. Dirk Blade wondered what kind of message it had delivered. If he had the management running scared, they might blunder into some kind of mistake. Add in the stress of having a missing kid and who knew? He really might be able to turn this to his advantage.

There was a phone ringing behind a closed door. Dirk Blade had been in that room earlier. It was small and dark and very neat, but there was nothing useful to his investigation. The phone though. He should have had them tapped a long time ago. Technically, it was illegal for him to do that without a warrant, and it was next to impossible for a private citizen, even a private investigator such as himself, to get one. So it would have been hard, which was a big part of why he hadn't done it. He still had some friends down at the courthouse, but they weren't likely to help too much. But answering the phone? That would be easy. The door to the tiny room was locked, but jimmying a lock had never been a problem for Dirk Blade. But just as he grabbed the handle, the phone stopped ringing. Damn.

Dirk Blade went into the bigger office. A large faux-mahogany desk dominated the space. It screamed cheap Chinese import. He had seen one just like it earlier in the office-furniture section of the store. Ditto with the pleather chairs that lined the walls. It made some sort of sense that they would outfit their offices with their own products, but why choose the cheap, ugly stuff? Idle speculation was not the key to good detective work. He needed to make a careful observation of the whole space, to use all his senses.

There was a small pool of liquid on the desk. Dirk Blade went over and sniffed it. Ack! Bodily fluid of some kind. Thank goodness he hadn't tried to taste it. He pulled the desk drawer open. He found the same thing in there that he had earlier that morning, a half-eaten bag of candy, a bottle of SuperMart-brand painkillers, and a smut mag. He closed the drawer in disgust. Dirk Blade wasn't a feminist, per se, but there was no honor in that drawer. No justice. The kind of man who succored himself with a smut mag was the kind of man Dirk Blade would delight in taking to the clink. If only he could find some hard and fast evidence.

The phone in the other office started ringing again. Dirk Blade made to go answer it but stopped. He could hear footsteps. Someone was coming up the stairs. He had to turn on his inward-looking eye. He stood in a corner and stayed very still.

TIM

During a Code Bobby, Tim's job was to secure the store. That meant double-checking that all doors had been double-locked, making sure no one went in or out, and continuing to manage things like squirrels and phones and customers. After initiating the Code Bobby over the PA, he hustled around the store's perimeter, making sure all the service and emergency doors were bolted. He finished at the front door, disabling the automatic sliding-glass doors that separated the entry vestibule where the shopping carts lived from the rest of the store. That way the abductor couldn't get out, if in fact that's what was going on. Golly. Tim hoped it wasn't actually an abduction.

Securing the store was the easy part. The hard part was waiting by the front door and explaining to customers why they couldn't leave. It was a paradox of sorts. If the customer was always right, how could Tim tell them they couldn't leave, if that's what they wanted? Tim really didn't like conflict.

Initially, it wasn't that bad. "It'll just be a little while. We have a missing child," was all Tim had to say, and people would generally be understanding.

The magic words seemed to be *missing child*. Once people heard that, they usually calmed down and asked what they could do to help. Mostly, what they could do was sit quietly in the café and enjoy a complimentary coffee. The words *complimentary coffee* tended to help people adopt a positive disposition as well.

But as a half hour stretched toward an hour, even complimentary coffee's power to mollify began to wane. It really started to turn when a guy in a gray State Univeristy sweatshirt came over and asked him how much longer he thought it would take.

Tim made the critical error of saying, "I don't know exactly. I hope not long."

Honesty was supposed to be the best policy. But this guy, judging by his reaction, didn't seem to know it.

"You don't know? Whattaya mean, you don't know? Look, buddy, I gotta get to an important ga—uh, meeting. It starts in half an hour. So how 'bout you just bend the rules a little bit, and let me out?"

The snowball started to roll, as it were.

"What?" said a woman with a lot of makeup and swept-up— and, Tim suspected, dyed—blond hair. It certainly wasn't as beautiful as Ms. Newman's—Sandy's. "If you let him out, you gotta let me out. He's probably just trying to go watch football. I've got a doctor's appointment!"

"Hey, lady, watch what you're saying. I'm sure your tanning session or whatever is real important, but let's not belittle State football," the State University sweatshirt guy said before Tim could answer.

"It's not tanning! The nail doctor's a real doctor," the woman said, snarling back. She marched up to the guy and began shaking her finger in his face. Despite being twice her size, the guy looked scared. Tim didn't blame him. He thought he should probably intervene but didn't know what to say. More darn conflict. Maybe they would work it out on their own. He chewed the nail of his left pinky. Maybe he needed one of those nail doctors.

"Scuse me," a rumpled-looking man who was holding a jar of pickles said to him.

"Yes, sir? May I help you?"

"Yeah, look, I don't want to cause trouble, but my wife's pregnant. I gotta get out of here and get back to her. My cell phone won't work in here, so I can't even tell her I'm running late. Can you please let me out?"

"I, uh, congratulations, sir. You must be excited. I can—"

"You're gonna let him out but not us?" the made-up woman said, interrupting.

"I—" Tim began.

"Because you can forget about that. If anybody gets out, it's me."

"And me," State University said.

"Please, my wife's pregnant," said Rumpled Man.

"Yeah right," Made-Up Woman said. "You're just inventing a story like this guy."

"No, I'm not. Honest. I just—"

"If he goes, we all go," State University said.

"I'd like to go too," another man said.

"Yeah, me too," said a woman.

"And me."

"Yeah, me too."

"And me."

"Yeah, this is dumb; let us out."

"My wife's pregnant!"

"So's mine!"

"Let us out. Let us out. Let us out," State University started to chant. The made-up woman and a couple of others took up the cry.

"Let us out! Let us out!"

The whole crowd was shouting now. They were closing in on Tim, and it began to feel very claustrophobic. All he had been about to do was offer the guy with the pregnant wife the use of a telephone! His pinky nail was bitten down to the quick. So Tim did the only reasonable thing he could think of in the situation.

"Complimentary coffee!" he shouted and pointed toward the café. When the crowd looked that direction, Tim ran away. He went to find Mr. Spooner.

***

Tim's first thought was to go to the office. There were few better places to weather a storm than there. It was elevated, so that would give them a good vantage point. And it was off limits to nonmanagement, so Tim would have space and time to figure things out. That's where Mr. Spooner must have gone to take command of the situation. When Tim arrived, the office was dark. The cinnamon-vanilla plug-in potpourri was doing its job. It smelled like Christmas. Tim sneezed.

"Oh sorry," Tim apologized. "Mr. Spooner, the crowd at the front door. I..."

Tim trailed off. Mr. Spooner wasn't there. Tim could hear the phone in his own office ringing.

"Oh golly!" he yelled, remembering that Mr. Spooner had told him to answer the phone. Surely Mr. Spooner would understand why he hadn't, if he didn't answer now, what with the Code Bobby and all. But Tim was in the office, so maybe he should just answer the phone? Maybe it was something to do with the missing child! Except he couldn't get into his own office, obviously: he was still locked out. So he ran to Mr. Spooner's office and paused at the door. Mr. Spooner's office was off limits without explicit permission. But surely an order to answer the phone was implicit permission. Right?

Tim took a deep breath and pushed open the door. He ran over to the desk and picked up the phone. Dial tone.

"Oh, jumping juniper berries!"

Tim remembered he would have to transfer the call back to this phone. He punched a couple of buttons, hoping it wasn't too late.

"Please hold for Mr. Wallace," a friendly feminine voice said. Before Tim could say anything to her, she was gone, replaced by a not-so-friendly masculine voice.

"Hello? Hello?" said the not-so-friendly man.

"Oh, I, uh, hello," Tim said.

"Mitch Spooner?"

"Oh, uh, no, sir. I'm—"

"I don't care who this is. Put Spooner on the phone."

Mr. Spooner had told him not to say he wasn't in the office. What was he supposed to do?

"Mr. Spooner's, uh, wait, may I ask who's calling?"

"You know damn well who this is. I shouldn't have to identify myself every time I call my own goddamned store. Now put Mitch Spooner on the line, god dammit."

Tim gasped. He had just...twice!

"Hurry up, for Christ's sake. I don't have all day."

"Yipes!" Tim said. The guy was blaspheming all over the place. He took a deep breath. He had to stay in charge.

"Sir, I don't know who you are, but that type of language isn't appropriate for a phone call—or anywhere for that matter. If you give me your name and a message, I can be sure that Mr. Spooner gets it."

"All right, small fry. Think you're clever, do you?"

Tim had never considered himself particularly clever, but being called clever emboldened him.

"The name is Tim, sir. Timothy Phillips. Assistant manager—"

"I still don't care. Listen, Phillips. I don't know who you are, but—"

"I tried to say, sir, I'm the assistant—"

"Don't interrupt me, Phillips. I don't know who you are. I'll find out if I want to. Listen up: The message is that Mitch Spooner better call me. ASAP. And he better have news. This is C. Franklin Wallace. I'll be arriving in an hour. And, Phillips?"

"Yes, sir?"

"You better think long and hard about whose side you're on."

"Side, sir?"

"Yes, Phillips, side. Good day."

The mean Mr. C. Franklin Wallace hung up. Tim did the same, confused. He wondered if Mr. Spooner was in trouble with the mob. Or drugs? Oh golly. Tim looked around. Mr. Spooner had a nice office. The shutters were down, but if they weren't, he could probably have seen the whole store from there. Mr. Spooner had apparently moved one of the floor mannequins up to a corner of his office. It was dressed in a goofy hat and a trench coat. Was it there to scare off members of organized crime? Gosh, it was so realistic it was practically alive.

"Yipes!" Tim yelped when the mannequin blinked at him. "Who are you?"

"Nobody," said the alive mannequin. It stepped out of the office and ran away, knees high and arms pumping.

"Hey! Come back here! You're not allowed in here!" Tim chased after him.

Tim saw the tail of the man's coat swishing out of sight as he ran down the stairs. Tim ran after him.

"Let us out! Let us out! Let us out!" The mob was still going strong. If Tim hadn't been so intent on catching the trespasser, he might have been offended that they hadn't even noticed he was gone. But the trespasser was more important right now. He might have something to do with the Code Bobby! And the trespasser...was gone. Tim stopped running in the middle of Aisle 4: Candy. Things were getting out of control. He adjusted his tie and gulped some air. He had to find Mr. Spooner.

LEE

Lee Rigg had jumped the gun, so to speak. He chuckled. He'd have to remember that one for later. But now was not the time for jest. Lee had run toward the screams only to get turned around in the washer-drier section. By the time he reached the screams, there were no screams, only a crowd listening to the well-endowed lady preacher who had been so into him by the front door. She was giving a sermon.

The sermon did not seem to have a great effect on the crowd. The digression about squirrels and the stuff about salt and pepper and smoked paprika were confusing. But Lee Rigg was sharper than the average pencil; he had gotten the point: some sick bastard had kidnapped a kid! The woman had pretty much said that it was up to Lee to save him, or they'd all get turned into squirrels or illegal immigrants or something. And she had huge knockers, so it had to be true.

Well, frig. He had a gun. There wasn't nobody gonna stand in his way. He'd show 'em. But he needed ammo. That sales guy, Brian. He'd promised free ammo. Lee should have grabbed it before running off. That much was obvious. But he had jumped the gun. Heh. Oh well, nothing he could do now but go back and collect it.

Lee headed back through the fishing pole forest to the gun counter. It took him a little while, but he got there. Why had they made the store layout so confusing? If Lee had been in charge, things would have been a lot more straightforward. Guns front and center, for a start. Friggin' hell.

When he arrived back at the gun counter, it was unmanned. Sonofabitch! Lee had seen the pimply teenager back at the speech. That kid was never where you needed him to be. Lee would have to go find him. He ran from aisle to aisle, peering down, hoping to catch sight of the kid, or better yet, Brian. Brian was all right. Lee had his gun under his arm. It made running difficult. He passed a couple of redheaded teenagers in the Bedroom Furniture section of the store. They appeared to be testing futon mattresses.

"Hey!" Lee said.

They hurriedly sat up, and their faces were as red as their carrottops. Neither made any eye contact. What the hell was wrong with teenagers today? They were turning into a bunch of meek little toerags. When Lee had been seventeen, if some adult had spoken to him, he would have answered with a *yessir* or *no, ma'am*. Unless the adult had seemed like a loser, in which case Lee would have told them to screw off. But these two...

"Hey! I'm talking to you. You know a kid who works here? Alden or Anton or something like that? Your age. Covered in zits."

Neither answered him. They looked embarrassed. Or simple. Both. Lee knew he could totally beat the snot out of them, no problem, but that wouldn't help him find that other brat who could give him ammo.

"Hey! I asked you a question. You know the guy or not?" Lee shouted a little louder. Maybe they were also deaf.

"Yeah," the boy mumbled.

"Well, where is he?"

The kid shrugged. Maybe he should beat the snot out of him, make an example of him, punch him in the eye; then people would start giving him a little respect around here. If he'd have had a loaded gun, they wouldn't be pulling this crap.

"You know?" he asked the girl. She was, literally, as red as a beet. Her face clashed somewhat harshly with her hair, which was more the shade of a ripe pumpkin.

She shook her head no.

"C'mon, carrottops, this is important," Lee said. What was their problem? Yep, when Lee was their age, if some dude had come up and started asking questions, he would have looked him in the eye and answered. Or told him to screw off. Probably the latter. But he would have responded.

"Maybe he's on break. We didn't come here to see him," the boy said, the words barely getting out of his mouth, catching on his braces most likely. Or maybe he had a speech impediment... in addition to being a brace-faced ginger. Poor bastard. Lee almost felt sorry for him.

"Cool," Lee said. "Which way's the break room?"

"We don't work here. Sorry," the girl said.

"Well what the hell good are you?" Lee said. "Naw, just kidding. You guys have a good day. I'll see you later."

Lee didn't like the little punks, but he still wanted them to think he was cool. He turned to go and then stopped.

"Oh wait," Lee said. "You guys want a cigarette?"

There was no surer way to make them think he was cool.

"Don't smoke."

"What?"

"We don't smoke cigarettes," the girl said.

"Seriously?"

"It's not good for you."

"Or cool," the boy said. "But if you have any weed, we'd take that."

"That friggin' hippie shit? Hell no!"

What the hell was wrong with teenagers today? Lee gave them a disgusted look and left them there. Little pricks.

The break room, Lee reasoned, must be at the edge of the store. By process of trial and error, he made his way to an exterior wall. The Mega SuperMart was massive, a real one-stop shop, just like their TV commercials said. If only you could find someone to help you.

And meanwhile, that poor boy! His freedom had been taken from him. If there was one thing Lee hated, it was those goddamn crows. But worse even than crows were those who impinged on the freedom of others: he had to do something about it.

Lee followed the wall and soon found his way back to the gun counter. Pimple Kid was there! Lee looked at his nametag. Aidan!

"Hey," Lee said.

Aidan looked up from his phone.

"Look, I need some ammo."

Aidan stared at him. What was wrong with this kid?

"I can't give you any."

"What?"

"You bought the gun today. There's a waiting period for ammo. It's a safety measure."

"C'mon, bud. You gotta be kidding me."

"I'm not kidding. Bud."

That was sarcasm. Little dink wouldn't be so friggin' snippety if Lee had some friggin' ammo.

"Aidan! What are you doing?" A chubby guy ran up. It was Brian. He was covered in sweat. In fact, Lee might not have recognized him all disheveled like he was, if not for the nametag.

"Brian, my brother. What's up, bud? This guy won't sell me any ammo. Can you hook me up?"

Aidan sniggered. Lee was really fed up with pissant teenagers.

"Oh, sorry, man. I'd really love to, but I can't. In fact, I'm supposed to ask all customers to go to the front café area and wait until we've swept the store. We've got a Code Bobby. And we still haven't found the kid. C'mon, Aidan. C'mon!"

Brian dragged Aidan out from behind the counter, and they hurried off. Lee shook his head. And he had thought Brian was all right. Plus, he was trying to go find that kidnapper without a gun. What a moron. One thing was certain: it was Lee who was going to have to bring the degenerate kidnapper to justice. And he sure as shit wasn't going to find him by going to the front café area. And another thing was just as certain: he needed bullets for his gun.

There was no one at the counter anymore. Lee knew the terms of his probation. And according to them, he was not supposed to steal. Or appear indecent in public. Or intoxicated. The friggin' government was taking away all his basic rights. But Lee also knew that there were Good Samaritan laws. They would probably protect him in this case. And he had tried to do the right thing and get ammo through normal channels. Plus, there was no one there to see. He probably wouldn't even get caught. Besides, the cavalry was not coming. Lee was the cavalry. Of the people, by the people, for the people!

Lee leaned against the counter, looking casual, like he was just taking a rest. He whistled a little tune and reached back under the counter and felt around until his hand closed on a clip. It took a little while. He picked it up and brought it to the top of the counter. Bingo! First try a match. Attaching the clip was not as easy as it looked in the movies. But Lee figured it out. He wasn't one to get outsmarted. He should probably grab a spare, in case it turned into a shootout; you never knew. But there was only one of this kind of clip on display, and he was running out of time. So he reached back under the counter and grabbed a box of bullets. He wasn't sure they would work but stuffed a bunch in his pockets just in case. Better to try than not to try. He leaned back over and replaced the now-empty box where he had found it.

Then Lee Rigg flipped the safety to live-fire mode. He was ready.

TIM

Tim ran up and down the aisles, no longer bothering with the dignified walk-skip. None of the associates he passed had seen Mr. Spooner.

"Any sign of anything? Mr. Spooner? The missing child?" Tim said to young Scarlett, the cashier, and Clem, the old greeter. They weren't his favorite pair, if he was being honest. Clem had contributed to this trouble by forcing Tim to bring Ms. Newman—Sandy—into the store. And Scarlett, well, Tim knew what Scarlett had done. And he knew he probably should have fired her for it. But well, *that* would have been an awkward conversation. Darned conflict, always rearing its ugly head where it was least wanted. And, otherwise, Scarlett seemed all right. Clem too. And maybe they had found something. That would be enough to redeem anyone on this day.

"No," Scarlett answered. "Tim, I'm getting really worried about him. Is it time to call the police?"

"I..." Tim was pretty sure it was past time to call the police. But he couldn't take that step without Mr. Spooner's say-so. Code Bobby had pretty specific top-down protocols. And Tim liked to follow the rules.

"Can you guys do me a favor?" Tim asked.

Scarlett and Clem looked at each other. They seemed to have some sort of telepathic connection. Tim shuddered, involuntarily. Sorcery really did make him uncomfortable. Witches were the last thing he needed added to his plate.

"What is it, Tim?" Clem asked. His voice was deep and calm. Clem would probably be awesome at reading bedtime stories.

"Well, gosh, thanks guys. There's a crowd of, uh, somewhat-perturbed customers. They're, uh, a little antsy. Over by the main entrance. Could you two, uh, go take care of them?"

Clem groaned.

Scarlett raised her eyebrows.

"Why don't we just let them out and call the police?" Scarlett said.

Tim was torn. But they had to follow the rules. That was the right thing to do right now. That's why there were rules.

"We can't. The protocols say that we—"

"Who cares about the protocols? To hell with them, Tim. A kid is missing. I'm gonna call the cops," Scarlett said. Were all ladies so scary when they were angry?

Her language decided it. He hated conflict, but sometimes it couldn't be avoided. He straightened his back, and he straightened his tie.

"I'm sorry to say this, Scarlett," Tim said. He was sorry. But it had to be said. "But if the police are called before I say so, you will be the one to talk to them. And it won't be about the missing child."

"What? What are you talking about?"

"You know exactly what I'm talking about, Ms. Jackson. You can tell them all about the deluxe top-of-the-line infant furniture that's wandered off lately. You're lucky you still have a job. No one should steal from this store. No one! Now go help the customers at the front!" Tim's voice was a little shriller than he would have wished. It was not how Mr. Spooner would have handled it. Of course, Mr. Spooner probably would have fired her as soon as he found out about the stolen crib.

"I...I..." Scarlett looked at her feet. "I'm sorry. Yes. We'll go."

"Now wait a second," Clem said. His voice was deep and rumbling; it would have been comforting, if it hadn't held the promise of prolonging the conflict.

"Please!" both Tim and Scarlett said, looking at him.

"All right. All right. But, Scarlett, we're gonna talk about this later. And Tim: you should call the police."

Tim didn't look at Clem. Anything to avoid continuing the conflict. Keep calm and carry on.

"C'mon," Scarlett said and pulled Clem away, toward the front of the store.

So there was one problem solved. Maybe. Tim really needed to find Mr. Spooner, and soon. Maybe Ms. Newman—Sandy—would know where he was. Tim knew he was mostly using that as an excuse to talk to her, but, well, there was nothing sinful in talking. Tim headed for Sandy's pulpit of soda. Rounding the corner, he crashed into someone. They both fell to the floor.

"Jesus Christ! What the hell, Timmy?"

It was Mr. Spooner! What luck! Tim was so relieved to have found him that he didn't even point out that Mr. Spooner had taken the Lord's name in vain.

"Well?" Mr. Spooner said, picking himself up. He looked like heck.

Tim got up too.

"Oh, Mr. Spooner, am I glad to find you. I've been looking for you all over. You haven't found little Billy yet, have you?"

"Who?"

"The missing child!"

"Oh, that little brat? No. I'm sure he's around somewhere. His mother's been giving me a real earful though. Ungrateful bitch."

Tim gasped. She was a customer, after all.

"Look, Timmy, I gotta go do some stuff. Don't worry. You got this, right?"

Tim was pretty sure he did not have this. But he didn't want to disappoint Mr. Spooner, so he nodded. Mr. Spooner gave him a thumbs-up and started to stride away.

"Wait!" Tim said. "Mr. Spooner! There's a pretty angry crowd of customers at the front. They want to get out. And we haven't found Billy yet. And the Golden Snacks truck is probably here by now. Shouldn't we call the cops?"

Mr. Spooner pulled Tim into a little cul-de-sac of televisions. Some sinful teen pop star was gyrating her sinful hips in a way that Tim knew he should despise, but he was somewhat hypnotized.

"Timmy. Listen to me. Hey, Timmy! Eyes on me." Mr. Spooner shook Tim by the shoulders to get his attention.

"Huh? Yes, Mr. Spooner, sir. I'll call the police then."

"No! You absolutely will do no such thing."

"But, Mr. Spooner, the Code Bobby protocols! We have discretion to call the police, and I think we—"

"Who gives a flying"—Tim cringed, waiting for the profanity—"hump"—there it was—"about the protocols? We've got a situation here. Several situations. Multiple fronts. I need you to help me here. Getting the police involved is just going to create a bunch of red tape and paper work. It will not help us solve our problems. Timmy, eyes on me. You get me?"

Tim tore his eyes away from the teen temptress, who was now rolling on the floor and groping herself in ways Tim was sure he was not supposed to find as enticing as he did.

"You mean we'll find the missing kid faster on our own?"

"What I mean is, if you call the police, I will cut your balls off. Got that?"

Tim reflexively covered his man parts. Why did cool guys have to be so mean?

"Uh, yes, sir. But, Mr. Spooner—"

"I mean it, Timmy. Now look, I got stuff I gotta take care of. You got this?"

Tim was pretty sure he still didn't have this and that the police would be a big help. But Mr. Spooner was the boss, and he wanted to keep his balls. He nodded.

"But, Mr. Spooner?"

"Timmy, I've really got other problems more important than holding your hand right now. You said you got this. Now get it."

"But, Mr. Spooner—"

"Timmy—"

"There was a guy in the office! Pretending to be a mannequin. He ran away when I confronted him. Oh yeah and the phone was ringing; a Mr. Franklin Wallace called for you. He was not pleased, sir. He told me to think about which side I was on. What was he talking about? Whose side are you on? What sides are we even talking about? Are you in trouble, sir?" Tim let it all out in one breath, not stopping for fear that Mr. Spooner would forestall or forbid further speech. Or cut off his balls. By the end, he was shaking a little bit. He felt like something bigger than himself was going on—not divinely inspired...but perhaps from the other side? Holy Jeepers! The devil in the SuperMart? This could be worse than he had imagined.

Mr. Spooner was quiet for a long time. He looked at Tim. Tim tried to stand up straight. If the devil was in the SuperMart, he knew which side he was on. The harlot on the televisions was no longer important.

"Oh, thank you, Lord, for showing me the way," Tim said.

"What? Speak up, Timmy," Mr. Spooner said.

"Oh, I just—"

"Never mind. Look, Timmy, I don't know who that guy was, but he sure as shit shouldn't have been in my office. As for Mr. Franklin Wallace—Mr. Wallace—don't worry about him. I want you to focus on securing the office. This is bigger than I thought. Unplug the phones. I don't want that asshole to be able to reach me. Then find the kid. You've got to handle this, Timmy. I've gotta check a couple of things. Then I'll meet you back at the office. It pains me to say it, but I'm counting on you, Timmy. Make me proud."

"I should kill it, Mr. Spooner?"

"What? No. Just take care of it. You got this."

Mr. Spooner clapped him on the shoulder and then turned and walked off, leaving Tim no chance to ask the questions burning in his head. It was still more than Tim could handle on his own, no matter what Mr. Spooner said. At least he could still follow instructions. He went and disconnected all the phone lines from the big box behind the customer-service desk. That was a job done. But now what? He needed help. Ms.—Sandy. She'd help. He had been going to look for her before he ran into Mr. Spooner. He'd go find her. Sandy. She'd provide all the help Tim would need!

BILLY

They had a new mission. The princess's sense of justice had kicked in while they were in the Castle of Hello Kitty.

"Will, we've got to help that poor kid!"

Billy wasn't so sure. He was also still getting used to his new name. He waited a little too long before realizing he should say something in response to Willow's statement.

"Will?" she said again.

Billy shook his head.

"What about the treasure?"

"Will! I thought you had a sense of honor! Some poor kid is lost out there."

"Oh, I'm sure he's fine."

Billy was fine, after all. Of course, he couldn't tell Willow that. She might mess up his escape plan. She might be cool, but she had only just turned seven.

"Well, I'm not looking for treasure until we find him. And good luck moving from castle to castle and fort to fort without my powers."

She had a point there. And if she thought they were looking for some other kid, then she wouldn't suspect him of being that kid. That way she couldn't turn him in. Fairy princesses could only be trusted so far.

"Okay. We can look for this kid. I don't know how we're gonna find him though."

"Well, he'll probably be hiding from the ogres, won't he?"

"That makes sense," Billy said. He certainly was, so it made sense that this fictional missing kid would too. This was going to be hard to keep straight.

The ogres were out in force, patrolling the aisles two by two.

"Unless..." Billy said.

"Unless what?"

"What if they've already captured him?"

"Oh, Will, that'd be terrible!"

"It's a possibility we have to consider."

"But there are so many ogres out there. Why would they still be looking?"

"What if they're looking for us?"

Willow looked very serious.

"Well, we can't let them find us," she said. "We'll have to be careful. But how are we going to find him?"

"That part's easy," Billy said. "We just follow the ogre king."

In their brief reconnaissance, Billy and Willow had identified the ogre king, a big lump of a guy with slicked-back hair. He smelled awful. They could tell that even from inside their castle. He seemed to enjoy giving orders. Especially to a smaller, cleaner ogre named Timmy. They both felt sorry for Timmy, though not so sorry that they tried to help him. He was still an ogre, after all.

They moved from castle to fort to castle. The Fairy Princess Willow froze time before each move, naturally. She had wanted to hold Billy's hand while running from one place to another, but he had to draw the line somewhere. He was almost eight, for crying out loud. Following their noses and the general commotion of the ogres, they were able to find the ogre king again without too much trouble. He was arguing with someone.

"Oh, crap!" Billy said.

"Ooh, you said a bad word," Willow said.

"So what?"

"Well, aren't you worried you might turn into an ogre?"

Billy had always taken pride in his knowledge of and fluency in swear words. He was pretty sure it made him cooler, smarter. But he didn't want to turn into an ogre. At least *crap* wasn't a real swear word. Not the kind he'd have gotten punished for before he ran away, only reprimanded. But even still...Willow might have a point. Maybe he should cut back for a little while. But that was a matter of semantics, and he had bigger problems: the ogre king was talking to *his mom*!

"Let's move back and come up with a new plan," Billy whispered.

"Why? We're hidden here, and we might be able to overhear them."

"It's just...I sense great power in the female ogre."

"Oh, I dunno. She looks nice to me."

"Trust me," Billy muttered.

"My son is missing!" his mom screeched. "You better start taking it seriously! And if you're trying to be funny, well I'll be happy to tell the police your little joke. We can see if they think it's amusing."

She turned on her heel and stomped off. Billy almost felt sorry for the ogre king. His powers were clearly inferior to his mom's.

"Where's he going?" Willow whispered.

Billy watched. The ogre king walked down a row of refrigerators. He kept looking over his shoulders and all around. Billy recognized that behavior. This guy did not want to be seen. He stopped next to a bright-red refrigerator. He opened the door. Then he climbed inside and was gone, having pulled the door closed behind him.

"Did you see that?"

Billy nodded. Willow would know just as well as he the story of little Alice, who gained notoriety after she had gotten trapped in her refrigerator and died. It had been a national tragedy when Billy was in kindergarten. They now had to have yearly refrigerator safety lessons at school. It was so dumb that Billy wasn't positive that the loss of little Alice was such a huge one for humanity. You had to be pretty dumb to climb inside a refrigerator and get trapped there. And whatever else he was, the ogre king was not dumb. There was something more to that refrigerator than met the eye.

"I don't think that's a normal refrigerator," he said. "We gotta get closer and check it out!"

RUSTY

The straight path was better in theory than in practice. The lattice of sprinkler pipes would sometimes just end, leaving a gap too large for even a flying squirrel to cross with ease. And Rusty wasn't that kind of squirrel. So he had to zig when he wanted to zag.

Which is how he found himself perched in a macabre section of the store—above fishing gear, staring down at a counter behind which were rows and rows of guns. Rusty froze. Those things would kill you faster than rabies. Faster even than bird flu! He checked involuntarily for hawks. Safe. There was a human down there. Adult male. He was leaning against the counter. And unless Rusty was hallucinating, this guy was up to something. Was he hallucinating? Rusty tried to breathe shallowly. There was no telling what kind of diseases existed in this strange human ecosystem. Nope, no hallucination. The guy was definitely up to something. Rusty saw him stick one arm behind the counter, then the other. Soon the human was lying on the counter on his belly, flopping around, like a pigeon whacked-out on rancid popcorn...or suffering from bird flu.

Were all humans diseased? They always seemed to be sniffling and sneezing and coughing; add to that their general behavior, and well...there was certainly ample evidence in favor of that thesis. Rusty held his breath. A reasonable precaution against airborne pathogens. The human violently twisted himself back upright. He had something in his hand. The human fiddled for a while and eventually jammed the thing in his hand onto a big gun. Then he threw himself back on the counter and flopped a bit more. Was it a mating ritual? Rusty couldn't see any females of the species around. Perhaps a practice mating ritual? It certainly needed work.

This time, when the human straightened up, he had a little box in his hand. Rusty watched as he dumped it out and began stuffing the pellets that fell out into his pockets. Oh, pockets... the human was stuffing his pockets so full Rusty thought they might burst. Then he folded the box back up and put it back under the counter. It was a bizarre performance.

Rusty was feeling a little dizzy. Was he sick? The cinnamon smell was gone. So was the vanilla. He swooned. Breathe! Rusty had been holding his breath for a long time, especially for a squirrel, whose lung capacity was not tremendous. He gulped and took a deep breath of air. He was okay. The cinnamon vanilla was back, and he felt less dizzy. It had just been good old-fashioned oxygen depravation.

Guns were bad. What was it Raccoon called them? WRDs? That was it. Weapons of Rodent Destruction. Raccoon left himself out of the equation—him not being a rodent and all. He probably thought he was too smart to get hurt by a gun or something like that. Maybe he was. Focus! Rusty had to focus. Nuts! He shouldn't have been anywhere near that human and his gun. He took another deep breath and tried to remain inconspicuous. He had to get out of there. Sooner rather than later. It was an unhealthy place. He sure could use a hit of electricity right now. No. He was going to quit. For his family. Just like he was going to get those nuts. For his family.

The human jogged off through the fishing pole forest.

Rusty headed left. He crossed a branch that held up one of the fluorescent suns. He slipped. He scrabbled. He swung his tail to counterbalance his body. He scampered. He made it to the next sun. It was warm on his paws. It was a pleasant feeling. He could feel the electricity pulsing too. With effort, he ignored it.

From his vantage point atop the artificial sun, Rusty had a 360-degree view of the store. He couldn't quite see to all

horizons though. Some of that was blocked by rows and rows of
metal towers with stuff on them. So much stuff. Though Rusty
supposed that if he were a goofy, naked ape, he would need a lot
of stuff too. But this seemed obscene.

Rusty could see two male humans standing close together
surrounded by boxes with moving pictures of other humans on
them. Rusty had learned through observation that these boxes
were semidivine, precious objects to humans, much like nuts. Or
electricity. No! Stay on the wagon. Rusty had never seen so many
of the moving picture boxes in one place before. Judging by the
amount of gesticulating going on down there, the two humans
were engaged in some kind of dispute. Probably territorial.
Given the regard with which humans venerated the boxes, he
imagined they were in some pretty valuable real estate, kind of a
human equivalent to a big, old, hollow oak. It was pretty easy to
see who was going to win. One of the humans was much bigger
and louder. His head fur looked wet with water, but Rusty could
see no droplets. It wasn't natural.

Sure enough, the loser slunk off, head down—a submissive
pose, Rusty knew, meant to acknowledge the winner's
superiority; those were pretty standard across various species—
while the winner went the other direction, toward a row of large,
freestanding boxes of some kind. These did not have moving
pictures on them, but Rusty knew they were still valuable to
humans. They kept such boxes in their food-preparation areas.

Ooh! To the victor go the spoils. A female human had gone
up to the dominant male. Well, he wasn't the victor yet. She
was yelling at him. Poor sucker. Perhaps this was a matriarchy.
Certainly the big male human looked a lot smaller after the
female had finished with him. She marched off, and he skulked
off down the row of food-holding boxes.

Rusty was pretty sure he would never understand humans.
But he was also pretty sure he didn't want to. He could see a
couple of human kits down inside a rack of human clothes.
Hiding the young. It made sense. But if they were old enough

to leave the nest, they were old enough to learn to gather nuts. Why weren't any of the adult humans paying attention to them?

Rusty shook himself. He needed to get his head in the game. Now was not the time to play the naturalist. He craned his neck and looked around. He checked his tail. Still bushy. Silky. Sexy.

Stick to the plan. Zig or zag, those nuts would be his.

MITCH

Mitch extracted himself from Timmy and set off, finally, for his subterranean bunker, hidden under the Kitchen Appliances section of the store. The Mega SuperMart had expanded the original Patterson's store that had occupied the site previously. The Patterson's had been built at the height of the Cold War and included a fallout shelter. Mitch knew only sketchy details of the Cold War—memorizing the playbook and trying to flick crumpled-up balls of paper down Melinda Carlson's shirt had occupied most of his thoughts during US History—but he was glad it had resulted in the bunker. It was a perfect secret lair. And no one else knew of its existence. Certainly no one was going to discover it now: Mitch had installed a hideous bright-red refrigerator over the entrance and taped a "not for sale" sign to the refrigerator. It was kind of the perfect plan to keep his secret hideout secret. But to be completely sure, Mitch also oversaw the shipping and receiving of kitchen appliances himself.

Mostly, Mitch used his secret lair to catnap and watch football, maybe play a little bit of Madden. He had dreams of making it something of a sex grotto, but sadly that had not come to fruition. Yet. But the reason he was going there now was that it was also where he kept all the "unofficial" SuperMart paper work. He had been extremely careful, but he had to be sure he hadn't accidentally left a noose for Corporate to hang him with. Though, if he were being honest, Mitch would also be glad for the peace and quiet, away from Timmy and all the other—

"Well?"

It was frickin' Soccer Mom. Her kid went missing, and she thought the whole world should stop. She certainly was succeeding in impeding Mitch's progress. Maybe she should have paid a little more attention to her brat. How about trying that? Mitch had attempted to be professional with her, but that seemed only to make the woman harass him more. He needed time and space to be alone. He had bigger problems than her stupid kid. But she didn't seem to get that. Of course, on the other hand, Mitch had to consider the possibility that she had the hots for him. It seemed crazy that she could think she had a chance but...he had seen a special on Psych TV about stressful situations and how it made chicks hornier. She was probably bored with her marriage, saw Mitch as a young, unattainable stud, and so her only way of expressing that sexual tension was to harass him. He got it. But even if that were the case, Mitch thought he probably wouldn't. But, hey, maybe. She was probably like a five and a half/six, and with a couple of beers and a wine cooler or two, she could easily be a seven or an eight.

"Look, lady," he said, "I think I know what this is about. You're upset, and naturally you're drawn to me because I'm the biggest dick in the store. And you want some of that."

He gave her a roguish grin. How could she resist him, really?

"Oh, god, no. You've got to be kidding me. I mean you are. For sure. Definitely the biggest dick in the store. By a mile."

She was sending mixed messages. Did she want him or didn't she? Whatever. He could really go either way. If she wanted him, better to make her wait for it a little longer. Soccer Mom kept talking.

"But I absolutely don't want anything to do with you except for the fact that somehow you have become the manager of this store, which is a complete joke as far as I'm concerned. But my son is missing, and you are the person responsible for finding him. That's why I keep coming up to you!"

Yep, she was into him. Mitch wasn't really paying attention to her words, but her body language was pretty clear. Flushed, pupils dilated, Mitch knew the signs. But then, how could she not be? He was a goddamn stud. Even still, now wasn't the time. She'd be there later. Or someone else would.

"Look," he said, "I'd love to take you up to the office and show you an awesome time. To tell you the truth, I'm even kinda into older chicks, so it wouldn't even be that big of a hardship. But right now just isn't the right time, you know?"

The woman lowered her eyebrows. No doubt she was trying to be seductive.

"My son is missing!" she said, the pitch of her voice approaching fingernails-on-blackboard level of screech: not very seductive. "You better start taking it seriously! And if you're trying to be funny, well I'll be happy to tell the police your little joke. We can see if they think it's amusing."

Blah, blah, blah, funny, blah, blah, police, blah, blah—Mitch didn't hear most of what she said; he just smiled at her as she continued to rage at him. A lot of pent-up sexual energy there. And she thought he was funny. Yeah, he decided. He would. She was talking about police, which meant she was into bondage and stuff. Kinky as hell. She finished speaking, turned on her heel, and stamped away. Clearly she expected Mitch to give chase. But that wasn't how this was going to go down. Now wasn't the time anyway. And she was realistically only a six. Mitch smoothed back his hair and wiped the residue on his pants.

"Okay, then," he said.

Now, maybe, finally he could get to where he was going. He waited until Soccer Mom turned a corner and then headed for the red refrigerator. He gave a quick look over his shoulder. No one around. He yanked the handle of the fridge and stepped inside.

It was a short flight of stairs that took him down to the bunker. Mitch opened the heavy door at the bottom and stepped inside. He always felt more relaxed once he was down there. He didn't regret not bringing Soccer Mom at all. He was playing it right. Besides, if you were in a place that no one knew about, no one could bother you there. And as fun as the first fifteen or so minutes with her might have been, at a certain point, he would have needed some privacy.

It was a pretty sweet man cave. There was a dope leather couch, a recliner, mahogany desk, sixty-inch flat-screen, Xbox. All freebies from work, of course. He hoped they were still free. How the hell had Corporate sniffed him out anyway? Mitch had been trying to figure that one out for months, but was no closer to understanding.

Mitch went over to the desk and unlocked the drawer on the top left. He pulled out a file folder full of papers. It was thick and slightly disorganized, with crumpled receipts sticking out at various places. Mitch opened it up and began leafing through the contents. Five percent a month. That didn't seem like much. Starting...wow. He'd been at this a while. Where had all that money gone? Still, all his tracks were covered. Nothing could tie him to the missing money. So that was good.

But clearly the financial discrepancies were starting to be a problem. Giving up the extra income was absolutely out of the question. He needed a way to get Corporate off his back until he could refine his system a little further. It was like he was swimming in a shark cage. He needed to toss some dead fish to distract them while he got out of the cage. Then they'd see who the shark master was.

Mitch smiled and leaned back. He crossed his hands behind his head, pleased with his metaphor. Mitch Spooner, Shark Master. That'd be a pretty sweet tattoo. He'd been thinking about getting a tattoo for a while. Chicks dug them. An idealized portrait of himself astride a shark? Bad. Ass. Should he get it across his chest or his back? Maybe both. Could they do 3-D tattoos yet? He'd figure that out later. For the moment, he was still in Corporate's shark cage. He had to get out. How did you get out of shark-infested water? Dead fish, what did they call it? Chum! He needed chum. Chum...

Mitch chuckled to himself again. You couldn't spell *chump* without *chum*. And as it happened, the chum and the chump in this case were one and the same. Timmy shared his office. Timmy was a naive idiot. Probably a virgin. Definitely a pussy. Which was ironic, if you thought about it. Mitch laughed at his own cleverness. Timmy had wanted to call the police. Fine, if it was the police he wanted, it was the police he would get. And Mitch Spooner, Shark Master, would serve them up just what they needed. Chum. Timmy. But not until Mitch Spooner, Shark Master, said so. It would take a little time. Fortunately, he had a little time. Nothing too pressing. It would even be easy to explain. No one could possibly believe Timmy's oafish, golly-gee-whiz persona was real. Clearly, he—poor, innocent Mitch Spooner—would have been taken in by the charade, while Timmy had skimmed and stolen. The paper trail would start in Tim's office and back up Mitch's story. He would just have to plant the evidence. Of course, Mitch might lose his man cave for a while. But he had always suspected there would be sacrifices.

They couldn't stop Mitch Spooner! They couldn't hope to contain him! He was the Shark Master! He pulled out a paper at random.

"Order received...blah, blah, blah...signed...Timothy Phillips."

Mitch was not an idiot. Not by a long shot. He had covered his tracks all the way. Mitch hadn't thought that anyone would ever need to find out about this file. But that was changing.

"Yeah, baby," he said to himself. He pumped his fist, so pleased to have found a solution so quickly and easily.

"I'm not a baby," a young boy said. "I'm almost eight!"

Mitch nearly jumped out of his skin. He had been followed! The man cave was compromised.

"What are you doing down here?"

"We're searching for the secret ogre den! We saw you go in the refrigerator. So we followed. And we found it, didn't we? What's that you're looking at anyway?" said a small girl who stepped out from behind the boy.

Mitch slammed the folder shut and stuffed it back in the drawer.

"Uh, nothing. Look, kids, you can't be down here. Where are your parents anyway?"

SANDY

She never should have gotten down from her pulpit. Up there, Sandy had had the crowd's attention. Now? Everyone was gone, and the few shoppers who did wander by weren't even making eye contact. She wasn't helping people this way, and she wasn't selling any DVDs. She needed a captive audience. And since the SuperMart shoppers couldn't leave the store, her captive audience had to be around somewhere.

Timothy was hurrying over to her. Good. He ought to know where the people were. He had a length of cable in his hand. Phone line? What was that about? Didn't matter. He was favorably disposed enough that he would probably help her set up on a good piece of real estate near wherever the crowds had gone.

"Ms. Newman? Oh, Ms. Newman, am I glad to see you."

"Well, shucks, Timothy. I'm pleased to see you too. But call me Sandy. Look, can you—"

"Ms. Newman—Sandy. I need your help. I need...guidance, I guess."

Sandy was somewhat taken aback. She'd never really been asked for guidance before. She figured it was part of the job but kind of always assumed it was secondary, that people would get guidance from her videos and DVDs and stuff, for which she would be paid handsomely. She knew that wasn't strictly the Lord Jesus's way. But the Lord Jesus didn't live in a time where the internet and the mortgage and the water bill all came due at the same time that his piece-of-junk car needed major exhaust work.

"Oh, Timothy. I...well...I guess my role is really more to inspire folks to get closer to God. I don't really know if I can help you with this missing kid. Now, what I'd like from you is—"

"Ms. Sandy. Please. I've seen all your YouTubes. I...I know you're the one who can help me. Please?"

Well, it probably wouldn't hurt. He was looking at her with such earnestness in his big blue eyes. He was sweet, almost cute, in a dorky kind of way. She could try to help him.

"Oh, all right. I'll try. Here, let's go over here and just talk."

Sandy led the way over to a bench in Women's Shoes. They sat down. Sandy tried to focus on Timothy and what he was saying—not on the DVD sales she was missing out on, on the cable special those sales might launch, on how the cable special would make her fame and fortune. It was hard to tune that stuff out. But she tried.

"What's on your mind?" she said.

Timothy burst forth. Boy, was he a talker. Wound up tighter than a top too. Holy Moses. Timothy talked and talked and talked. And talked. Sandy did her best to follow along.

"So what you're telling me is you think your boss might be involved in some kind of drug smuggling?"

"Yep. Nope. I don't know. It's just he's being so secretive, and I think he's in trouble, but I don't know what kind, and you hear all the stories on the news about bath salts and crystal meth and all sorts of other drugs I don't even know about! Not that I know about those. Just their names, you know, from the news? And he seems so tired and distracted. I mean, what if it is drugs? Oh, gosh, I must seem all sorts of dumb to you. But I can't work out why we haven't called the police, and golly, it's just a lot."

"It sure is. And you're not sure what to do because you think he's a 'cool guy'? Despite the fact that he treats you like dirt?"

"That's not so true, Ms.—Sandy. I mean, sure, he sometimes rides me kinda hard and makes me do the jobs he doesn't have time to do—"

"Like opening and closing the store. Every day? And cleaning the bathrooms? And sweeping his parking spot? Think about true friends. Like"—Sandy searched for inspiration. She had long had an idea for a sermon she had never tried out. It could work here—"like Big Bird and Snuffleupagus. Did you ever watch Sesame Street?"

"Every day!"

"Would Big Bird treat Snuffleupagus the way Mr. Spooner is treating you?"

"No! I mean, yes. Well, sometimes. Big Bird would sometimes forget to be nice."

Curses. Sandy had never really paid that close attention to the show.

"And the parking spot I do just to be nice. But that phone call and thinking about drugs. It makes me worry about him."

Timothy was chewing his nails. Sandy took his hand, as much to make him stop as to offer comfort. She couldn't abide nail-biting.

"Look, Timothy, you gotta start standing up for yourself. Not just for yourself but for what's right. I mean, that's what's going on here, right? We all need a Snuffleupagus. And that's the point of Big Bird and Snuffy. When you have your Snufleupagus, you've got to treat him right."

Sandy wasn't totally sure where she was going with the Snuffleupagus thing, but she was trusting her instincts. It was what made her an effective preacher.

"I guess. I guess Jesus would say Mr. Spooner's not helping anyone if he's doing drugs and stuff. But I...it's just...golly."

Poor thing, he really was in a state. And he really was kinda cute in his dorky way.

"Well, he certainly isn't behaving much like Jesus. And you can't let him bully you."

"You think?"

"I do. But maybe we should pray on it, because that never hurts."

"Together?" Timothy asked.

"Of course." Sandy smiled.

Sandy got down on her knees and clasped her hands, her elbows on the bench they had been sitting on. The hard floor hurt her knees, but she endured. Timothy did the same. Sandy searched her mind for the right prayer, the right words. She couldn't help this poor, sweet man. She couldn't even pay her bills. Jesus was supposed to be her savior, but he had certainly put her in a box. She looked over at Timothy. He had his head down, his lips moving silently. That was pure. She didn't have to say anything. Her heart swelled. The talk and the walk. It was all the same.

"Amen," she said out loud.

"Amen," Timothy echoed.

He looked up.

"Timothy, can I tell you something?"

"Anything."

"I woke up this morning, and I had a feeling today would be different; today would matter. Now I barely have two dimes to rub together, and all my bills are coming due at once. I was thinking that today I would make some money, that that was the Lord's plan. But I've only made about twenty-five dollars. And I was getting close to despair."

Timothy's face was open, innocent. He was hanging on her every word. What a sweetheart. And it sure felt good telling someone about her troubles.

"But now I think maybe his purpose was to bring me here, to bring you here too. To bring us here. Together. What do you think?"

"Golly, Ms.—Sandy. I guess maybe. I mean, I could help with your bills if you wanted; I've saved lots from my paychecks."

"Oh, Timothy, you are a dear."

He turned red.

"But I could never accept your charity. Besides, I think what's happening here is bigger than us."

"You can say that again," Timothy said.

"I think what's happening here is bigger than us," Sandy repeated.

Timothy looked confused.

Sandy took his hand in hers.

"You have reaffirmed my faith," she told him.

"You've more affirmed mine!" Timothy said.

"Feel better?" Sandy asked.

Timothy smiled. Sandy's heart hammered in her chest.

"I...I..."

They were kissing. Sandy couldn't say who had made the first move, but neither could she say it felt wrong. Oh Lord, she could not. Preaching to the crowd could wait.

Timothy pulled away. "Oh! Ms.—Sandy. I...I'm so sorry. I don't know what came over me. That was sinful. I never meant...I just...I'm sorry."

Sandy looked at him. He was such a dear.

"I'm not," she said.

"You're not what?"

"Sorry," she said. "C'mon."

She grabbed him by the wrist and dragged him over toward a changing room.

"That's ladies only!" Timothy sputtered.

"Oh, please," Sandy said. She pulled him into the booth and dragged the curtain shut behind them.

BILLY

"Where are your parents anyway?" the ogre king said. He pushed the chair back and started to come around from behind the desk.

"Run!" Billy yelled. They had cornered the ogre king. But it had been a mistake: a cornered ogre was a dangerous ogre, and now they had to escape.

The door through which they had entered had closed behind them. Billy jumped for the handle and hung from it. A clever trap. The handle mechanism was clearly responsive only to brute ogre force, or perhaps it was biometric, and Billy's kid DNA couldn't trigger it; either way, they were trapped. He dropped to the floor. Willow was being brave. But she had only just turned seven. She couldn't be expected to hold out for long.

"Where are your parents? How'd you get down here?" The ogre king had come over and was crouching in front of her, asking the same questions again and again, like she was dumb or deaf or both.

"Don't tell him anything!" Billy shouted.

The ogre king looked over at him. Billy shivered.

"Hey," the ogre king said. "Don't worry. It's just a kid has been missing in the store. Danny or Johnny or something. Are you Danny or Johnny or whatever?"

Billy shook his head. He wasn't saying anything. This ogre king might be playing dumb, but Billy suspected he knew. And soon he'd try to return him to his mom. And *that* would be bad.

"Oh, but we're looking for him too!" Willow said. Her tone was too chatty by half.

The ogre king crouched in front of Willow.

"That's nice. Do you want to help us find the missing kid?"

Billy groaned. That's what you got with an only-just-turned-seven-year-old. No spine.

"No! We're gonna find him ourselves! Like he'd trust you—ogre!" Willow shouted. She slugged the ogre king with a pillow and ran over to Billy. That's what you got with an only-just-turned-seven-year-old! She might be young, but she had pluck. Together they crossed their arms and stood shoulder to shoulder, defiant.

The ogre king tossed the pillow back on the couch. He seemed unfazed. That was worrying; Willow had swung the pillow hard.

"Look, kids, first of all, don't swing couch cushions. Second of all, that's fine; you can leave it to us grown-ups. We'll find him. Though I almost feel sorry for the poor kid. His mom is a real piece of work."

"Hey!" Billy said in spite of himself. But the ogre king didn't seem to notice.

"But whatever, look, I can't let you guys get lost either. One missing kid's enough, you know? And you definitely can't stay down here. In fact, if anybody asks, this place doesn't exist—you got it? You were never here. Now, let's take you back upstairs and find your parents, okay?"

The ogre king smiled. His teeth were distractingly white. And yet his breath smelled like Billy had expected ogre breath to smell: stale coffee mixed with some kind of rotten, fermented something. It combined with the ogre king's body odor and a sickly sweet, overhanging must. It was brutal. Billy held his breath. He felt the Princess Willow tense up next to him. She must be doing the same.

"Time freeze!" she yelled and pushed Billy away from her. He understood immediately. He regained his balance and sprinted for the desk. They could hide under it. The ogre king wouldn't be able to reach them. He heard Willow squeak and looked over. The ogre king was in front of her. The time freeze hadn't worked. The ogre king's magic was too powerful! Billy watched as he scooped her up and put her on the couch. Prison!

Before Billy knew what had happened, he was plopped down next to her. The ogre king was as quick as he was ugly. Willow was giggling. It had been kinda fun, flying through the air and landing on the couch.

"Again! Again!" Willow said, delighted, and she took off again. Again the ogre king grabbed her and tossed her back to the couch. As he did, Billy attempted to escape. Yet once more, the ogre king was too quick; he grabbed Billy and tossed him back on the couch. Maybe the ogre king was all right; this was pretty fun.

"Stop this." The ogre king was panting. "Listen—"

Billy and Willow did not listen. They kept escaping and being tossed back onto the couch until finally the ogre king raised his voice to a roar.

"CUT IT OUT! I'M TAKING YOU UPSTAIRS, AND WE'RE FINDING YOUR PARENTS! NOW TELL ME YOUR NAMES, YOU LITTLE BRATS!"

This guy wasn't playing with them and having fun. This guy was mean. And scary. Billy felt Willow grab his hand with her small one; he didn't pull away.

"Names!" the ogre king said, growling. His slicked-back hair was even greasier now that he was sweating.

Neither Billy nor Willow said anything.

"Look, I'm gonna find out somehow. Don't make it worse for yourselves."

"I thought...I thought..." Willow's voice trembled. She was squeezing Billy's hand hard. "I thought we were playing."

"Don't cry. Jesus Christ. Here. Take this teddy bear. Here, it's yours! A nice teddy bear for a nice little girl. God dammit. Don't cry. Look, kid, let's just get out of here and find your parents? Oh for Christ's sake."

Billy barely bothered to catalogue the swears, except to recognize that if the ogre king was doing it, it was not cool. Tears shimmered at the corners of Willow's eyes. The teddy bear that the ogre king had given her didn't seem to help. Billy felt like doing the same. But he was almost eight and had to stay strong and focused. Otherwise, he was going to end up back with his mom. And that really would be bad. Billy tried to focus on what he could control, which, as the ogre king marched them up and out of his lair, was precisely nothing. They were prisoners.

Something was bumping in his pocket. The signaling device from the man in the trench coat. A distress signal! Billy took it out, slowly and secretly. He pointed it away from him, back down the stairs and pulled the ring.

There was a fizzing, then a screech, and then *kaboom*! It was the Fourth of July!

"What the hell!" The ogre king dove and squashed them with a flying tackle.

The air was driven from his lungs. Billy tried to breathe and felt a sharp stabbing pain. His eyes unfocused for a second. The ogre king rolled off of them, and Billy gasped for breath. The air was thick with smoke, and behind them, the ogre king's lair was in ruins. It looked like Billy had scored a direct strike on the desk.

"You little shits," the ogre king *swore* at them. Willow started to cry. Billy tried not to. The ogre king dragged them to their feet and pushed them ahead of him out of the refrigerator. Billy waited for help to arrive. None came.

DIRK BLADE

It had been a near thing in the office. Too near of a thing: Dirk Blade had almost been made. But it had been worth it. He had learned a name: Tim Phillips. He couldn't be sure who this Phillips was, but he had some possibilities. The earnest-looking fellow who chased him out of the office? The unknown on the other end of the call? A third player? He could guess, but a good detective didn't rely on theory and conjecture. You needed to go with your gut, but it worked a lot better if that gut was backed up by some facts. And facts were harder to find if you were running pell-mell out of an office.

It had been easy enough to escape: he had melted into the crowd and even managed to get a cup of free coffee. He wasn't a customer, but they hadn't asked. The coffee was lukewarm and as weak as a two-day-old baby, but it was coffee. Dirk Blade's stomach rumbled. Breakfast hadn't been very good, and it had been a long time ago. Maybe he should listen to his gut...and the facts would come to him? It was so crazy it just might work. What did his gut tell him? His stomach rumbled, more loudly and uncomfortably this time. His gut told him...his gut told him...he had to find a restroom. Fast.

***

The restroom had been a near thing. Too near of a thing. The Denny's breakfast had wreaked its revenge. It had taken some time, quite a bit of time, in point of fact, but Dirk Blade was better now. Well, no one ever said this job was easy. His stomach was better, but he wasn't any closer to solving the case. He made his way back into the warren of the store. He needed a bright idea. A bright idea, like a light bulb. He should go to the floor lamps. It didn't make sense, but Dirk Blade was listening to his gut.

RUSTY

Shipping/Receiving! At long last, Rusty had a lock on where he was going. He was glad he had bothered to learn to read human. He had worried it might have been a waste of time while he was completing the correspondence course, but now he could tell Shipping/Receiving was back behind Tools. Easy as fir-cone pie.

Those nuts were gonna be his. Rusty scampered along one of the metal branches holding up the artificial suns. This was good. He was good. Better than good. Great. Nothing could bring him down. He paused, just above one of the artificial suns. It warmed his paws. He felt the pulse of electricity. No! Eyes on the prize. Get the nuts. He had to quit now, become a family squirrel.

He watched a man come out of one of the red metal food boxes; he was pushing two small human kits in front of him. Like that. Rusty was gonna be like that. A good family squirrel. Bring his kits with him everywhere. Teach them right from wrong, good nuts from bad. How to watch out for predators. The important stuff. Rusty reflexively looked around for hawks. It was clear. No sky. No hawks.

Rusty wondered how many of the little rascals he'd have. Squirrel average was four to five a litter. Since it would be his and the missus's first batch, maybe a little lower was to be expected? If the numbers were lower, was that normal? Rusty wanted to be virile. He wanted to be more than average. Six. Six would be a good number. That way he could even lose one or two to hawks and still have a healthy number. Not that he wanted that. It's just, well, that was life as a small mammal. You did your best to stay alive, avoid rabies and whatnot, but reality was reality. That's why these nuts were so important. They would give him

173

security. Independence. He'd be out of the rat race. Literally: he wouldn't have to race rats for food anymore. They'd come to him. And, boy, would he make them pay through the nose. Avaricious murids.

But he had to focus. He knew where the nuts would be. And they'd probably be there pretty soon now; maybe they already were. It really was impossible to tell time in here. Raccoon had said the nuts would arrive in an enormous truck just before noon. And Shipping/Receiving was where he would find the truck. Ships were seafaring craft. Rusty had never seen the sea, but he had read about it. The nuts were arriving in a truck, and he was gonna take them before they could go off on any ship. Tough luck, pirates: he was too quick, too smart. The prince of squirrel thieves. Pirate of the land! The king! Those nuts were gonna be his!

Bang! Bang!

They were shooting at him! Did they have some kind of thought-intercepting machine? How much did they know about his plan?

Bang! Bang!

Get down! Rusty flattened himself against the top of the artificial sun. Electricity pulsed by him. Oh, sweet temptation. These were extreme circumstances. Just a little nibble. Then he'd quit. Last time. Rusty gnawed through the plastic covering of the wire. Oooh. Main line. This was going to be good. The shooting had stopped. Rusty couldn't see where it had gone. Somewhere below. Maybe they'd thought they'd hit him. Ha! Can't hit what you can't see. Rusty sampled the wire some more. So good. He was getting a pleasant tingling from his whiskers to his tail. Mmm. This was good juice. Rusty hoped the human kits were okay. He wouldn't want them to get hurt. He liked human kits. But as the electrical charge suffused his body, he cared less and less for the concerns of the humans. He felt good. Better than good. Great! Nothing was gonna stop him.

Rusty knew he should probably disengage. Let go of the wire. Too much of a good thing and all that. Plus, hadn't he read somewhere that excessive wire chewing could lead to mouth ulcers? Or cancer? He should let go. It was so good though. He didn't want to let go. He couldn't let go.

He couldn't let go! Physically, he was held, mouth and paws to wire, by some invisible force. So this was addiction. Rabid chicken poo! Here he was, about to become squirrel-thief royalty, only to be trapped by his own vice. Stupid! Dumb! Idiot!

Rusty heard a crackling. His tail—still bushy—extended straight out as if by magic. Rusty's eyes stared into the artificial sun. The light! Not the light. Sonofachipmunk! The nuts. He'd never get them. He could smell a faint burning. His tail? The crackling got louder. Then there was a *fizz-bang-pop*. A jolt like he had never experienced ran through Rusty. His gums were on fire. His toes curled. Glass shattered. The artificial sun exploded. Rusty was blasted backward through the air. He was flying! But, but...he wasn't that kind of squirrel. Everything went dark.

CLEM

Clem was definitely getting too old for this shit. His beloved store was infested with kidnappers, squirrels running amok, and now an angry, overcaffeinated mob that he was supposed to calm down? This was too much. Whatever was going on here was not worth giving up his peaceful retirement for. The world seemed to have gone crazy, and he'd somehow missed it. Thank goodness for young Scarlett. She was a godsend.

She was patient. The big lug who kept jabbering at them about State football: Clem would have liked to whack him in the shins with a broom handle. But Scarlett had just smiled at him and, with just a few words, sent him back to the café.

"How'd you do that?" he asked her.

"Oh, I deal with creeps like that all the time at my other job. And this guy's sober, so he really wasn't that much trouble."

Clem watched as she placated a woman who wanted to go to see the "nail doctor," which Clem didn't even know existed. Next she was scolding a redheaded teenage couple, probably not too much younger than herself, about the dangers of teen pregnancy. That ended with her giving them a box of prophylactics.

"Don't worry. I'll pay for them," Scarlett said.

"I wouldn't bother," Clem told her.

"No, I gotta pay for them. Tim...never mind. Guys, guys, if you could please just calm down. We'll let you out as soon as we can." She turned from the teenagers to a clump of noisy customers. What was she doing working here? She should be working for the UN or something.

But even Scarlett was having trouble with a shabby-looking man who claimed his wife was pregnant and that he needed to get back to her.

"What do I say to this guy?" she asked Clem. "His wife's pregnant."

"I'll take care of it," he told her. It was about time he started pulling his weight in this partnership.

Clem ambled over to talk to the guy.

"Can you do anything?" the guy asked.

"We're in lockdown, sir. I know you want to be there for every minute, but if you want my advice, take this little break as a blessing. You'll have precious few breaks after the child arrives."

Clem didn't know from personal experience, but he had observed a number of his friends over the years, so he was pretty sure he was right. The guy looked at him for a minute, then nodded. He didn't look completely reassured.

"How far along is she anyway?"

"It'll be six months on Tuesday."

"Man, come on. You don't need to be rushing back. She'll be fine for a little while without you. Six months? Shit."

Clem hadn't meant to say that last part out loud. But he wasn't going to handle this guy with kid gloves either.

"You don't understand," the guy said. He reached out and grabbed Clem's shirt. "She's crazy. She wanted pickles. If I didn't get back twenty minutes ago with pickles, there's no telling what she's gonna do. You gotta help me."

Clem pushed the guy's hands off him. This fool had bigger problems than getting out of the store, and that was for sure. But no sense in telling him that.

"Just try to be patient. I'll give you a second jar of pickles, and maybe that will help."

"Oh, man, that really might. Thanks, man."

Clem walked away, shaking his head.

Scarlett was talking to a woman with long, flowing skirts and hair nearly as long and flowing. Clem ignored the nail-doctor woman and made his way over to Scarlett.

"We've got another missing child," she said, keeping her voice low.

The woman spoke up, "My daughter, Willow, she hasn't turned up. I try to let her wander; it helps to build creativity, you know? But I worry she may have wandered too far and can no longer feel our connection."

"Connection?" Clem asked.

"You know, *sambandha,* the mother-daughter bond? We drink herbal tea together every morning, ginseng and astragalus root. It enhances our psycho-emotive connection. Everyone always goes on and on about the heart-healthy benefits of astragalus, and of course that's true, but what they don't understand are the psychic benefits in the roots, which are of course multiplied when it is brewed with ginseng. And yet today, in this place, our connection seems to be lost."

Clem scrutinized the woman. Was she putting him on? Or was she just out of her mind?

"Yes, well, we'll make sure you get that back," Scarlett told her. "Could you give me a moment to discuss a couple of things with my colleague?"

"Of course," the woman said. She clasped Scarlett by the upper arms. "Thank you."

Then she turned to Clem and did the same. She stared at his eyes with her green ones. Her eyes were striking, but the depth of her gaze made him more than a little uncomfortable. He couldn't be sure, but her pupils were maybe ever so slightly different sizes.

"Thank you," she said.

"You're welcome," he said, disengaging as quickly and as gracefully as he could manage.

"Christ," he added under his breath as Scarlett pulled him away.

She guided him over to the sliding-glass doors that were the entrance to the store. Clem pulled halfheartedly at the frame. He wasn't going to be able to budge it. The doors were locked. Locked and immovable.

"We've got to call the police," Scarlett said. Her voice was urgent. She was worried. She was right.

"I agree. Where are Rog and Sam?"

Rog and Sam were the internal security team. They weren't too bright, but they had a direct connection to police dispatch.

"They never showed up today. Oh, god. You don't think it's anything more than a coincidence, do you?"

"No, no. Rog and Sam aren't clever enough for that."

Scarlett gave a giggle in spite of herself. Clem smiled at her.

"Look, Scarlett, we don't know these kids are in trouble. They could—hey, wait a minute, is that Rog and Sam?"

There were two men with their faces pressed up against the glass of the outer vestibule doors.

"Oh my god, it is! They must have just showed up late. Guys! Hey, guys!" Scarlett waved at them.

"Po-lice. Po-lice. Call. The. Police." Scarlett mimed a phone with her hand at Rog and Sam. The two security men had their brows furrowed; comprehension did not seem to be dawning.

"Why are they asking what kind? There's only one kind of police. Oh, forget it; we're just gonna have to call ourselves." Scarlett sighed and turned back to Clem.

Clem nodded.

"We could just leave, you know. This isn't my problem, and it certainly shouldn't be yours, my dear. You're too young to be carrying the burdens you do. You don't need to be carrying this."

"Clem!" Scarlett scolded him. "We've got to help those kids. If it were my nephew, I'd want good-hearted strangers to do the same."

Ahh, the nephew. Julian or something like that. The girl doted on him. Well, he couldn't fault her for that. She was right.

What had happened to his morals? Just because the world had gone crazy didn't mean he had to as well. Now he was a little ashamed. But that didn't stop him from looking longingly over at the emergency exit behind customer service.

"Police!" Scarlett pantomimed to Rog and Sam one more time.

Rog and Sam smiled and waved and gave the thumbs-up.

"I think they got it!" Scarlett said, then covered her mouth, embarrassed. "Sorry. I got a little overexcited. I don't need to be shrieking. I'll keep it together."

"You're doing great," Clem told her.

"You think?"

"Yes, I do."

"It's just, I keep thinking about Julius and how I would feel if he disappeared. Those poor mothers!"

Julius. That was the nephew's name. He'd almost recalled it correctly.

Bang! Bang!

"Ohmygod, were those gunshots?" Scarlett managed to keep her voice down, and somehow the crowd of trapped shoppers took no notice. But it wasn't a good sign. No, sir.

Bang! Bang!

More shots. They definitely sounded like gunshots. But how? Shit. Scarlett was whipping her head around in a barely contained panic. He couldn't blame her. If he could move his neck that quickly, he might do the same thing. Instead, he looked over at the crowd. They were drinking the brownish liquid that passed for coffee and grumbling among themselves. Were they all deaf? Or just dumb? Didn't matter. Better to not schedule dental exams for gift horses and to thank goodness for small miracles.

The lights in the back half of the store went off. This the crowd did notice. Apparently they weren't blind. The volume went up, and the grumbling turned to yelling.

"What's going on?"

"The lights! The lights went off!"

"You sure we shouldn't just leave?" Clem asked, only half joking.

Scarlett didn't answer. The mob was coming toward them. He really was too old for this shit.

SANDY

Minutes (or was it hours?) later, when they came up for air, Sandy gasped. Timothy gasped too. Surely he felt the connection she did?

"Gosh, that was wonderful," Timothy said. "Maybe this isn't cool to admit right now, but I've never even been to second base before."

Sandy smiled at him.

"Is this right though? I mean, is it strictly proper?" Timothy said. He fidgeted a little bit with his hands.

Sandy smiled at him again. He was so sweet. And cute, when you looked at him long enough.

"Oh, don't be silly. I told you: I think we were meant to meet each other today. Don't you think?" she said.

He smiled. He looked a little dizzy. Sandy had to confess she felt a little dizzy too. They leaned in and kissed again. She guided his hands toward her breasts. She'd teach him to like baseball.

Bang! Bang!

Timothy snatched his hands away.

"I'm so sorry," he said, growing a little red in the face.

"No, Timothy, it's fine. I put them there, after all."

Sandy grinned at him. He was adorable.

"But, what was that noise? You don't think it's a sign of the Lord's displeasure? I mean, it is kind of sinful, what we're doing."

"Oh, Timothy," she said. But what were those sounds, if not divine disapproval? She had just tried to give spiritual comfort and ended up giving carnal satisfaction. Oh, she was going straight to hell. But maybe that didn't matter. This felt good. This felt right.

"With the games the Lord's been playing with me lately, I doubt he'd mind this. Besides, even if it is technically sinful, that doesn't mean it's wrong."

Sandy wasn't sure of that, but it sounded okay. Maybe she could work a sermon out of it. People loved permission to sin. She wouldn't want to lead people astray, but a popular message could make her a popular figure. And popular figures got their own cable shows.

Bang! Bang!

There were a couple more bangs. Gunshots? Sandy couldn't be sure. But they had stopped making out, so it couldn't be more divine displeasure, could it? Then the lights went out.

"It's the end times!" Timothy squeaked. "Oh forgive us, Lord Jesus, for our trespasses and our sins. Oh Jesus, please, we didn't mean it."

Sandy glanced over at him in the half dark of the emergency lights. The end times did not have emergency lights.

"Didn't mean it?" she said.

"Well, I..." Timothy trailed off.

Sandy looked at him. Didn't mean it? He hadn't felt the connection at all? And now she had debased herself. For what? Timothy leaned in and tried to kiss her. But she turned away.

"If you didn't mean it, I wouldn't want to give you the wrong idea."

"I...I..." Timothy fell silent.

"I did mean it," Timothy said after a moment. "I...I just don't want Jesus to be angry with me. I'm sorry. It's just...I don't want to screw up. Especially not with you."

Sandy looked at him. Only the back half of the store was in darkness. The front of the store still had lights. Timothy was waiting for an answer, poor thing. He was so uncertain. Well, she would be a hypocrite if she didn't admit that sometimes she was uncertain herself. He was a dear. Sandy gave him a quick peck on the cheek. His smile and the flutter in her belly let her know she had made the right decision. She checked her hair in the mirror. Still perfect.

"Let's go find out what's going on," she said.

She and Timothy made their way toward the front of the store, where they could hear something of a clamor.

TIM

Minutes—or it could have been hours—later, when they came up for air, Tim gasped.

"Gosh, that was wonderful. Maybe this isn't cool to admit right now, but I've never even been to second base before."

It was the truth. Before just then, he hadn't ever so much as kissed a girl. Well, except for his mom, but he was pretty sure that didn't count. He hadn't even really given much thought to second base: he had never really liked baseball. But maybe he should give the sport a second chance. He hoped he hadn't been too much of a fool admitting that to Sandy. To think, that morning, she had just been a vision on a computer screen. Now she was real flesh and blood, and that flesh was pressed into his own! Really pressed. Tim worried it might not be strictly proper.

"Oh, don't be silly. I told you: I think we were meant to meet each other today. Don't you think?" Sandy told him.

He smiled. He was a little light-headed. Sandy smiled too. She kissed him again. He was the luckiest guy in the world. She guided his hands back to the region of her breasts. Tim worked hard on keeping his mouth moving in what he hoped was a pleasurable way. His hands seemed to be doing fine on their own.

Bang! Bang!

They decoupled at lightning speed.

"I'm so sorry," Tim said, pulling his hands back.

"No, Timothy, it's fine. I put them there, after all."

Sandy's smile was wicked.

185

"But, what was that noise? You don't think it's the Lord's displeasure? I mean, it is kind of sinful, what we're doing."

"Oh, Timothy," Sandy said. She paused. "With the games the Lord's been playing with me lately, I doubt he'd mind this. Besides, even if it technically is sinful, that doesn't mean it's wrong."

Sinful but not wrong? That gave Tim something to think about. To think, that just this morning, she had been a face on a screen. His heart felt like it was skittering around his chest, so fast he worried it might end up stuck in one of his lungs or something. He forced himself to hold on to each breath a little longer. Stay in control.

Bang! Bang!

A couple more bangs. Then the lights went out.

"It's the end times!" Tim hollered. "Oh forgive us, Lord Jesus, for our trespasses and our sins. Oh Jesus, please, we didn't mean it."

"Didn't mean it?" Sandy said.

Oh fiddlesticks. Tim had screwed up. He had only just met the woman of his dreams, and already he was screwing up.

"Well, I..." Tim didn't know what to say. Either he was lying to Jesus, or he was lying to Sandy. He just didn't want to screw up. Maybe if he kissed her again? She turned away. Dumb-dumb head! He'd really done it this time.

"If you didn't mean it, I wouldn't want to give you the wrong idea," Sandy said.

Tim couldn't answer. He mumbled something that probably sounded dumb. Sinful without being wrong? Maybe that was it. He had really liked second base. Maybe it wasn't wrong. But now Sandy was mad at him. And probably Jesus was mad at him too. What to do? Tell the truth.

"I did mean it," he said. "I...I just don't want Jesus to be angry with me. I'm sorry. It's just...I don't want to screw up. Especially not with you."

Sandy waited an uncomfortably long time to answer. Tim was pretty sure that meant doom. Just as he was trying to decide between flinging himself prostrate on the floor to plead with her and just running away, she swooped in and gave him a peck on the cheek. She liked him! She really liked him! He *was* the luckiest guy in the world. Golly. He gripped the bench they were seated on—if not he might float right up through the ceiling. Sandy turned away from him, patting her hair. Tim admired her admiring herself in the mirror. Their eyes met in the reflection. She smiled. An angel.

"Let's go find out what's going on," she said.

They headed for the front half of the store, which was still lit. There was shouting and chanting. Tim hoped they weren't walking into a riot.

LEE

Lee Rigg was locked and loaded. He wasn't gonna let some degenerate mess with kids on his watch. Not when he could stop it. It was like he was in a *Die Hard* movie. But first, he had to find the bastard.

Lee ran down the fishing aisle. When he got to the end, he stopped. How the hell was he gonna find him? Admittedly, there weren't many people in this part of the store. In fact, there weren't any. That was good. Civilians would just muck things up. A systematic approach would probably be best. But he was in the middle of the store. How was he supposed to apply a system to that? He looked left and then right. Might made right. And Lee Rigg was mighty: he had a gun. Right was right.

He sprinted off to his right, his heavy-soled boots making a pleasant thud on the linoleum-tiled floor. He whipped his head left and right to look down rows of shelves: blenders, remote-controlled cars, baby cribs, plumbing supplies, all manner of amenity for house and home flew by. When Lee reached the end of the passageway, he threw himself into a hook slide, like he was coming in from third and trying to avoid the tag at the plate. The butt of his gun jabbed him in the ribs and knocked the wind out of him a little.

"Oof," Lee said. That was why you didn't run with the bat. But his ball-playing years were behind him now anyway. He had more important things to do. He pulled himself up. He was in produce. The bananas looked terrible. But the apples looked delicious. Lee knew the terms of his probation. But no one was around. He selected an apple: big, juicy, and red. This was what America was about. Apples any time of the year. Big and tasty.

Freedom wasn't free. And this apple was a small payment for the service Lee Rigg was about to render. He took a bite. It tasted like a fresh, juicy fall day—all wax and crispiness. Just as God intended.

Lee walked back the way he'd come. Maybe slow and steady was the right approach: less Navy Seal and more John Wayne. He'd find that degenerate sonofabitch. He'd take him down. Lee took another bite of apple and continued to walk. It was certainly easier to peer down aisles at a stately John Wayne pace. They were totally empty. Where was everyone? Didn't matter. Lee could solve that problem later. One thing at a time.

Lee finished his apple as he reached Home Appliances. He opened a display-model trash compactor and tossed the core in. As he pushed the bin back under the display counter, he heard a muffled shouting. Lee tensed and gripped his gun with both hands. They were over by the refrigerators! Lee crept over, crouched in covert-ops mode. He peered down the row of refrigerators. Nothing. They had to be there somewhere. A bright-red refrigerator a little more than halfway down the row was moving! Lee rubbed his eyes. They weren't tricking him. Holy crap. This was it. They were in the refrigerator. It was just like little Alice! Sick bastard.

Lee marched toward the red fridge. He stopped about ten feet from it, next to a big silver three-door model. Lee couldn't understand why anyone needed three doors on their fridge. But before he could ponder that mystery further, the door of the red fridge swung open. Two small children climbed out, a boy and a girl. The boy looked angry, the girl worried. Wisps of smoke trailed them.

"Hey, kids, over here!" Lee called. But before they could move, a man climbed out behind them and put his hands on their shoulders.

"You sonofabitch," Lee said.

"What? Who the hell are you?"

The guy had greased-back hair and rings under his eyes. But he was dressed nice. They never looked like you expected.

"I'm your worst nightmare. That's what I am," Lee said. "Get your hands up."

"What? You don't understand. I'm Mitch Spooner. The store manager."

"I don't give two craps who you are!" Lee said and squeezed the trigger on the gun. He was gonna fire a couple of warning shots to show that frigger he meant business.

Bang! Bang!

"Jesus Christ!" The kidnapper raised his arms.

Damn straight. Might made right in the land of the free and the home of the brave. America! Did the boy just roll his eyes? Probably just a trick of the light.

"C'mon, kids," Lee said. "I won't hurt you. That was just a warning shot. But there's plenty more where this comes from. So don't try anything, Mitch. Or I'll make you my bitch."

Lee was killing it with his word choice. That rhyme could have come straight out of a *Die Hard* movie. He kinda wished there was a camera crew there.

The kids didn't move.

"Look, man," the kidnapper, Mitch, said. "Put your gun down, and let me explain. I was just—"

"Shut up!" Lee yelled. The kids still weren't moving. Were they simple? Or were they suffering from that friggin' Sacramento syndrome or whatever? He was at an impasse.

"Look, I'm totally sure we can clear up this misunderstanding." Mitch was talking again. Lee needed him to shut up. He needed quiet to think, to figure this out. So he squeezed the trigger to let off another couple of shots in quick succession—*Bang! Bang!*— to send the message that he was in charge and that Mitch should only speak when spoken to. It didn't work.

"Aaah, shit!" Mitch collapsed clutching his shoulder.

"Ah, shit," Lee said and sprinted over.

"My arm, you idiot!"

"I didn't mean to! It was supposed to be a warning shot. To show you not to speak until spoken to. Why didn't you just shut up?"

"What? Why didn't you just put the gun down?"

"'Cause you're a goddamn child abductor!"

"What? No I'm not. I found the kids and was bringing them back to their parents. I work here! Ahh, my fuckin' shoulder. Jesus Christ!"

Oh crap. Was he telling the truth? If so, Lee might have made a grievous error. But that was just the sort of song and dance degenerates like this guy would tell to try and get away. Lee wasn't going to be fooled. The kids would tell him the truth.

"Yeah right. Shut up. Kids, what do you have say about this?"

They didn't answer. There was a small fizz and then a bang, a tinkling of shattered glass overhead, and then the lights went out.

"Kids?"

Lee turned his head, keeping the gun pointed at Mitch to see what had happened to the kids. He thought he saw a small object fly through the air from an extinguished light. Or maybe he was imagining it. It was dark now, and he never heard anything land.

"Crap. Kids!" Lee shouted louder. The kids were gone.

"Get back here, you little brats!" Mitch was sitting up and craning his neck around. The auxiliary lights came on, but most of the store was still in shadows. The kids were nowhere to be seen.

"You idiot!" Mitch said. "You let them escape. C'mon, we gotta find them."

Mitch got up. Lee jammed the barrel of his rifle into his belly. Mitch grunted.

"Not so fast, asshole. Those kids're safer without you. You're coming with me."

"Jesus, be careful with that thing."

"Jesus's got nothing to do with it. Shut up and walk. I'm the people! I'm taking you in. Citizen's arrest."

"No, you don't underst—"

"I said shut up!" Lee jabbed Mitch again and elicited another grunt. "Towards the front. There's light up there."

Mitch had finally shut up. Good. Lee frog-marched his prisoner toward the front of the store.

MITCH

Mitch clutched his shoulder as the lunatic with the assault rifle shepherded him toward the front of the store; he clenched his jaw in a tight grimace. Christ, it hurt. He was really going to have to curtail his activity at the gym. His shoulder was on fire and the needle-dicked little prick kept poking and prodding him from behind with the barrel of a loaded assault rifle. He hadn't had a chance to put away the files in the man cave. That was the little brats' fault. Little shits. Of course, they might have saved him the trouble by destroying everything with that firework. But he needed to know for sure. One thing at a time though. The crazy hick needed to be separated from his gun before Mitch could do anything.

"Keep walkin'," the man said. "If you so much as fart, I'll blow your ass away, you sick sonofabitch. The action on this thing is frighteningly responsive."

Mitch couldn't disagree with that last statement. He kept looking for an opportunity though, as they moved toward the lighted portion of the store.

Help came in the form of an old guy and...his granddaughter? No. They were store employees. SuperMart's corporate policy was to never hire family members. But still. This could work. And more. Damn, she was fine. She worked here? Mitch made a mental note to peruse the personnel files a little more closely when he next had the chance. She had a furrowed brow, and when she saw him, she looked down and away. Did he know her from somewhere? Duh, she worked there. It was sweet of her to avert her eyes, what with him being the boss. He hoped she'd look at him when they were getting freaky though. Deepen the connection and shit. But that was for later. Right now he needed to not get shot.

"Hey," the gun-toting dumbass shouted to Mitch's employees. "Hey! I got 'im!"

The old man and the young hottie came slowly toward them.

"Oh, Mr. Spooner," the old man said.

"Naw, I'm Lee Rigg. What's crackin', grandpa?" the gunman said.

"Excuse me?" the old guy said.

"I caught the kidnapper, gramps! What'd you think—I shot him for fun?"

"No, I'm sure you did not." The old guy had a deep voice, with a slight southern inflection. Soothing. Mitch wouldn't have minded if he read him bedtime stories. "Look, uh, Mr. Rigg. This man is the store manager. I hardly think that he would have abducted the children."

"Naw, man. I saw 'im with the kids."

"Kids?" the hottie said.

"Yeah, boy and a girl. Coming out of a refrigerator. Only the kids've runnoft again. But I brought back this bastard for justice. Citizen's arrest! Of the people, by the people, for the people! America, baby!"

Mitch rolled his eyes. He didn't have a whole lot of hope for the old invalid and the pretty face to get him out of this mess.

"Now, where's security?" Lee Rigg said. "We can hand this guy over and then find the kids. They were so scared of him they wouldn't speak to me."

"Maybe they were scared of you too?" the hottie said. Oh to get freaky with her. All night long. Where did he know her from?

"What? Naw. Frig, you sure are pretty. What's your name?" Lee Rigg was also distracted by the hot chick. Was this his chance? No, the dumb hick's finger was still on the trigger. Patience.

She didn't answer him. Instead, she said, "Look, maybe if you put the gun down, we could talk about this?"

"What? Frig no! You might be pretty, but you sure ain't too bright, are you? If I put the gun down, then what's to stop him gettin' away? Let's just hand this guy over to security and be done with him."

The young woman's scowl deepened. That's how he knew her! Mitch smiled in spite of himself. She hadn't done the corporate cheer this morning. Mitch would give her something to cheer about. Most definitely.

"This young woman is about the smartest person I know," the old guy said. "Do not speak to her like that again."

Mitch snorted. Like that chick was the smartest person he knew. The old guy knew him!

"Clem, don't worry about it," the hot chick said, antsy and anxious to smooth things over. Clearly she wanted him to be free. Aw yeah, she did. Babe.

Lee Rigg said, "C'mon, grandpa. I was just pointing out the flaw in her plan. I don't mean nothing personal by it."

"Security, ahh, well, they're actually..." The hot chick was stalling.

Mitch groaned. Those oafs hadn't shown up again. He could tell by the tone of the hot chick's voice. Of course, Rog and Sam were idiots. And there was the distinct possibility that, if they had been there, someone else might get shot. As long as it wasn't him again, Mitch didn't really care, but he also wouldn't have placed money on him not being the one who got shot just based on the sheer number of idiots involved. On balance, it was probably just as well they hadn't shown up. But Lee Rigg didn't have to know that. Mitch needed to turn the tables in his favor.

"They're in my office," he said. Quick thinking would get him out of this mess. Well, that and the Glock he kept taped to the underside of his desk. He had put it there just in case. And it seemed like today that case had arrived.

"I said shut up!" Lee jabbed Mitch in the ribs with the butt of his rifle.

"Ahh!" Mitch grunted as the air was driven out of his lungs, replaced by a searing pain.

"Please be careful with that," the old guy—Patterson, that was his name—said.

"Don't worry, old-timer. I've got the hang of this thing now. Now let's get this guy to security."

"Security..." Patterson said.

"...Is in Mr. Spooner's office," the hot chick finished for him. She was pretty and clever? Mitch's admiration grew. And not just his admiration. Mitch shook his head. Now was not the time.

She kept talking, "So let's, uh, bring him up there. Clem, can you go find Tim and bring him up there?"

Mitch did not approve of that part of the plan. Adding another moron to the mix wasn't going to help. So the hot chick was more hot than clever, but that was fine. Mitch didn't say anything. His shoulder already hurt like hell and his ribs were probably going to be black and blue as it was. Besides, if he got to go to his office, everything would be fine.

"Who's Tim?" Lee asked.

"He's the assistant manager," the hot chick said. Mitch realized he'd have to learn her name at some point, if for no other reason than it would give him something to shout when they were getting down to business. She was still talking. "He told me once that he had some first aid training. So I thought he could try to do something about Mr. Spooner's shoulder. You know, while security gets stuff straightened out."

"That's more than this asshole deserves, but if you say so. You're apparently the smartest person gramps here knows, so whatever."

Mitch didn't bother contesting the statement, never mind how wrong it was. He needed to get to his office. There, his Glock would solve all his problems.

"Wait a sec," old Patterson said.

Christ, what was the matter now? This guy should be retired. Or at least not making trouble when things were finally moving in the right direction.

"What?" Lee and the hot chick said at the same time.

"Jinx, you owe me a Coke," Lee said and winked at her.

She ignored him.

"I'm gonna go with these guys," Patterson said. "You go find Tim. And security."

"I...but security..." the hot chick said.

"You know who I'm talking about, remember? You saw him first thing this morning. No arguments, now. Good luck. We'll be counting on you."

WTF? What was he talking about "him"? Rog and Sam were two people. Two morons. Maybe the old guy was senile. Mitch wouldn't hold his breath for a heroic rescue. This was all on him. Christ, it would be so much easier if his head and shoulder didn't hurt.

"Okay. All right. Take care of yourself, Clem," she said and went off.

Great, a moron with a gun and a senile old man. But maybe this could work out. After Mitch had heroically delivered the old guy from the clutches of this maniac, she'd be so thankful that...

Yeah, this could work out.

SCARLETT

Clem didn't deserve this. No one deserved to be stuck with the crazy, gun-toting redneck and that d-bag Mitch Spooner. But especially not Clem. It had happened so fast, how Clem had taken her place. He was trying to protect her, but he didn't deserve to be in that situation. No one did. And it would be her fault if something happened to him. She had to find help quick. The police. She had to call the police.

Scarlett picked up the phone at the end of Aisle 7 and pressed *9 for an outside line. Nothing. No dial tone. She slammed it down and went across to Aisle 13. Dead too. Maybe the power had knocked out their phones too? And meanwhile, poor Clem! Security. The gunman was willing to hand Mitch Spooner over to security...who had locked themselves out. So that was out. But Clem wanted her to find that federal investigator or auditor or whoever he was. But she had no idea where he might be hiding or what help he might actually provide. She needed to buy him time. How?

Tim. He could go to the office and buy Clem some time while she found help. That must have been what Clem meant by "get Tim." She swallowed. It hurt a little; her mouth was so dry. Tim. The same guy who had intimated he would fire her the last time they spoke. She couldn't afford that. But she really couldn't let Clem get hurt.

Scarlett hadn't seen Tim since he had foisted front-door duty on her. But front-door duty was his job in a Code Bobby, and Tim liked to follow rules. Scarlett didn't relish facing the mob again. She and Clem had only just been able to extricate themselves from it by offering free pastries to go with their free

198

coffee. And those pastries were not good. She couldn't believe that it would placate the crowd for long. But the coffee wasn't any good either, and the crowd hadn't seemed to care about that.

Scarlett took a deep breath and made her way back to the front. Amazingly, she found Tim almost immediately. He and that pushy blond preacher came spilling out of the Super Sale section. They were holding hands and giggling like mad. Scandal! It would have been funny in a different circumstance. When they saw Scarlett, they stopped both giggling and hand-holding. They looked rather unkempt, though the blond woman's hair was still perfect. It wasn't natural.

"Heh...hey, Scarlett," Tim said. He seemed dazed and...guilty, maybe? Scarlett tried to meet his eyes, to see his pupils, to make sure he wasn't high or something. Tim was the last person she'd expect, but it was getting to the point where nothing would be a surprise. And a drugged-out assistant manager was the last thing she needed.

"What's...what's going on?" Tim was stammering more than usual; his face was flushed and seemingly growing more and more red by the second. Tim couldn't actually be on drugs. Right...?

"Look—" Scarlett said. But Tim interrupted her.

"Oh, how rude of me. Scarlett, this is Sandy. Sandy, Scarlett."

"Hi there. Sandy Newman. Pleased to meet you."

The preacher had a vaguely empty gaze. Like she was on autopilot and her mind was elsewhere. Coupled with her unmoving blond hair, the overall effect was somewhat unsettling.

"Scarlett," Scarlett said. She shook the offered hand. It was greasy. Sweaty? Scarlett wiped her hand on the back of her pants.

"So, answer Timothy's question. Don't let me get in the way of important company business," Sandy said.

Scarlett didn't like her tone. But she also wanted to get back and help Clem as soon as possible.

"Right," she said. "So here's the deal: Mitch Spooner's been shot by some nutcase with an assault rifle."

"Terrorists!" Tim shrieked. Sandy put her arm around him.

"No. It's not terrorists. It's just one moron with a gun," Scarlett said. Tim seemed reassured. Scarlett wasn't sure that was any better.

"We've got to get out of here," Sandy said. "It's one of those mass shootings like you always see on the news. He's gonna kill us all!"

Tim started shaking. Sandy rubbed his shoulders.

"Stop it!" Scarlett said. "It is not a mass shooting, and no one is going anywhere. You guys are going to help me."

"No!" Sandy said. "You said it was a nutcase with a gun. We've got to escape. C'mon, Timothy."

"Wait, stop," Scarlett said again and moved in front of them. "The gunman. He's crazy—you have to be to shoot a gun so cavalierly like that—but he's not unreasonable. Does that make sense? We were able to get him to go to Spooner's office to wait."

"So it's not a mass shooting?" Sandy said.

"Or terrorists?" Tim added.

"No."

"Well thank the Lord for that," Sandy said.

"Amen."

"Please!" Scarlett said. "Spooner's been shot—"

"Poor Mr. Spooner," Tim said.

"Yeah, I guess," Scarlett said. "But I'm not sure he didn't deserve it."

Tim gasped. Scarlett continued, "The guy with the gun insists Spooner kidnapped the kids—"

"Mr. Spooner would never!" Tim said.

"Yeah. I agree; whatever else Mitch Spooner is, he isn't a kidnapper. But the gunman didn't want to hear it. He says he found the kids—there's another one missing, by the way, but apparently she's with the first one—and that he found Spooner with them. And when he was apprehending Spooner, the kids ran away again. He won't take his gun off him until security shows up."

"This is bad," Tim said, finally coming to grips with the obvious. He was even more pale than normal.

"Yes, it is. The gunman wants to hand Spooner over to security. But Rog and Sam are idiots and showed up late and got themselves locked out. They may or may not have gone to get the police. Clem—Clem Patterson, you know, the greeter—is stuck with Spooner and the gunman. That's why you can't leave. We gotta help him. He's old and sweet and shouldn't be involved in stress like this."

Scarlett paused. Tim was just mouthing *gun* and *man* silently to himself. It was not the reaction she was hoping for. Might as well tell him the rest.

"Also, the crowd at the front door is restless and almost riotous. I've done everything I can think to calm them down. But the best thing we could do would be to find the kids and be able to let the people out. Actually. Do you think maybe we should just let them out? Spooner found the kids. I don't think they've been kidnapped. And call the police. We should definitely call the police."

Scarlett watched Tim, trying to judge his reaction. It hadn't gone over so well last time she had told him what he needed to do, but now, surely he couldn't protest? He didn't say anything. He just sort of stood and stared. Was he in shock? Well, she couldn't blame him. But he was also the defacto boss and needed to make decisions. Especially if he was going to threaten to fire people if they did things without his permission.

She pressed on, "So, yeah, we should call the police because nobody's done that yet. Except the store phone lines are down, and cell phones don't work here, which I guess you know. So I don't see how we're gonna do that.

"Oh, and you can also see there's been some kind of power surge, and half the store is out of power. Maybe that's what happened to our phones. Plus, it's gonna make finding those kids that much harder."

Scarlett took a deep breath to recover. It was insane. This day was insane. It couldn't be real. And yet, here she was. She waited for Tim to tell her what to do.

"So, what do we do?" Tim said.

You're the assistant manager! You're in charge now, you doofus! Scarlett wanted to shout at him, but she managed to contain her reaction to a single raised eyebrow.

"Just who do you think you're raising your eyebrow at, missy?" the blond evangelical—Sandy—said to her in a loud voice. "Show some respect. Timothy has been through a lot today, and the last thing he needs is disrespect from his underlings. Don't worry, Timothy. We'll figure this out. Together."

Scarlett wanted to slap the condescending smile from the preacher's condescending face. She was what, maybe five years older than her? Being close to Jesus didn't give her the right to be a bitch. But again, Scarlett managed to tamp down her emotions and limited herself to a cool smile.

Tim gave a sheepish smile. But he didn't say anything.

Scarlett straightened her back. If no one else was going to take charge of this situation, she wasn't just going to stand there like a chump. Not while the kids were missing and Clem was in mortal danger.

"Look," she said, "Tim, you've got to go to the office and try to talk some sense to the guy with the gun. I'll come with you. Not you"—she was speaking to Sandy, who had grabbed Tim's hand and looked to be coming with them—"you're going to the front door to try to calm down that crowd. That's your job, right? To shepherd the huddled masses?"

"Yeah, but...you're not going with him!" Sandy said. "You're not gonna steal my man, you little minx."

Scarlett could not contain her reaction this time. She laughed out loud.

"Think it's funny, do you, you hussy? Well let me tell you what. It's the devil's own work that sends pretty little things off to flirt with honest men like my Timothy. And you two aren't going anywhere without me."

Scarlett had had just about enough sexual harassment in the last twenty-four hours. The ravings of a jealous preacher were pushing her dangerously close to the edge.

"Look, Sandy," Scarlett said, "I don't know what you're talking about, but Clem is my friend. I'm going to help him. To do that, I need Tim. You are a preacher. Go preach. Tend to your flock or whatever. 'Your Timothy' will be back soon enough."

Sandy's eyes flared. For a moment Scarlett wondered if she was about to get hit by a preacher. That would be a first. But no blow was forthcoming. Instead, Sandy bit her lip and flashed her eyes under that blond helmet of hair: back and forth between Scarlett and Tim.

"It's okay," Tim said, finally ending the indecisive standoff. "She's right. I've gotta go. And don't worry. You're the only lady for me. You're my gal. I'll be back as soon as I can."

They gazed into each other's eyes, and Scarlett did her best not to groan.

"You better be," Sandy said and kissed him. Passionately.

"Oh my god, get a room. I'm right here," Scarlett said, which seemed to bring them back to reality.

Tim smiled and grew red again. At least he wasn't on drugs.

Sandy was flushed but composed when she turned to Scarlett. "Don't even think about it. Or else."

"I won't; don't worry. My god."

"And don't take the Lord's name in vain."

Scarlett bit the inside of her lip and held it between her teeth until her sarcastic retort passed. She had to stay composed. For Clem.

"Can we please just go?" she said.

Sandy nodded and started to walk toward the front doors.

"Sandy!" Tim said.

Sandy stopped and turned.

"I'll be your Snuffleupagus! I love you."

Sandy blew a kiss in return.

"Oh, Jesus, c'mon," Scarlett said.

The preacher and the assistant manager both rounded on her and started talking at once.

"How dare you!"

"Don't take the Lord's name in vain!"

"Show some respect—"

"ENOUGH!" Scarlett cut them off. "I'm sorry. I didn't mean to offend you, but there are more important things right now. Let's GO!"

That seemed to do the trick. Sandy gave Tim one last peck on the cheek and went off to soothe the mob. Tim watched Sandy go, then, finally, came with her toward the offices. To try to sort out the madman with the gun. She wasn't overly optimistic about their chances.

BILLY

"Grown-ups are crazy!" Billy said. "They're crazy. Out of their minds. *Non copos mentis.* Insane. It's the only explanation."

Willow nodded.

"I mean, my mom is bossy and makes me do stuff I don't want to do, but compared to these people, she's totally cool!"

Willow nodded again, not saying anything. She was pretty shaken up, and Billy couldn't blame her. They had just seen a man shoot another man, with a gun. A real gun. Right next to them! There was nothing heroic about that. It was terrifying. Then the lights had gone out, and they had escaped. They were sitting in between the row of refrigerators and a row of washing machines. It had the advantage, in addition to keeping them well hidden in a place grown-ups couldn't fit, of being somewhat bulletproof. That was important now. Billy shook his head. No longer were they in a fairyland of wonder. This was more like a postapocalyptic wasteland. The power was out, and the only law of the land was lawlessness. It was time to leave. Which was good, because that had been his plan all along.

"What are we going to do?" Willow whispered.

"The way I see it, we have two options: we can try to find our moms"—Willow nodded furiously. Billy gulped, then continued—"but that would mean going back through the store the way they went."

Willow shook her head in fear. Again, Billy couldn't blame her. The gunman and the ogre king had headed toward the front of the store, where there was still light.

"Or we could try to find our way out of the store. I don't know about your mom, but my mom is twice as fearsome as that gunman. She'll find her way out no problem. I just hope she doesn't kill me when she finds me."

"Yeah, moms can usually take care of themselves. Maybe we should get out of here?"

Billy nodded. Not that that was going to be straightforward. The darkness in the back half of the store offered good cover, but it didn't mean it would be easy to find a means of egress. And then there was the million-dollar question of whether he could return to his mom. It was what he wanted, sure, but was it right? Did it make him spineless? Gormless, craven, weak?

"At least we've liberated a prisoner," Willow said, holding up the bear and breaking up his train of thought.

"Yeah, that is good. He didn't deserve to be down in that ogre cave. What's his name?"

"How about Leroy," Willow said. "That means the king in French."

Billy could see it. Leroy was a good name for a bear. And Willow had been a princess, so it made sense for the bear to also have royal connections.

Billy wriggled between two washing machines to peek out. The coast was clear.

"C'mon," he said.

Billy, Willow, and Leroy crawled out into the dark washing machine aisle. They headed farther down it, away from the light, and passed by a forest of floor lamps, all extinguished.

"Do you think, when all this is over, we could have a play date sometime?" Willow asked. "This has been pretty scary. But it's also been fun."

Billy looked at her. He never called them play dates. That was an affection the grown-ups had started and was therefore lame. Why couldn't it just be "getting together to play"? Stupid grown-ups. But Willow was right. It had been fun, gunplay aside.

"I could show you my tree house."

She had a tree house?! Billy had always wanted a tree house. But his technology was limited, and his parents were stupid.

"Yeah! That'd be fun. Once we get out of here."

He didn't mention that he'd probably be grounded from then until eternity. But there was no need to get into all that with Willow right now. Right now, they had to keep their focus.

There was a rustling to their right, from the forest of floor lamps.

"Hey, kid. You all right?"

"Run!" Billy shouted. "No wait! I know this guy. He's okay. Sort of."

It was the man in the trench coat who had given him the mission, which seemed like such a long time ago.

"We set off your stupid rocket," Billy said. "It exploded and almost killed us, by the way. Thanks a lot for that."

"Why would you give that to children?" Willow asked, widening her eyes.

The trench-coated man blinked and adjusted his hat.

"I thought you could handle it," he said. "I didn't see the signal though. And I've been watching. When'd you set it off?"

"Just now! What are you, blind?"

"No. I just...I guess I didn't see it. Sorry. Oh well. You seem all right. Any news?"

"You gonna pay up?" Billy asked. If this guy was going to be an obtuse ignoramus, Billy was going to get something out of him. Maybe with enough money, he could buy his mom's forgiveness.

The man looked at him.

"Look, kid."

"Will," Billy said.

"Look, Will. This is bigger than you and me. We never talked about payment. You were just doing your duty as a junior gumshoe. And you were a big help to me. And to Uncle Sam."

"Maybe, but that was before your exploding rocket almost killed me. And I don't have an Uncle Sam."

"And my dad says the government should stay out of people's business," Willow said. Billy was confused for a second and then realized that, of course, this guy must be working for the government.

"Well, isn't he smart," the man said. "But as it happens, I'm not the government; I just mistook you for the patriotic type. But if that's not the case, how about this? How about you tell me what you know, and I'll give you each a thousand dollars?"

A thousand dollars! Billy tried to control his face. That was more money than he'd ever seen. Maybe he really could buy his mom's forgiveness. The only question was whether he should buy her something or just hand over the cash. He could figure that out later.

"Plus candy," Willow said. She was a genius!

"Yeah," Billy said. "And candy."

The man patted his myriad pockets and drew out a wad of cash.

"Don't get greedy, kids. I'm fresh out of candy—you could grab some from Aisle 4 if you want—but here's two thousand dollars. Now show me what you found."

Billy took the money, divided it in half, and gave Willow her share. The remaining wad of bills was thick in his hands. A thousand dollars! He could buy so many things. Xbox games. Legos. His mom's forgiveness. What if he put it toward a new fort?! The sort of technology he could afford now would make it indestructible! He ran his thumb over the bills, and the cash purred. Willow fanned herself with her money. Billy grinned. Willow giggled.

"You kids gonna show me something interesting, or you gonna give me that money back?" the man in the goofy hat said.

Billy's money wouldn't all fit in one pocket. He divided it and filled both his pockets. Willow's dress only had the one ladybug pocket. But the money fit; the ladybug bulged.

"This way," he said, and he and Willow took the man to the red refrigerator, which still smelled faintly of exploded-rocket dynamite.

"Crackerjack work, kids. You might have a future in this game. Here, take my card."

Billy took the business card and read it:

Dirk Blade, Master Private Investigator. No case too big or too small.

"All right, now scram, kids. I got work to do."

Billy didn't like his tone, but before he could put the private investigator in his place, the man had disappeared down the steps inside the refrigerator. Billy was not about to follow him down there. Besides, he was rich! But it wasn't time to focus on the money. They were still in the store, and they had to get out. They headed deeper into the gloom of the darkened portion of the store.

Before too long, they could see light in the distance, pouring through a window slit into the dark store. A red fluorescent EXIT sign glowed above. They were almost out. It was quiet. Too quiet.

"Hold on," he told Willow and pulled her back behind a display of vacuum cleaners.

"What? That's the door right there."

"Yeah, I know. I just wanna be sure nothing else is going to jump out at us."

"Oh, yeah. Good idea."

They peeked out from behind the vacuum cleaners. To the left were tall shelves with boxes and boxes of home-cleaning products, which gave off the faint odor Billy associated with school bathrooms. To the right was Aisle 41: Hardware and a display of hammers and other tools. It looked deserted.

"Are you ready for this?" Billy asked.

"I think so. Are you?"

"I..."

Billy paused. Was he ready for this? An hour or two ago, it was all he wanted. To be free of the stupid tyranny of his stupid mom. He had been bold, seized his chance, and become admiral of his own fate, and now...the world was big. And he was alone. He didn't want to run away anymore. How would he eat? Where would he sleep? Did that make him weak? Did he have to stay the course? He...he couldn't. He'd just have to find his mom and hope she didn't kill him. But first he had to get out of the store. Whatever was on the other side of that door had to be better than what was going on in here. His mom was a grown-up. She'd find her way out fine. What about Willow? Would she get in trouble for this? That wasn't fair. She had never been running away. Billy felt bad for not telling her the truth.

"What's wrong?"

Willow clearly was endowed with that particular feminine quality that allowed her to read minds. His mom had it and his sister too, sometimes.

"I..." Billy hesitated. How much could he tell her? She had stuck with him this far. She was all right. She had a tree house! He should come clean.

"I'm the kid they're looking for," he said. "I was mad at my mom, and so I ran away."

He slumped his shoulders and looked at his feet. He kind of wished he had the cool light-up shoes. They wouldn't have helped him keep a low profile in a darkened store, but they would have been a distraction from this conversation. Willow would probably be mad at him. She would maybe even leave before they had made good on their escape. Lying was bad. Not that he had lied exactly. But he hadn't told the whole truth. It didn't feel good.

"I'm sorry," he said, still looking down. He dragged his right toe along the floor.

"Oh, that's okay," Willow said. "I figured it was you."

"You did?!" Billy snapped his head up to look at her in the half dark. She was serious. But not in an angry way.

"Well, yeah."

"Why didn't you say anything?"

"Well, I mean, at first I thought maybe it was some other poor kid. But then once I figured it out, I thought you must have a good reason. And it was fun playing. Do you have a good reason?"

Billy thought about that for a second. He had had a good reason. Now...

"I don't know," he said. "Running away seemed like a good idea at the time. My mom was being really bossy. And she destroyed my fort."

"That seems like more than enough reason to me," Willow said. She crossed her arms across her chest and nodded, once and firmly, like that settled it.

"I know! Right? But now...with guns and explosives and crazy grown-ups all over the place? It's too much. It's too crazy. I don't think I want to run away anymore."

"Yeah, I know what you mean. Today has been pretty crazy. And moms can be kind of crazy too, sometimes."

"Do you think that...that if I don't run away, it means I'm weak? That she'll just go back to bossing me around like before?"

Willow kept her arms crossed and furrowed her brow. She didn't say anything for a minute, then spoke.

"I don't think so. Moms can be kinda bossy. And they almost never think of us first. Sometimes they forget that their kids have feelings that need to be respected."

Billy nodded. Willow was right. But try explaining that to his mom.

"And moms do good stuff too," Willow said.

"Yeah, like cook."

"And keep us safe. They love us. They might not always be good at showing it, and so we have to remind them."

"By running away?"

"Drastic times call for drastic measures."

"But if I don't follow through?"

"It's okay. You sent the message. Your mom will understand."

"You don't know my mom..."

"Trust me," Willow said, uncrossing her arms and extending her hand to Billy.

Billy took it and felt Willow give him a strong squeeze. She nodded again, one time, like that was settled. Billy squeezed her hand back and then let go.

He looked down at his feet. He also hadn't told her his real name. He should probably come clean about that too. No one liked liars.

"Willow—" he said. But before he could say anything more, there was a muffled sliding and then the boxes of cleaning solvents started to fall all around them.

"Ahh! Look out!"

Willow had already jumped back. The boxes smashed open. The school-bathroom smell was overpowering.

"Hey!" Willow said.

"What?"

She was pointing. It was a small red squirrel. Was it the squirrel from earlier? It looked freaked out. All its hair was standing on end.

"It looks scared," Willow said.

"Yeah, should we catch it and take care of it?" Billy had always kind of wanted a pet squirrel. And his superhero identity was The Squirrel, after all.

"I dunno. Aren't you supposed to leave wild animals alone?"

"But we can't leave it in the store; it'll die."

"You're right. Okay."

They moved toward the squirrel. It took off. Billy and Willow took off after it. Up an aisle. Left. Along a row of lawnmowers. The squirrel was gone.

"Hey, where'd it go?" Billy said, looking around. The squirrel had disappeared.

"I don't know, but look—it led us to the door!" Willow said.

In their escape from the falling boxes and their pursuit, the squirrel had led them right to the door. Billy was worried for the squirrel; this store was no place for it. This store was no place for anyone. But then again, maybe the squirrel just didn't want to hang out with humans. Billy couldn't blame it. Hopefully it'd be all right.

"Well," he said, "should we do it?"

Willow nodded. They both took a deep breath and pushed the door.

It didn't move. The door was stuck. Billy turned to Willow and saw the panic he felt rising in his own stomach in her eyes. They pushed again. Stuck. Nothing.

"Wait! It's locked," Willow said, pointing up at the deadbolt. "I don't think I can reach it."

Standing on his tiptoes, Billy could reach it. He was almost eight, after all. And he understood how locks worked. He flipped the latch.

"Right," he said.

"Right."

They took another deep breath and leaned on the door. It swung open, into the warm world outside.

RUSTY

Rusty's whole body felt drained, like someone had pulled the stopper on his energy. So this was overdose. He wondered if it was like late-stage rabies. He didn't even have the energy to lift his head and check the bushiness of his tail. What a way to go out. A junkie. A loser. Not the prince of squirrel thieves. Nuts.

The power surge and subsequent explosion had been the rush of Rusty's life—a life that was likely to end right there in the semidarkness of that unnatural human habitat. It smelled like fox pee. Were there foxes around? Rusty couldn't summon the energy to be scared. There probably weren't foxes around. Not in this environment. Hopefully there weren't foxes around. Stupid foxes. What a way to go. He thought of his wife, who would be expecting him to come home this evening with all the nuts she had ever dreamed of. How long would she wait? His children. Rusty realized they'd never know him. Without his scavenging, they'd probably die before they made it out of infancy. His genetic material would pass with him.

Rusty was crying. Stupid Raccoon. He had said it would be so easy. Easy his tail! In fact, if he ever got his paws on Raccoon, he'd scratch him limb from limb. And if that seemed too dangerous, which, given their relative differences in size and mass, it did, he'd chatter at him incessantly until he went insane. Of course, that would require the energy to get out of his current sorry state and not expiring right where he was. And Rusty just didn't see it happening. Fade to black. That had been some hit of electricity. No. Electricity was bad. It had ruined everything. Life was over now.

Or was it? Did he have strength after all? He felt something shift. Was it his leg muscle? Nope. Not the leg. Tail? Something was definitely moving.

"Aah! Look out!" He heard a human-kit voice shout.

The ground. No, he was inside. The floor. The floor was moving. Which meant...

Rusty was falling again. Weightless. But he wasn't that kind of squirrel! In midair, Rusty could see his tail. It was bushy, silky, sexy; it rippled in the air as he fell. He flexed his paws. Come on, squirrel! He landed. It wasn't a graceful landing, but no one was there to see it. Plus, it was dark. He had landed in a puddle. It smelled like fox pee. Foxes! Run! Self-pity was banished as instinct took over. He twisted, leapt up, and sprinted, heedless of the young human kits shouting and chasing him. Were they running from the foxes too? He bobbed and weaved, sprinted like lightning, skittering around corners, his claws scrabbling on fresh-polished floor. He lost the human kits. And the incontinent foxes.

He was alive! He was back! He paused to get his bearings. It was just as confusing without any artificial suns as it had been with them. His legs were trembling. He supposed that was normal, given the circumstances. Between the near overdose and heroically evading a skulk of foxes, surely it was normal if his legs trembled just a bit. Where was he? From the floor, he couldn't see much. Rusty climbed the nearest shelf and perched in the seat of one of those superloud things that humans drove over the grass. He'd always wanted to drive one of these. He had the theory down, from hours of observation, but didn't know how to turn the machine on. Oh well. Now wasn't the time. He'd had enough adventure for one day, and the day wasn't over yet. Rusty was wobbly. That was the electricity's fault. That was it. For real this time. He was done.

"Hey, where'd it go?" the male kit said from below.

Ha! Rusty had outsmarted him.

"I don't know, but look—it led us to the door!" the female kit said.

Rusty looked to see what she was talking about. A vertical shaft of light was pouring through a tall, narrow window. It was a door! Above it, Rusty could read a single word: Shipping/ Receiving. He had made it. Now he had to dig deep and finish the job. Be the change you want to see in the world! Be the squirrel! Rusty tensed, waited; the human kits were having a little trouble with the technology of the door. Rusty understood. Doors were tricky if you didn't understand the theory. But he remained alert, alive, ready, and when the human kits finally got it open, he bolted, brushing the legs of the male kit as he burst into the sunlight.

Outside there was a smell of burning something. Maybe skunk? Could be burning skunk. But Rusty didn't have time to help hapless skunks. He had to find cover.

"Whoa, dude, a squirrel. I'm so tripping balls right now."

"Word, dude."

"No! Don't let it shut!"

There were a few adolescent humans and a fully grown male human outside. They all began talking at once. Rusty didn't wait to find out what they thought of squirrels. Nor did he have time to bask in the sun's warmth. He was outside; there were hawks. He needed to find cover, fast. He ran under a big truck and took stock of the situation.

He was alive. That was good. He didn't seem to have rabies. Also good. His tail was bushy. Silky. Sexy. And...Rusty scented the air with his nose and whiskers. Through the haze of burnt skunk, he could detect nuts. Peanuts, walnuts, even those fancy South American nuts. Preshelled. Roasted *and* salted! Rusty darted to the side of the truck and looked up. Jackpot! On the side of the truck were nuts the size of Raccoon himself! Good old Raccoon. Rusty wouldn't have even needed to know how to read to know that this was it. He darted back under the truck to plan his next move.

He had the schematic of the truck's hydraulic system memorized. It would be the work of a moment to adjust the brakes to his advantage. Getting the nut-carrying trailer portion to decouple at just the right time would be tricky, but he'd come this far. Raccoon's information had been good. Mostly good. The job was not the simple walk in the park that Raccoon had made it out to be. But walks in the park rarely were simple. Maybe for Raccoon they were, but for a squirrel, a walk in the park was dangerous and fraught with peril. Maybe that's what Raccoon had been trying to say. He should have just spoken plain. Too late now. Rusty had no choice but to trust Raccoon's information about coupling mechanisms. That didn't mean he shouldn't be careful about it.

Rusty had no idea how much time he had before the truck would be moving again. He felt bad for the skunk. But he couldn't see him, and he didn't know how to help an invisible burning skunk anyway. He had to look out for number one.

Rusty got to work.

TIM

"Oh, you're so dumb, Timothy; why'd you go and say that? Now she's gonna think you're desperate. You big dumb-dumb head, Timothy." Tim was berating himself as he and Scarlett headed to the executive offices of the Mega SuperMart.

"Don't be so hard on yourself," Scarlett said.

It was nice of her to try to cheer him up, but there was no point. *I'll be your Snuffleupagus?* Why had he said that? *I love you?* That was not what cool guys said. Tim knew he'd never be like them, but he also didn't want to chase away his one true love. He wondered what Sandy was doing now.

"Maybe I should go check on her?" he said.

"No," Scarlett said firmly. "If there's one thing women can't stand, it's a guy who thinks he has to check up on her and is always up in her business. It's controlling, and she'll never trust you if you don't trust her."

That made sense, but still.

"It's just...I miss her already."

That was true. That morning, Tim never would have imagined he'd even meet Sandy Newman, much less reach for a higher plane of existence with her. How could he not miss her now?

"Tim." Scarlett stepped in front of him. She was slightly taller than he was, which wasn't saying much, since Tim only stood about five foot seven. Her next words snapped him out of his reflections about their respective heights.

"We've got a situation here. It's real and it's now. There's a man with an assault rifle in your office *as we speak*. He's already shot one person. And we've got to go up there and convince him not to shoot anyone else. Focus, Tim. Our phone lines are down, and no one's cell phone works: we can't call the police. It's on us. On you. I'm happy for you and everything, really. But that'll all work itself out, but right now, we've got more important things to deal with."

Tim didn't believe her that anything was more important than Sandy. But he did have to admit that it was a serious situation.

"Well, I could fix the phones," Tim said.

"What? I thought the power surge must have fried them."

"No. I, uh, Mr. Spooner asked me to disable them earlier because he keeps getting harassing phone calls from this really mean guy. I disabled the phones so he wouldn't be able to call back. I can fix them. It'll just take a minute."

"That'd be awesome, Tim."

Tim glowed. Today was the day when people finally started to notice him! Hopefully Mr. Spooner would be proud too.

"I think I can make the cell phones work too," he told Scarlett.

"What?! How?"

"We have a cell phone–spiker machine in our office. It jams the signal so people can't comparison shop on their phones. Mr. Spooner says it's just a way of leveling the competition with the internet vendors."

"I think that's illegal."

"Oh no, Mr. Spooner says—"

"I'm sure he does," Scarlett said. "Look, Tim, fix the landline phones. Then call 911. I'm gonna go try to find reinforcements. I'll meet you in the office, and we can turn off the spiker and try to do something about the gunman."

Reinforcements? Hadn't she just told him it was up to him and her? Besides, he couldn't just call 911. It may have been an emergency, but the protocols were still there to follow. Plus, Mr. Spooner had made it clear that he couldn't call the cops if he wanted to keep his balls. And now it was even more important to keep them, what with his new status with Sandy and all.

"Oh geez, I...it's just...it's really clear in the manager handbook. The decision to call 911, unless there's a life-threatening medical emergency, can only be made by the manager. It's not my call. Oops, no pun intended."

"The manager is a hostage! It is your call! Do it, Tim. And then get up to the office. I'll be there as soon as I can."

Yipes, she was so scary when she was angry. But wait a minute. He was the assistant manager here. She didn't have the right to give him orders. And she had stolen from the store!

"Wait just a second. I'm still the assistant manager here."

"Tim, we don't have time for this."

"Just like we don't have time to discuss the certain light-fingered habits of certain employees? Because it's not just luxury children's furniture going missing. Towels and soap and PowEnergy bars and Xboxes and lots of other stuff besides. I can put two and two together. So don't think you're getting away scot-free! You want to talk about what's important? I'm still the assistant manager."

"Not now, Tim!"

Yipes! She sure was scary.

"If you want to fire me after this, fine—fire me. But that baby crib was damaged and going back to the warehouse to probably get thrown away, 'cause that's how this place rolls. I'm sorry. I had a need, and I took it. I sure as hell can't afford a three-hundred-dollar crib on what I'm getting paid. It's not like I was jacking Xboxes by the pallet. In fact, I don't know what you're talking about with the other stuff, but that wasn't me. Now can we please try to solve this problem?"

Tim bit his lip. He needed to stay in control. But she had just said he could fire her if he wanted—it wasn't strictly true; only Mr. Spooner had that power—but if she didn't know that, maybe it would keep her from being so bossy.

"All right, we can solve this problem," Tim said. "But we might have to have a performance-review meeting when it's all said and done. And I can't promise you you'll keep your job."

"Yeah, okay, whatever. Please, Tim. The phones."

Well, that was settled then. Tim adjusted his tie and went to fix the phones. But he wasn't going to usurp Mr. Spooner's authority and call 911. Scarlett wasn't the boss of him. No, sir. That was still Mr. Spooner's call to make. But to check with Mr. Spooner first, he was going to have to face the gunman.

The phone panel was behind the customer-service desk. He'd be able to glimpse the front door. Maybe he'd be able to see Sandy. The thought cheered Tim greatly. If he could see her, why, he'd be able to do almost anything. Even talk down a crazy gunman. At least it wasn't terrorists.

The Customer Service Department was normally where Tim spent a big part of his day. Servicing customers' problems really put an extra skip in his step. But today was not a normal day. If he could just fix the phones and save Mr. Spooner, then he could get back to...to servicing Sandy. He plugged all the lines back in, double-checked that the colors of the plugs matched the colors of the outlets, then headed for the office.

He looked back toward the front doors. He could see Sandy, her blond head shining like a beacon of hope. She was standing on a table by the café, waving something over her head. A sweater? No, that wouldn't make sense. A sea of people surrounded her, listening to her spread the word, no doubt. Gosh, what a lady.

A staccato burst of gunfire broke him out of his reverie. How long had he been standing there watching her? He swallowed. He fixed Sandy's face, her hair, and her smile in his mind. If he was about to get shot, it was a good memory with which to die. Tim squared his shoulders, tightened the knot of his tie, and climbed the stairs to the office.

LEE

Lee Rigg's life had complicated since arriving in the office. First of all, security was not there. The old guy claimed that the hot chick had gone to get them, but she had been gone a while and Lee was starting to wonder if she had just runnoft. It confirmed his general view of women, and it did not help him in bringing his prisoner to justice.

His prisoner was another problem. This was pretty clearly his office. Nothing about it shouted child abductor. And the child abductor in question—Mitch Spooner, that was his name—kept shouting how he wasn't one. Lee wished there were citizens' Miranda rights. The guy wouldn't shut up about his innocence. The hardest part was that Lee couldn't help believing him a little bit. Spooner was obviously a pretty cool dude. In other circumstances, they'd probably have been friends. Lee didn't want to think bad of him, which was probably exactly what a manipulative child abductor would want.

Lee needed to think, to figure things out. Vigilante justice was a lot harder than Bruce Willis made it look. But concentration was impossible. At first, the old guy—Clem, he was called— kept trying to get him to put his gun down. Like that was gonna happen. He was starting to think that this Clem guy might be a commie-pacifist wuss. He wondered if maybe he should arrest him as well. That was another thing he needed to figure out. But then he found that he could shut Clem up by waving his gun at him; it worked on Mitch as well. So that was good. Guns ruled. His probation officer was probably going to take a different view, but Lee couldn't worry about that. As long as he had the gun in his hands, he was in control.

But now the goddamn phone wouldn't stop ringing. It was impossible to concentrate. He wanted to answer it, just to make it stop ringing, but if he answered it, it would distract him from the problems at hand. And if he let Clem or Mitch answer it, then it was a variable he couldn't control.

"Can't you silence that thing?"

Mitch answered, "Sorry, no. Company policy, no ring silencers. Do you want me to answer it?"

"Yes. But don't. I'll answer it. Stay where you are, or I'll blow your balls off. Both of you. You know how gentle the action is on this thing."

Lee moved over to the desk, keeping his gun wedged under his arm. Mitch was slumped in a chair in front of the desk, clutching his shoulder. Lee didn't feel sorry—but hoped he hadn't misread the situation. Clem was seated in another chair, over by the door. He was sitting quietly, with his hands folded in his lap. Old fella probably needed a nap. Lee could see them both. And they could both see his gun. They wouldn't try anything. He picked up the phone.

"Please hold for C. Franklin Wallace," a feminine voice told him.

"Huh? Who are you?"

"What? This is C. Franklin Wallace. Is this Mitch Spooner?"

"No, he's, uh, on the crapper right now. I'm Lee Rigg."

"Well, Rigg, you have exactly ten seconds to get Mitch Spooner on this phone or else."

"Or else what? I don't think too much of your tone, bud."

Mitch was waving his good arm and motioning for Lee to give him the phone. Fat chance.

"Or else you're gonna be fired! Jesus Christ, you're even more witless than that last idiot I spoke to."

"Oh yeah? Well guess what. I don't even work here, asshole, so good luck firing me. Who's the idiot now?"

Lee didn't get to hear the reply because Mitch had leapt up and grabbed the phone away from him.

"Mr. Wallace, sir? Mitch Spooner here. Sorry, sir. I—"

A string of profanity interrupted whatever Mitch had been about to say. Lee didn't wait for it to finish; he raised his gun and squeezed the trigger. The result was instantaneous: the phone was like an icicle that, having let go of the high edge of a roof, plummeted several stories and splintered into a thousand shards on the frozen asphalt below. Fragments of plastic showered Mitch, who shielded himself with the receiver, which was the only bit that remained intact.

"What the hell'd you do that for?!" Mitch yelled.

"That guy was an asshole. I did you a favor, which is more than you deserve. Now sit down. And shut up."

"A favor? That guy is in charge of the whole goddamn SuperGroup. You probably just cost me my job."

"You got bigger problems than that, you prick. And you lost your job when you took those kids. You're lucky I don't do to you what I did to that phone. Now sit down. And shut up, 'fore I change my mind."

"For Christ's sake, I keep telling you: I didn't kidnap anyone!"

"And I keep saying sit down and shut up!"

Lee waved his gun and finally got some obedience. Christ, no respect for anything but guns. Fortunately, he had a big one.

"What are you smiling at, old man?" Lee was peevish, and Clem's serene smile stuck in his craw like a grasshopper in his truck's grill.

"Oh nothing," Clem said. "It's just, that's the first thing you've said that makes sense."

"Sit down and shut up? You're damned right!"

"No, that Mr. Wallace is an asshole. And that Mr. Spooner here has bigger problems than his job."

Lee was unsure what to do with that statement. It sounded like a compliment. He scratched his head and then said, "You're damn straight. Now shut up!"

The door opened. Finally. Hot chick was back with some reinforcements! Thank god.

Lee was disappointed to see a short, slender man in a white short-sleeved shirt and black tie step into the room. This guy was not reinforcements. The guy's tie was knotted so tightly Lee wondered how he could breathe.

"Who the hell are you?" Lee asked, waving his gun.

"Yipes! Don't shoot! I'm Tim, Timothy Phillips. Sir. I'm the assistant manager."

"Assistant manager? You head the security team here?" Lee asked, just in case. This guy was more likely to be the coach of a powder-puff-football team than head of a security team. But things were not always what they seemed. Especially today.

"Security team? We don't...no, I'm not." Tim Phillips stopped talking. The whole business was fishy. Bruce Willis sure made vigilante justice look a lot easier than it was all right. But if it was easy, then every country would be as great as America!

"Well, what the hell are you doing here?" Lee asked Tim.

"You're right; I should go. I—"

"Hold on, Timmy," Mitch said. "Didn't I tell you to take care of the phones?"

"I...yes, Mr. Spooner, sir."

"Well, why the hell did my office phone start ringing minutes ago? You useless piece of garbage. I gave you one simple task, and you find a way to fuck it up. And now you pop in here like a turkey with its head cut off. Jesus Christ, Timmy! I told you it was—"

"That's enough," Lee said. Whoa, his voice had gotten deep. Then he realized that Clem had said the same thing at the same time. Their synchronicity had taken him by surprise. He looked at Clem, who shrugged. Tim had visibly shrunk under the barrage of verbal abuse. Lee wasn't sure how Tim fit into this whole picture, but one thing was clear: he didn't deserve that abuse from a child abductor.

Lee went on, "That's enough out of you, cockhead. You don't have the right to criticize anyone else. Stop being such a dick.

You've got enough problems. From now on, Tim's under my protection. C'mon over, Tim."

Tim hesitated, then crossed over to the desk and stood just behind Lee. Lee didn't like the idea of someone standing behind him, even someone as puny as Tim.

"Stand next to me, Tim. You, Spooner. Apologize."

"Oh c'mon, for what? Giving my employee direct feedback; you don't understand management, man. You've probably never been in my position, where you're in charge of—"

Lee had heard enough; he rolled his eyes and raised the rifle to his shoulder. He got the desired response.

"Ah, mister," Tim said to Lee. "Mr. Spooner doesn't need to apologize to me. He's been under a lot of stress lately, and I'm sure he didn't mean it. I should have left the phones the way he told me to."

"What? Gimme a break. Don't make excuses for this guy," Lee said. "Otherwise, dicks like him will walk all over you your whole life and inhibit your freedom. Now, tell this piece of crap to apologize."

"Oh, I don't..."

"See, man, Timmy doesn't want to. Right, Timmy? Plus, he effed up and he knows it." Mitch Spooner had a grin on his face. It took a certain amount of control for Lee not to shoot him again. At least he was no longer conflicted about arresting him.

"Shut up, prick face," Lee said. "Grandpa, tell him."

"Mr. Spooner isn't treating you like a good boss should or would," Clem said.

"What would you know about it, you senile sonofabitch? Watch what you say, or you'll be out of a job."

"I said quiet, you." Lee waved the gun for silence and turned to Tim. "Ask for an apology."

"I...uh...well...geez," Tim stammered. "Okay, I guess, it would be nice, if maybe you didn't yell at me quite so much. I was only doing what I thought would be best for you. And maybe if you'd just trust me a little more, that...golly...that'd be nice?"

"No, Tim," Lee said. "That's not how you ask for an apology. Makes you seem weak if you say it like that. Strong response, that's what you need. Otherwise, you sound like those liberal wussies in Washington who bend over and take it every time some Arab says so. Now, repeat after me: Mitch, you piece of crap."

"Mitch, yipes, golly, mister. I don't like to use curse words."

Who was this guy? He was trying to do him a favor.

"Oh c'mon. It's the only thing dicks like this guy will understand."

"No, I try to live a good, clean life, and so, nope, I can't change now, even if you do have a gun."

"God dammit, Tim. I'm on your side!"

"And please don't take the Lord's name in vain," Tim Phillips said, straightening up and facing Lee.

Well, he had tried. If the wimp didn't want a lesson in toughness, Lee had other things to worry about.

"Fine, have it your way," he told Tim. "You can sit in that chair over there."

Lee pointed to a chair against the wall over by Clem.

"Now where the frig is that hot chick and the security personnel?"

SCARLETT

Reinforcements. The problem was that Clem hadn't told her how or where to find them, or rather, him. She had been lucky finding Tim. But he seemed to think he could fix the phones. So that was something, even if it did get her fired. How would she get a job somewhere else if she were fired for stealing? What if Tim pressed charges? Shit. He probably wouldn't, but still. If she lost her job, she would lose her apartment. Tips from Applebee's didn't get you very far. And if she lost her place, then what would that mean for Rose and Julius? God dammit. Scarlett shook herself. Now wasn't the time to worry about that. She had to help Clem. To help Clem she needed to find the government agent. Just going to the office alone wouldn't do any good. How long would it take for the police to get there after Tim called?

She headed past the checkout counters and scanned the crowd. The preacher woman was up on a table, doing... something. She was waving her sweater around and dancing. It was borderline suggestive. But the crowd seemed to be in rapt attention. So there was that. Scarlett didn't see the government agent. How was she supposed to find him?

Scarlett ran down Aisle 6: Greeting Cards. She reached the end and stopped. This wasn't the way to do it. Stop and take stock of the situation, not run around panicked; that was what they said you should do in an emergency. Scarlett thought. Had Clem told her anything? Something useful about the store that she was supposed to remember? No. She had always been too busy talking about herself and her problems. She had to stay in the moment. Clem hadn't told her anything. Had there ever been a pointless training video about it? Tim had them watch a lot of pointless training videos. But no, there hadn't been. A video about how to react if you or a child got trapped in a refrigerator, yes—that was because of poor little Alice Sansom, a tragedy to be sure, but Scarlett had not learned much from that video—but no video about how to find a questionable government agent. Wait. A refrigerator. That's where the gunman had said he had found Mitch Spooner with the kids! It wasn't much, but it was all she had. Scarlett headed for Home Appliances.

It was especially dark in that part of the store. There was only the faint light from the emergency-backup system. It was eerie. There were droplets of some liquid on the flood at the end of the refrigerator aisle. Scarlett realized with disgust that it must have been Mitch Spooner's blood. Her stomach churned a little. That sort of thing didn't usually bother her, but in this half light, and after all that'd happened, the sight was chilling. The fact that she hadn't eaten in forever probably didn't help. Focus. Scarlett took a deep breath and straightened her back. She walked down the row of refrigerators. The features fridges had these days! A touch screen with smart technology? Three doors? Why would you waste your money on crap like that? Scarlett shook her head.

Halfway down the row, there was a refrigerator door open. In the shadows, it was hard to tell, but maybe it was red? Scarlett could smell something acrid in the air. Maybe a bullet had damaged one of the refrigerators' compressors? But this smelled like smoke. It was sulfurous, like fireworks almost. Weird. The smell grew stronger as Scarlett approached the refrigerator. Her breath got shallow, and only partly because of the smoky smell. She was scared. Why was she scared? What was there to be afraid of? The Mega SuperMart was lots of horrible things, but scary wasn't one of them. Not usually, at least. But looking for an unknown government investigator in the murky gloom of the emergency-backup lights was creepy—no one could deny that. But she couldn't be a baby about it.

She thought of Clem. He needed her help. She thought of the missing children. The best way to help them was to get the mess in the office sorted out. She had to pull it together. She peered around the door of the refrigerator and found herself looking down a stairway. There was a light on at the bottom. The hell?

Scarlett knocked, somewhat ineffectually, on the refrigerator door and called down, "Hello!"

No one answered, but she thought she might have heard movement. Scarlett took another deep breath, resisted the urge to cough, and headed down the stairs.

DIRK BLADE

It had been a long day for Dirk Blade. He was ready to get out of this store, out of this Podunk town. The only thing he'd had to eat all day was the 4:00 a.m. breakfast at Denny's. It hadn't been very good, and boy, had it wreaked havoc on his GI tract. He still hadn't touched his e-cigarette.

Everyone wanted to focus on the runaway kid. Dirk Blade understood that. Missing kids freaked people out. Not Dirk Blade. Other people. Dirk Blade was cool as a mountain stream in springtime. And by itself, a missing kid wasn't that big of a deal: the kid had a good head on his shoulders and had proved quite useful. He'd shown Dirk Blade the underground office where the private investigator was currently standing, photographing everything he could. The problem was that there wasn't much there; it looked like a bomb had gone off. Destroying evidence: that was another felony. Even still, Dirk Blade had found one piece of evidence that was pretty damning. It was a falsified order slip, signed, rather messily, by, surprise, surprise: Timothy Phillips. Dirk Blade was gonna nail him like a thesis to a church door. No one wanted to talk about systemic fraud. Wasn't a "sexy" crime. Well, Dirk Blade would show them.

He was thirsty. But his flask was empty. He thought about a smoke, but the e-cigarette was doing its job; he wasn't tempted. Smoke. He had found the smoking ruin of another faux-mahogany desk, but what he needed to find was a smoking gun, to back up the admittedly pretty strong circumstantial evidence of tax evasion and fraud. But to prove it, he'd need more than a scrap of paper and a gut feeling, which, thankfully, had calmed down after the near disaster earlier.

231

It had been a strange day. Squirrels running through the store, runaway kids. A strange day indeed.

The issue with the runaway kid was that it made everyone else freak out. Certain stereotypes existed about lone men in trench coats and fedoras. But Dirk Blade wasn't going to change his style. Trench coats were dead useful: he could fit so much in his pockets; though, he had to admit, the utility was lessened if you forgot your side arm. And his fedora, well, he wasn't about to give that up. It was classic, and classic never went out of style. He smoothed his thin moustache with his thumb and forefinger. To be the part, you had to look the part, and Dirk Blade looked the part.

Leaving his nine mill at home had been a mistake. But hindsight was twenty-twenty, and he was investigating a white-collar crime: he couldn't have known. Not that his wife wouldn't give him an earful when she saw him. Nothing he could do about that. Besides, she was going to have such a conniption about the two grand he had given those two kids that maybe she wouldn't even bother second-guessing him. He could expense the two grand though. He really hoped he could.

The store manager was in deep trouble. And only some of that had to do with the bullet in his shoulder. Dirk Blade could tell by looking at the math. Someone had stolen hundreds of thousands in the last quarter alone. And he wasn't even being very careful about hiding it. The bomb to destroy the evidence had been crude, childish even. But it hadn't gotten rid of everything. He had the scrap of paper with a name on it. This Timothy Phillips should have done a better job covering his tracks.

There was a knock from above, someone called out "Hello," and then there were footsteps coming down the stairs. Dirk Blade couldn't have his cover blown. Not now, when he was so close to solving the case. There weren't many places to hide. So he tore a lampshade off a desk lamp and thrust it over his own head. He held perfectly still, looking inward. Not his best disguise but not so bad for improvisation.

"Hello?" a voice said from up the stairs. Dirk Blade continued to hold perfectly still. With any luck...

"Hello? Hello. Hey!"

The voice belonged to a young woman. Probably around twenty. Probably a looker. They usually were. Dirk Blade focused on remaining statue still.

"I can see you," the voice said. Dirk Blade held his breath.

"Seriously." The voice was nearer now. Dirk Blade hoped it was a bluff.

"What do you think I am? Blind?"

The young woman pulled the lampshade off his head. Not a bluff, then.

Dirk Blade took a look at his assailant. It was a young woman. She was indeed a looker. His age-by-voice-recognition skills were still sharp. He decided there was too much intelligence in her eyes to play dumb. So he tried to play it cool.

"Hello," he said.

"Are you the undercover agent?" she asked.

Hell's teeth! His cover was already blown. Probably those pricks over at the FBI. They never liked his solo skills. What if she worked for them? Wheels within wheels. But now was not the time to figure out how or why—he had to limit the damage.

"Who wants to know?"

"I do."

"And who are you?"

"I'm Scarlett. Now are you or are you not the undercover agent? Because if you are, I need your help. If you're not, I'm going to have to ask you to leave."

Dirk Blade's fingers twitched toward his jacket pocket, where his e-cigarette lay hidden. If he had had real cigarettes, he would have pulled them out, offered her one, then said, *The name's Blade. Dirk Blade. I'm a private investigator.*

But lacking real cigarettes, he was limited to, "Call me Dirk Blade. I'm a private investigator. What do you need, Scarlett? I'm in the middle of an important investigation—that is to say, I'm in the middle of an important case. So tell me what you need, and make it snappy."

"Well, Mr. Blade—"

"Please, call me Dirk Blade."

"Okay...Dirk Blade, is that your real name? Never mind. Doesn't matter. Look, we've got an armed gunman holding some hostages—"

"Terrorists?" Dirk Blade said, his heart revving up like an inline-eight waiting to drag race off a red light.

"No, it's just a moron with a gun."

Dirk Blade's heart eased off the throttle.

"I don't know that that's necessarily better," Scarlett continued. "Our security team is locked out, because we're in a Code Bobby on account of a couple of missing kids. Our telephone lines may or may not be down, and help is probably not coming for at least a little while. My colleague thinks—I can't believe I'm saying this to someone who just tried to pretend to be a lamp but—my colleague thinks you're the only one inside the store with the skills and knowledge to help us out of this situation."

Dirk Blade nodded slowly. He could work this to his advantage.

"All right, Scarlett, if that's *your* real name. I'll help. But in return, you gotta help me. You work here?"

"Yes."

"Great, then I want all you know about Timothy Phillips. He's been stealing from this store and from the government. He's been stealing from you."

"Tim?" Scarlett laughed. "Oh, really. How the tables have turned..."

She stopped speaking, and her face split into a wicked grin, eyebrows arched, danger flashing in her eyes. What was between her and Tim Phillips? Did it matter? It was times like these you had to ask just the right question. One false step meant the difference between solving the case and chasing your tail for weeks.

Before he could speak, Scarlett went on, "But, Mr.—Dirk Blade. Are you sure you've got it right? Tim is a real stickler for rules. And seems as innocent as a baby. Well, maybe a little less after today, but that's not important. I can't really see him stealing from the store."

Unfortunate information. It didn't fit the case he was building. Still Dirk Blade pressed on. "Maybe he's just pulled the wool over your eyes. I just saw him come up from here; well, I didn't see it, admittedly, but I have it on impeccable authority that your Tim was down here not a half hour ago, arranging papers. He ran across the wrong kids though and then got himself shot—not by the kids; that'd be absurd. Anyway, it'd take too long to explain now. Plus, I've got hard paper evidence. See?"

He waved the order slip in front of her. To his surprise and consternation, she grabbed it from him and took a look. She rolled her eyes.

"First of all: he's not 'my Tim,' so let's just nip that in the bud. Second of all: I don't know that this slip of paper 'proves' anything. And third: the guy who got shot? That's not Tim. That guy is named Mitch Spooner. And he's exactly the type who would try to steal a bunch of money and then pin it on someone else. I bet that's what happened."

Wheels within wheels within wheels! An open-and-shut case had just gotten a whole lot more open. Had she ever considered becoming a sleuth? Dirk Blade didn't ask; instead he pulled out the e-cigarette and offered the first puff to Scarlett.

"No. Gross. Plus, you can't smoke inside the store anyway. Not even e-cigarettes. Sorry."

Couldn't smoke in stores? It was an e-cigarette for Chrissakes. This was supposed to be America! Guess she wouldn't make that good of a sleuth after all. Without the proper alkaloid cocktail in your body, you couldn't do proper detective work. That was part of what had made this day so difficult. Alas. Dirk Blade spun the e-cigarette around his fingers, then stuffed it back into his pocket. It really had been a long day.

"So what do you want me to do?" he asked Scarlett.

"You're the private eye! Use your private eye skills to get the gun away from the nutcase!"

Dirk Blade wondered what sort of private investigators the young woman knew. He wished he had known them.

"You know I'm unarmed, right?" he said.

"What kind of a PI are you?"

Dirk Blade winced. That was a low blow. Leaving his nine millimeter home had been an oversight—he got that—but she didn't have to remind him.

"Look," Scarlett said, "can you just come with me and try to talk to this guy? He won't listen to us. Maybe he'll respect your authority."

Dirk Blade kind of doubted it. What authority? Typically, lone gunmen didn't think much of private investigators.

"You say this perp had Mitch Spooner with him? What about Tim Phillips?"

"Yeah, they both should be there; can you just hurry up, please?"

Maybe it was time to stop pussyfooting around and come out of the shadows, confront the elephant in the store, as it were.

"All right," said Dirk Blade. "I'll come."

BILLY

Three things happened when they pushed the door and stepped out into the sunshine. None of the three were what Billy might reasonably have expected. The first was that the small red squirrel darted between his legs and scampered under a big Golden Nuts Salted Snacks truck parked outside. That was good. That store was no place for a squirrel. Or children. As he had tried to tell his mom before they had left home. If only she had listened.

The second thing was a man who shouted, "No! Don't let it close! Aw, dammit!" Neither Billy nor Willow reacted quickly enough to keep the door open. Why would they? They had been trying to get out all morning. It slammed shut behind them. There wasn't even a handle on the outside to open it. There was no going back. Billy knew from the man's choice of swear word that this was a semiserious situation. Nothing dire but also nothing to take lightly.

The third thing was that he could smell a heavy scent of a sort of skunky, burnt cabbage. It reminded Billy of the way Thomas smelled. Thomas was his sister's boyfriend. She insisted to her parents that Thomas was just a friend, but Billy knew better. Thomas was a drummer in a bad band. He said things like "dude" and "word, bro" all the time. Billy was convinced he was a little dumber than average. Mary seemed to think he was "so cool" and "totally awesome." Billy was positive she became a little dumber around Thomas. Was getting progressively dumber just a part of growing up? He would avoid that fate for himself—there had to be a way.

The burning skunky, cabbagey smell was coming from three teenagers, two boys and a girl, who were leaning against a wall. The girl and one of the boys had red hair. They could have been brother and sister or cousins or something. The other boy had bad acne and was wearing a SuperMart apron. None of the three seemed to have avoided the get-dumber-as-you-get-older fate. They were giggling and talking about the squirrel.

"Dude," the acne-faced one said. "It was a squirrel."

"I know. I know. That's so rad," the other boy said.

The girl was compulsively giggling. Billy shook his head. Teenagers. He turned from them to the only other person there. The guy who had yelled and sworn. He had a round face and short black hair. He was big in all his dimensions.

"Kids!" Even his voice was big.

"Yeah," Billy said. The guy was apparently a master of the obvious.

"Hell, I hoped you were store employees. Where is everyone anyway? I was supposed to unload a half hour ago. But the only people here are Tweedledum and the Ginger Twins. And they're too blazed to tell pretzels from wood chips. What's going on in there?"

Billy wasn't sure how far he could trust this guy. Trusting Dirk Blade, Private Investigator, had been a mixed bag, like on Halloween when you dug your hand into your bowl hoping for Swedish Fish or Sour Patch Kids and ended up pulling out ginger chews that you got from the MacPhersons. Stupid MacPhersons. But what was this guy's angle?

Billy also wasn't sure, now that he was out of the store, that he was necessarily better off. Though at least he hadn't seen a gun outside yet. The flaw in his plan was obvious. This would have been the right move if he were still running away. But now that he was decided against it, he had placed an impassable barrier between himself and his mom. He was trying to figure out what to say when Willow spoke up.

"It's like this, mister: There was a power outage, and in the dark, we got separated from our parents. The store employees are dealing with the power, I guess. We saw this door and came out. Plus, there was a guy with a gun in there. So we thought it was smarter to get out."

Captain Obvious struck again, with expletive-laced eloquence. Willow, shocked, widened her eyes and formed a big O with her mouth. Indeed, from the man's choice of swear word, Billy could tell that the seriousness of the situation had ratcheted up tenfold; he raised an eyebrow in acknowledgment.

"Scuse my language. It's just...that's crazy. A gunman in there? Is it terrorists? I mean, you hear about these things on the news, but you never think...wait, where are the cops? I've been here a half hour, and I haven't been able to get in. Has anyone called them? We gotta get you back to your parents. Are you brother and sister?"

The man was panicking a bit. It wasn't reassuring. He was a grown-up, so he probably wasn't too bright—that was a given. His diction and his cadence indicated he probably wasn't a man of great emotional depth either.

"No, we're friends," Willow said.

"And dude, we're totally dating; we're not twins," the redheaded boy said, putting his arm around the redheaded girl, who giggled.

"I wasn't talking to you nitwits," the man said. To Billy and Willow he said, "Are your parents inside?"

"Yeah," Willow answered. Billy was glad that she was doing the talking. This guy hadn't impressed him much so far, and he would have been tempted to respond with sarcasm.

"Oh, man. Okay. Look, we gotta get you back with them. My name's Pete, by the way. I drive that truck. Why don't you come with me, and we'll walk around to the front. I bet that's where everyone went. If there's a gunman in there, they'll be trying to get out."

Billy looked at Willow. They knew the rule about not going anywhere with strangers. Pete was obviously not very bright, but also, he didn't seem like a bad guy—for a grown-up. Willow shrugged.

"All right," Willow said.

"Yeah, okay," Billy said. "But don't touch us, or we'll scream."

"And I'm a really good screamer," Willow said.

Pete held up his hands. "Look, kids. I'm just trying to help."

"Now you three, stoner triplets." Pete turned to the three teenagers. Billy didn't see what they had to do with rocks, except they seemed as dumb as rocks and about as active as rocks too. The girl was still giggling about the squirrel. The squirrel had disappeared under the truck. Billy was glad. He liked squirrels. In fact, the biggest positive about the day, as far as he could tell, was the large number of squirrels he had seen.

"Hey, listen up!" Pete yelled at the teenagers. They stopped giggling.

"Dude," the pimply one said. Billy could read his nametag. He was Aidan, apparently. "Dude, stop killing our buzz."

What did bees have to do with anything? Seriously, Billy would have sworn teenagers and grown-ups were speaking an entirely different language sometimes. He'd have to start cataloging nature metaphors as well as swears, if he ever wanted to understand them. He wasn't sure that he did.

"Yeah, dude, not chill, bro," the redheaded boy said.

"Listen, meatheads. What you're doing isn't 'cool' or whatever. It's dumb. And it makes you dumb and boring. But since you're here and obviously too lazy to go anywhere, you're gonna watch my truck. And if anyone from the store comes out, you're going to keep them here until I get back. And then you're going to help unload. Or else. Got it?"

"Yeah, whatever," the girl said and flipped up the hood of her sweatshirt.

"Good," Pete said. "I'm taking these kids around the store to find their parents."

So with Pete the truck driver, Billy and Willow set off on a circumnavigation of the Mega SuperMart. It was huge. Billy hadn't really appreciated just how big it was from inside it. He was also hungry.

"Hey, Pete, do you have any food?" he asked. "I haven't eaten since breakfast."

Pete was looking at his cell phone.

"Damned thing can't find a signal. What? Food? No. Sorry, kid. Hey, what are your names anyway?"

"Oh I'm Bil—Will."

"I'm Willow."

"That's funny," Pete said. "Your names are almost the same. You're sure you're not brother and sister? Just a joke, guys. Sorry, I don't have any food. But once we get you guys back with your parents, I'm sure they'll get you some."

Billy swallowed. He had been trying not to think about that. Sure, liberation from the tyranny of his mom wasn't all it was cracked up to be, but she was going to be mad. Epically mad. Historically mad. He glanced at Willow. She didn't seem too worried. She was looking up at the sky as she walked.

"I think I can see a hawk," she said.

Billy squinted up into the bright sky. There was some kind of bird up there, but it was too far away to tell what kind.

When they rounded the corner to the front side of the store, there were two guys walking across the parking lot. They were big and burly. They could have been Pete's brothers or cousins or something.

"Hey!" Pete called out to them.

The two men headed toward them. They both had shaved heads, which, combined with their sheer size, made them kind of intimidating. They were carrying boxes of something.

"Pizza!" Willow said, clearly pleased by this turn of events.

Billy shared her excitement. Hopefully these new guys were sharers. Billy wasn't really much of a sharer himself, but that had more to do with his dumb sister than his moral code.

"You guys work here?" Pete asked. Billy could tell by the tone of his voice that Pete didn't think it likely that they did.

"Sure do," said one.

"We hope anyways. We were a little late today. Got locked out. Don't know why. A girl—cashier—on the inside was yelling at us to go get pizza, so we did. Don't know why. Maybe there's some kind of surprise party no one told us about or something. Course that don't make much sense, if they're not gonna let us in. But if there's one thing Rog and Sam can do, it's go for pizza. Right, Sam?" The one elbowed the other one in the side, in a friendly sort of way.

"You know it, Rog. So we went and got pizza. Don't see how it's helpful though, seeing how we can't get inside," Sam said.

Billy got the impression that Rog and Sam might be particularly dull, even for grown-ups. But they didn't seem particularly harmful for it. Plus, they had pizza.

"So what're you guys doin' out here," Rog asked. "You want some pizza?"

Yep, Rog and Sam were all right.

"Yes, please," Billy said before Pete had a chance to mess it up. Sam set a pizza down in front of Billy and Willow.

"Pepperoni!" Billy said. "The best!"

But Willow was picking the pepperoni off of her piece. He gave her a quizzical look.

"I'm not supposed to eat processed meat," she told him.

"What?" Billy said. "Pepperoni's awesome! When was the last time you tried it?"

"I haven't tried it. My parents say it's not good for me."

Billy couldn't believe what he was hearing.

"Well, they're wrong. You gotta try it. It's delicious."

Willow picked up a piece and stared at it.

"...And so the store's in lockdown, apparently. I don't know if it's because of the gunman or these guys." Pete was talking to Rog and Sam. Billy almost choked on his pizza. Pete wasn't half as dumb as he looked: he was on to them!

"Geez," said Rog.

"Wow," said Sam.

"So what do you guys think?" Pete asked.

"The lockdown is for missing kids, no doubt," Sam said. "How's the pizza, guys?"

"Good," Billy said.

"I like pepperoni!" Willow said, popping another piece into her mouth.

"Hey, Sam."

"Yeah, Rog?"

"D'you think that instead of saying pizza, Scarlett was saying police?"

"Hmm, that would make more sense. Unless she knew we'd meet these guys out here. She might have. She's pretty smart."

"Yeah, I guess we'll never know."

"Can't know the unknowable," Sam said, nodding and smiling, his dark skin punctuated by his bright-white teeth.

"But shouldn't we call the police anyway? You know, knowing what we know now? I've been trying, but my cell phone won't work here," Pete told them.

"Oh yeah," Sam said. "Cell phones don't work here."

"Mitch Spooner's got one of those cell-jammer things. Doesn't want customers comparison shopping on their phones," Rog said. He had picked up a piece of pizza and seemed to be trying to finish it in the least number of bites possible.

"Huh. Thought that was illegal," Pete said. "Well. What do we do? Should we go find a landline? Drive down the road? We wouldn't have to go far."

"Naw," Rog said.

"Yeah," Sam said. "We've found the kids. Fastest way to end the Code Bobby will be to show they're out here."

"What about the gunman though?" Pete asked.

"Is it confirmed that there's a gunman? There are lots of things that can go bang."

"We saw him!" Willow said, indignant. Billy had given up trying to correct grown-ups when they were wrong; it wasn't like they listened to him anyway. Plus, there was pizza.

"Well, if there *is* a gunman, the last thing we need is to get the blue hats in here. They'll just make things worse. Probably end up shooting me or some BS," Sam said.

Billy knew what BS stood for. The situation was still grave.

"We'll deal with him," Rog said. His face changed from open and happy to dark and menacing. Sam cracked his knuckles and pounded his fist into his hand.

Billy didn't really see how that would help against a gun, but he was still glad he wasn't the gunman.

"You kids done?" Pete asked.

Billy nodded, and Willow licked her fingers.

"Well, let's go then."

They walked with Rog and Sam over toward the front door.

"I guess it's over," Willow said in a whisper to Billy.

"Yeah," Billy said. His mom was going to be so mad.

"What's the matter, Will? Didn't you have fun?"

"Yeah," Billy said. "I did. It's just, my mom might actually kill me for this."

"Oh," Willow said. "Don't worry. I'll tell her you were helping me. I'll pretend I was lost."

"You don't have to lie."

"I don't mind," Willow said. "Besides. It was fun. And it's not a total lie. And it'd be better for me if you weren't grounded forever so we could play again sometime soon."

"Yeah, I guess you're right."

"Of course I am."

Well, he couldn't argue with her if she was right.

They had crossed the parking lot and were beside the front doors. Rog and Sam were peering in. They looked funny with their noses scrunched up against the glass.

"Whoa, Pete, buddy, check this out! No, kids. Not for you, why don't you, uh, see how high you can count or something."

Billy ignored them and went to see what was so important inside. But before he could get to the window, he heard a scream.

"Biiiilllllllyyyyyy!"

RUSTY

The scent of nuts wafted down to Rusty as he chased wires and cables along the underside of the trailer. It was heady, intoxicating even. It was the sort of smell that made a squirrel forget all about electricity. The trailer had a stiff, metal exoskeleton, which was almost as tough to crack as some nuts. But the underbelly had some vulnerabilities. It would be short work to bust through, and then he'd be like that duck, what's-his-name, the one who bathed in piles of gold. Ducks were weird. It'd be like that, except with nuts. All the nuts! Shelled, roasted, salted. Say what you will about humans, but they did their nuts right. The work of a moment...but then how would he get them back to his family? He didn't have pockets. No, he had to stay strong, resist the temptation, and stick to the plan.

Rusty pawed at a collection of wiring. He had to disable enough of the coupling apparatus to be able to loose the trailer at a moment's notice yet leave enough so that it wouldn't uncouple at the *wrong* moment. He picked out a red-and-yellow wire. They reminded him of snakes. How did it go? Yellow before red, you're as good as dead? Red before yellow, you're a fine fellow? No, no, no. It was: red or yellow, just stay the hell away from snakes! That was definitely it. But did mnemonics of that sort apply when you weren't dealing with serpents? There was so much he didn't know. So much Raccoon hadn't told him.

Rusty had spent hours watching the humans over at Dave's Diesel. So he had some familiarity with engines and commonly associated problems. He knew the theory of the carburetor, and that it didn't really apply to diesels. He had a solid working knowledge of trailers and how they attached and detached, which, together with the schematics Raccoon had supplied, gave Rusty a pretty good overall picture of what he was up against. Of course, Raccoon had also provided schematics of the store, and those had only been partially useful. The problem with the truck and trailer was that everything was built to human scale. And Rusty knew that even Dave himself couldn't really work on these machines without tools. But failure was not an option. He had to do the best he could with what he had. Rusty picked up both wires and bit clean through them. Nothing. No explosion. No poison. Not even a hint of electricity. No rabies. Rabies? Rusty checked his tail. Still bushy. Silky. Sexy. All good.

The bolts were going to prove more difficult. Not even Beaver could chew through solid metal. Rusty wrestled with the head of the bolt, but it was unyielding. Probably overtorqued. Dave would not approve. Nuts! It didn't budge. Tools. Rusty had always assumed they were just another crutch of weak humans. But maybe they were more like pockets, mostly unnecessary, but at times, pretty sweet. Sweet, sweet pockets. Or an arc welder, for example, he could really use an arc welder. He could forgo the bolts altogether and just cut the main attachment point clean off. That'd make it so much easier. Maybe tools *could* be useful. Dave used tools, and he was just about the only human Rusty really respected. The diagrams had shown a basic tool kit stashed right forward. If he could get in there, maybe he'd have a chance.

He scampered over. Yep. Right where it was supposed to be, held closed with just a flimsy plastic buckle. Rusty placed his hind paws on the buckle and braced his back against the underside of the trailer. He pushed; the buckle budged but didn't give. Rusty coiled and sprung. The buckle was no match for his squirrel strength. The tool kit sprang open, and various socket wrenches and spanners tumbled to the ground in a metallic waterfall. There was no arc welder. So much for the easy way.

Rusty leapt down, searching for the three-quarter-inch spanner.

"Dude, do you see the squirrel?"

"Yeah, ohmygod, he's, like, humping that wrench!"

"Dude, it's so funny."

Rusty ignored the adolescent humans. Their brains weren't fully formed, so they couldn't be held responsible for what they were saying. A door slammed open, and a shadow passed across Rusty. He froze. Hawks! No. It was just a male human. Adult. He and the adolescent humans began to engage in some sort of banter. Rusty ignored them and resumed his search. Five-eighths inch. Ten millimeter. Adjustable. That'd work in a pinch but...

The truck's engine rumbled to life. Rusty could feel the vibrations pulsing through the ground. He was running out of time. Three-sixteenths inch. Another ten millimeter? Sockets, useless without a driver. The truck stalled out. A male human's voice cursed from the cockpit. He had gained precious seconds. He pushed sockets and spanners this way and that. The engine rumbled to life again. Aha! There it was. Three-quarter inch! Rusty wrenched and tugged. It was no easy task for a twelve-ounce squirrel to pick up a twenty-ounce spanner. But he managed. The truck's gearbox groaned and ground. Dave would not have been pleased. But by the time the truck lurched forward, Rusty was in place, leveraging mechanical advantage to loosen some bolts and to remove others completely. Dave would have been proud. The truck picked up speed, but Rusty stayed perched underneath the trailer. So close to his goal. So close to the nuts.

CLEM

Lee Rigg was the only one who moved, pacing back and forth behind Mitch Spooner's desk. He had pulled the shades up, and the store behind him was split into light and dark halves according to where the power was working. Lee Rigg stopped pacing and stood, the light half of the store on his left, dark on his right, drumming his fingers on the stock of the assault weapon. Who knew what was going through the man's head? He was dimmer than the lights at that new, overpriced French bistro downtown, and his gun was way overpowered—like a hand drill driven by a jet engine. The man by himself wasn't probably all that dangerous. With a gun like that though...

Mitch Spooner was slumped in a chair opposite the desk. He was watching Lee pace, and Clem could tell he was looking for an opening, a way to get out of this mess. Criminy. Didn't he realize he had already been shot once? That this wasn't a game? That they could all be one movement, one wrong word away from another bullet? And maybe this time it wouldn't just hit a shoulder? Mitch was as dumb as Lee Rigg. But at least he didn't have a gun. Of course, who was to say he himself wasn't the dumbest one out of the bunch—he had volunteered to come up here with them.

There had been a moment, after they had both defended Tim, when Clem found himself allied with Lee. It had been odd, but it had been a moment. And it meant, maybe, that there was a chance to reason with him. It didn't seem likely, but he had to try.

"Lee. Mr. Rigg," he began.

Lee Rigg swung the gun on Clem.

"No, please. Put the gun down."

There was a bang and a crack. Some drywall plaster from the wall a foot above Clem's head crumbled and fell on him.

"Whoa, frig! Sorry! Well, not really. When I say quiet, I mean quiet."

Clem didn't dare brush the drywall powder off his head. Fear gripped him. He could feel it physically, creeping up through his stomach, toward his heart. His head was hot, but empty, like he hadn't had enough to eat or had too much to drink. He didn't move a muscle. He'd heard some people felt fear more— stronger or more often or both—as they got older; others felt it less. Clem felt it about the same. But he felt it, and it wasn't pleasant. Death, it was coming, sooner or later, for all of them, and he wasn't blind to the fact that his mortality was closer than most people's. But not like this. It was so pointless. So stupid. It'd be a story in the papers, and then everyone would forget about them. Just another tragic footnote. Else. She wouldn't forget. But he wouldn't be there to comfort her.

Clem felt the tear form before it was actually hanging on the corner of his eye. He didn't dare to reach up to brush it away. Next to him, Tim was whispering something under his breath. Praying? Well, no atheists in a foxhole. Else. She would probably be getting lunch together now. Soup and half a sandwich. It'd been the same for fifty years, and why not? It was a great combination.

Thinking of his wife was calming, but it didn't make him happy. If Lee Rigg was that quick on the draw, when an old man just said his name, what hope was there that this wouldn't end terribly? Damn it all.

Time ticked by, and no one new came through the office door; tension filled the room like a balloon, expanding, pressing everywhere, filling the gaps, making the office smaller and closer than it already was. Clem felt it at the base of his neck, in between the tops of his shoulder blades. He tried to sit up a little straighter and leaned his head back, pressing it against the wall. It didn't help much. Bits of drywall tumbled from his head onto his shoulders and to his lap. His breath was shallow, and so was everyone else's. The remnants of the phone lay scattered about the floor. It hadn't so much shattered as exploded when the bullets hit it. A piece had hit him on the thigh and fallen next to his shoe. It was still there, now covered with a fine dust of drywall powder.

This was so stupid—waiting for something to happen, and as likely as not, that something would be a gunfight. The office wasn't big enough to stay out of the way of flying bullets. And him sitting there in the middle. A foolish end to a foolish old man. No. That was too stupid. Maybe Scarlett would come. Better that she not come though. Better that she had made good on her own escape; at least then some good would come out of this. The waiting, the pacing, the tension, the silence, it all dragged on. Unbearable.

If he just stood up and walked out? Would that surprise the idiot so much that he wouldn't shoot? Was it worth the risk? Was he brave enough to try? Yes. Anything was better than this. Quickness was no longer an arrow Clem had in his quiver, but that was just as well. As jumpy as Lee was, grace was a better weapon. He'd have to muster all he could. Clem shifted his weight forward from his hips to his feet, preparing to stand.

There was a knock on the door.

Clem whipped his head to look at it, even as his heart sank, knowing whom it must be.

"Who's there?" barked Lee Rigg.

"It's Scarlett! I brought help."

Clem slumped back against his chair again.

SANDY

Sandy felt her pulse racing as she walked toward the crowd by the café. She was on cloud nine. She had thought her higher calling was to preach the message of the Lord to the masses in the most lucrative way possible, and it might still be, at least in part, but it was no longer her main deal. Not now that she had met Timothy. He was so sweet and brave. And he had said he'd be her Snuffleupagus! She'd always wanted someone to say that to her. She was pretty sure that her highest purpose was to be with Timothy as much as it was to serve the Lord. It was confusing and thrilling at the same time. And now she was going to confront the mob again. Her second sermon of the day! Maybe this was her chance to get noticed. All part of a greater plan. A blessed plan! The Lord had given her a platform, and he had given her Timothy. Her Timothy, who had gone off with that temptress to confront a gunman. Oh, if either one of them disturbed so much as one hair on his head...but she had to trust the plan. It was hard sometimes.

"Oh, help me, Lord Jesus, and keep my Timothy safe and true to me," she whispered as she clambered up onto an empty table. It was a slippery surface, and her high heels almost let her down. But she bent her knees and was able to brace herself and stand up. She took a deep breath and spoke.

"Hi, y'all! Over here! Yes. Hi! Hi."

People turned toward her from their grumbled conversations and sullen silences.

"Not you again!" a man shouted from the back. Sandy furrowed her brow.

"Now that's not all that nice. That's not Christian," she said. "I'm here, at the request of the store's management, to talk to y'all."

"Save it for tomorrow," the man shouted.

"Shut up!" someone told him.

"You shut up!"

"Come over here and make me, tough guy."

The crowd began jostling. This was not how Sandy had envisioned the start of her sermon.

"People! PEOPLE!" she shouted, a little more shrilly than she had intended, but it was effective in stilling the crowd.

"Now is not the time for fighting. No matter our differences, we've got to come together, not break apart."

The crowd seemed to be listening.

"Now, let me tell you a story. The Lord Jesus, he—"

"I'd rather you take your top off," a guy right at the front of the crowd said. He was wearing a gray State University sweatshirt. Sandy glared at him. She was spoken for.

"A story," Sandy went on, "about how one man, faced with the suffering of his brothers, the suffering of his sisters, how he made a choice."

"No, seriously," the guy interrupted her again. "I'll give you fifty bucks to take your sweater off. Keep going and I'll double it."

Sandy paused. That was sick, demeaning, immoral. She thought of Timothy. He wouldn't want her to...but then again, it was a heckuva lot of money. She thought about the water bill and the gas bill. Her car. Her mortgage. She undid the top button on her sweater.

"Yeah!" State University shouted. She undid a few more buttons and pulled her sweater off. He handed her a fifty-dollar bill. A couple of other men whistled, and some more money was thrown on the table. In a fit of inspiration, Sandy twirled her sweater above her head. More whistles. And more money. It was demeaning...but lucrative? And at least people were paying attention to her now. That was a darn sight better than what they had been doing back during her Sermon on the Mount of Pop.

"No! Stop! This is disgusting. Don't debase yourself for these losers," a woman said. It was Ms. Uppity, who had lost her kid and caused this whole mess in the first place. Always butting in where she didn't belong.

"Money talks," Sandy said.

"What? Fine. I'll give you twenty bucks to put your sweater back on," Ms. Uppity said and handed over a twenty.

"Thank you, Jesus," Sandy whispered and put the sweater back on and started to button it up. The Lord truly worked in mysterious ways. But she would be able to pay the internet bill on time now.

"Booo!" State University shouted. "Show us something!"

He threw some more bills on the table. Sandy took her sweater back off.

Another woman threw some money on the table, and Sandy put the sweater back on. Back and forth they went, showering Sandy with money. Sandy was surprised to see that who gave her money wasn't determined by sex. Some of the women wanted her to take the sweater off; some men wanted her to keep it on. Sandy didn't really ponder it too closely, as long as the money kept flowing to her feet.

"Money talks!" she shouted, twirling the sweater and doing a little dance. She hiked up her skirt to show her knee. Whistles. She dropped the hem back down and put the sweater on. "But we must remember, that as loudly as money speaks, we cannot ignore the spiritual. Jesus Christ might not always speak loudly, but he is always there."

Sweater off.

"Not like a creepy stalker but like a dear friend. He loves us dearly and will forgive all manner of sins."

Sandy sincerely hoped she was right about that.

"And we should work hard to please him. That he might not have to forgive us."

Sweater on.

"So think about that with your every action."

Sweater off.

"With your entire being, know that Jesus is with you. As a dear friend."

Sweater on.

"As I am with you. Let's raise our hands in prayer."

Sandy ripped off her sweater and lifted her hands over her head. She patted her hair. Still in place. Good. Shouts and whistles and green paper greeted her. She pulled up the hem of her skirt again. Sandy looked down. There had to be close to a thousand dollars there.

This was the most audience participation she'd ever experienced. It was even more gratifying than comments on the YouTube.

"I will give you five hundred bucks to take it all off and show me those—ow!" State University shouted.

Sandy spun on the table and caught the cretin in the side of his head with her foot—she had been a fair turn back in middle school on the soccer field, and she hadn't forgotten everything, so she was able to make it appear reasonably accidental—surely Jesus wouldn't mind too much.

"Oh I am so sorry," she said, feeling sorry not at all. He was lucky she had used the instep and not her three-inch heel.

State University recovered quickly. He had a wad of cash in his hands and was waving it at her with a somewhat manic glint in his eye. "Praise Jesus!"

"Oh, well, bless your heart." Sandy took the wad of bills as he thrust them her way; with his other hand, he was miming the act of lifting the heather-gray State University sweatshirt. Sandy accepted the money, and in lieu of mimicking him, she shot him a withering smile. She was not about to go that far. She had already sinned enough for one day, and no matter the Lord's mysterious plans, she was pretty sure that sinning further for a meathead who rooted for State was not part of them. However, she was a savvy enough businesswoman to know that she could milk the five-hundred-dollar offer for a considerable counter offer from the prudish delegation to keep her clothes on. That was just smart business.

Before she had time to do it, however, Ms. Uppity screamed. "BiiiILLLLLLLYYYYYY!"

She had burst through the back of the crowd and started to hurl herself against the locked door. The time for talk was over; Sandy had to act.

"You and you." She pointed to State University and a woman who had been giving generously for Sandy to keep her clothes on. "Don't let her hurt herself. I'll be back in two minutes with the manager.

"You," she said to a frumpy man holding two jars of pickles, who had been among the most enthusiastic patrons of the sweater-off movement, "come with me."

Sandy scooped up her earnings—she supposed they were earnings, after a fashion—and stuffed them into her bag. She climbed down off the table.

"Where are we going?" Pickle Guy asked.

"To get the manager." Sandy didn't think this guy would be that useful, but it made sense to have backup, just in case.

"Why do I have to come? I just want to go home."

"You will. Hurry up."

Sandy looked over her shoulder at the front door. Ms. Uppity was giving State University and the woman a run for their money. Good. The three of them would keep each other busy for a while.

"I'm married," Pickle Guy said. "My wife's pregnant. I'm sorry. I shouldn't have paid for you to take your...I'm...I just...I don't know. It's just...it's just been so long since—"

"Congratulations," Sandy said, cutting him off. She did not want to hear more. "Marriage and children are truly blessings."

"Yeah, I guess, but look. What you were doing—strip-preaching or whatever you call it?—I'd go to church twice on Sunday to see that."

Sandy was equal parts flattered and creeped out.

"Let's get the manager," she said.

As she put her foot on the first step of the stairs up to the executive office, she heard shouts. It wasn't Ms. Uppity. Timothy! She put her foot on the second step. Gunshots! Not again! The crash of plate glass breaking. It came from the office, not the front door.

"Timothy!" Heedless of the danger, she ran up the stairs as fast as her high heels would carry her. Pickle Guy followed at a somewhat less enthusiastic pace.

MITCH

Mitch slumped in his chair. He had been trapped—a prisoner in his own office for what felt like hours. His shoulder hurt. His head hurt. And he was powerless to do anything about it. The asshole with the assault rifle—Lee Rigg, the moron always referred to himself by his first and last name, like a nerd—had blown the phone apart. Mitch had been thinking about making a dive for the Glock taped under his desk, but the phone's fate had caused him to slow his roll. The hole blasted in the wall above old Patterson's head had stopped his roll completely.

He was pretty sure his career as the manager of the Mega SuperMart was over. He could probably talk his way out of it—he was still Mitch Spooner after all—but he'd definitely have to cut back on the freebies. That would adversely affect his lifestyle, and he couldn't accept that. No, it was time for a new start. He had some cash put away. It was wrapped in plastic and disguised as a rock inside Charlie the piranha's tank. He'd have liked to see some bastard thief try and take it. It was a sizable chunk of change, enough to get him started somewhere else.

Like Mexico. The money he had might even be enough to make him a man of means there, like a baron or whatever they had in Mexico. Heck, once the Mexicans recognized his awesomeness, his lifestyle might even improve. Nothing but piña coladas and señoritas on the beach. All day every day. Hell yeah. He could get into that. But he had to get out of this office first. Preferably without getting shot again.

Timmy wasn't going to be any help. He was sniveling in his chair. What was he doing? Praying? Pathetic little bitch. And old Patterson was practically asleep. He had barely moved since Lee Rigg had fired at him. Coward. Mitch was on his own. Ordinarily, he was pretty sure he would have been able to kick Lee Rigg's ass. He probably had a wiry sort of strength, but he was definitely a loser. He hadn't played football. But with his shoulder wound, and his ribs, and the assault rifle...no, it would be better if he had a way to even the playing field. And he did—it was taped to the underside of his desk. He just had to reach it.

There was a knock at the office door. Everyone's heads snapped up, even old Patterson's. Lee Rigg lifted the assault rifle and barked, "Who's there?"

"It's Scarlett! I brought help."

"Well, about friggin' time," Lee said and lowered his gun. "Come on in."

The hottie—Scarlett—and some guy Mitch had never seen came in. Damn, she was fine. Mitch wondered if, maybe, she'd want to come to Mexico with him. Her sneer left him feeling like it was probably wishful thinking. Or maybe she was just playing hard to get. That was probably it. Didn't want to let on how much she wanted him. Chicks. Mitch smiled.

"What are you grinnin' about, dipshit?" Lee Rigg gave a yellow-toothed scowl and slapped the back of Mitch's head. The reverberations echoed around his skull. His smile turned to a grimace.

"That's what I thought," Lee continued. "You're about to have your time of reckoning. Who're you, mister? Security?"

These last questions were directed to the guy who had just come in. He was wearing a trench coat and an old-timey gangster hat. He had a thin mustache that looked sketch as hell. Mitch clenched his jaw and willed the headache to pass. He could have pulled that hat off. But this guy just looked like a jackass. He definitely wasn't Mega SuperMart security. Where were Sam and Rog anyway? Probably skipped work or were late and got locked out or some shit. Worthless. It was amazing to Mitch that he was able to make as much money as he did, really, given how much incompetence surrounded him.

"The name's Blade. Dirk Blade. I'm a private investigator."

The man sounded like a pompous buffoon, a caricature. Mitch wondered if that was even his real name. Dirk Blade? Sounded like a porn star. But if he was actually a private eye, that could be good. Maybe he'd use his authority to get that gun away from Lee Rigg.

"You sonofabitch!" Lee Rigg said.

Maybe not.

"You come here to give me my money back?" Lee asked.

"What money?" Dirk Blade said.

"All the money the government steals from me every year!"

"I, uh, no. I think you're thinking of the IRS. I'm sorry. I'm a private investigator. It's different. But I am here to help."

"Help? IRS or FBI or private friggin' eye, it don't make no difference! We don't need your help. Tellin' me what to do and impingin' on my freedoms! That ain't help. Now get lost!"

"Well, I guess I could. I—"

"He's not going anywhere," Scarlett said. "He's here to help."

"Oh, sweet cheeks. He done pulled the wool right over those pretty little eyes of yours. He ain't here to help. Government don't ever do nothin' but steal and rob and try to push us around."

"He's not the government," Scarlett said.

"Really, I'm not," Dirk Blade said. "And I'm not here to take away your freedom either."

"Friggin' right you ain't," Lee said. "'Cause I got a big-ass friggin' gun."

"Exactly," Dirk Blade said. "I'm here to question Timothy Phillips."

"Yipes! Me? Why?"

An uncomfortable thought occurred to Mitch: if he wasn't here because of the gun, what was he doing in the store in the first place?

"And Mitch Spooner."

Fuck. His cover was blown. For sure he could make whatever the private eye had stick to Timmy, but his hand would have to stay out of the till for all time now. Unacceptable. It left him no choice. Mexico, baby, Mexico. Drastic times called for drastic actions. He was gonna have to go balls to the wall, all in for the win. It would hurt. But if the private eye was here to put him in prison—and he sure as shit wasn't there to deal with Lee Rigg; that much was obvious—Mitch wasn't going to make it easy for him. Who had hired him anyway? Fucking Corporate? Hadn't C. Franklin Wallace, that prick, mentioned something about that?

The private eye, Dirk Blade or whatever, was still trying, with limited success, to calm Lee Rigg down. It seemed all he had managed was to learn the gunman's name. Useless. Mitch had figured that out in no time. He would have made one badass detective. But that wasn't his path. He took a quick survey of the room. Timmy was in a chair against the wall, looking at his feet. Useless. The hot chick, Scarlett, was bent down, whispering with old Patterson. Mitch wouldn't mind bending her over; goddamn, she made it hard to focus. But that would have to wait.

Lee Rigg was waving the gun around. Dirk Blade was holding out his hands, attempting to be nonthreatening. Mitch shook his head. Sometimes you had to fight fire with fire. And guns with guns. No one was paying any attention to him. All he needed was a clever ruse, a subterfuge. Fortunately, he was the master of clever ruses.

"Ooh, ooh." Mitch groaned and put his good hand to his head. He didn't really have to pretend that his head hurt. It still did; it was just that his shoulder hurt more. No one paid him any mind. He collapsed to the floor.

"Hey," Lee Rigg yelled, "git up!"

"Is that guy Tim Phillips?" Dirk Blade asked. Timmy looked up from his feet, but before he could say anything, Scarlett spoke up.

"No," she said. "That's Mitch Spooner. He's the one you want. I told you."

She was giving him up. What a bitch. Well, he'd forgive her in time, but she'd have to beg. Besides, his little act was accomplishing what he needed it to. The room was confused, and he was on the floor within reaching distance of his Glock.

"I said git up!" Lee Rigg said again and came around to kick him in the ribs.

"Ow! Fuckhead!" Mitch said.

"Git up then!"

"I think he's hurt," Timmy said. "Mr. Spooner! Are you all right? I know first aid. Can I be of assistance?"

Mitch ignored him. He reached up with his good arm, his bad shoulder pressed painfully into the floor. The grunt of pain was not simulated. He closed his fingers around the butt of the Glock. Mitch gave a tug, and the gun came free.

"Git up, or I'm gonna shoot you again!" Lee Rigg said.

"Rigg, put the gun down," Dirk Blade said.

"Too late, losers!" Mitch cried. He rolled out from under the desk. Pain lanced through his shoulder. Play through it like a champion. He squeezed off three quick shots in Lee Rigg's direction.

He heard screams and knew he had hit his target. There was a crash to his left. More shouts. There was the sharp *rat-a-tat-tat* of semiautomatic gunfire. Lee Rigg was shooting back. Asshole! But he couldn't hit Mitch. It was probably dumb luck, but Mitch would rather be lucky than good. Well, he'd rather be both. But it wasn't time for a philosophical debate; it was time to escape. The door was too far away. He had only one chance. Balls to the wall. No regrets. Mitch raised the Glock again and shot out his office window. Not like he would be needing it anymore anyway. Then he hauled himself up, gritting his teeth in pain. Timmy was screaming. Lee Rigg was yelling. But Mitch didn't look back. No regrets, no looking back. Two steps and a leap—just like hitting the hole on a two-yard dive for the end zone—and Mitch was out of the office through a cascade of glass.

What Mitch hadn't calculated was just how far ten feet—the distance between his office window and the store's floor below—was. He landed on his feet but felt a snap as his left ankle rolled under him. Pain followed almost instantaneously. He hoped there was a good clinic in Mexico. With hot nurses. Superhot nurses. The kind that would be totally into him and wouldn't stab him in the back and give him up to the authorities.

Mitch stood up. Ow! That asshole had just thrown the clip from that assault rifle at him. It hit him in his good shoulder. Well, better than getting shot. He had half a mind to go back up for more revenge, but Lee Rigg was a small fish. And Mitch Spooner was the Shark Master.

There was a mob of some kind over by the front door. What the hell was going on today? Definitely time to cash out. But he couldn't shoot his way through that crowd. Plus, his truck was too fly and noticeable. It would suck leaving it—it was his baby— but he could always get another one, something even more boss. For now, he'd have to take an alternate means of transport. He checked his watch. Wasn't that Golden Snacks truck supposed to be here about now? Perfect.

Mitch checked the safety on the Glock. He wanted to be sure it was on. Then he stuck the gun in his pocket. The last thing he needed to do was shoot his junk off like that NFL player a few months ago. And given the way this day had been going... on second thought, Mitch pulled the gun out and decided just to carry it. His ankle was already broken, no need to add injury to injury. He limped off toward the back of the store and the Shipping/Receiving door.

As he limped through the darkened store, Mitch ran through a mental checklist: wallet, gun, passport, money, Charlie. Shit, how was he going to get a piranha across the border? Didn't matter. He'd figure that out. Should he pass by the man cave? He had another batch of cash stashed down there. The stairs were gonna suck on his ankle.

The stairs did suck on his ankle.

"Play through it like a champion!" Mitch grunted to himself as he hobbled down.

He had a sizeable reserve of cash in the man cave. But where was it. The man cave was a ruin, his desk splinters and ash; there were scraps of papers and feathers from couch cushions everywhere. Mitch limped over to the painting—it was some sort of classic, not original of course, but it looked classy, with its gilt frame—covering the safe on the wall. It had miraculously escaped damage. The painting was a pretty good reproduction. Maybe he could bring it to Mexico.

He took the painting down and spun the combination.

"Fuck!"

Before he finished spinning in the combination, Mitch remembered. The other day, he had transferred the man cave's cash reserves out of the safe, just in case Corporate had somehow sniffed it out. It wasn't paranoia; it was smarts. But he had transferred them into that goddamn teddy bear he had given to that goddamn little brat to make her stop crying.

"Fucking fucking fuck!"

Mitch drew back to punch the wall but stopped himself. Enough of his body was in pain already. Enough self-pity. No looking back, no regrets. He still had the piranha money and his platinum company credit card. He'd be fine. And once he was safely in Mexico, he could probably hire someone to go get the bear back. Maybe they could also grab his Hummer while they were at it, because if he was being honest, he wasn't sure a vehicle more boss than his Hummer even existed. What about the painting? It was pretty sweet, with the centaurs and storm clouds and stuff. He could probably sell it for good money in Mexico. Art was always a safe investment. And if he didn't have to sell it, it'd look sweet on his cabana wall. Better to bring it now. Mitch grabbed the painting, took a breath, and gritted his way back up the stairs.

In short but painful order, Mitch made it to the Shipping/Receiving door. It was unbolted. Timmy really was an incompetent moron. Whatever. Not his problem in Mexico.

"Hold the door!" someone said at him as he pushed through. Mitch paid no heed, and the door slammed shut behind him.

"Hey! Why'd you—"

"Dude, shut up. That's my boss."

"Oh, shit, dude. Ha-ha. You're screwed, bro."

"Bummer."

Three teenagers were slumped against a wall. High as Buzz Aldrin. Mitch shook his head. He'd have loved to get high right now. For one thing, it'd numb the pain. His ankle, his shoulder, his head: more parts of him hurt than didn't, at the moment. But it'd also numb his wits, and he needed his wits.

He ignored the teenagers. Skater punks and losers. He needed to get out of there. And there was his ride: the Golden Snacks delivery truck. The teenage dipshits were too blazed to realize all the munchies separated from them by just a door.

"Hey, mister. Dude, you can't take that truck. Oh shit, he's got a gun!"

Mitch tossed the Glock and the painting into the cab ahead of him and hopped in. Lee Rigg had a point—people did respect you more when you had gun.

"Dude, I told you, shut up. He's the store manager. Mr. Spooner, uh, that truck isn't—"

"You losers are out here smoking weed," Mitch said. He had hated losers since high school. These dweebs were probably in some crappy band or something. And the acne and the red hair weren't gonna help any of them get laid, unless it was with each other. Gross.

"That's a felony, as you know."

"No, man, it's just a misdemeanor, and the cops don't even—"

"Shut up, dorkus. It's a felony. It's fine: you're too young to know the laws. And don't worry; I'm not gonna call the cops on you though. Just shut up, and stay where you are. And you never saw me. If you tell anyone otherwise, I'll come back and fuck you up real bad."

Mitch knew he could take him. All three of them. The potheads nodded and shrank back against the wall. All you needed to do was talk tough to losers. Then they'd be eating out of your hand.

The keys were still in the ignition. Finally, some luck. Mitch had always wanted to drive a big rig. What was that old saying? The bigger the truck, the bigger the dick? That wasn't quite it. How did it go again? Didn't matter. The point was Mitch was driving a big truck, and he was hung like a goddamn Clydesdale. That was what was important. He was glad the driver of the truck had backed up to the store though. With the truck's gears crunching and grinding, Mitch pulled out around the store. Mexico bound!

CLEM

Clem let out a long breath. It was a miracle no one was dead.

Mitch Spooner had just leapt through his office window, indiscriminately firing a gun—where he had gotten it from, who the hell knew—over his shoulder as he went. It really was a miracle no one was dead. Tim was wounded, but it seemed a small price to pay, given the alternatives. Lee Rigg had been about to go after Mitch when the private eye had tackled him. Scarlett had done some quick thinking—and moving—and picked up the assault rifle and thrown the clip out the broken office window. Smart girl. The danger—the immediate danger of an idiot, two idiots, with guns—was gone.

Clem breathed again, long and slow, the tension he had been holding in his neck and back sailing out after Mitch Spooner, the fear evaporating as Lee Rigg was wrestled into submission.

"You sonofabitch! You can't do this! I know my rights!" Lee Rigg was yelling and kicking while the private eye, Dirk Blade, who had produced duct tape from somewhere, bound his hands. It was like he had no concept that he was, in all likelihood, going to prison for a good long time, and all of the struggling was only going to make things worse.

He shook his head. Else was right. It was time to retire for good, to go on that vacation. He'd always wanted to see Italy, and Florence was supposed to be lovely this time of year.

The blond preacher burst into the office. She went immediately to Tim, alternately sobbing and smothering him into her bosom. Tim, despite the bullet wound in his arm, looked happy enough. Clem hoped he was getting enough air.

"Clem!" Scarlett said. She had been talking to a dumpy-looking guy with a jar of pickles, who had slunk into the office after the preacher. Clem recognized him, the expectant father. "They found Billy!" Scarlett was excited; she looked happier than she had in months.

"That's great," he said. "Where is he?"

"He's apparently outside the store, with Rog and Sam. They went and got pizza. That's what this guy says." Scarlett jerked her thumb at the rumpled man holding the pickles.

"I don't even know why I'm here," the expectant father said. "But I certainly didn't come up here to watch her give a private show to that doorknob. He didn't even pay!"

Clem blinked and shook his head. What was this guy talking about? Tim and the preacher? Granted it was weird, but...Clem sighed. World sure had gone crazy all right.

"Let's get you downstairs," Scarlett said to the man holding the jars of pickles. "If Billy's been found, we can open the door and let everybody out."

Clem agreed. Anything to get out of that office, small and crowded, hot and sticky. Anything to get out of that store. He was tired, and it was time to go home. With any luck, Else'd still have the sandwich fixings out.

They trooped down the stairs, leaving Tim and the preacher and Lee Rigg and the private eye to their various exertions.

"Do you know how to open the doors?" Scarlett whispered in his ear as they got close to the mob.

"Yeah. That I do know.

"Good people," he said, raising his voice like a modern Demosthenes to project it out over the crowd; it felt good to do so. And the crowd—except for the hysterical woman who was still fighting to throw herself through the glass doors—grew quiet. "The missing child has been found."

"We know that! He's out there eating pizza!" the big lug of a State University football fan shouted back. Demosthenes he was not. He was trying to restrain the woman, who, Clem realized, was the mother of the missing Billy. The big lug had his hands full. Clem almost smiled. Served him right.

Clem squinted through the glass and into the parking lot. Sure enough, there they were.

"Let us out! Or bring back that chick with the huge knockers!"

Scarlett walked over and slapped the big lug across the face. The crowd cheered. The big lug looked shocked, but he shut up.

"We don't have the key," Clem said, his voice still stentorian.

"We're never getting out," the expectant father with the pickles said, the whine in his tone of voice no doubt presaging his offspring. The rest of crowd groaned, and a couple of people started to shout.

"But"—Clem raised his voice as loud as he could—"we do have this!"

He picked up a stool from behind checkout number eight.

"Step back please, ma'am," he said to Billy's mother.

"Oh, thank you, thank you, thank you," she said.

Clem hefted the stool. It wasn't too heavy. He wasn't too old for this. He swung the stool into the door. With a mighty crash, the window shattered. Clem reached through and pulled the manual-release lever—in keeping with building codes, the lever was on the outside; he had always said it was an ill-designed system—and the doors slid apart. The crowd whooped and clapped and stampeded ahead. Clem stampeded with them, out and away into the bright sun of the parking lot.

LEE

"You got the wrong guy!" Lee Rigg struggled against the weight of Dirk Blade, who had tackled him just as Lee was about to save the day. So this was government oppression. Lee Rigg had always felt it but in an abstract way. To have the stench of nicotine in your nostrils, to actually feel the warmth of coffee breath on the back of your own neck, this was different. Lee Rigg wanted to hurl. Friggin' government.

"You sonofabitch! I know my rights!" Lee tried to bust free. In a fair fight, he would have beat the snot out of him, but the g-man wasn't fighting fair! He had sneak attacked him when Spooner jumped out the window! What the hell?

"Shut up. I gotta bring you in."

Lee Rigg struggled harder. He knew the terms of his probation. Arrest was bad. And this guy was sneaky strong. Lee couldn't free his arms from his iron grip. How was it possible? Dirk Blade was off him and standing right there. Was he a friggin' X-Man? Lee twisted his head around. Nope. He had just taped Lee's hands together! Sonofabitch! Lee struggled against his bonds in vain.

Over against the wall, the blond preacher with the huge knockers was cradling the nerdy assistant manager who had just been shot. It looked like the guy might be having trouble breathing. Lucky bastard.

Lee was in a tight spot. Dirk Blade hauled him to his feet. Lee had to admit that Dirk Blade was a pretty badass name. In other circumstances, they might have been friends. That seemed to be happening a lot today.

"Man, I tell you, I'm not the one you want. Friggin' pig! Friggin' FBI!"

"Save it," Dirk Blade said. He bundled Lee out of the office toward the stairs.

Lee fought him every step of the way. If he was going to jail, he wasn't going easy.

"Knock it off," Dirk Blade said.

Lee dug in his heels. Dirk Blade elbowed him in the ribs. He had to acquiesce. If only he could get his teeth around something. Lee Rigg had an iron jaw. He thought about biting Dirk Blade. No. He knew the terms of his probation. He didn't need to make things worse.

DIRK BLADE

Nothing was ever easy. That fact had been driven home today more forcefully than a bases-clearing double. Dirk Blade was no longer dealing with a world of black and white; no, the world was innumerable shades of gray it seemed. The man he had apprehended, this Lee Rigg, he seemed like an all right guy. And he certainly wasn't the one stealing from the SuperMart. But now Dirk Blade was in a tight spot. Tim Phillips had been a false herring. That much was obvious. Years of private detective work gave Dirk Blade the ability to size people up at a glance. He was almost always right. So the private investigator left Tim in the office with his lady friend.

But the guy who had leapt out the office window, Mitch Spooner? He had the look about him. The young woman, Scarlett, maybe she had the right of it. But his training had taught him to always take out the guy with the gun first. It was a point of emphasis with all the government agencies right now, and even though he was a private contractor, taking out a shooter would still be big. He'd get more cooperation when he needed something from Uncle Sam. Yep, bringing in a gunman would be a real feather in his cap. Losing Mitch Spooner would be a black eye, especially since that was what he had been hired to do, but Dirk Blade hoped that maybe the one would cancel the other out. It was about as much as he could hope for. Lee Rigg was still struggling. Normally, Dirk Blade wouldn't have cared. But there was something gnawing at the pit of his stomach. Maybe it was just an ulcer—thanks for nothing, Denny's—but he doubted it. Something about this didn't feel right.

They were downstairs in the now-deserted SuperMart. It was quiet, except for the occasional outburst from Lee Rigg. Dirk Blade reached for his e-cigarette. He needed to think. Nicotine would help, even delivered via this gelded mechanism.

"Oh, jeez. Can I bum a smoke?" Lee Rigg asked.

Dirk Blade stuck the e-cigarette in his prisoner's mouth and turned it on for him. There were still courtesies to be observed. Lee Rigg raised his eyebrows at the e-cigarette but puffed away contentedly enough. His hands were taped together behind his back, so Dirk Blade had to tend the man's e-cigarette for him and tap off the ash. It might have been an e-cigarette, but it was top of the line, with simulated ash, made out of plastic or something, which did help. It fell to the shiny tile floor, like little ashen flower petals.

"What am I supposed to do?" he wondered aloud.

"Don't friggin' arrest me! I ain't done nothin' wrong!" Lee Rigg shouted. The e-cigarette fell to the floor and smashed. Luckily, Dirk Blade had a backup. He pulled it out and took a puff. Nothing. Batteries were dead. He tossed it away, useless piece of junk.

"Here's the thing," Dirk Blade said. "I gotta have something to show for today. I believe you're a good guy."

"Friggin' right I am!"

"Anyway, be that as it may, I gotta have something to show for today. And right now, you're it. I could bring Phillips in for questioning, but that's not going to accomplish anything; you and I both know he's innocent."

"'Cept for how he had his head between that preacher lady's boobs, you mean. Heh."

Dirk Blade paused. Lee Rigg was not wrong.

"Exactly, but of fraud on an industrial scale? It was Spooner. There are few doubts about that now. But if I go back to my client and tell them he got away, well, that could be the end of the case for me. I've got bills to pay and mouths to feed. This job is gonna pay big. And if I return with you, a gunman? You know how that sort of thing plays on the news. I might even get a bonus or something."

"But that ain't justice! That ain't America! I'm not the problem here! The only friggin' guy I shot was friggin' Spooner! C'mon! You gotta do the right thing!"

"But what is the right thing?" Dirk Blade kicked the broken e-cigarette aside. It skittered away and disappeared under a display of on-sale Styrofoam coolers.

"Are you kidding me? Let me the frig go! We'll go after Spooner together. He's only been gone what, like five minutes? I shot him in the shoulder, and he probably broke his ankle jumping out of that window. He can't be moving fast. Let's go get him!"

It was tempting. And Dirk Blade, in spite of himself, kind of liked Lee Rigg. He was a simpleton, but his motives were honest, if somewhat misguided. But there was no way they could catch Spooner now. That ship had sailed.

"No, he's probably halfway to Mexico by now. There's no way we could catch him. I'm sorry."

Better to just take Lee Rigg back and hope to spin the story his way, maybe get that bonus. It didn't feel like justice, but sometimes you had to play the cards you were dealt.

"Mexico! How do you know? And anyway, that's like a thousand miles from here! C'mon. Let's get him! You can make me a deputy. It'll be like one of those old west movies. I'll even let you be John Wayne. C'mon!"

"I keep telling you I'm a private investigator, not a government agent."

"Oh yeah? Then how the frig you know he was goin' for Meixco?"

"They always head for Mexico. Sorry, Rigg. Let's go."

Lee Rigg struggled and fought. He managed to get his teeth around a shopping cart handle—which was just gross—and clung there for a good thirty seconds before Dirk Blade could pry him off. Then, by pushing and prodding and occasionally by dragging, he brought Lee Rigg out of the store and into the sun where he would soon have to face the harsh light of justice. Dirk Blade shook his head.

Justice.

It wasn't what it used to be.

TIM

Tim was exhausted. He must have lost a lot of blood. It didn't really look like it, but why else would he feel so light-headed? Maybe he was in some kind of psychological shock. By golly, that was probably it. A lot had happened since he arrived in the office. Mr. Spooner had shot him, for one. It probably wasn't on purpose, but still. The Mr. Spooner Tim thought he knew—the cool guy, the good boss—well, he sure as heck wasn't the Mr. Spooner who was revealing himself today. It felt like...betrayal? Maybe that was too mean. Whatever it was, it was unsettling.

Then there was Sandy. She had held him against her...against her boobs, pressed his face right in and held him there. If it was a sin, why did it feel so good?

Tim wondered if he had died and gone to heaven. He expected heaven would be pretty much like this, except more cloud-like and less office-like. Also Dirk Blade wouldn't have just bundled out the cursing, yelling gunman—not Mr. Spooner, the other one; gosh, this was confusing—Tim couldn't remember his name. Though maybe this heaven was still getting set up because Tim was so recently dead? But if that were the case, why was Sandy there?

"Is this real, Sandy?"

"You bet your sweet bippy. All real."

She gave Tim an affectionate squeeze, and Tim's arm lanced with pain. He yelped. Maybe he wasn't dead.

"Holy jeepers! I got shot! Mr. Spooner shot me!" Tim said. The pain had jolted the recent events into focus.

He still couldn't believe it, any of it. Mr. Spooner had gotten a gun from somewhere and shot him right in the arm. At first, the pain and the blood loss seemed enough to kill him, but actually, now that he looked down at it, his arm wasn't that bad. And then Sandy had been there and smothered him, with her...with her love. That had been kinda wonderful though. And it hadn't killed him. Then they had kissed. She was quite a gal.

"Don't worry, darling. I'm here now." Sandy was patting his head.

They were still in the office. When he had started kissing Sandy, the place was full. But now they were alone.

"Holy buckets," Tim said.

"You said it," Sandy said. "And guess what."

"What?"

"I found a way to make some money. Real money. To make money and spread the word of Jesus."

"Gosh. That's terrific. I knew you would be doing great things, even in the middle of a crisis."

"Aw, thanks, darling."

She squeezed him again, but—Tim was glad to notice—she was careful not to involve his wounded arm.

"Holy cow!" Tim yelped.

"Oh, darling, did I get your arm? I was trying hard not to," Sandy said.

"No!" Tim said, panic rising in his chest like water in a clogged sink. "But the kids! Code Bobby! The store! Sandy, we...I...have been derelict in our duty! Mr. Spooner isn't here; the place is probably falling apart without me!"

Tim stood up. He wobbled. He was light-headed. He smiled. That's what love was like. Sometimes you were light-headed. Sometimes you wobbled. Sometimes you got shot. Sandy stood up too. She didn't seem to wobble. But she hadn't lost a bunch of blood like he had. That had to be it.

"Well," Sandy said.

"Well, what?" Tim asked. Or did she not feel the way he felt? And that was why she didn't wobble. Oh, fiddlesticks.

"Is my Snuffleupagus gonna go save the store or not?"

Tim blushed. Maybe she did like him as much as he liked her. He dared to hope.

SANDY

It had been a good day, all things considered. Lucrative. It hadn't been quite what she had expected, and it certainly hadn't started off so great, but well, the Lord worked in mysterious ways. And now she had a pocketbook crammed near to bursting with cash and a new...what was Timothy? Her boyfriend? That sounded too common. Her beau? Yes, that had a nice ring to it. French, so it was classy. He was a little worse for wear, but she would nurse him back to health—yes, she would. But first they had to get out of that office. Timothy was a little wobbly, but his face was regaining its color a little. He was no longer so bluish.

When they reached the store floor, they found the place deserted. Well, except for the FBI or CIA or whoever-he-was guy—it hadn't been totally clear to Sandy his exact affiliation. In any case, he was still there struggling with the gunman over by the shopping carts. Sandy didn't spare a thought for them though, for she was with her Timothy, and she was going to nurse him back to health. The power was still off in the back of the store, and there was a warm breeze coming from somewhere. As it turned out, the warm breeze was coming from the front doors of the store, which had been smashed. Timothy wobbled, then started yelling.

"My store! The doors! The Code Bobby! Oh, turnips! Now you've really done it, Timothy! You screwed it up! It's all your fault. Dumb-dumb head! Idiot! Moron!" He started to beat his fist into his thigh.

"Whoa, whoa, darling, stop that." Sandy had to calm him down. He had been placid enough in the office with his head nestled on her chest. At least, until he had started turning blue.

Poor thing had lost a lot of blood. "Let's just go outside and figure out what has been happening down here."

"Yeah, yeah. Okay, that makes sense. Okay," Timothy said.

Timothy leaned on her as they stepped out through the broken glass and into the bright parking lot.

BILLY

It had been pretty impressive when the old guy had smashed the door: the shattering glass was cool. And the old guy hadn't even gotten in trouble for it! If Billy had smashed the door, he never would have heard the end of it. But it wasn't the time to make a scene about that particular injustice.

A flood of people poured out into the parking lot. They were so relieved—just to get out of the store. Now they understood. Most people headed to their cars and drove off, creating a traffic jam in the parking lot. Billy's mom, however, came directly to him. Close on her heels was a woman with long hair and long skirts, who he assumed to be Willow's mom.

"Oh, Billy," his mom said, dropping to a knee to hug him.

"Oof," Billy said as the air was knocked out of him. "Mom, c'mon."

"Oh, I was so worried. So worried. Are you all right? What happened? Did someone try to hurt you? Oh, my darling."

She was crying. She was actually crying! But she was also smiling as she alternately squeezed the air out of him and patted his head. Moms.

"Mom! C'mon. Jeez. I'm fine. I just...I'm sorry. I told you I didn't want to go."

His mom stopped crying and got a more serious look. Billy gulped and prepared himself for the boom.

"He was helping me!" Willow said. "I got lost and was scared, and so he stayed with me."

His mom looked at her.

"My Billy? Really?"

"Yeah, we were gonna try and find you, but then there was a man with a gun, and the power went out, and so we ran, and then we got locked out."

Willow had been right: it wasn't a very big lie at all. His mom was either completely gobsmacked by the story, or her mendacity detector had failed to find the slight fib that they hadn't actually started out trying to find her. Or both. Willow's mom stepped into the silence.

"Hello." Her voice was slow and dreamy. "My name is Moonbeam. I'm Willow's mother. Thank you, Billy. And you, mother of Billy. You are raising a fine boy."

"Billy?" Willow said, raising an eyebrow at Billy.

Billy shrugged.

"My real name's William," he said.

"But Billy's so cool. Like the goats! Why would you change it?"

"You like Billy?" he asked.

"Yeah! It's a great name."

"Well, thanks, I guess I was just...I dunno."

He looked at his mom; she was stunned, clearly confused by the goat remark, and also struggling what to make of Willow's mom and wanting to be polite.

"Oh, well. Thank you. You're welcome," his mom said. "The important thing is that everyone is all right. I guess we can just go home now."

"No one's going anywhere yet," said a stern man with gray hair and a blue pinstriped suit. He exuded power and prejudice. Billy took an instant dislike to him.

"Is there a problem?" the old guy who had smashed the glass door said. Billy recognized him as the nice man who had given him the sticker way back when he had first come into the store. He had come over to their group with a young woman who looked like she was maybe his daughter or granddaughter. She was wearing a store apron and a nametag. Her name was Scarlett. Her eyes sparkled with intelligence. Billy liked her immediately.

"Oh yes, there is," the fancy-suited man said. "There was a Code Bobby at this store. And Code Bobby protocols say that no one leaves until the child is confirmed back with his family. And I say no one is going to leave until I get to the bottom of what's going on here. And you, sir. You will pay for that door. Now where's Mitch Spooner? I want to speak to him face-to-face."

The guy seemed to be accustomed to having his words obeyed. He was like a mom. Except he wasn't a mom, so that just made him a bully.

"Well," Billy said, "this is my mom. And that's Willow's mom. So we're back with our parents. Now we can go."

"We're not trusting the judgment of a child," the man said, speaking over him to the other grown-ups. Billy seethed. This guy wasn't showing him proper respect. If only he had a piece of lasagna or some other sort of projectile.

"Code Bobby will end when the store manager confirms that this is the woman who filed the complaint," the man went on. "And I will let you all go after I've spoken to Mitch Spooner."

"Well Mitch Spooner's not here anymore. I can vouch that these are the children's mothers," Scarlett cut in. Somehow she had managed to avoid the stultification with aging that was so epidemic at the SuperMart. Could she share the secret with him? Would she? Maybe she could babysit next time his mom got it into her head that he couldn't stay home alone. Not that he needed it, but with Scarlett, it might be kind of fun. With some people, you could just tell.

Scarlett was still talking. "And who do you think you are to come in here acting like you own the place?"

"I'm C. Franklin Wallace. With my stock options, I do own this store. And your job, missy. So don't take that tone with me, thank you. Now where's Spooner?"

C. Franklin Wallace? That was the dumbest name Billy had heard in a while. And he had heard some dumb ones. No wonder the guy wasn't too nice. He'd probably had a chip on his shoulder since childhood. Was he a biter?

No one answered C. Franklin Wallace. He turned to Willow and said, "And where'd you get that teddy bear, young lady; did you pay for it?"

"I...I...it was given to me," Willow said.

"Well in that case, you can give it back easily enough."

"No, Leroy is mine now."

"It is stolen property, and I'll have it back."

C. Franklin Wallace grabbed one of Leroy's arms as Willow tried to pull him away. There was a brief struggle and then a big *riiiiiiiip*. Leroy was bisected down the middle, his entrails exposed to the world. His entrails turned out to be hundreds and hundreds of hundred-dollar bills! A breath of breeze swirled them into a cloud among the crowd in the parking lot.

"Oh, more money?" The blond preacher woman had arrived. She started grabbing the bills and stuffing them into her bag; she was quick, her motion smooth and efficient. Clearly, she had some practice in the activity.

"Stop that! Stop that! That's my money! Chauncey, collect my money!" C. Franklin Wallace said. A man who had been leaning against a shiny car with tinted windows leapt to attention and started grabbing the bills. Well there was the problem: this Chauncey guy did whatever C. Franklin Wallace wanted without question. No wonder he had turned into a bully.

Chauncey was big and fast. He was even better at collecting the floating bills than the blond preacher woman. Between the two of them, they had Leroy the bear's entrails pretty well collected in about two minutes. Billy didn't bother to grab any of the money. He had a pocket full of cash already. What he really wanted was to just go home.

SANDY

Well, when he decided to provide, he really decided to provide. The odd tug-of-war between the well-put-together gray-haired man and the little girl had ended in a cloud of cash. Benjamins!

Sandy stuffed the money as fast as she could into her already-overstuffed purse. She had competition, from a big, ugly brute who wasn't afraid to use his body to shield her from the money. Well. She would just have to be more efficient. To heck with the purse! She grabbed fistfuls of cash and tucked them into her bra straps. It wasn't elegant—the French certainly wouldn't do it—but it was functional. Soon all but a couple stray bills were collected. The big, ugly brute went over to the gray-haired man and gave him the money he had collected. The gray-haired man patted him on the shoulder, like he was a dog; then he walked over to Sandy.

"Just what do you think you're doing? That's my money. I'll have it back."

He made to grab it back. Sandy stepped back and slapped him. Not hard, but enough to make him stop. No one reached for that part of her. Except for Timothy. Well, Timothy and that squirrel this morning, but with any luck, it was a hawk's lunch by now. The gray-haired man stepped back and looked her up and down. Sandy wondered if she would have to employ her self-defense training.

Timothy stepped between them.

"If you would please leave the lady alone. I won't let you treat her like that."

A true gallant! A knight in shining...a knight in a nice white slightly bloodstained shirt and tie!

"I'll treat her however I damn well please! Who the hell are you, you little pissant?"

"I'm Timothy. Timothy Phillips. Who are you?"

"Who am I? I'm C. Franklin Wallace, and I want to know what the fuck is going on with this store. Who is in charge here?" The man's voice was calm, but his eyes flashed in anger. Sandy didn't like this guy. Not one bit.

"Let me just try and explain. Mr. Spooner was in charge, but he's, well...he might not be who I thought. But there was a runaway child. And a gunman. It's been kind of a big day." Timothy was talking fast. He looked nerve-wracked. Well, he had reason to be.

Sandy had to stand by her man. But she couldn't do it with cash sticking out of her underclothes. It wasn't classy; it wasn't elegant. She was in a pickle. It was a good pickle—like one of those sweet butter pickles that went so nice on ham sandwiches—but it was still a pickle. At least she'd be able to pay this month's bills. She had enough there to do that and then some. Maybe she could even fix that leaky window. But what to do with the cash for the moment? She looked down at her purse. If she took out her makeup and compact, the money would fit. It would be a risk. But her hair had held thus far. And besides, with that amount of money, she could buy lots more makeup. She emptied her purse of everything but money. She had to really force it—she clamped the bag between her elbow and her body to get a little extra give out of the green faux leather—but she was able to just get the clasp closed.

"Oh really? Where is Spooner? Where is this gunman?" C. Franklin Wallace said.

"I...I don't know, sir. I...Mr. Spooner left, and the gunman... he...he...please, sir. I've been shot," Timothy stammered. Sandy straightened up. Time to set the record straight, for her man.

"I've got him right here." The detective walked up, pushing the gunman in front of him.

"Well, there's that taken care of," Sandy said. "Isn't it just the most blessed day?"

It really was. Everything had just worked out. C. Franklin Wallace was talking to the detective. So that would clear that up. She had money, employment opportunities, and a great beau. Truly, it had been a blessed day.

SCARLETT

"I've got him right here." The private eye walked up, pushing the gunman in front of him. The gunman's hands were duct-taped together. That was for the best.

"I'm not him! I keep telling you. I'm Lee Rigg. I was making a citizen's arrest! I'm the good guy here. Stop taking away my freedom." The duct taped former gunman struggled, but Dirk Blade, private investigator, held him tight.

"Pay no attention to his ravings. I always get my man."

"Who are you?" C. Franklin Wallace asked him.

"I'm Dirk Blade. I'm a private investigator. I'm investigating a not insignificant amount of white-collar crime at this facility. Here's the evidence, right here." Dirk Blade handed C. Franklin Wallace a burnt scrap of paper. Scarlett recognized it as the one that Mitch Spooner had crudely forged Tim's signature on.

"I'm afraid the perpetrator got away, but I have apprehended a dangerous gunman," Dirk Blade said.

Scarlett couldn't argue, but she also couldn't help but notice how Dirk Blade kept looking down and wouldn't make eye contact with anyone. She recognized that body language. What was he feeling guilty about? Yeah, Mitch Spooner had gotten away, but the guy was an idiot. They'd catch him in about five minutes.

C. Franklin Wallace. Tim, Sandy. Rog and Sam and the guy who had found the kids. Now Dirk Blade and Lee Rigg. But still no police. WTF? A confederacy of fools, if she had ever seen one. Thank goodness there weren't any guns present. A little way away from the confederacy were the kids and their mothers. And Clem. He looked as wearied by the day's events as she felt.

She wondered how he was doing. He was eighty-one after all. And it was his store, once. Poor Clem. Maybe she should see if he wanted to go get a sandwich or something.

C. Franklin Wallace had rounded on Tim again. He was yelling at him. Poor Tim. He really wasn't such a bad guy. Kinda overmatched and hopeless but not a bad person. C. Franklin Wallace, on the other hand, he maybe was a bad person. Certainly, he had done nothing so far to dissuade her of that opinion. Why didn't Tim's preacher lady friend help him out? Scarlett wondered if she should step in.

"Of course you're fired," C. Franklin Wallace said. "You're all fired. The only question is, who is going to jail? Cooperate and I might be lenient."

Well, damn. That sucked. Though at least this way it wasn't for stealing, so maybe she would be able to get some other crappy retail job now. Still. God dammit. Maybe she should have grabbed some of that money from the bear. Scarlett's stomach rumbled. She hadn't eaten much all day. Maybe Clem really would want to go get a sandwich. Before she could ask, a white semitruck with Golden Snacks written on the hood and on the trailer came lurching around from behind the store.

"That's the guy!" Lee Rigg shouted. "He's driving."

"The guy" was Mitch Spooner. He was honking, grinding gears, and giving the finger to anybody who was looking. Scarlett shook her head. The way he was driving that truck, it might take a little more than five minutes to catch him, but only a couple of minutes more.

"That's my truck!" the guy who had found the missing children shouted. "Those stoner punks! Somebody call the police."

He went running after the truck. But only about ten steps. He wasn't going to catch it. Mitch Spooner turned recklessly toward the street, careening off a couple of cars that were parked by the old Coffee Xpress. The high-pitched squeal of metal on metal made the hair on the back of Scarlett's neck stand up. The parked cars were mostly destroyed. The Golden Snacks truck and Mitch Spooner, however, carried on, over the curb and into the street. It might have just been her imagination, but the trailer looked pretty precariously attached.

RUSTY

Rusty sat perched on a stay on the undercarriage of the Golden Snacks trailer. The wind whipped through his whiskers and ruffled his tail. He was moving! He was going to do it! The final part of the plan was in motion. He was gonna go down in history: the prince of squirrel thieves! The king!

Rusty could tell that the driver of the truck was inexperienced. It had been a lurching start, and Rusty could smell burning. A different burning from the burning smell that normally accompanied these trucks. It was probably the gearbox, though without seeing, Rusty couldn't say with certainty. He wasn't actually a diesel mechanic, after all. He was, however, the prince of squirrel thieves, and an inexperienced driver played to his advantage.

Rusty flexed his paws, one by one. He felt good. Better than good. Great. He was on his way. Stay loose. Stay sharp. No hawks down here. No rabies. Rusty felt a tingling from his ears to the tip of his tail, a rush that came from the flawless planning and execution of a genius caper. It was better than electricity. The couplings were fixed. The spanner was positioned on the final bolt. One good yank and the trailer would roll free and down into the ravine behind his tree. What a day!

The driver honked and shouted—acclaiming Rusty's triumph. Rusty chattered fiercely. But he had to stay focused. Light as a feather, quick as squirrel. Agile. He was on it. Rusty chattered again. It was drowned out by a grinding scrape of metal on metal as the truck's gears found a new position. The trailer stopped and then lurched in a slow arc out onto the main road. It banged against a couple of parked cars, jostling and jolting Rusty, but he held firm. The last thing he needed was to fall off and get run over just before getting home. That'd be worse than rabies and bird flu at the same time. Rabies! After all this time in the human world, Rusty had to remember to wash his paws really, really well as soon as he got home. And maybe again before eating. You couldn't be too careful. Raccoon was always washing his paws. And that guy knew stuff. Rusty checked his tail. Still bushy. Silky. Sexy. He felt good. Better than good. Invincible.

The truck hit a pothole and bounced. Rusty clung on for dear life. Not quite invincible then. The trailer clipped a curb; it jumped and listed. Rusty and the spanner were knocked clear of the final bolt. Rusty chattered with rage as the spanner clattered to the ground and out of sight. Nuts! He was only able to just keep himself secure by hanging on to the snow chains, which were tucked up under the trailer for safekeeping. They swung wildly. The quickest there is. The prettiest. Rusty twisted out of the snow chains and made his way back to the bolt. It was stuck. If only he had brought explosives. He and Raccoon had debated the merits and drawbacks to a small packet of C-4 and, ultimately, decided it wasn't worth it. But that was before accounting for an inexperienced driver and the loss of the spanner.

He needed to do something. The truck slowed to a crawl. Rusty detected the unmistakable perfume of coffee. He had tried coffee once. It was like weak, bitter electricity. That humans were so dependent on the stuff was just another sign of their shortcomings as a species. But if he couldn't get this bolt free and the trailer loosed, what would history say of his own shortcomings?

Coffee. It was basically liquid acid. Maybe it could melt away the bolt. Rusty stuck his head out from under the side of the trailer. The coffee odor was overwhelming. The truck cab had pulled up next to a building with a window. It was a delivery system, Rusty knew, for food, coffee, what-have-you; humans were quite often too lazy to gather their own foods. It held no interest for him. But on top of the building—holy nuts!—there was the biggest cup of coffee Rusty had ever seen! It was at least as tall as an adult human and had writing in diagonal cursive across the front. Rusty squinted. *Cup-a-Joe.* Joe. That was slang for coffee. Like the way some electricity junkies would talk about jolt, or spice, or fluffles. Rusty gave a shiver. That could have been him. But no more. The coffee in that cup would surely be enough to corrode the bolt away. All he lacked was a means for delivery. A pipe or garden hose would be ideal.

"I said mocha latte! This is a goddamn mocha frappé. There's too much goddamn foam. Do it right. I'm in a hurry."

The driver of the truck was berating the food-delivery window. A window. That just gave you food! How could you yell at it? Humans took so much for granted.

How to get the coffee from the enormous cup onto the bolt? There was no time to engineer an elaborate coffeeduct. He'd have to go up and just tip it over and hope. To the bold go the nuts!

Rusty sprinted out from under the trailer and flew up the brick wall of the building with the food-delivery window, as if gravity had no hold on him. His balance was immaculate, his agility sublime, his tail glossy. Faster than a falcon with its tail on fire. Falcon! Hawk! Rusty froze. He felt the buffeting of wings and heard a screech as fear washed over him. Unfreeze! Bob and weave! Sprint for cover! The hawk swooped away, talons empty. Rusty crouched under the enormous cup of coffee, quivering from ear to tail. Had the beast been tracking him this whole time? Were the hawks and humans in league? Success wasn't assured until it was accomplished.

The trucks gears gnashed. No! He had to get the cup tipped over. The truck stalled. Precious seconds. Rusty peaked his head out. Coast was clear. He sprinted up the cup to its lip.

Empty. Empty! This was so like humans, to have all this space and to just waste it. The truck rumbled to life again and began to creep forward.

No way. Those were his nuts. Rusty jumped to the roof of the building and from there to the top of the trailer. Can't stop. Won't stop. Especially not there, in the open. With a roll and a slide, Rusty barreled down the side of the truck, he latched onto a handle with his tail, and using his momentum, swung himself back under the trailer. Ninja. Now to master that final bolt.

TIM

Just when Tim thought the day couldn't get any more stressful, C. Franklin Wallace, the CEO of the entire SuperGroup, had appeared. And he was talking to him! And he was mad. He was yelling at him. Tim's head was spinning. He had just been trying to defend Sandy, who had just been trying to pick up the litter from the parking lot—she truly was a woman after his own heart. And now accusations were flying—at Tim! He didn't even know what a double-blind receivables 35(f) securitization was, but Mr. Wallace seemed to think he did. And the private eye, Dirk Blade, he kept saying he had evidence on Tim. Oh, this was a bad, ugly, unexpected turn.

"Of course you're fired," Mr. Wallace said. "You're all fired. The only question is, who is going to jail? Cooperate and I might be lenient."

Jail? Oh, turnips! He hadn't even realized that SuperGroup had its own jail.

"So where's the money?" Mr. Wallace stepped closer to Tim. He smelled like fake lemons and salt.

"Yeah, you'll make this a lot easier for yourself later if you cooperate now," Dirk Blade said. He was on Mr. Wallace's side. Tim hadn't realized just how many sides there were. The only person who seemed to be on his side was Sandy. But that was just fine and dandy with Tim. She was all he needed.

Mr. Wallace and Dirk Blade were still going on about missing money. Tim didn't really know what they were talking about.

"I...I really don't know what you're talking about. That bear had a lot of money in it," Tim said.

"Forget about the bear; that bear was chump change," Mr. Wallace said. His gaze ran over Tim's head, like he wasn't even there.

"Look, you're Phillips. Your name was on the document," Dirk Blade said. He kept looking down; Tim looked down too; there was just SuperMart parking lot asphalt and a stray hundred-dollar bill.

"Oh, who cares who he is?" Mr. Wallace said. "All that matters is, what did he do with my money? And you better hope it shows up, Blade; that's what I'm paying you for. No money for me, no money for you."

"Well, it wasn't in the underground bunker," Dirk Blade said.

"I'm telling you. That ain't the guy!" the duct taped gunman said. "It's that greaseball who jumped out the window. Let go of me, and I'll go get 'im, you goddamn fascists."

A tractor-trailer truck slowly ground its way along the outer edge of the parking lot. Oh, fiddlesticks! The Golden Snacks delivery! Tim had screwed it up.

"That's the guy!" the gunman yelled. "He's driving!"

It was Mr. Spooner! What was he doing in the truck?

"That's my truck!" the guy who had found the missing children—Pete—shouted. "Those stoner punks! Somebody call the police."

Pete went running after the truck but only about ten steps. He wasn't going to catch it. And it was true—Mr. Spooner was driving. He honked and waved out the window. Tim waved back, but Sandy pulled his arm down.

"He's not being friendly, darling."

Tim thought she was wrong but stopped waving. There was a line of cars blocking the exit to the parking lot, but that didn't stop Mr. Spooner; he turned right past the Coffee Xpress, crashed through some parked cars, jumped the curb, and swung out into the street. He honked and waved again and chugged off into the distance. Where was he going? Tim involuntarily waved back again.

"Stop waving, you idiot," Mr. Wallace said, his jaw barely moving as he spoke.

"Don't you talk to him like that," Sandy said, then lowered her voice and said to Tim, "but stop waving, darling. Really."

Tim couldn't help it. Why was Mr. Spooner leaving? That seemed suspicious. Maybe he really was the guy that everyone was saying he was and not the cool guy that Tim knew.

"Oh, but I was just being neighborly, returning the wave," Tim said.

"That's not a wave, you moron. He's giving us the finger," Mr. Wallace said.

Tim pulled his hand back and pretended he had an itch to scratch on his head. The world was confusing.

BILLY

All the grown-ups were arguing. Billy was tired. He didn't want to be there. He had never wanted to be there. He looked at his mom. She looked the way he felt.

"Hey, Mom?" He pulled on her hand.

"Yes?" she said.

"Can we go now?"

"I...I don't know. I think we're supposed to check out or something."

Billy didn't know *which* swear word would properly express his frustration, but he knew that one existed, or some combination of swear words. Probably a combination actually. While he searched for just the right words, a big tractor-trailer truck drove by honking and grinding gears. The driver was giving everyone the finger as he bounced off of curbs and small cars. Billy knew that the finger was supposed to mean the f word. But it seemed to be more socially acceptable, especially while driving.

"It's fine; you should just go." Scarlett had overheard them. Thank goodness!

His mom turned to him and said, "Billy, you were right."

"Wait, what now?" Billy couldn't believe what he was hearing.

"Don't get smart. Let's just get out of here."

"No, I'm not being smart; it's just, you so rarely recognize—"

"We can stay longer if you want."

Billy shut up. He was finally going to get out of there. But Willow!

"Wait!" Billy said.

"What now, Billy? If you say you want to stay, I swear I'll—"

"Mom! Relax. I just have to say good-bye to Willow."

Billy ran over to Willow and her mom.

"Willow, I gotta go. These people are crazy. You should probably get too, while the getting is good."

Billy wasn't sure Willow's mom was a woman of action. She might not recognize that this was their chance to escape.

"Yeah, okay. Well, bye, Billy. Remember, you have to come over and play in my tree house. Next weekend?"

"If I'm not grounded," Billy said, scuffing his toe on the pavement.

"Oh, no, I'm sure that won't be the case," Willow's mom said. "Here."

She gave Billy a small business card. It was his second one of the day, along with the one he had gotten from Dirk Blade: Master Private Investigator. This one read:

Yoga and Meditation with Moonbeam

"I'm actually fine, thanks," Billy said, handing the card back.

"No, silly. It has our phone number on the back. That way you can call, and we can figure out when you can come and play," Willow's mom said.

"Oh." Billy took the card again. "Thanks."

Billy saw his mom coming over. If she started to talk to Willow's mom, he would literally never be able to leave. He had to head her off.

"Thanks," he said again. "I'll call you! Now, I gotta get out of here. See you soon!"

"Bye, Billy!" Willow said.

"Bye!"

Billy ran over to his mom, and together, they headed back to their car. It wasn't until he was safely buckled in the back seat and his mom was pulling out onto the main road that Billy let out a sigh of relief. He was finally going home.

LEE

"I'm telling you, we can friggin' get 'im!" Lee Rigg turned to his captor. There was hesitation in Dirk Blade's slate blue eyes. But also something else. A spark? A glimmer? Lee couldn't be sure, but he thought maybe the cop was weakening.

The semitruck smashed through a couple of parked cars and into the street. The spark went out of Dirk Blade's eyes.

"No, we can't," he told Lee.

"What do you mean? He's right there! And you saw how he was driving. He ain't gettin' far fast. Mexico ain't for a thousand miles! Let's go!"

"No, we can't," Dirk Blade said again. "That was my car."

Lee followed his finger toward an older Ford Taurus. It was tan and rust colored. The front end was all stoved in. It wouldn't be going anywhere soon, unless it was on the back of a flatbed tow truck. Ordinarily, the destruction of a cop car would have lifted Lee's spirits. Back in the day, he might have even done one or two himself. But these were not ordinary times.

"Well, frig. Let's just take my truck then!" Lee Rigg found a solution. His freedom depended on it.

"Could we?" The glimmer had returned to Dirk Blade's eyes.

"Hell yeah! All you gotta do is release me and, uh, maybe not press charges about the whole gun thing? I had a misunderstanding with the law a couple of years ago, and it would be better if I could keep a clean record for a while."

Dirk Blade was quiet. Lee held his breath.

"Yeah, okay. Let's go get that guy."

Hell yeah! Lee Rigg was going free. And now he had the law on his side.

"Could I have a badge?"

"What? No. I don't even have a badge."

"Whattaya mean, you don't have a badge; are you a friggin' cop, or ain't you?"

"I've been trying to tell you. I'm a private investigator."

"Oh, so that's different?"

"Yeah. It is."

"Well, frig. So what does that mean about my badge? Do I get one or don't I?"

"Tell you what, Rigg. We get this guy, Spooner, I'll make sure you get a badge."

"Sweet beans. How about no taxes too?" Lee figured it wouldn't hurt to ask.

"I'm not the IRS! C'mon, Rigg. Let's go!"

Well, shoot. Dirk Blade sure was an ardent sonofagun when the spirit moved him. He cut Lee Rigg's hands free and headed off toward Lee's truck. Lee brought his arms in front of him and stretched. The duct tape was still wound around each wrist. It looked pretty cool, and Lee didn't mind saying so. But there was no time to stand and admire himself. That would have to wait. There was a sonofabitch child abductor to catch.

"Excuse us," he said to the assembled SuperMart employees. He hadn't been paying much attention, but it looked like the old guy in the suit was putting moves on the little dweeb's, Tim's, woman. Lee wouldn't have put up with that. He would have beat the snot out of anyone who so much as looked at his woman the wrong way. But whatever. Not everyone was Lee Rigg.

"C'mon," Dirk Blade said.

"Coming!" Lee said. "My truck's over there."

He sprinted over to his truck. It was just the way he had left it: a monument to coolness in a vast desert of lame. He jumped in to find himself wedged right next to Dirk Blade.

"I'll drive," Dirk Blade told him.

"You'll move the frig over," Lee said. "There's no friggin' way anybody but me's driving my friggin' truck."

They locked stares for a moment. Then Dirk Blade moved over.

"You can shoot out his tires when we get close," Lee said to smooth over the controversy.

He turned the key. The roar of the engine blocked out Dirk Blade's reply. It looked like he might have said that he didn't have a thumb, which was patently ridiculous. There wasn't time to worry about that right now. Lee slammed the truck into reverse and did a sweet power turn to straighten the truck out. Then he floored it. The four barrels kicked in, and he shot past Dirk Blade's ruined Taurus and into the street. Lee kinda wished there had been an explosion or something. In a movie, there would have been an explosion. Adrenaline coursed through his body. Friggin' justice! Friggin' America!

SCARLETT

At least she had done one good deed for the day, Scarlett thought, as she watched Billy and Willow and their moms make their way to their cars and escape. Escape. That would be wonderful.

She turned back to the group and wished she hadn't. Dirk Blade had freed Lee Rigg, and they sprinted off and jumped into a big red truck with bright-chrome stand-up exhaust pipes. Scarlett wasn't sure that was such a great idea, but there was little she could do to stop it. At least Lee Rigg no longer had a gun. So there was that. The roar of the engine echoed around the parking lot, drowning out pretty much everything. Someone needed a new muffler. Then the two vigilantes tore out of the parking lot in the direction the semitruck had disappeared. Scarlett smiled in spite of herself. She might have to watch the news tonight.

C. Franklin Wallace, Tim, and Sandy were involved in some kind of three-way argument that Scarlett couldn't bother caring about.

"How're you doing?" Clem asked.

Scarlett turned to look at him. She wasn't sure how to answer. It had been a kind of surreal day.

"I could ask you the same thing."

"You could, but I asked first."

He always asked first. She really had to get better about asking him.

"I'm all right, I guess. I'm tired. And hungry. Do you wanna go get a sandwich or something?" Scarlett said.

"That would be lovely. Shall I drive?"

"I don't have a car."

"I guess I shall then."

C. Franklin Wallace had disappeared along with most everyone else, leaving only Tim and Sandy in the parking lot. Scarlett was glad to leave them behind. After their display in the office, she didn't want to hang around. People like that needed each other. Good for them. She did not need people like them. She needed a sandwich.

TIM

"Excuse me, y'all," Sandy said.

His angel, coming to the rescue.

Mr. Wallace turned from Tim to Sandy. Dirk Blade and the gunman had run off and jumped in a big pickup truck. It seemed they were going after Mr. Spooner. Did that mean the detective didn't think Tim was guilty? The world sure was confusing sometimes.

"Well, hello again. You wanna play nice now?" Mr. Wallace said. Tim didn't like his tone.

"I can vouch for Timothy. He's a good Christian with impeccable character."

Tim loved the way Sandy used big words.

"Would you now?" Mr. Wallace said. "Well, let me say, I'd believe almost anything you'd tell me. And I'm always looking for a new secretary. Do you type?"

Mr. Wallace stepped forward and took Sandy's hand and kissed it.

"Yes, well, you've heard her." Tim stepped between them. "Now please take your hands off her."

"Step aside, pipsqueak. The lady and I are getting to know each other."

Mr. Wallace put a hand in Tim's chest and pushed him. Tim stumbled backward and fell. He sat on the ground. His arm hurt, his neck hurt—his tie was too tight—and his heart hurt. Mr. Wallace was reaching for Sandy's...for her boobs! Again! Tim bit his lips. Nothing ever worked out for him. Even Sandy Newman, a woman he loved with all his heart, had turned out to be false. She was consorting with a richer, more powerful guy

305

right in from of his face. How fickle the heart of a woman! Just twenty minutes ago, his head had been using those same boobs as pillows!

"Gosh! Oh, galldarnitall, heck!" Tim swore and blinked back tears. He knew he was sensitive but didn't want to give anyone—not Sandy, not Mr. Wallace, not the truck driver, none of them—the satisfaction of seeing him cry. So he didn't see what happened next. Somehow, Sandy had spun, or Mr. Wallace had. In any event, she was now standing behind Mr. Wallace, whispering into his ear. Tim would have been elated for her to be speaking to him like that. But Mr. Wallace didn't look happy. His brow furrowed, and his lips peeled back to reveal clenched teeth. Tim could only see one of his arms. The other was behind him, doing who knew what—it wasn't right. Mr. Wallace must have been some kind of gymnast. Tim had been an idiot to think it would work out for him with Sandy.

"Mmm-kay, darling?" Sandy said.

Tim sighed. Time was, he had been Sandy's darling. How fickle the heart of a woman indeed.

Mr. Wallace grunted and then stepped forward, releasing a blast of hot, stinky breath into Tim's face.

"Let me help you up," he said, shaking out the hand that had been fondling Tim's beloved. "It seems I misjudged you, Phillips."

He offered his other hand to help Tim up. Tim pushed it away and stood up.

"Get off! How dare you touch her! And how dare you let him touch you!"

"Well, I won't again," Mr. Wallace said, still massaging his groping arm. Tim wanted to cut it off and burn it. "Your, uh, lady friend made certain of that."

"She's not my lady friend. She's my Snuffleupagus!"

"Whatever," Mr. Wallace said.

"What he means is, if he ever so much as thinks about trying to touch me again, I'll break his arm clean off, instead of just giving it a twist. And the Bible says I can. I'm more of a New Testament gal, generally, but I think Old Testament applies here." Sandy smiled at Mr. Wallace, but it wasn't a friendly kind of smile.

"So you didn't. I mean, you're not leaving me for him?" Tim felt relief from his head to his toes. He was wobbly again. Must have been the blood loss.

"Of course not, Timothy. You're my Snuffleupagus. We've got a good thing going on. Plus, I got a way to make money now. And so do you."

"I do?" Tim said. He had just been fired, after all.

"Yes, you do. It seems that this branch needs a new manager. And as your special lady just pointed out, you might be qualified," Mr. Wallace said. "More than qualified, to take over."

"Golly, Mr. Wallace. I don't know what to say. Thanks."

"Well, isn't that just a blessed outcome for everyone?" Sandy said.

"Yes, quite," Mr. Wallace said. He didn't seem to appreciate the blessing as much as Sandy. He was just a big, old sourpuss, Tim decided.

"Just remember, Phillips. Pull any of this embezzlement crap like your predecessor, and you will be out of a job and in prison faster than you can say chateaubriand. Speaking of which, I'm starving. Good day to you all. Come, Chauncey."

Mr. Wallace went and got into a black car with black windows. Ooh, it was a BMW. Mr. Spooner was always talking about how cool those cars were. Tim shook his head. No, what Mr. Spooner said wasn't cool anymore. The world sure was confusing all right.

Tim sat down again.

Sandy came over and sat next to him. She ducked under his arm and put her head on his shoulder.

"Sorry I doubted you," Tim said.

"It's okay, darling. God tests us all. And you've been tested more than most today. You don't have to be Jesus."

"Jiminy Cricket! I'd never compare myself to him."

"It was a joke, silly." Sandy kissed him on the cheek. "And I like you the way you are."

Tim liked sitting there, just holding her. But he knew he should also be polite and interested in her new job.

"So, what's your new job?" he asked.

Sandy hesitated.

"We'll talk about that later," she said and kissed him again.

DIRK BLADE

Dirk Blade was holding on for dear life. But that served him right for messing the whole thing up in the first place. He felt bad for trying to pin the crime on Tim Phillips, for agreeing with C. Franklin Wallace. Where was his integrity? It had been a long day, but that was no excuse for compromising his detective work. And now he was paying for it.

Lee Rigg swerved in and out of traffic. A pack of cigarettes skittered across the dashboard. If he had had a free hand, he would have grabbed one. He could really use a cigarette right now or coffee—the lone contentments of life. But in the current circumstances, either would just lead to someone getting burned, probably him. It was bad enough that his car had been destroyed. His wife would be seriously ticked off. He didn't need coffee or cigarette burns on his legs or arms or face on top of it. His poor car. Who knew what Wallace would pay for—nothing, more than likely, unless he returned with Mitch Spooner. And that looked like a fifty-fifty proposition at best. Given the way Lee Rigg was driving, it was better than fifty-fifty that they'd end up wrapped around a telephone pole. It was probably just as well he couldn't reach the cigarettes. He gritted his teeth.

The red truck zoomed down the median. Its exhaust growled, deep and throaty. The median in this section of road was a left-turn-only lane. Fortunately, no one else seemed to want to turn left. Though they may just have been terrified of the way Lee Rigg was driving. The semitruck had turned right at the end of the avenue. At some point, they would have to cross two lanes of traffic to make that turn. But they couldn't lose the truck. They had to catch Spooner.

The turn was coming up. Dirk Blade grabbed the door handle and braced. The force he expected to toss him across the seat into Lee Rigg never came. They kept going straight.

"Where are you going? He went that way!"

"Naw, I'm gonna cut him off. Fastest way to Mexico is I85. Fastest way to I85 is down Second," Lee Rigg told him.

"We don't know he's going to Mexico!" Dirk Blade shouted. He really should have driven.

"What? Course we do! You said so yourself. Don't worry. He'll show up on Second. Now hold on."

Dirk Blade didn't have time to retort. Rigg took a hard right and then a quick left and then another right. Dirk Blade was jostled and thrown sideways. He pushed himself up. Lee Rigg had stopped the truck. The deep gurgle of exhaust kept time with the bounce of the engine as they idled. They were in a little side alley looking out onto Second. The semitruck wasn't there. The seconds ticked by.

"You idiot," Dirk Blade said.

"Hold on; it'll be all right. You said so yourself."

"I said I thought he'd be headed for Mexico. I didn't know! What am I, a mind reader? God dammit. God dammit!"

"Well, frig. Excuse me for thinking you knew what the hell you were talkin' about!"

"Don't push me, Rigg. We gotta find him, or you'll be under arrest again. I don't like it, but that's the way it's gonna be."

"Not friggin' likely! You ain't even real police! I don't gotta listen to you!"

Dirk Blade turned to argue, but before he could say more, the Golden Snacks truck rolled by...right where Lee Rigg said it would. Well, sonofagun. It was better than a poke in the eye with a sharp stick.

Dirk Blade and Lee looked at each other. Lee gave a golden-toothed grin.

"Yeah, yeah, yeah," Dirk Blade muttered.

Lee threw the truck into gear.

"Wait," Dirk Blade said.

"He's right friggin' there! Let's get the bastard!"

"I need a cigarette first. You want one?"

"Do bears crap in the woods?"

Dirk Blade dug out a couple of cigarettes from the pack on the dashboard. He lit Lee's and then his own. Finally. He took a long drag. He immediately started coughing and hacking. He couldn't stop. Finally Lee Rigg gave him a slap on the back, and Dirk Blade was restored. He flicked the barely smoked cigarette out the window. There were so many small tragedies in life. Sirens wailed in the distance. Someone had called the police.

"Not on my watch. Rigg, those guys are not bringing in our perp."

"No friggin' way!" Lee Rigg shouted and slammed the accelerator. The tires on the truck gave a sharp squeal as they left behind some rubber; the private eye and his self-appointed deputy tore after the semitruck. It didn't take long to catch up. The sirens were louder. The police were gaining.

"Go, Rigg! We gotta stop that truck!"

"Okay! Shoot out the friggin' tires!" Lee Rigg shouted.

"I don't have a gun! I told you that already."

Dirk Blade had recognized his mistake already. Why did everyone have to keep pointing it out?

"What the hell kind of government agent are you?"

"I'M A PRIVATE INVESTIGATOR!"

"Oh yeah, frig. I keep forgetting. Don't worry, bud; I got your back on this one."

Lee Rigg reached over and popped open the glove box. In it was a Smith & Wesson semiautomatic pistol. Dirk Blade took it out. Ready, aim, fire.

"Holy crap!"

Dirk Blade couldn't have put it better himself. With his first shot, the trailer decoupled from the truck and went rolling over the embankment and down into a wooded ravine. He had never been much of a shot, but he wasn't about to complain.

Unencumbered from its load, the truck sped up.

"I don't friggin' think so!" Lee Rigg said and trod harder on the gas pedal.

Dirk Blade leaned out the window to better aim at the tires. The police had caught up too.

"Pull over! Pull over!" one of the local cops was shouting at them through a megaphone. Dirk Blade paid them no mind. He had to stop Mitch Spooner. He had pushed all his chips to the middle of the table. He took a deep breath, steadied his hands, and squeezed the trigger twice in quick succession.

A direct hit! The back right tire of the truck exploded in a hiss of rubber. Maybe he was a good shot after all. This day was full of surprises. The truck fishtailed, and its back tires went over into the soft sand at the side of the road. Dirk Blade knew from his own experience that the only chance for the truck now was to slam the accelerator and hope. But...nope, Spooner stepped on the brakes! The wheels stopped spinning; they were locked up. Given the speed at which it had been traveling and its top-heavy design it should...yep. Timber! The truck tipped over on its side.

"Hell yeah! Gimme five, bud!" Lee Rigg held up his hand. There was an awkward half second as Dirk Blade tried to figure out how to shake it. But it ended well with a clasping high five and some enthusiastic hooting and hollering. They had done it.

Police cars screeched up, and local cops poured out. Oh no they wouldn't! Dirk Blade leapt out of Lee Rigg's truck. It was his perp! He had to reach him first. As long as he did, then the local cops would cooperate. Fair was fair. That was how it worked in procedural dramas on television. That was how it would work in this Podunk town.

Dirk Blade sprinted to the tipped-over tractor-trailer cab. Lee Rigg was right with him. The cops seemed content to let them go in. They usually were, if they thought there was any risk at all. Dirk Blade knew there was risk—Mitch Spooner had already fired his gun in his general direction once today—but there was also reward, a cool fifty grand. It would be worth it.

RUSTY

The coupling was still stuck. Rusty ducked his head to get his bearings. Holy nuts! It was time! They had just passed Big Pine Tree. It was time.

Rusty chattered unprintable squirrel swears and wrenched at the bolt.

There are stories, in rodent lore, of outstanding virtues that enabled incredible feats: the magical left paw and vision of Ratòn, the rat who led RFC Barça to four league titles in five years and lifted the World Cup for Spain; the prodigious appetite of the mouse Augusta, who singlehandedly caused the great almond shortage of '15; the vision of the Marquis de Porcupine, the fashion icon, who inspired a generation to follow his own spikey, subversive style; the bravery of Marmotta, the marmot, who served on the Dolomitic Front in World War I; the heartache of Lemmy, the lemming who didn't jump, whose story was a tragedy to which Shakespeare had no equal. To those would be added the story of the strength and determination of Rusty, prince of squirrel thieves, who, with the strength of ten squirrels, managed to loosen the bolt and then knock it free.

The coupling let go. There was a bang, and then the trailer full of nuts was loose. His timing was perfect. On the slow curve—around the house through which he had started his adventure that morning—the trailer let go. The cab of the truck continued down the road, south. The trailer continued west. It hit the soft dirt and started to roll over. Time to bail. Rusty leapt off and landed on a bush, light as feather and quick as a squirrel. The trailer rolled once and then slid down the ravine and stopped. There was a little damage, but most of the nuts would be okay. It was right at the base of his tree. Wow, he was good. Better than good. Great. Prince of squirrel thieves. King. Legend.

Rusty leaped off the bush in a twisting double somersault. He rushed to his tree and sprinted around the trunk, circling it three times, paws scarcely touching bark. Then he shot up and inside.

"Honey!" he chattered triumphantly. "I did it."

CLEM

Clem drove in silence back to his house, which thankfully was the opposite direction from where Mitch Spooner—and an increasing number of emergency vehicles—had gone. Scarlett seemed content to sit in the passenger seat and look out the window. It was a companionable silence. He should have invited her over for a sandwich long ago.

He heard Scarlett give a little gasp as he pulled onto the property and the crushed-stone drive and up the tree-lined hill to the house. It was a bit grand. Hopefully she wouldn't judge him too harshly for it.

"This is beautiful," she said, her voice soft.

"Yes, it is. I've been lucky," Clem said, stealing a look at Scarlett out of the corner of his eye. She was gazing up at the oaks, which had only just started to leaf out. He was lucky.

He pulled around the circle by the front door instead of into the garage. It was grandiose, but Scarlett didn't seem to mind. Before they had gotten two steps to the house, Else came flying out.

"Oh, Clem! I was so worried! The news has been saying the most awful things!" She ran up to him and threw her arms around his neck, hugging him hard. He hugged her back, feeling stronger than he had in years. She smelled like rosemary. It was good.

When Else released him, her eyes were damp.

"I'm all right, Else."

"I know. I'm so glad. Sorry. Who's this?"

Scarlett was standing back by the car, one leg crossed behind the other, hands in her pockets, pretending to be really interested in the brickwork leading up to the front door.

"This is Scarlett. I've told you about her. Scarlett, this is my wife, Else."

"The Scarlett? I am *so* glad to meet you. Welcome."

Before Scarlett could say anything, Else had hugged her too. She was a hugger—nothing he could do about that. Scarlett didn't seem to mind.

"Come in, come in. I've finished lunch, but there's plenty more if you'd like something to eat."

Clem followed the two women into the house. In the kitchen, the little TV was on. It was showing live footage from a helicopter of a flipped-over tractor-trailer truck. It was surrounded by police cars and a big red pickup truck.

"*...Again, shocking scenes as a high-speed chase has ended with a spectacular semitruck rollover on Route 202 South, just short of the on-ramp to I55. It appears the truck began its journey at the Mega SuperMart in West Greenville where there have been reports that an armed gunman had taken hostages. It is unconfirmed if these are unrelated incidents or part of a coordinated attack. To recap, the hostage situation appears to be over, but this is an evolving situation, and law enforcement will neither confirm nor deny that they have taken two suspects into custody...*"

The reporter sounded breathless, excited, almost giddy. Clem scowled and found the remote. He jabbed it at the television. The screen snapped to black.

"A lawyer? Yes, I agree that a right-functioning justice system is critical to a prosperous society. But your eyes, deary, your eyes have a doctor's look to them. I don't know if Clem has told you, but we have a Foundation..." Else had already gone to work fixing Scarlett a sandwich, and fixing more than a sandwich, it seemed. Clem smiled and went to the fridge and got out some lemonade.

MITCH

Everything had gone dark. Mitch didn't remember much, but he supposed all the adrenaline, all of his awesomeness had caused him to black out. He didn't even remember reaching Mexico. Nor had he realized that Mexico was all sideways. Huh. Mitch shook his head. It still hurt. He squeezed his eyes shut and then opened them again. Maybe this time he'd see the beach and a Corona. God, he would love a beer right now.

"Dos cervezas, por favor."

Instead of receiving his beverages, when he opened his eyes, he saw the thin mustache and dark-blue eyes of that weak-sauce private investigator, Dirk Blade. What was he doing there? Oh well, he was outside his jurisdiction. He couldn't touch him. Hey! Why was he touching him? He was pulling him forcibly out of his seat.

"Hey! The fuck, man?" Mitch swore as he was dragged through the truck's window. His shoulder hit the door. "Ahhh-ow! Jesus Christ. Get off me."

This wasn't right. Dirk Blade did not unhand him. And why was that goddamn hillbilly Lee Rigg there, grinning like a goddamn idiot? And a bunch of cops? Though one of them was a lady cop. Maybe it was some kind of stripper-gram? But there were a lot of dudes. That didn't make sense.

"Let go of me, man," Mitch said and tried to shake the private eye's hands off of him.

"You have the right to remain silent. Anything you say can and will be used against you...blah, blah, blah."

Mitch was forced to his knees and handcuffed. He shook his head, and the world swam in and out of focus. What the hell was happening? He needed to think.

Now he was in the back of a cop car. The lady cop was in front. What the hell? Lee Rigg was forced into the seat next to him, swearing and struggling. Seriously, what the hell?! This was so unreal. Mitch shook his head again. Unreal, duh. He must have been asleep. One of those Lucite dreams. Aware but unaware. It was trippy. Probably brought on by all the painkillers he had been taking. And the stress. It didn't quite explain Lee Rigg, but dreams were messed up sometimes. It *did* mean that lady cop was probably Ms. MacFarlane. Any second now, she'd tear her top off, the police cruiser would transform into a bed, and everyone else would fade away. And this time they would do it, for real. Then he'd wake up in the Mexican sunshine. Yep, it was all a dream. Mitch settled in to enjoy it.

BILLY

He was home. He was home! Billy flopped on his bed and looked at the ceiling of his room. It was a nice ceiling. It was a nice room. Yes, his mom had told him to go straight there when they had gotten home, so it wasn't, strictly speaking, his choice. But it was where he wanted to go. It was where he wanted to be.

Billy got off his bed and went over to his window. He had a view over the park. He looked out the window and grimaced when he saw that his fort was no longer there. But somehow that didn't matter as much anymore. The wind had come up. Maybe it would rain. There were more clouds now. Billy could hear sirens coming from somewhere on the other side of the park. Yep, his room was right where he wanted to be.

Whoa, cool! Billy watched as a raccoon trundled along through the bushes at the edge of the park, then disappeared behind an old sycamore, heading sort of toward the sirens. Raccoons were so cool.

His mom hadn't given him his Xbox back. But that didn't really surprise him or even make him that mad. He hadn't given her his thousand dollars. And she had left his books and his Legos and given him a snack of cut-up apple and goldfish crackers. He was pretty sure she wasn't really that mad. Billy wondered what Willow was up to. Was she in her room? Probably her tree house. That made the most sense. But his room was pretty good. For now, at least.

Billy dumped out his Legos. A thousand dollars would go a long way toward a new fort. A Lego mockup would help him perfect the design. He pushed the pile of Legos around, spreading it out, digging through the pile, looking for the most important piece. Aha! He took the cannon and set it on his bed. Now to figure out exactly where it should go.

ACKNOWLEDGEMENTS

Throughout the writing of this book I benefited from the input and suggestions of a number of wonderful, intelligent readers. Had I listened to all of their advice the result would have undoubtedly been better. But thanks to them it's not any worse. I'm nothing if not stubborn.

Liz, Annie, Woody, Megan, Ryan, and Rick, thank you for reading earlier and worse drafts than this, offering suggestions that improved the story, and for giving me encouragement when I needed it most.

Thanks also to Molly Schulman and Lindsey Nelson, whose editorial expertise saved me many times. Your wisdom, skill, and expertise made this story so much better. I am lucky to have had your help.

And of course finally thanks to Alicia, without whom everything would be less, particularly the number of squirrels in my life.

ABOUT THE AUTHOR

Ben is from Maine and returns there whenever he can. *Code Billy* is his first novel. When not writing he likes to explore mountains. He has a (very) sporadically tended website: www.benhuber.net

CPSIA information can be obtained
at www.ICGtesting.com
Printed in the USA
LVHW090058240320
651002LV00004B/1203